THE
ANVIL OF
SOULS

BY: JOSHUA C. COOK
THE FORGEMASTER CYCLE
BOOK TWO

Published by Joshua Cook

Email us at josh@joshccook.com

First published in 2020 / First printed in 2020

https://www.joshccook.com

Cover Art by A.M. Bochnak

info@misadventurepress.com

www.misadventurepress.com

"MAGIC IS A MYTH, A LEGEND, A RUMOR. POWER ONLY FLOWS FROM THE GODS, AND THOSE THEY BLESS..."

The First Lesson, a handbook for new priests.

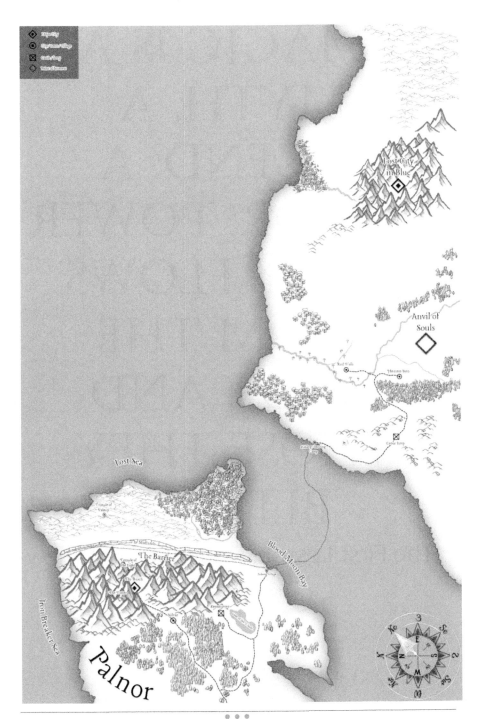

Chapter 1.

Pain. Everything was pain. The man struggled to open his eyes, awareness of anything but how much he hurt seemed to fall off if he tried to think about it. Where was he? Who was he? Why did he hurt so much? He fought to find anything other than the agony that came in waves. Dust there, dust. His mouth was full of it. And his nose, dust and... something else. Something rich, slightly metallic. Blood. The dust in his mouth fled before the moisture in his body produced at the smell of blood.

He opened his eyes finally enough to see, and he wondered if the effort had been worth it. He was on a red dust filled plain; the light was dim, maybe dusk? Dawn? He couldn't see a moon or the sun, or even a sky. The air was full of that same red dust. The pain still came in waves, some stronger, some weaker, but the man pushed past them, at least enough to be aware. Who was he? The knowledge skittered away as the information was about to come to him.

"Mine..." The voice came out of the dust, a hiss, angry, but weak. The man knew that voice, and a fear gripped him, terror. *"You... are mine."* The voice seemed nearer, and less like a hiss. It was throatier now, and the sound of it brought unfamiliar emotions to the man. The terror changed to anger? Hate bloomed in his mind. Betrayer. The word echoed inside him. Betrayer. False. The man didn't know the voice, did he?

"My pet. My vessel." The voice changed again, feminine this time, a voice the man knew. A flare of rage followed by a deep sadness. Love, love lost. The red dust swirled around the man, dancing into a shape. The shape of a woman. *"My revenge. My way back."* The shape paused. *"Do you know me, pet?"*

A name formed on the man's lips, a name he knew. "Rache" WRONG. Not that name, the other name. What was the other name?

A laugh greeted his answer. *"No pet. My actual name. I have had many. Rache was only one, and not an excellent one at that. Think again."* As the figure spoke, it shifted from a woman's shape to a man. The voice changed with it, rougher, old.

The man licked his lips. The dust, the dust was dried blood. The rich iron taste filled his mouth. How had he not realized this before? The blood brought an additional level of anger and rage. The pain which he had been forcing away faded before this hate. Kill, kill and maim. Tear the flesh, rip the skin. Hear the screams and the power, the power of feeling a person's life, fade away.

"NOOOO!" the man screamed, falling to his knees. The anger faded, and with its fading, fresh memories came. Of a town, snow, the sound of hammers. The Reach. The name brought a weary joy. Home.

"WHAT IS MY NAME?" The voice came, roaring, echoing around the man. The surrounding dust shuddered and twisted away from his prone form. The figure in the dust broke apart, and he stood in the swirling wind. He knew the name, a name he hated, and a name he feared. "Zalkiniv. Your name is ZALKINIV."

A scream came from all around him, one of anger and triumph. The man wanted to run away, but he couldn't move. Why couldn't he move? He felt as if the world was pressing down on him. The pain returned, more pain than before. Pain and weight. He was being crushed. As he opened his mouth to scream, the figure flowed and moved into the very air he breathed. The man screamed then, all other feeling fell before this, he was on fire. Every part of him was being burned away.

"You are mine. My vessel for revenge. I was betrayed, and I will wreak my vengeance." The voice was inside him now. Who he had been was being burned away. *"You cannot resist me. You are weak. I am strong."* The voice spoke, and the man knew it was right. Zalkiniv was right.

As the man felt himself being destroyed, he knew. His name, his name was… Duncan Reis.

***

Myriam sat back and watched William as he walked through the Reach. It had been four days so far. Four very long and sad days, mostly. When they had brought Amder back, she had foolishly thought that all their problems were over. They had brought a God back to life!

They had named William as the Forgemaster. All had heard the voice of Amder and known. But William had learned of the fate of Duncan, his only family, and had fallen into a deep sadness. That melancholy had only grown when they had gotten back to the Reach. William, Regin, her, and the few Reacher's who had been at the Temple to help guard the place came back to a town that was more dead than alive. The Valni, the blood-crazed monsters of the Blood God, had torn through the place trying to get to the Temple.

It had saddened her; the people here were good people. And no one deserved what the Valni did to their victims. Regin had reacted the same, but William had given in to grief. A deep grief. For the last four days, all he had done was help bury the dead. He, the anointed Forgemaster of Amder, had put down his hammer, and helped bury every dead Reacher. He had dug graves; he had held the living in his arms and wept with them.

"They died to save me. They died because I asked them to." Will had answered when she tried to speak to him about it. "Myriam, I have to. I cannot bury Duncan. I could never bury my father, my uncle, or my mother. But these people, these I can bury, and these I can weep for."

Now, four days in, she hoped that this would be the last day. The smell of death and blood was finally leaving the Reach. A stiff wind, but a fresh one had started that morning and blown the miasma away. The wind held the smell of fresh snow, evergreen trees, and for all the world, a fresh start.

"Do you think he gets the message?" Regin appeared from inside the Golden Chisel, holding a hot mug of soup in each hand, along with a small hard piece of bread. He offered one to her, which she took graciously.

"I don't know. William is trying to do the right thing, and I know he mourns for his cousin, but life moves on. I'd bet you two ingots of Drendel steel that this wind is a reminder from Amder that his time of mourning is over." Myriam took a sip of the soup, the salty, meaty smell making her almost sigh. Better than nothing, but still four days of the same soup was getting old. All the cooking staff for the Chisel had died in the Valni attack, along with the innkeeper. His wife and daughter, and youngest son, had survived, but supplies were limited until the wagons came.

She felt guilty for complaining, even to herself, though. Reachers were remarkably able. Even though they mourned the losses to their families, and to the Reach they still kept moving forward. A little salted meat soup wasn't an enormous price to pay for everything that had happened here.

"I know. I spoke to him about it yesterday. He admitted Amder had tried to speak to him twice, but he'd ignored him. Ignored the God he gave so much for. He had seemed at peace with Duncan's death that night, but after?" Regin shook his head.

"Well, hopefully this wind will get him moving. He's the Forgemaster of Amder now. He needs to take up his hammer and get to work." Myriam held up her mug and motioned Regin to do the same. As he did so, she clinked their mugs together. "And we will help him, Companions to the Forgemaster it is."

Myriam watched Regin laugh. Such an unfamiliar man now. When they had traveled before, to the Guild with William and Master Jaste, Regin had been an insufferable ass. Arrogant, rude, and any time he opened his mouth, he spoke down to you. She'd hated him and had been more than happy when Master Jaste had sent him ahead to Ture.

William had filled her in about what had caused the change in the man. He had, along with William, Duncan, and their old Priest friend, Haltim, had been captured by the former High Priest of Amder. Who had beaten and tortured them all. That experience, and the knowledge of who William really was, had burned out the arrogance and pettiness. Regin had become a fresh new man. One she liked.

Regin took a bite of his bread and pointed at William. "Ah, the Forgemaster approaches."

***

Will was tired. Bone soaked, tired. Tired of burying bodies, tired of holding weeping survivors, tired of the smell of death that hung over the Reach. This is victory? All the old stories and legends he'd heard growing up here in the Reach had never gone into what it was like to survive the great turning points of the world. They had led the readers or the listeners to believe that everything was wonderful afterwards. This was decidedly not wonderful.

Amder was back. The power of the Priesthood was shattered, and the Guild could once again be what it was supposed to be, a place for learning and skill, not fighting for scraps that the Priesthood gave them. And the Blood God, may the sparks burn him, was never coming back. *Thanks to Duncan. Not you. Duncan.* Will felt himself push that pain away. He wasn't ready to deal with that hurt yet.

Will wiped his face with a cloth from his pocket. It wasn't warm here, but enough effort would make anyone sweat. He spied Myriam and Regin sitting in front of the Chisel, watching him. They'd done that every day since the night Amder returned. They'd both offered to help bury the dead, but they weren't Reachers. They had helped clean up and repair the town the first two days since that night, but after that, they waited. Waited for him.

He knew what they were waiting for. Amder was waiting too. The God of Craft and Creation had tried every night to contact him in his dreams, and every night, William didn't answer the call. Last night's call had been harder to ignore. He was sure tonight it would be harder still. One man, even the Forgemaster, can't ignore a God forever. He wanted to, though. He didn't want to admit it, but he William Reis, Reacher, Forgemaster of Amder, was scared. Scared of this unknown life, scared of the path in front of him. He didn't feel ready; he wasn't ready.

He'd taken up this burden to save Duncan. Now that was over with, some of that old self-doubt had come back. He knew that it was all in his head. He had brought a god back to life. A god that had named him the Forgemaster. *One reluctant Forgemaster.*

Will's eyes fell on Myriam again, and he felt his heart thud for a moment. Did she know how beautiful she looked sitting there? The light shining in her hair; the wind blowing it out of her face. A kind face, and wise beyond her years. A face that made him smile every time he saw it. Myriam always knew the right thing to say to Will. She believed in him. *And yet, you lied to her, and she hasn't forgiven you yet.*

And sitting next to her, Regin. Master Regin. This version of the man was someone that Will would have never expected when he met him at first. Once an arrogant, spiteful man, Regin had changed so much, Will wondered if he should have a different name. Will never would have made it out of Ture if it weren't for him. And he was a full Master of the Smithing Guild, waiting on him!

Will watched as yet another family stood, weeping at a mass grave. There wasn't enough room in the town cemetery for all these bodies. He didn't like the idea of a mass grave. *They deserve better.* Though he couldn't think of any other option. At least a few of the survivors who had the talent had already talked about what kind of monument to build here. He had let it be known he didn't want to be in it. He'd not done anything but bring them death.

Yet, every day, those who still lived came up to him and thanked him. He had seen more than a few small children peek around corners at him as he walked by. Whispers of awe. He didn't like it. He was still only William Reis. Granted, he was Forgemaster William Reis. Forgemaster. He still had a hard time thinking of himself that way. Maybe it was time to accept it, it would not go away.

The wind came down the street again, pushing away the smell of death. Will could almost feel the note of spring and renewal in that wind. Despite his melancholy mood, he smiled.

"About time, I was wondering if you'd fallen into a pit you'd never get out of lad." Amder's rumble filled his mind. *"And don't ignore me. You have work to do. I gave you this time because I knew you needed it. But my Forgemaster can't be doing this forever. I need you in Ture, at least at first. You must help the Guild get settled."*

"The Guild? But…" Will wanted to say, couldn't someone else do that. But there wasn't anyone else. He was the Forgemaster. *"I will have to get used to this. Won't I?"*

"Yes. But if it's any consolation, every single Forgemaster I've ever named, regardless if they were a Reis or not, has had the same fears and doubts. At least at first. I had one who hid in a cave for nearly 15 years before he finally accepted what he had to do. Do not worry William, you're doing a lot better than most." Amder's rumble was felt more than heard.

Will smiled at that. Well, I'm not screwing it up already at least. *"Amder, sorry I didn't answer, I…"*

"I said it was fine, William. And it is. But that time is past. I'll give you one more day here, then I need you heading to Ture." Amder's rumble paused. *"And really, you could have never ignored me if I didn't let you. You may be a Forgemaster, but you're not a God."*

William felt a stillness settle over him and the voice of Amder left him. *I wonder if I'll ever get used to a God, an actual GOD speaking to me on a first name basis.* Will took a deep breath and, instead of going to comfort yet another weeping survivor, approached his companions.

"Myriam, Regin." Will paused for effect. "Amder, the God of Craft and Creation has laid forth my first task."

Regin stood instantly. "Where are we to go? To the southern lands? Spreading the voice of Amder? Or maybe to the villages of the Grey coast?"

Myriam shot William a smile, a smile that brought a thrill, as usual. "We will go wherever he commands, of course."

"Amder, has ordered us to Ture. I get to put the Guild back in order. And make sure that factions of the old Priesthood aren't trying to latch onto the Guild to make it into something else." Will shrugged. "How I'm supposed to do that, I have no idea. But Regin, you will be an immense help there."

Myriam stood and stretched, her shirt accenting parts of her as she did so. Will averted his eyes.

"Ture? Well, not the most exotic and fantastical location, but it works, I guess."

Regin studied Will for a moment. "Forgemaster Reis, I hesitate to say anything, but we may need to wait a few days."

Will paused, looking back at Regin. His eyebrows crunched together a bit. "What do you mean? Amder said to go, so we go."

Regin sighed and rubbed his head. "Look Forgemaster, I know the Guild. I know Ture. Even though I'm sure things are more than chaotic in the city currently, there is one thing I know well. You don't look the part of a Forgemaster. Not yet, at any rate."

Will opened his mouth to complain, then closed it. Regin was right. He looked like a young blacksmith. Which he was. But he was also the anointed Forgemaster of the reborn God, the God of Craft and Creation. *I will never get used to that.* "Well, what do you suggest then?"

"Armor. Fancy armor. Show them the truth." Regin waved his hands around the courtyard. "We are here in the Reach. We can get materials easy enough, you have a god touched hammer, and we can, I'm sure, find a Forge to use."

Will hated the idea as soon as Regin said it. *I'm not a warrior. I fight only if I have to. But Regin is also right that I need to do something.* "No. Not a full set of armor. One, we don't have the time. Two, I'll never wear it."

Regin opened his mouth to argue, but snapped it closed. "As you say Forgemaster."

"Don't be so formal, Regin. You're not wrong. While I'm not doing a full set of armor, how about this? I'll get an additional set of blacksmithing leathers, the best we can find here, and we will make a breastplate. Only a breastplate, but one embossed with Amder's symbol. We can make it out of the best materials we can find, and you and Myriam can help forge it." Will clasped Regin's shoulder. "I need your advice, but please, call me Will."

"Forge... ok... Will." Regin nodded. "A breastplate it is. Can we at least do bracers as well?"

Will rolled his eyes in mock pain. "Fine, breastplate and bracers."

Myriam, who had said nothing, laughed, a happy sound that brought a smile to Will's face. "Well then, William, should we not get started?"

She still calls me William. A twinge of sadness clouded his smile. "Yes, let's."

"Well done, a breastplate and bracers I approve of. The armor isn't an awful idea really, but there isn't time. I could make it myself, I suppose though?" Amder's voice echoed for a moment in his mind.

"I'd prefer to do this myself; I need to make something. Create something. After all this death, I need it." Will looked forward to holding a hammer and making something that wasn't a god.

Chapter 2.

The man shuffled through the dry and baked landscape, heading north along the edge of the valley. From time to time, he would glance down, inspecting the valley floor. Red mist still flowed, but the white crystals, the blood of the cursed one, no longer filled the valley. Unfamiliar patterns had emerged in the mist, ones that the man watched with interest.

He was Zalkiniv; he was the master of the blood and was in full possession of Duncan's body. Somewhere, deep in his mind, there still existed a scrap of a man. A man who cried out to be free of this world. *Foolish man.* Zalkiniv drove his new form north. He would have his revenge on his betrayers. Then he would hunt down the ones who had brought back the soot god. He knew them. He had had the man in his grasp once. He could do it again.

A tingle on the edge of his mind snapped him back to the now. A Valni. There were less of them now. You would have never seen a lone Valni before his betrayal. The fools wasted too much time after killing me. If they had struck fast, Valnijz would have returned. Though if they had succeeded, he would not have been able to get his revenge. They had thrown hordes at the city of the Reach. Many had died there, but many more had died trying to escape the barrier's return. Once, many years ago, they had forced a Valni to contact the barrier. The resulting sound and the burning of flesh had echoed across the valley.

The tingle grew closer. *Good, I am hungry.* Zalkiniv sat back and let the beast take over this body. A hunger surged through him. Blood, Blood and power. The beast crouched down behind some rocks nearby. The Valni would have his scent now. That was good. It wanted its prey closer.

A crouching figure came over a nearby rise, sniffing the air. Loosely garbed in a chain shirt that was more holes than chain, the figure was thin, dirty. The rest of its clothes were ragged, dusty, and ripped. More than half its hair was missing, ripped out by the look of it.

Blood surging, blood rich, blood touched by a mad god. The beast took a sniff of its own. Closer. Prey must come closer.

The beast purposefully shifted a foot, making sure the sound could be heard. A soft sound, but enough to draw the prey closer. The scent of blood grew closer. The beast could hear the prey breathing now, a hitching sound that all Valni had.

The beast leaped out from behind the rocks, his arms wide, ready to grasp the head of his prey. The Valni scrambled back to get a better angle to attack. The smells of this man, this creature confusing it. A man, yes, but something like the Valni, but not.

The beast landed and, faster than its prey could react, grasped the head of the Valni and pushed its hands together. Its prey lashed out its legs and arms trying to find purchase to escape. But the beast was powerful, stronger than the Valni. Its hands pressed again, and the beast could feel the bones trying to stay where they were. Bones shifted as the pressure grew. An audible crack and the Valni went limp. The beast did not care, pushing further, feeling the bones shift and the skin tear as it pushed its hands tighter. Blood covered the beast's hands and forearms before it stopped. The beast looked down and, with a growl began to feed.

Zalkiniv waited until the beast was done and, with the power his spirit could gather from the blood of the Valni, pushed the beast back into the back of the mind and took the body over again. Blood and other things filled his mouth. He took a scrap of cloth off the rags the Valni had worn and wiped his face.

That should hold the beast, for now. Zalkiniv moved forward again, ignoring both the screams of rage of the beast, and the fainter weaker retching that came from the last scrap of the man who had been Duncan Reis. Zalkiniv wondered how the man held on. But some stubborn scrap, some tiny remnant of the man clung to life. Powerless, but still there. At least it will be entertaining to torture that scrap. Next time, he'd talk to it as Rache.

With that thought, the man, Zalkiniv, moved faster. He wasn't sure how much farther it was to what he was looking for, but it couldn't be too far. His suspicion was correct as he finally spied them in the distance. Three huge pipes, leading from the blood mist, into the blasted landscape. They led to one place, one very special place, the Temple of Valnijz. *And I will release the beast on them all.*

Settling into a distance eating run, he ran next to the pipes, remembering the days of using the mist. After the Godsfall, things had been chaotic. He'd had to kill multiple challengers in the days and weeks following that cursed day. Once his grip had been secure, and they had known the knowledge of the effects of the mist, they had built these pipes.

They had pumped the mist and tested it on slaves, animals, anything. Learning how it changed people, seeing the effects on animals, even trying to imbue food and drink with its properties. All the experiments had failed, save one very special one. One that once it had been completed, all who had known of it had been given to the blood god by himself personally. The results had been hidden and sealed away.

The Blood God had ordered it destroyed. But that they had been unable to do. Zalkiniv had never questioned it before, but now, betrayed, he no longer cared to follow the orders of a dead god. If Valnijz feared that result, then Zalkiniv would reclaim it.

The day wore on as Zalkiniv ran, before finally, in the early evening, he spied the tops of the twisted black and red spires of the Temple. Wait. Wait till dark, then turn this body over to the beast, and lay waste to those who huddle inside. He knew the perfect time to strike.

As he waited, his thoughts turned inward, finding the speck of Duncan that still clung to existence.

***

"Duncan... I miss you." Rache's voice came to the huddled man.

"Rache?" Duncan tried to look around, but all he could see, or at least perceive, was the same dull red mist. *She's not real. Remember.* The barest hint of a whisper that he more felt than heard came to him.

"Rache? Where are you?" Duncan couldn't remember anything much anymore. Not since leaving the Reach with Haltim. Pain, pain and anger. Rage even. Everything was so foggy, but those feelings were all he knew.

"Duncan… I'm with you always. We will never be apart." The voice of Rache came again, so close this time, but he still couldn't see her.

She's not real. She's the enemy, Duncan. She's playing a game with you. That whisper came again. The voice was familiar, but he couldn't place it. Where was he? Even the ground below him felt odd. Sticky and cold. Blood? Was it blood he was lying on?

"Duncan…." Rache's voice turned what little attention he had back towards the mist. There! A female form, young, beautiful, came out of the mist. She wasn't wearing any clothes, but the mist swirled around her, hiding her nudity. "My poor Duncan."

"Rache? Why do I hurt so much? Where are we? I can't remember anything." Duncan struggled to sit up more. His body didn't want to move, but finally he seemed to sit up. *I feel so strange. Like I'm not real, except for the hurt.*

"My poor Duncan, don't you remember?" Rache smiled then, and Duncan's breath caught. The smile was wrong. Her teeth, they were filed as sharp as a Narmors. And her mouth... was it growing??

"You're mine forever, Duncan. My toy, my pet. I will make sure that every kill, every death you feel. You are nothing more than a shadow of a memory, one that will scream for release." Rache's mouth grew bigger, stretching to obscene proportions, as her voice changed into his tormentors.

Duncan screamed in fear as the holes in his mind filled. He knew her now. He knew the truth for this moment. He knew why he hurt; he knew where he was. He was dead, and somehow, someway, this thing, this creature, had taken his body. *I will never be free.*

***

Zalkiniv nearly laughed. He had been worried at first, with that shred of Duncan left behind. But after that brief interaction, he was more amused than anything now. Something to entertain him when he was bored. The sun was almost down now, and the air, before hot and dry, was rapidly cooling. Fires and large torches lit up at various points in the Temple. *The screams will echo tonight.*

Finally, he heard the sound he'd been waiting for. Three booming hits reverberated through the air, carrying over the distance. The call to worship. *They will all be in one place, such an easy target for the beast.* Standing finally, Zalkiniv felt more than heard the joints pop as he stretched. He could feel the power from the Valni kill still inside. *Good, the more power, the better.*

He moved towards the temple, keeping an eye out for anything unusual. There hadn't been guards before. Why would there be? Who would be foolish enough to try to attack the Temple of the Blood God? But he didn't get to where he had been by not being aware of what was going on around him, and who knew what the current High Priest, whoever it was, was trying to do.

Finally, he arrived at a side door that had always been very seldom used. Its major advantage this evening was the fact it was almost directly connected to the sacrificial heart of the complex. He would enter, release the beast and watch from inside as the beast feasted and killed those who had betrayed him.

Valnijz would be angry, but Zalkiniv no longer cared. For a thousand years, he had worked to bring about the return of his God, and in his moment of triumph, his God had betrayed him. All because he hadn't gotten both cursed Reis men. He'd had them both in his hands, but the other one, the one who must have become a 'Forgemaster', had slipped through his fingers.

Zalkiniv pushed those thoughts away. It was time. The door wasn't locked as usual. Once inside, he took a deep breath. The tang of blood overlaid everything. Salty, metallic, he found himself hunger and his mouth watered. Soon enough, there will be blood for days. Zalkiniv mentally pushed himself back and let the beast take over. His last act, before releasing his control, was to point it down the hall. KILL.

The beast howled, but its voice didn't overwhelm the sound of chanting and screams that echoed down the hall from the heart of the temple. The smell of blood brought forth a rush of hunger, a hunger that could never be truly filled. With a guttural roaring, the beast ran down the hall and burst into the main chamber.

For a moment, none of the assembled priests or slaves even noticed, as all attention was upon the altar. Standing there, a Priest stood, holding a black iron dagger, and a slew of bodies hung, throats slashed, and hung upside down. A small stream of blood flowed down the raised platform and into a pool below.

The beast cared nothing for this, but the fresh blood so near drove it even madder with hunger. It grabbed the nearest acolyte, and with a snap broke his neck with such strength his bones burst through on one side. Then the priests and slaves noticed, and panic set in. The beast ignored the frantic yells and killed more. The beast thrust its hand through the abdomen of a nearby slave and disemboweled the screaming man. On another, the beast ripped the throat out of a frantically chanting Priest with its teeth, the warm salty blood full of fear and hate making it smile.

Blood magic washed over the beast, as older, more powerful Underpriests attempted to stop it. The beast ignored the attempts to command it, and as one priest after another fell to its rampage, the more senior priests tried to flee. The beast was too fast for them all, and each died in its attacks.

Finally, all that was left was the new High Priest, wielding his dagger. The Priest's face was white, and fear shone upon its face. To his credit, he slashed out at the beast. Untrained in combat, he might have been, but a wild swing can still sometimes hit. And this one contacted the arm.

The beast screamed in pain and hunched away for a moment; the dagger cut hurt! Nothing in its mind should cause it pain, but this dagger, this cut, burned with a fire unequaled. The Priest smiled for a second, thinking he had taken control of the situation, lashed out with the dagger again, aiming this time for the beast's chest.

The beast was fast though, and after the first shock, the pain only enraged the thing more. With a nearly impossible twist to its form, the beast dodged the attack and before the Priest could react grabbed its attackers' arm and with the sound not unlike the breaking of a tree limb broke the elbow in half.

The Priest screamed and dropped the dagger, falling to his knees as the beast twisted and ripped the arm off the man, his screams stopping as the shock and pain overwhelmed him, and he fell dead, his blood mixing with his victims from minutes before.

The beast fed then, though it avoided the blood-covered dagger that had clattered to the floor.

***

Zalkiniv watched from inside. He found himself somewhat in disbelief. His order was soft. This many Priests should have put up more of a fight, but the beast had made quick work of them. Even that new High Priest had fallen to the beast with little of a fight. Zalkiniv tried to remember the man's name but failed. He recognized him as one of the twenty, the leaders of the Underpriests, but what he had been called, he had no idea.

The dagger, though, that was worth paying attention to. The beast's hunger was still strong, but the feasting had slowed for now. Zalkiniv gathered his strength and pushed the beast back, taking over the body once more. The feeling of flowing back into control was one he relished. The pleasures of the flesh weren't unknown to him, but this, this was far better.

Locking the beast back into the part of the mind, he fed it delusions of death and destruction to keep it there. A useful tool the beast was, as long as he kept it in control. Turning his attention back to the dagger, he carefully took the handle of the dagger, but no pain greeted him. Only the blade hurt, then, good.

Zalkiniv knew this weapon. They had created it in the first experiments with the blood mist. The Priest who had created it had died, and no one was sure what he had done. Even the rites of the dead had failed to get an answer. He knew the dagger could break almost any defense, as his own death attested. He had woven protection into his very soul so many times the dagger should have never been able to even wound him, yet his death had been easy.

Of course, Valnijz wanted me dead, so how many of those protections bound with blood workings would have worked, anyway? The pale leather of the handle was stained red brown, the blood of countless victims having turned it so years ago. Searching the body of the now former chief priest, Zalkiniv found the sheath for the dagger and put it away. *Another useful tool.* And better the dagger where he could use it himself, and not left behind.

One last thing to acquire, and the first part of his revenge would be done. Then he would, with the beast under his control, cut a swath of death and destruction from here to every corner of the world. But first, every scrap of the worship of his former lord would die by his own hand. Valnijz betrayed him, and so the God must pay.

But where to go? In the blasted lands here on this side of the barrier, there wasn't much in the way of power outside of where he was right now. To the south it was. He would cross the Lost Sea and head south. The lands there held followers of the Blood God, though this had been the center of his worship. But the southern cults had secrets of their own. And power he could use.

The cut on his arm still burned, and it was raw, even gleaming. That should have healed by now. Zalkiniv frowned at the pain but bound his arm in a torn piece of tapestry. *If I work the blood, the effects would be unknown. Better to wait.*

Making his way off the platform, Zalkiniv carefully made his way through the various hallways and rooms, heading down, down to a room that only he knew of. He passed the occasional slave who wisely fell to their knees and waited for a death. He didn't bother killing them, though. He didn't need to, and for now, his bloodlust was filled. The Priests had betrayed him; the slaves were there to be used for power.

Finally, he stood before what appeared to be a plain stone wall, with a small carving of the Spear of Valnijz upon it. The spear. Where was it now? He'd have to question Duncan again, to see if the wretch knew. Touching the carving four times in the right order, the wall shifted and slid off to the right.

Light thrust out of the room; light so bright, he blinked in surprise. He had forgotten the light in his room. In his mind, the beast howled, afraid. Interesting. That could be a useful side effect if I need it. For there, on a pedestal, sat a crystal in a small metal box. The crystal was golden and blue, with moving lights of brilliant green swimming under its surface, a crystal that terrified even a God.

Zalkiniv didn't like the thing. His skin prickled as he entered the room, and something, some sound, came to him, but was out of reach to hear. An experiment, but why this result? It had seemed a sound and interesting idea back when proposed. Could the blessed mist be forced into a crystal of the blood of the soot god?

In the holy valley, the mist and crystals intermingled to the naked eye, though the priests had studied the mist closely and had long ago realized that the mist never touched the crystals of the dirty one. The idea had come to force it, a sound idea they had believed. If they could turn the blood of a god, what powers would this have? Could they use this to bring the blood god back, and even more powerful? The plan had been run by the most powerful of the priests under him. They had used slaves to gather the sample crystal, which in of itself had taken several weeks. Nearly twenty slaves had been chosen by the mist in the attempt and risen as Valni.

But finally, one had taken a small crystal and transported it here to the Temple. They had built a vast machine afterwards. One that was attached to the pipes outside, sucking in the blessed blood and increasing the pressure inside its vessel. Slaves, captured travelers, and even Valni had been sacrificed to increase the power inside the machine.

Finally, nearly a month later, an explosion had rocked the Temple. The machine had burst open and all in the chamber at the time had either died or become Valni instantly. Three days it had taken to get all the blessed mist out of the room.

And there, in the wreckage, had been this crystal. Changed. The blood god had been weaker then, and had to Zalkiniv's surprise immediately spoken to him, cursing the crystal as an abomination and demanding its destruction. It had been the first time the blood god had spoken directly to him since the Godsfall. Destroying it proved impossible. Scores of Priests had died trying, and the slaves had vanished. As soon as one touched the crystal with their skin, or with something else, the slave had faded out as if they had never been there. They had only one semi success during this time. A captured merchant had been successful in putting the crystal in a small metal container he had with him. He'd been a jewelry merchant, if Zalkiniv remembered correctly. That the crystal had allowed.

It could be picked up by anyone once it was in that little chest, but touching the crystal itself still caused the death of any loyal followers of Valnijz, and the slaves still vanished. *We cleaned up the room and put the crystal here and sealed it away.* But something that scared a God? Zalkiniv wanted it.

To keep the secret, he had sacrificed anyone who had knowledge of what had truly happened. Zalkiniv had done that personally. The one thing that had surprised even him was that the blood god had never mentioned the thing again. It was almost as if he didn't even want to think of it. Useful now.

The feelings the thing gave him increased as he entered the room. His skin was now sweating, and he itched badly. The beast howled in terror and for a moment attempted to wrest control. Zalkiniv forced it back with effort. Even the tiny speck of Duncan that existed still reacted, though differently. His weeping had stopped, and he felt more real. It seemed whatever this crystal was; it was giving him some strength.

Closing the lid to the box with some effort, the feelings ended.

Chapter 3.

Will stepped back from the family forge, smiling at the work. He, Regin, and Myriam had spent the last two days forging this breastplate and bracers, and he had to admit, they had turned out beyond his hopes. When the word had gotten out that William Reis, the new Forgemaster, needed metals to make something, Reachers had appeared with options that surprised even him.

Lanzinite, Drendel Steel ingots, Blue Cobalt, and even three small Wight Iron ingots. And for inlay, more goldlace, silverlace, and even rarer crimsonlace. He'd picked his metals and thought about where to make this extra equipment. The house forge had come to mind at once, but he'd hesitated. He wasn't sure how he would feel stepping back into the place. No Duncan anymore, and that fact still hurt.

"It's the right choice, William. Bring some joy back." Amder's voice had echoed in his head, a whisper, but still there. When he'd first led Regin and Myriam to his childhood home, he'd been worried. He should not have been. Myriam had immediately taken to the place. An enormous smile had broken out when she'd realized what the building was. And Regin had nearly laughed out loud with the enormous carved relief of Amder on the side of the building.

Will had gone first, and stepping into his home felt odd. As if someone else lived there now. *I guess I've changed. Will I ever live here?* He shook off the thought. *One Day, I'll settle down here. Have a family. One day.* Will glanced at Myriam, but she didn't notice. Her eyes were darting around the house, taking in its size.

The place was a mess. After Duncan and Haltim had fled, the Priest who had been here then ransacked the place searching for clues of their whereabouts. But thankfully, the forge had been untouched. The bedrooms were easy to put back together too, though Will kept the door to Duncan's room closed and untouched. He wasn't ready for that one.

Now, looking at the bracers and breastplate, the choice to do it here felt right. Making things again felt right. No more death and destruction, but creation felt good. The hammer on metal, the sounds of the quench, the smell of the forge. Will's melancholy had faded with the work. *I needed this.*

***

Regin wiped his forehead with his glove, giving a whistle as he checked the last piece over. "Well, if I hadn't been a part of it, there's no way I would have thought we made this in only two days."

"I agree." Will clasped Regin's shoulder. "I couldn't have done it without you."

Regin laughed. "Well, it's a strange feeling, a full Guildmaster, reduced to forge helper!"

Will laughed with him. Regin wasn't lying. It was odd to have a full Guildmaster being the assistant. But then again, he was the Forgemaster, right? Still strange, Amder, still strange.

"If you two will stop congratulating yourselves, you could let me get to work? I have the inlays ready, and if we want to get on the road tomorrow, I have to get started." Myriam pointed towards the house. "Go in there, and I'll let you know when I'm done."

"Yes Myriam." Will smiled at her and gave a mock bow.

Regin said nothing, but mirrored Will's bow.

Myriam snorted and turned towards her work as Will and Regin went inside. Will's eyes readjusted to the dim interior. After they had cleaned up the place the first day, he'd gotten more used to being back here. He had to admit he loved this house. No, this home.

The first night had been hard for him, though. He kept expecting Duncan to walk through the door and sling a bag of scaving treasures onto the table and regale him with stories of his adventures that day. He knew that would never happen, but he missed it, though at the time he'd missed a lot and only half listened. A lifetime ago.

"Myriam is wonderful, isn't she?" Regin said as he settled down into a chair. "Few others could do the work she does in that small a timeframe."

Will's ears perked up at Regin's wording. Wonderful? "Yes, she's very talented." Will looked at Regin, trying to read the man. But as usual, Regin was already unreadable. The man had both an interesting and irritating tendency to say something and leave it out there. It made trying to figure out where he was going with an idea rather annoying.

He waited for Regin to say something more, but the Guildmaster only took the occasional sip of water out of a mug and said nothing. The sounds of Myriam working by the forge occasionally worked their way through the house, otherwise quiet settled over the place.

Some time passed, and Will gathered some food. Bread, Cheese, a few sausages. He wanted korba fruit, but about any fruit was hard to get in the Reach. You had to pay nearly a week's wages to get anything fresh. He knew if he asked for it, they'd give it to him for free, but that was the thing he was actively trying to avoid.

"Let me go get Myriam, and we can eat something. I'm curious how well the work is going." Will waved to Regin. "You start, but leave some for us!"

Regin nodded as he ripped some bread in half. "Sure, sure. Don't take too long."

Will went back out to the Forge to find Myriam critically eyeing the breastplate. "Food's ready if you're hungry." Will said, clearly startling the girl as she gave a slight jump at his voice.

"Oh... Sorry. Yes, food, food is good." Myriam put down the Breastplate. "But William, can I talk to you first? Alone?"

"What do you need?" Will leaned back against one anvil.

Myriam looked down for a moment and when she raised her head, Will could see the dampness in her eyes. "William. I wanted to say how sorry I am about your cousin. I know you did everything you could to save him, and yet he still didn't live. I really am sorry."

Will nodded. "Thank you. I haven't quite come to terms with that yet. I keep expecting the sparks blessed man to walk in the door half the time. But why the tears? You didn't even know Duncan."

"William. It's about... you. Us. What was? Who you were? Markin Darto." Myriam sighed and looked down for a moment, wiping her eyes. "Sparks burn me, I hate this."

Will could feel his stomach fall as she spoke. *Let her stop talking right now. Please.* "We don't have to talk about this now." Will let the words slip out. *I'll give her an out. I can still show her I'm the same man, right?*

"No, William. I need to do this. If I don't, it wouldn't be fair to you, or me." Myriam's voice stopped for a moment. She looked up at the sky and let out a lengthy breath. "The man I knew, the man I met traveling with Master Jaste and Regin, that man, Markin, was a lie. I know why you did it. I really understand. Even more so now, with you being the Forgemaster. But this new you, well new to me you, I don't know. And I find myself not being interested in the same way I was before. I like you, William, but as a friend. Nothing else, nothing more than that."

Will wanted to say something, but what? He didn't share her feelings. In fact, his attraction to her had only grown since he had stopped living that lie. Markin Darto, damn that name. But he couldn't say that now. She'd thrown out anything she had felt for him and left him with friendship. He realized he was clenching his jaw when he saw Myriam's face pale a bit. *I must look like I'm about to explode in anger at her.*

"I." Will took a breath himself, feeling it catch for a moment. "I understand. Food is ready if you're hungry." Will tuned as fast as he could away from her. His thoughts a mixed jumble of emotions. *If we are still friends, maybe I can show her I'm the same person. No, that's stupid. Send her away. Clean break is how I should handle this. No, she's earned the right to be here with you. She helped you bring a God back to life!*

"Myriam coming?" Regin asked as he was eating, but as he raised his head, he took one look at Will and stopped mid-chew. "Everything all right?" Regin craned his head past Will. "Is she hurt or something?"

"She might be here, but I've lost my appetite. I will rest upstairs for now. I'll be back down later." Will could taste a hint of sour bile in his mouth. *I wish Duncan were here. He would at least make me laugh about it.*

Will could hear Myriam come in as he went up the stairs and the muffled conversation she and Regin were having. He even heard a peal of her laughter, a sound that only made him more confused.

*****

Regin watched William go upstairs. Hard to believe he was the Forgemaster of Amder, if you didn't know the man. Talented didn't describe him. Regin had nearly dropped the billets more than once in their work, from shock. William was that good. Every hammer blow seemed to line up exactly right, with the perfect amount of force. Regin was an anointed Guildmaster, and compared to the skill William had, he might as well be an oaf hammering scrap iron.

Regin could tell that whatever Myriam had said to Will outside was, it had made the Forgemaster more than a little unhappy. And considering William was a man, and Myriam was a woman, Regin could guess what she had said. It was obvious how William felt about her. Will would look at her and then drop his eyes and look away. He doesn't have much experience with women; I think.

Myriam came in, wiping her face and forehead with a fold of her cloak. "It may be cold in the Reach but being at a Forge all day still gets you sweaty." Myriam glanced at Will's empty chair and Regin saw the slight frown cross her face.

"Food I see?" Myriam threw a smile and sat down, grabbing a hunk of some bread and the pot of Klah. "At least one thing here has some flavor." Regin watched as she smeared a thick layer of that spread on her bread and took a bite.

"Be careful there, Myriam. Stuff's potent. The only person who would want to be near you after eating that will be William." Regin shot a smile at her, trying to cheer her up.

A small, sad frown crossed her face before vanishing. "Probably not him, not right now."

"So how is the inlay work going?" Regin forced the conversation away from what was obvious. *He may be the Forgemaster of Amder, but I have to remember he and Myriam are still young for all this. Looks like William's having some heartbreak.*

"Great actually. The pieces you both made are fantastic work, and the inlay seems to flow perfectly." Myriam answered in between bites of bread and cheese. "Must be that Guildmaster training."

"William did nearly all of it, to be honest. I merely assisted. It's incredible to watch him work, but you probably know that from that night in the Temple." Regin sat back for a moment. "How was that for you, anyway? Will doesn't like to talk about it, considering he found out his cousin died at the same time. He might want to talk about it later, but I think it's too fresh for him, too raw."

Myriam swallowed and washed down a second large bite of bread with Klah. "Incredible. Terrifying. Worrying. Exciting. And I know what you mean. Will looked like some kind of God himself. The Forge of Amder lit up with a white flame unlike anything I'd ever seen, swinging that Hammer of Amder, the light catching all the gems on it. I've seen a lot of metalworkers in my brief life, but none seemed to BE the work they were doing the way he was."

Regin nodded. He'd caught glimpses of that himself in the last two days. "In some ways I wish I could have been down there with you all, but I was doing what I needed to do." *My last act of penance for being such a cod for so long.*

"You might have been more help than I was. I'm not even a fully trained first year Guild apprentice. You're a full Guildmaster." Myriam gave a slight shrug. "If I wasn't here, I'd probably be back at my father's inn now, working the tables and my dream of being a Guild Smith, a dead one."

"You know, now that Bracin is apparently gone, and William is the Forgemaster, I'm sure he can get you back into the Guild." Regin took a long drink of his water. "That would mean you wouldn't be traveling with us anymore, but you'd be able to finish."

Myriam sighed. "I thought about asking him. But I enjoy traveling with you all." Myriam started for a moment and raised her eyebrows. "You know, you're a full Guildmaster, you could tutor me. Master Jaste did always say you were a very good smith. We travel with William and you teach me the things I don't know. About Metalwork and Smithing I mean."

Regin frowned for a moment. Her idea wasn't a bad one. He could tutor her as they traveled, and when they had time to do metalwork, having one-on-one training would be good. "I guess that could work. I can talk to William. It's kind of obvious that he's not overly happy right now."

Myriam sat back in her chair. "That might be for the best. I told him something he didn't want to hear. I told him that while I liked him as a friend, whatever feelings more that were developing have gone, along with that name he used back in the Guild, Markin Darto."

"You know he's the same person, right? He apparently hated being Markin Darto." Regin studied Myriam for a moment. She's a smart, talented girl, and, yes, attractive. William could do a lot worse.

"I know that. And I told him I understood why he used that name. But he's the Forgemaster of Amder now. And that's a whole different person that I don't know." Myriam stood and took a long drink of water. "I better finish the work if we are to get out of here tomorrow."

Regin watched her leave. *Hopefully, this resolves itself. The last thing we need is an emotionally wrecked Forgemaster, not now.* His mind turned towards one other thing Myriam had said. Master Jaste had always told them he was a good Smith? Regin looked out the window for a long moment. *Thank you for that, Master Jaste. That's another thing I owe you.*

Chapter 4.

William awoke, still fighting his sadness. He'd not come back down at all after that conversation with Myriam. *I'm bad at these things.* It wouldn't get any better now that he was the Forgemaster. Will had little experience with romance, but even he knew that being powerful and important drew people to you, but usually the wrong people. For a moment, he considered flaunting a series of women in Myriam's face when they got to Ture, but discarded the idea almost as fast as it came. *My feelings might be hurt, but I'm not that kind of person.*

Duncan would have known what to say. He'd had half the Reaches eligible young women after him. He'd never picked one, and he'd been very careful not to get himself into serious trouble. Will had never had that knack. A few girls their age had shown some interest, but he'd always screwed it up. Usually by showing too much interest, too fast. He didn't understand the rules of the game of courtship. If you were interested, just say it. Why waste all that time with flirting and pretending?

Will's stomach reminded him with a noise that he also hadn't eaten last night. He had, however, packed up what he was bringing to Ture, outside the extra armor items. *Gave me something to do while I felt sorry for myself.* He grabbed his pack and his hammer and headed down the stairs. The morning light was streaming in as the sun got high enough to not be blocked by the mountains.

"Morning William." Myriam's voice came from the door to the Forge.

William turned around to find her waiting there, wearing a set of travel clothes and a new leather apron. "Inlay work done?" Will kept his voice as plain as he could.

"Yes, everything is ready. There's food in the kitchen, most Regin packed up already. He's outside with a cart. He got up early to get things organized." Myriam didn't react to Will's tone.

She's still my friend, but I still wish it was more. "You should have woken me. I would have helped." Will headed to the kitchen to find a few fresh and still warm bread rolls. Helping himself, Will wandered outside to talk to Regin.

He found the man sitting in the cart and deep in conversation with Captain Tolin.

"William! The person I wanted to see. Captain Tolin here is insisting on coming with us. Says it's not safe for us to travel alone with all the recent changes in Palnor. I explained you're the Forgemaster, but he's not buying it." Regin waved at Tolin. "Maybe he will listen to you."

Captain Vin Tolin turned to William and came to attention. "Forgemaster Reis."

"Captain. You need not do that. I'm merely William." Will liked the Captain. He was an honest, if somewhat hard, man. But he had to be in his line of work. And his defense of the Reach during the attack of the Valni had been a miracle of Amder.

"Forgemaster." Captain Tolin ignored his request. "You may be the Forgemaster, but it's not safe out there. I've been in places where there is a change in power. Things can get messy for a while. Besides, I'm not needed here now. Ture will give me a place to decide what my next step will be."

"Take him." Amder's voice whispered in Will's head. *"I don't expect you to be a warrior, but there might be a time you need to pick up that hammer to do more than shape metal. Take him and let him teach you some on the way to Ture."*

Will frowned at that message. He didn't want to fight anyone anymore.

His frown must have been a bad one though as Regin sort of moved back a bit, and even the Captain inhaled.

"I don't mean to offend Forgemaster Reis. I am only trying to do what I believe to be the right course." Captain Tolin seemed to stand even straighter.

"No, you didn't offend." Will let go of the frown. *Fine, I'll do it your way.* Will thought at Amder, not even sure if the God could hear him. "You can come with two stipulations. One, you call me Will or William. And two, on the trip you teach me combat. I don't want to fight, and I don't want to be a soldier, but it could be useful to know how to swing this hammer of mine in other ways." Will let his hand rest on the Wight Iron of his hammer, the symbol of his office as Forgemaster.

Captain Tolin raised an eyebrow and then, with a slight bow, accepted. "I agree with those terms, William. I will be back in less time than it will take you all to get finished here."

Will watched Captain Tolin head back towards the Chisel. Well, looks like another person is coming with us.

"Sparks above William. Do you really want to get trained with weapons?" Regin's face held that somewhat familiar look of surprise on it.

"No, I don't want it. But Amder gave me some advice. Said it would be good for the Captain to come. I was going to turn him down." Will shook his head. "I might be the Forgemaster, but Amder is still a God."

Regin shrugged. "I like the man well enough. For a soldier, I didn't expect you to bring him along. But in a way, it makes sense. Even Journeymen in the Guild, before they go out and wander, learn to have some fight training. Not that many would willingly attack a Guild member, but it's happened that Journeyman who had stowed away their cloaks for the night or for whatever reason had been attacked. And wild beasts don't care about red cloaks." Regin half laughed at the last line.

"Did I ever tell you about the time when I was first heading out? I was passing this farmer's field, and this man's rooster..." Regin stopped mid-sentence as Will held up his hand.

"Tell me once we start down the road. Let's get the rest of the gear in the cart, and I'll put on that armor to try it on, grab Myriam and wait for the Captain." Will took a last bite of his breakfast. "Let's go see what Myriam has wrought."

Regin climbed out of the wagon and together they went back inside the Reis' home. And there, on the table, sat the Breastplate and bracers. The light of dawning sun lit up the metal and, for all the world, it looked alive.

Will held his breath for a moment. The inlay work Myriam had done was impeccable. The crimsonlace flames around the silver anvil and golden hammer of Amder seemed afire on its own. The metal under it shone itself, a unique shade of silver distinct from the Anvil, but yet everything was clear. *Sparks above, it's beautiful.*

"It's also blessed William. Nothing short of a God blessed weapon can get through that, and I've already removed my blessing from the things made before my resurrection, mostly." Amder's voice carried a trace of amusement. "They didn't like it much, though. I think there's more than one noble or rich merchant demanding the money back from the Priesthood right now."

Will stifled a laugh at that. Haltim had always maintained that there were still honorable people in the Temple, but Will had yet to see it. Serves them right. His eyes raised up and saw Myriam, the light off the armor reflecting in her eyes, and her smile. His momentary humor fled. "Don't take it hard, William. I'm a God, and the vagaries of the human heart mystify me. That was to be my brother's world, before he became what he became."

Will knew Amder was right, but the sting was still new. "All I can say is to be a loyal friend. Things may change down the road, you never know. I don't even know." Amder's voice echoed one last time before leaving him. Will always knew when he wasn't there anymore. He wasn't sure how, but it felt like someone leaving a room you were in.

"Well, what do you two think? You've not said a word, standing there like a fencepost in a field." Myriam pointed to the items. "Say something, making me think you hate it!"

Both Will and Regin spoke, but Will got his out first. "It's incredible, Myriam. Truly remarkable work. I knew you were talented, but this is amazing."

Regin picked up the breastplate. "You know, I think tutoring you would be easy. I saw your practice piece, and that was good, but this... are you sure you even need to be tutored?"

Will reached for the breastplate himself as Regin handed it over. "Tutoring?"

Myriam answered. "Well, basically, I'm still an unfinished first year, Smith William. Regin is a Guildmaster, and you're the Forgemaster of Amder. While technically I left the Guild, I hoped that you might get me back into it, in the future, not right now." The words spilled out of her faster the more she spoke.

"It's not like I want to leave, but Regin and I were talking and the subject of tutoring me came up so that if I go back into the Guild, I will not have to start over, at least that was the idea, I don't know if that's allowed or not." Myriam shut her mouth and looked at Will with a hopeful smile.

Will hadn't really thought about Myriam's rank. Myriam was Myriam. Even if his feelings for her weren't returned, she was a fantastic smith, and he trusted her. "Well, I hadn't ever thought about it, but now you say that I think it's an excellent idea."

Regin nodded. "We can start on the road to Ture. While William here is learning combat tactics, you will learn more about Forging and metalwork."

"Combat? What does that mean?" Myriam asked, cocking an eyebrow.

"Oh, Captain Tolin is coming with us. At least to Ture. Amder kind of pushed me into it. While I can swing a hammer, I know little about fighting with one. And I guess it's something I probably need to learn. You too at some point." Will picked up the bracers. "Let's try these on one last time, clean up and get out of here."

"I seem to remember being much better at combat than you already, William." Myriam remarked as she helped Will buckle the breastplate on, font and back. "Remember the Narmor?"

"Yes, yes. I remember." Will remembered it well. It had been the first time he had truly seen how remarkable she was, not that he could tell her that part, not now, at any rate. *I should have told her that a long while ago.*

Regin stepped back as Will finished the last buckle on the bracers. "Well, you stand out now. It may not be a full set of armor, but no one will mistake you for a work-a-day metal pounder. Once we get to Ture, we will add a cloak to the mix, have to finish the look."

Will snorted. "I'm not a noble, and technically in Guild terms I'm an Apprentice still."

Regin shook his head. "William, with this kind of thing, trust me. The appearance will matter. A golden cloak will bring it together. Approach the gate to the Guild at mid-morning, when the sun peeks over the buildings and lights up the road. You entering the Guild will make for a show of power that will help you an impressive deal. It may be all theatrics, but it will work."

Will forced his scowl down as Regin spoke. Fakery and tricks. But Regin was right. Will didn't have to like it, though.

A knock on the door broke Will's grumpy thoughts. Regin opened the door to find Captain Tolin standing there in his normal guard attire and a large rucksack. "Captain Tolin, we are about to leave." Regin waved him inside.

"Thank you, Guildmaster. And you Forgemaster Re… William. I approve of the armor. Where is the rest, though? A half decent swordsman could take you down like a hunter killing a lame deer. Your legs are completely exposed and neck. A cut to the back of the leg and you'd go down hard." Captain Tolin walked a slow circle around William. "Craftsmanship is impeccable, I'll give you that. How thick is it? If it is only ornamental, it wouldn't be much use in a fight."

"I want my legs free. I'm not the fastest mover, anyway. I'd lumber everywhere if I was wearing more. But you don't have to worry about its thickness. Its god touched Captain Tolin. Nothing short of a god-blessed blade will cut through this." Will thumped one of his bracers. "It's solid."

Captain Tolin started to answer but closed his mouth. "As you say, William."

Myriam had grabbed her rucksack as the four of them stood around the table for a moment. "Well, are we ready to leave for Ture?" Myriam ushered them towards the door. "Standing around here won't get us anywhere."

"You all head outside, I'll put out the fire and be right there." William answered grabbing a sand bucket.

Regin nodded as he, Myriam and the Captain headed outside.

Will poured the sand on the embers of the fireplace before looking around the great common room. Home. The last time he had left here, he'd been alone. Duncan had left before dawn, as to not have to say goodbye.

"I'm sorry, Duncan. I am so sorry. I tried everything I could to save you. I changed the world to save you. But it still didn't work." Will whispered, blinking away wetness. "I swear to you, though, I'll be the best Forgemaster this world has ever seen. I will continue our line, and I will destroy anyone who follows the Blood God."

The silence didn't answer, but Will felt better. *"Be at peace, lad."* Amder's rumble echoed one last time. Will stepped out into the morning light, leaving the ghosts of the Reis line alone once more.

Chapter 5.

Zalkiniv could feel the blood drying on his skin. The temple had been dealt with, and far quicker than he'd expected. He'd even taken a side trip before he'd left and smashed each and every vial of the blood memories. Though that had not gone totally according to plan. He'd used the dagger to break them, which might have been a mistake. For each time he had done so, the dagger thrummed with power, but as quickly it had faded back into a pitted black Iron dagger. *I will find the secrets of this thing, only not today.*

He liked to imagine Valnijz screaming in rage, in whatever hole a dead god lived in. The soot god back alive, his temple slaughtered, and his way back never returning. If Valnijz hadn't betrayed me, none of this would be happening. *I am Zalkiniv, and I will have my full measure of revenge.* He had a decision to make.

If he headed south now, he'd have to cross the wastelands, then cut by the swamps. There were several smaller villages on the coast or had been several hundred years ago. He'd never paid them any attention. Fisherman and smugglers held no genuine power. They were a source of slaves, though, which protected them from being totally wiped out.

He considered taking this body back under the barrier and hunting the Reach. That would be an enjoyable trip. Duncan would howl and scream as the beast slaughtered whatever was left of that dirty, stinking city.

No, please no. A whispered thought made Zalkiniv stop in his tracks. The man still existed enough to fight him. *Not the Reach, not home. Never.* Yes! That was the voice of Duncan! Impressively, the man still held that much of himself inside, enough to communicate.

"I will do whatever I want with your body my prize. You have already lost." Zalkiniv turned towards the Mountains. "Your pathetic begging has sealed the fate of your people. I almost wish you could watch as I do, as the beast kills every person you know. The place is already reeling from the Valni attack, I'm sure. Now, the lost Duncan Reis appears, and kills everyone else."

NO! The force of the metal yell made Zalkiniv stumble. *I WILL FIGHT YOU EVERY STEP OF THE WAY. NEVER THE REACH.* Duncan's voice was stronger now.

Zalkiniv gripped the dagger tight and pushed back against the growing strength of Duncan. "You have no power here now, Duncan. You are a fragment of a dead man. This body is mine. Mine and the beasts." The power of Duncan grew, forcing Zalkiniv to stop moving at all, fighting with all his strength and skill to stop this threat. "I AM ZALKINIV, I AM IMMORTAL AND YOU ARE NOTHING!" he screamed into the wasteland, his body rigid in effort.

I WILL NOT ALLOW YOU TO HURT THE REACH. Duncan responded, and the body Zalkiniv wore, Duncan's body, responded. Slowly he turned away from the mountains, towards the south again.

Zalkiniv thought for a moment. He could fight this, but this piece of the man was far stronger than he expected. Did he want to fight every step, every time? He wasn't sure what would happen if he allowed the beast to take over with Duncan fighting it. "Fine, not the Reach then." Zalkiniv said and as quickly as it had come, whatever strength that fragment of Duncan had faded away like water poured on the hot dry ground.

There was no response from that scrap of his victim. He could still feel it there, as before. South then, I will take more power, and to banish this last scrap once and for all. Then the Reach will fall to me, and finally, that Forgemaster of Amder. *I will be a living god. I will be what the Blood God should have been.*

***

The road out of the Reach was quiet, which Will was thankful for. He knew Amder needed him elsewhere. He accepted it, but leaving the Reach in the state it was still in was hard. Having to say goodbye to the survivors would have made it even worse. Not that anyone was angry with him that he could tell. In fact, they seemed to be proud of him more than anything else. *I brought ruin to them, and they celebrate me.*

He knew it was guilt making him feel that way. Duncan would have told him to stop feeling sorry for himself. Everyone knew what came that night, and they volunteered. No one was forced to fight. His cousin would have then probably have thumped him on the head and offered to buy him a drink. *Sparks above Duncan, I miss you.*

A sharp pain overwhelmed him, one that brought with him a torrent of terror and anger. His mouth, in an instant, tasted of blood and dust. Will gasped and nearly fell out of the wagon. Regin immediately stopped the horses.

"William! Are you all right?" Regin reached over, trying to right Will, who was hunched over.

Will struggled to answer. He couldn't move, he couldn't speak, and he could barely even breathe. Waves of pain flooded over him. He moved then, but into a spasm as the pain forced his muscles to contort in ways they had never done.

"Amder above, William!" Myriam scrambled to the front of the wagon and tried to help Regin. "William, say something?"

Captain Tolin stepped back but put his hand on his sword, scanning the area they were in. A few miles outside of the Reach on a trader's road.

Will felt the pain fade finally, his back unlocked as the spasms subsided. "Water." Will spat out the word. "Water."

Myriam grabbed a waterskin and held it up for Will to take a drink from. He took a sip and spit it out. That taste of blood faded, but the water was clear. No actual blood. Why had his mouth been full of the taste?

"William! Forgemaster! Are you ok??" Regin turned Will towards him.

"I think so." Will said, his voice cracking with effort. "I... I don't know what that was. All I could feel was pain. And I was so scared and angry." Will took another sip of the waterskin, taking it from Myriam, this one he spit out again with a grimace. "At least everything doesn't taste of blood now, and dust."

Captain Tolin came closer to the cart, but still scanning the surrounding area. "Have you ever felt that before?"

Will paused, wondering what to say. On his trip to Ture with Master Jaste, he'd had dreams similar, but nothing like that. "Not totally. I don't know how to describe it, but before, back when we made our way to Ture for the first time. I had dark dreams occasionally. But nothing like that."

Myriam wiped his forehead with the edge of her shirt, wiping some sweat that had sprung up now that the pain had faded. "I remember. You thrashed around a bit, grunting"

Will took one last sip of the water. "I seem to be fine now. Let's get moving."

Regin sat back. "Are you sure? That was not normal. Should we stop and let you talk to Amder?"

Will shook his head. "I feel fine now. And Amder has better things to do than talk to me all the time."

Captain Tolin got back into the cart. "I don't think I'll ever get used to knowing someone who talks to a God."

Myriam wiped Will's face one last time. "William, you should probably do that. Talk to Amder I mean."

Will felt some anger grow. "I said I was fine. Let's forget it and go. I can rest here in the cart." His voice snapped at her. "And stop touching me, I am fine."

Myriam moved back away from him, and Will could see a flash of shock as she answered. "Yes, Forgemaster Reis." And she turned away, back to him in the back of the cart next to the Captain.

Will immediately felt ashamed. She'd been concerned, and he'd snapped at her. *I should apologize.* Yet he held his tongue and said nothing. I'll apologize when we stop the cart for the night. Let us both cool off.

"Tonight, when we camp, I'll try to talk to Amder then. I want to get moving." Will turned back towards the road. "Please Regin, let's get going."

"You're the Forgemaster." Regin answered and started the cart again, heading towards Ture, and the new life awaiting Will there.

***

Myriam blinked a few times as she chewed her lip in thought. William had truly gotten angry with her. She knew he was still interested in her, and that had added to his frustration. She'd had a cousin like that. When he'd get hurt, usually doing something stupid, he'd lash out until the pain faded away. Add in his emotions about her, and it made for a terrible mix. But even so, she hadn't expected that from William.

"Don't worry about him, lass. He's an inexperienced man, embarrassed to show pain in front of anyone. It's not you." Captain Tolin whispered to her. "Forgemaster or not, he's still only a youngster. Blood full of fire, and not the wisdom to know how to use it."

"That could be." Myriam whispered back. She liked the Captain. He was who he was, and he reminded her a lot of her father. "Captain, any thoughts on what you will do in Ture?"

"Call me Vin." Vin sat back, leaning on his bag. "As for Ture, I'm not sure. I might ask the Forgemaster here if I can stay with him. Train him in combat, and I'm sure even the Forgemaster could use a bodyguard from time to time, at least for a while."

"Vin, it is then." Myriam smiled at that. "Why do you think he'd need a bodyguard? He's the Forgemaster of Amder now. Sacrosanct, right?"

Vin chuckled and shook his head. "If there is one thing I'm sure of, someone in Ture is plotting William's death. Maybe I don't trust people, but remember, he's upended a power structure that's been in place for hundreds of years. There's going to be chaos in Ture, I'm sure of it. And those who have lost power will be hungry to get it back. That might be impossible, but that doesn't mean they won't strike out if they can."

Vin turned and pointed at William's back. "That attack, whatever it was, I'd not be surprised to find out that someone in Ture was involved."

Myriam nodded slowly. The Captain might be right. She hadn't really thought about it that way. She'd been shocked at how much power the Priesthood had over everything in Ture. Would those same people now celebrate William's rise? What about the Tempered? They might be a disbanded order, but those people were anything but pious, anyway. They were thugs, and they fed on hate and violence. Would they turn tail and vanish?

Myriam turned to look at William. *I wonder if he knows what he is getting himself into.*

"And he's not the only one who could stand to learn combat techniques." Vin pointed at Myriam. "You could use them too, I'm guessing."

Myriam shrugged. "I guess. I'm used to having to knock a few heads from time to time. My father owns an inn, but actual combat I've not been in."

"Well then, you will join our esteemed Forgemaster." Vin glanced behind them again. "He's an odd one, that lad. But he tries hard at least."

"I'll try my best, but I'm also getting tutored by Regin. Since I left the guild so early on, I'm only a first-year apprentice." Myriam sighed. "William is an honorable person. He tries too hard to be one."

Vin nodded, but added nothing else. Myriam felt the conversation lulling away and closed her eyes to the rhythm of the cart, and felt sleep come to her.

"Myriam..." Myriam awoke with a blink. "Did you say something?" She turned to Vin to find him asleep. I swear someone said my name. She looked at Regin and Will, who still sat in silence. She'd been asleep for a bit, it seemed, by the position of the sun. At least it would be good to get out of the cold. William liked it, but she'd often thought the cold was creeping into her bones in the Reach.

She considered asking Regin where they were, but decided against it. Both men didn't seem like they had much to talk about, and even though she wasn't upset anymore with William about his snapping earlier, still it might be better to wait till they stopped for the night.

***

The shadows were getting longer when Regin finally pulled the cart over in one of the many cleared out alcoves along the road. They hadn't seen hardly any other travelers all day. Partially, that was because of the time of year. Late winter was still too early for much trade. William wondered if recent events had caused some of it. *I hope the Reach gets its supplies soon.* He didn't worry too much, though. If there was a profit to be made, merchants would come. And there was always profit to be made with the ores of the Reach.

"Thanks for driving all day, Regin. I'll drive the cart tomorrow." William got out of the cart, stretching, feeling his back crack in a few places. "I should have done some today."

"It's fine. I didn't mind, though I'll take you up on tomorrow. This would be faster, you know, if you could ride." Regin got down himself and stretched. He turned to the back of the cart where Captain Tolin slept and Myriam was asleep as well. "Our companions here seem to be down for the count though."

Will smiled at that. Walking over to the back of the cart, he gave him a thump with his fist. "We are here, stopping for the night of watchful Captain and fellow smith."

Captain Tolin popped an eye open. "A good guard knows when to get rest, William. We were not in a dangerous place, and since I plan on staying up late on watch, it was better to get rest now than later."

Will nodded. Can't argue with a man who's been a soldier most of his life about what is a good resting time. He thumped the wood again, harder. "Myriam?"

Myriam yawned and opened her eyes as well. "Sorry, the cart put me to sleep."

Regin laughed. "Well then, since the two of you got rest, then you two can set up camp and make dinner tonight. Will and I will do it tomorrow."

Will made a face. "Myriam will cook? Sparks above, do we have enough water? Last time I ate something she made, I thought I was sucking on a piece of lit forge coal; it was so hot."

Myriam said nothing in response, but rolled her eyes as she got out of the cart.

Captain Tolin joined her. "Please call me Vin. If I'm calling you William and Regin, call me Vin, and I think that's fair. Gives me a chance to set up a practice area for later, anyway."

William nodded, but didn't feel it. I had forgotten about that; I have combat practice. "Do you want help? Might do me good to figure out what I'm getting myself into."

Vin laughed. "No, I've got it. You're not a raw recruit, you know. You are the Forgemaster of Amder, so I don't think I'll be having to make you run leagues or haul rocks around."

Will blanched at the thought of running. "You do that?"

Vin smiled. "Be late for training and you'll find out." And with that he walked towards the tree line, making marks on the ground with a small metal rod he took from somewhere on his person.

Will turned to Myriam. "I wanted to apologize. I shouldn't have gotten angry, I... I don't know what that was."

Regin grabbed bags and took them out of the cart, avoiding both William and Myriam, leaving them alone.

Myriam nodded. "It's fine. It really is William. I get it. But can we not talk about it? Instead, we need to talk about what that was. Vin made a point; you are traveling into a nest of trouble; do you realize that?"

Will shrugged. "It might be chaotic, but I don't think it's dangerous."

Myriam paused and waited until Regin got back to grab the rest of the needed bags out of the cart. "You both should hear this. Vin pointed out something. You've broken a power structure that goes back hundreds of years. You may be the Forgemaster of Amder, but there are bound to be people in Ture who want you dead, and dead fast. You've ripped power from people who have had it all their lives."

Will felt a slight chill at her words. *I had never thought of that. I still have a lot to learn about being a Forgemaster.* He looked at Regin. "Well, you of all of us know the old power structure the best. Do you agree with the Captain?"

Regin hefted the bag in his hand and swung it over his shoulder. "Maybe. And before you get mad about me not voicing the concern before, I hadn't given it a lot of thought. And he may be right. While that Bracin person is gone, at least according to what we know, I can't promise that there aren't people around who want the old way back."

"But that's impossible. You know that. They only could do what they did because of the Heart of Amder. They don't have that now." Will shook his head. "How could they get back to what it was before?"

Myriam chimed in. "But how many people knew that? Sure, the High Priest did, and maybe some tempered, but I'd wager that more than a few rich and powerful members of the Priesthood did not understand how it worked. But they know that you coming into existence as the Forgemaster spelled the end of their power."

Will sighed. "This is the thing I hate. No offense, Regin, but I hated your class in the Guild. I want to be a smith, not rub elbows with nobles and the rich, and learn how to flatter them. All this lusting for power, I just don't get it."

"That's why you're my Forgemaster." Amder's rumble echoed in William's mind. *"And for the record, what happened earlier wasn't from anyone in Ture."*

Will held up a hand to Myriam and Regin. "Hold on, Amder is... well, doing his thing when he talks to me."

Well then, what was that? Will 'thought' back to Amder.

"I don't know if I should say. I only suspect, remember feelings and the mind were supposed to be the domain of my brother." Amder's rumble came again, this time with the distant sound of hammers.

Hammers? The only time he heard that with Amder was when the God was agitated about something. *What was going on? I wish you would say my Lord. I mean, it wouldn't be good for me to be trying to heal things in Ture and have one of those attacks again. It wouldn't inspire confidence, and based on the conversation we were having, there's already those who might be out to get rid of me.*

The hammering sound grew louder for a moment before fading off. *"You are right, but I fear that saying what I suspect might do to you."* There was a long pause. *"I believe now that I was partially incorrect. The night I was reborn, I told you Duncan Reis was dead. That might not be true."*

Will could feel his skin turn to ice as the words came to him. Duncan!?!? Alive??

"Not alive, not truly. I fear that someone or something is using his body. Some slight part of him must remain, however. There was always a powerful bond between you two. That brief episode you had; something came through that bond." Amder's blows were hitting harder, but yet each blow seemed to fall into the space between the words.

Duncan, ALIVE! Will felt tears come to his face. Tears of joy and relief. Duncan isn't dead!

Amder's rumble cut in. *"He's gone William. I said what I think, but your cousin is gone. Something might wear his shape, but it isn't Duncan."*

William blinked. *Then I must find him. I can save him. I didn't fail!*

Amder responded with a twinge of anger this time. *"No, I forbid it William. You are my Forgemaster, but I need you in Ture. You are not to go chasing after whatever it is that wears the shape of Duncan. This was why I didn't want to say anything."*

Not go after Duncan? Will knew he had to go. *My Lord Amder, I have to go. This is Duncan! My only family. There has to be a way to save him from whatever this is. He would do the same for me. I can't leave him to whatever is going on. If something has taken him over, if someone has taken him over, to leave him like that... I know Dunc, and that would be the worst thing in the world for him.*

Amder's response came loudly this time. Loud enough that William went to his knees, clasping his ears from a sound only he could hear. *"I have forbidden it! You are my Forgemaster, and on this you will obey me!"*

Will stood slowly, waving off Regin and Myriam, who both tried to help him up. *My Lord Amder, I will follow you in all things. All things but this. I will find Duncan. If I must renounce my title, I will leave my hammer here. But I WILL go after Duncan.*

Will could feel a heat now, like an open forge stoked to the point of melting down. Amder's anger flowed over him. *Answer me this, my Lord. If you could have saved your brother, if you could have saved Valnijz from what he became, would you have not done it? Duncan is my brother in all but name. I MUST save him.*

The heat, nearly unbearable, lessened. *"This is not a wonderful idea, William Reis. There is something here that I can't see. Something that makes me..."*

Will waited for the word to come. What could Amder be getting at? And he was a God! What couldn't he see?

A long minute passed as Will waited. He glanced over at his companions to find that Captain Tolin had joined them. All three were giving various looks of worry and confusion, though the Captain more looked grim, if that could be the word for it.

"Go. I give my blessing to this, but I do not think this is a wonderful choice. You are right, I would have done anything to save Valnijz if I had known what was coming," Amder's hammer blows slowed and tapered off.

Will nearly threw his arms up in triumph. He had no desire to stop being the Forgemaster, but saving Duncan was worth more to him. Still, one thing tickled at his mind. *My Lord Amder, you said before that Valnijz left after an argument. Did you ever remember what that was? If I may ask.*

For all the world, Will thought he heard Amder sigh. *"I did. We argued over who was older. It meant nothing really, but as the argument progressed, Valnijz swore to discover the truth, and the next day he was gone. Not merely gone, but unfindable. When he reappeared years later, he was now the thing you know of as Valnijz. But that does not matter. If you will do this, it's better to get started. All I can tell you is that the form of Duncan Reis is in the wastelands past the barrier and is heading towards the coast."*

Will pondered Amder's words. That was not close by, and traveling back to the Reach, then heading south, would put even more distance between them. But heading that way directly would require finding a pass through the Skyreach, something he knew nothing about. And those were Gorom lands, and the race wasn't exactly known to help travelers.

"I will see if I can help. Grimnor will listen to me sometimes. I will let you know. For now, head towards the coast and the southern Skyreach." Amder's voice faded away. *"Good luck, Forgemaster."*

Chapter 6.

The wastelands spread out before Zalkiniv in a flat plain of yellows and browns. Farmlands once, in years long ago, forgotten. Before the purge, before the blessing of the Scaled One, fell upon them and ended everything. As it should be. Zalkiniv smiled as the memories of those days came to him. The screams of the dying, the pyres of the bloodless bodies, drained for the power they gave. Those not worthy to enter the horde at least had some part to play.

There was no Valni in that time, his lord having still been alive. Instead, the forces that did this were human. A mix of tribes, cults, crazed and tormented volunteers. Zalkiniv had been an Underpriest then, but powerful. He had personally pulled the blood out of thousands of sacrifices. In the days that had followed the ground had been more blood-soaked mud than anything. *I was a fool, though, giving my life to a God who betrayed me.*

The memories faded as he ran, and a new thought came to him. Mere revenge for his betrayal was easy. There must be a greater punishment. He had spent generations working to bring back his former master. He knew secrets; he knew power. Valnijz doesn't deserve the power he has. A dead mad god. *I should take the power. I'd not fall victim to his crazed demented fantasies.*

Zalkiniv slowed his run and looked down at the dead and dusty ground. *I should be a god. Not Valnijz. Not Amder. Me. Not any of the other eight, either. None of them deserve the power they have. There must be a way, there had to be a way. I will not fail where he did. I will not fall to madness, and once I am a God, all will perish to me, and those who follow my steps.*

This body, fueled by the blood and power from the Temple, ran on, eating the distance. The only life seen was a rare bird in the sky, and once in the distance a swarm of iron flies, pests who in a swarm could kill a normal man, eating tiny bites as they flew around their victim. He had experimented with them as well in the past, studied them as they picked a man from skin to bones in mere minutes. But they had been hard to control, and he had ordered them exterminated.

They had been mostly successful. Fire killed them well. A few swarms had escaped, and it had taken years for them to regain their numbers. It mattered not, though a few swarms of them released in the rich fat lands of the east would be a joy to behold.

He ran on, day turning to night as he ran, the body not faltering, not tiring. In his head, he could still feel the echo of Duncan Reis, still somehow, some way clinging to existence. And there, also, was the beast. Trapped in a vision of death and rage, it slew phantoms and ripped them to shreds, screaming in joy as it killed.

It still bothered Valnijz that Duncan somehow existed. The spirit of the man had been tortured, beaten, abused, but yet he still held on, to still be part of who he was. He would have to find a way to rid himself of this vestige. But for now, he was firmly in control. Soon he would arrive on the coast, and from there cross the Blood Moon bay. He had not been south in a long stretch of years, but he knew he could find what he was looking for.

The Cruor sworn. A branch of the Blood God that frankly Zalkiniv had never liked, anyway. Even when he had been the High Priest, that sect rarely even acknowledged his existence. They had their own leader, though he wisely did not claim to be over all followers. They had their own rituals; they had their own skills. Zalkiniv would enjoy releasing the beast upon them.

The morning came to find him, finally crossing over a ridge, staring down at the harbor village. He did not know the name of the town, nor did he care what it was. It had boats, and it had blood. Several hundred fishermen and a rare merchant who was foolish enough to use the port here. More than enough blood for the beast to use and refuel this body for the trip across the sea.

You should watch this Duncan Reis. Your face will be etched into the legends of this place forever, assuming anyone escapes. A faint whimper was all the shred of the man could muster in response. Drawing the black iron dagger again, he ran a finger across its edge carefully. It seemed to hunger in response. He could almost feel a deep gnawing need to kill as its metal touched his skin.

He pushed the body forward into a run and, with one last command, released the beast from its delusions. KILL THEM ALL.

***

Will broke into a grin that, for the first time in a while, he actually felt. "Duncan is alive!" he ran towards his companions, as each of them registered the shock that this announcement brought them. Regin's eyes widened, and he swore the man might have even turned pale. Captain Tolin smiled back, giving him a nod, and Myriam, she actually ran towards him and hugged him!

"That's amazing! How? Where is he?" Myriam asked as she let go of him.

William flushed a bit at the contact, but answered the question. "Heading south. And well, we aren't going to Ture anymore, we are going after him. He's not well. Someone has taken his body over, and Amder wasn't exactly forthcoming. But he's alive!"

Regin and Vin exchanged glances. "William, Forgemaster, are you sure this is..." Regin asked.

"Yes, I'm sure. Amder was hesitant at first as well, but I MUST do this Regin. I can save him now. None of us might be here if he hadn't been the person he was. That Zalkiniv person would have won. I have to save him for that reason, if no others. But there are others, lots of others." Will spoke quickly the excitement and joy of Duncan being alive overshadowed any feelings of fear or disquiet over the rest of the information.

Captain Tolin stood still for a moment and then went to full attention and saluted. "Very well Forgemaster Reis. South I will go with you."

Myriam and Regin only nodded. "I might not think this is the best plan, but I swore to follow you, and I won't break that bond." Regin added.

Myriam shrugged. "Let's go then William. Where to the south is he? Is he near the south trading road out of Palnor? We can go that way and I can explain the situation to my parents. I'm sure they've heard of the chaos in Ture by now, and of my leaving the Guild. Probably torn between anger and worry."

"Sorry Myriam, but he's on the other side of the barrier, in the wastelands heading south." Will paused. "I never even thought about your parents, Myriam. I am so sorry. You can go to them, you know; you don't have to travel with us."

Myriam shook her head. "No, I'm going. If we find a way to send a message on the way, I'll do that, but I'm going with you all."

"If you are sure!" was all Will said out loud, but he couldn't help but be happy. *Maybe there's hope after all.*

"How do we get there? Do we go back to the Reach and head that way and once we are in the wastelands, head south?" Regin asked. "That could take a while, and I'm not all that interested in spending that much time in the Valni lands, even if there are less of them now. That would be a highly dangerous path. And who knows what else lives there?"

Vin nodded in agreement. "I'd follow you, but that's a damn fool of an idea."

"No, Amder has suggested we head for the Southern Skyreach, and he might be able to get the Gorom to help us." Will shrugged. "Said something about talking to Grimnor."

Myriam stepped back at that information. "The Gorom? They don't talk to anyone, I'm not sure they even LIKE anyone, not a Gorom."

Regin nodded. "I've only had contact with one once, and it didn't speak to me. I simply ushered it into Master Reinhill's office in the Guild. It was all robes, couldn't even see its face or even its skin."

Vin shrugged. "Don't have any idea. Only know they exist."

Will nodded. "I know. It's always rather interested me that we know little about them. I mean, I've met a Trinil, and a Saltmistress. We've seen evidence of the Drendel, even if they are all gone, but the Gorom keep to themselves to a fault. They live in the Skyreach, and even Reachers don't see them ever." Will paused for a moment. "But it doesn't matter. If Amder can somehow get us through the Gorom lands, it will save us days if not weeks, and should be a great deal safer than heading through the wastelands."

Vin nodded. "Speaking of safety, you do understand, William, that this means we will have to train even harder. Before the threat was simple, people who wanted power. Now? We are heading into lands very few, if any, Palnorian have ever seen. We don't know what kind of dangers we will face. You ALL need to be ready."

Regin groaned at the words. "I know what that means. But I'm a Guildmaster. Who is going to attack me?"

Captain Tolin hooked his thumb to the back of the campsite. "All of you need training. I don't think any wild beast is going to care about the Guild, and if we run into any Valni or worse, the color of a cloak will make no difference. Master Regin, you need to brush up. But you, Myriam and William, get ready to work."

***

Zalkiniv took in the sight that greeted him as he wrested control from the beast. It was harder than he expected, the resistance to the delusions greater. But no matter, the beast was blood drunk. The slaughter of the town had been more than complete. He was sure he could hear a slight whimper coming from somewhere, but he couldn't pin it down. A child, perhaps? Or a wounded fisherman?

The beast had torn through the place, and in a somewhat surprising turn of events, had used the dagger to kill about everyone. The more animalistic kills were nowhere to be seen. Throats cut, stab wounds, even a partial flaying of a man who had tried to fight back based on the spiked club in the man's hand.

The dagger. Zalkiniv eyed the thing, back again in its sheath. He wished he knew more about it. When he had taken control again, it had for a moment seemed to move on its own, almost breathe. But as he fully took control, it had stilled, once again, a dagger of pitted black iron. *What are you?*

He considered throwing it into the bay, either here or out in the sea proper. Things he could not control can be a danger. And this was the dagger that ended his old life, thrust into him by a scheming Underpriest. He could still feel that moment, looking down and seeing the point of the thing erupting from her chest, unable to move as the cord in her spine had been severed.

But no, it was a tool, a useful tool. And getting rid of a useful tool would be foolish. Zalkiniv raised his eyes, searching for a boat, and forgetting his momentary thought to destroy the dagger that hung on his belt.

He discounted several fishing boats right away. They were craft meant for hugging the shoreline, and not suitable for his needs. Small enough that I can make it work alone, but seaworthy enough that it will make it to the glowing lands, the places beyond the Blood Sea.

There had been two smaller merchants in port when the beast had attacked. He'd watched as both had fallen in a matter of seconds. More smugglers than merchants both had ships capable of crossing, but only one was the right size.

He stepped on board, passing over a deckhand that the beast had plunged the dagger into both of his eyes. Yes, this will do. He knew how to sail, at least somewhat. Before his ascension to the High Priest, he'd traveled this way twice before. And now, with the blood the beast had shed, he would have no need to eat or drink.

He quickly cast off from the dock and pointed the ship in the right direction. Thankfully, this wasn't the storm season, or this would have been far harder of a passage. As it was, one or two weeks depending on the wind, sailing due South would get him to the home of the Cruor sworn. His hand reached down to caress the dagger. Jindo Halfman. He looked forward to cutting the leader of the Curor's throat open with this dagger.

Jindo had refused most conversation with Zalkiniv and had ignored orders to sacrifice slaves and those captured by the sworn to assist Zalkiniv when he had been trying to summon the blade. It hadn't mattered in the end, but when Zalkiniv ascended to Godhood, Jindo would long be dead and gone, his blood used to steal the secrets of the Cruor.

They were his target for one reason. In their vaults, they held the first drop of blood ever spilled by Valnijz. A legacy of his birth. Unlike the blood mist, this blood was liquid, and based on what he had discovered through the years, it held powers. Jindo had flatly refused to give up his artifact, something that had driven Zalkiniv crazy at times. How dare he turn down the High Priest?

Valnijz had been no help. The God even at his best was not overly coherent. A master at killing and pain, but cared little for the trappings of the mortal realm. It had only been the crystal that Zalkiniv carried that had ever drawn the attention of the God.

He checked the bag tied on the opposite side of the dagger and felt the metal box still inside. Good. He trimmed the sails as best he could, and with a smile, sat down on the deck of the ship, the surrounding wind pushing his vessel towards the south, and towards his legacy.

Chapter 7.

Duncan shivered as he tried to block out the knowledge of what had happened. He still felt weak from the fight with that thing that had control over his body. He had, much to his surprise, managed to not have the Reach be the target. That had taken all of whatever he had. Why did he even still exist? Why could he not find rest and peace?

The screams and images of what his body had been forced to do still haunted him. No, not forced. When that thing took over, it was not forced. It was as if he had been tied up and thrown into a cart and taken for a ride. He could see everything, but he had no control. The thing that Zalkiniv called the beast, it reveled in the death and killing.

And it was getting stronger. Ever since the temple, ever since it had been allowed to use that dagger, it had been getting stronger. Duncan admitted he hadn't been as upset over the Temple attack. The death of the Blood God's followers had felt almost right to him. That made him uncomfortable, though. Who would ever want to be the same as Zalkiniv?

He wondered why the now former High Priest of the Scaled One couldn't see it, though. The dagger was more than a dagger, even he sensed that. What it was he did not know, but while he could feel everything the beast did, he didn't feel Zalkiniv doing the same. Could his enemy not see what the beast did?

Did it even matter? Despair crept around him, coalescing into ominous shadows and forms, whispering to this shard of a soul that there was no way out, no freedom, and no hope. *Why can't I die?*

***

Will, Myriam, Regin, and Vin practiced for far longer than Will had wanted to. By the time they had stopped, the night had fallen in full, and all of them stood, panting and sweaty. Will knew he'd be sore tomorrow. Swinging a hammer to fight used some same muscles as forging, but not all.

"Good Job overall. Myriam, use your quickness. You are strong for your size, but the fastest of all three of you. Use it." Captain Tolin pointed at Myriam. "You've got good instincts mostly, but don't hesitate to land a killing blow. Be assured, in a proper fight, your opponent will not think twice about landing theirs."

"Regin, I was right. You needed to brush up on your combat skills. But even so, all things considered, a decent job. You have got to watch the footwork though, you put yourself in situations where you are unbalanced, and that can end your life, fast." Captain Tolin waved the Guildmaster off.

"Forgemaster. Where to start." Vin shook his head.

"Um, start with anything good?" William asked hopefully.

"Good... You are the strongest of the three of you, and you are stronger than I am, actually. When you make contact, your blows can shatter or break bones." Vin paused for a moment, his eyes alighting on William's hammer. "And you've got that. I have no doubt that hammer will make a powerful weapon, assuming it hits anything."

"And that's the major weakness, Forgemaster. You are slow. When you go to strike, you strike as if you are hammering metal. Huge long swings. Powerful, but leaves you so open to attack you can never finish that swing because you will already be dead. Maybe you really need a full set of armor. At least that would make it harder to kill you while you setup such obvious attacks." Vin sighed. "But don't get too discouraged. I know it's your first combat lesson. I guess I sort of assumed being the Forgemaster you'd have more… skill in this area."

Will shrugged. "Truth? I didn't. I've never needed to. Even growing up, I avoided fist fights. Duncan always leaped into those things if the need arose."

Captain Vin Tolin nodded, but added nothing else.

"Well, let's get cleaned up, get some food made and get to sleep. We have a lot of ground to try to make up tomorrow, heading towards the southern Skyreach, and the Gorom held lands." Will waved everyone towards the fire, now barely alight.

"I call using the stream to clean up first!" Myriam nearly jogged to the cart, grabbing her pack. "You all can wait here."

"You know, I'm the Forgemaster!" Will called after her in protest.

"So?" her answer came with a slight laugh as she headed into the woods where a stream passed by, out of sight.

"I'm second!" Regin said before Will yelled out his retort. "I reek like I've been working a forge for half a day."

Will grimaced for a second, then broke into a smile. "All right then, you and Myriam can make dinner then again, since you will be the first all cleaned up."

"Bah," Was all Regin said, but he smiled as he did so.

Will sat down by the fire, the sweat on his skin cooling him somewhat in the evening air. He fed a few sticks into the flame and waited his turn. After a few minutes, he turned to Regin. "Can you see what's taking her so long? I'd go, but...."

Regin nodded. And headed into the same area that Myriam had gone.

***

Regin picked his way through the bushes. He didn't want to scare the girl though, so when he felt like she had to be in earshot, he called out. "Myriam! You almost done?"

"Don't rush me. I may not be a court lady, but I don't always want to smell like sweat and the forge!" her answer came from past a line of undergrowth where he heard the water passing by.

"I'm not. William sent me to check. Since I have a second, they have put you and me on cooking duty." Regin fiddled with a leaf on the bush in front of him, idly.

"I guess that's fine. I have some spices with me I bought in the Reach, liven up the meal." Myriam answered back.

Regin winced. "Let's, go easy on that, ok? For the rest of us? I don't want to have to sit in a cart all day after eating whatever dish you've created."

Laughter was his only response. *She does have a delightful laugh; I can see why William likes her.* He picked a leaf off a bush, idly examining it. Its edge fluttered in a breeze that had started up.

"Yes Guildmaster. Oh, after dinner, can we start my tutoring? At least going over things and figuring out how we will do it?" The bushes rustled where she must be at.

"Yes, I suppose we had better." Regin answered the rustle having taken his attention from the leaf in his hand. The moon was rising, nearly full, shining its pale white light everywhere. And then, the bushes where she stood opened with a light wind.

Myriam stood there; lit up by the moonlight. The light hit her profile perfectly. The outline of her muscles, long and lean. Even her hair shone. Regin watched as it fell in a long wave. He suddenly very much wanted to run his fingers through it. Was it as soft as it looked?

She's... stunning. Regin's breath caught as Myriam was putting her hair back into a serviceable ponytail. She was clad only in a clean white undershirt, not her normal leathers and wool. Regin forced his head away. She's your friend and travel companion, not to mention the fact the Forgemaster might be in love with her.

"I'll be there in one minute, let me finish getting dressed." Myriam called out. Regin didn't answer but turned around, keeping his eyes down, and walked back to the fire that William had by this time returned to a respectable cooking fire.

"She will be right here." Regin reported in. He kept his eyes away from William. *Why am I acting like a child caught in the larder?*

"Good. Then you can get cleaned up, then Vin, and finally me." William poked the coals with a stick. "And oh, don't let Myriam decide on the spices to use."

Regin smiled, some tension he felt running away. "Now that you mention it, she said something about having bought some spices in the Reach."

"Ha! I am warning you now, if she ever offers to make a chicken dish from back home, nicely decline!" William laughed as he spoke.

Put it out of your mind, Regin. It's just been a while since you enjoyed the company of an attractive woman, that's all. Regin joined in the laughter and put the image of Myriam away in his mind.

Chapter 8.

William chewed on his lip for a moment as the cart moved forward again. Too slow, this is taking too long. They had eaten what he still considered a meal that seemed on fire last night and exhausted from the travel and the combat training had fallen into a deep sleep. The morning had come fast, but now the cart was taking forever. He'd passed on breakfast. One, he didn't want to waste the time, and two, it was mostly leftovers from dinner, and he wasn't sure his stomach could take more of that meal.

"Is there any way to move faster? At this rate, Duncan's trail will be cold and gone by the time we get anywhere near to where he is now." Will rubbed his neck, the tension he was feeling making it stiff.

"The only way to move faster is to ride. And you don't know how." Regin answered. "I'm not sure you want a mad dash to the Skyreach to be your first time riding." He glanced at Will and gave a smile. "If you think you were tired and sore after the training last night, riding for the first time for miles in increasing hilly terrain will near kill you."

Captain Tolin spoke up. "I agree. But I may have a way to make this faster. I know of a few merchant roads that might help, but I can't promise anything. No traders go to the Gorom lands that I've traveled with."

"Anything." Will answered. He knew that he was on edge. Nevertheless, this was insanely slow to him now.

"When we stop for lunch and let the horses eat and water, I'll make some changes to the map." Vin answered.

"Do we have to stop? Can't we wait till nightfall? Can't you make the changes now?" Will blurted out.

"William. If we don't feed and water the horses, they will move even slower. You know that." Myriam spoke up. "I know you want to help your cousin, but you might burst into flame where you sit if the horses go without all day."

Will knew she was right. He didn't like it, but he knew it. "Sparks burn me, I know, I…" he trailed off with a shrug. There wasn't much else to say.

"It's fine, William. We understand, we really do." Myriam patted his back for a moment.

Her touch brought feelings he didn't want to deal with now. *Everything should be about Duncan now; I can try to prove to her I'm not a different man after that.* William gave a nod, but kept his mouth shut. *They wouldn't understand, I think.*

What had Haltim told him once? When you listen and don't talk, you do the world a favor? Something like that. *I miss you, old man.* At least Vin was here. He wasn't Haltim, but he had some wisdom that came with age.

The cart made its way to the southeast of Palnor, passing through areas that Will hadn't been able to see the first time he'd left the Reach. Most of this part of the country was quiet farmland, dotted with the occasional village or cluster of homes that didn't even have names most of the time. Rarely there would be a small inn or village drinking house, but nothing large. He had asked his companions to not bring up that he was the new Forgemaster in any place they went at the moment.

One, it worried him that any place they stopped right now, he'd have to deal with a lot of questions or have to help them. *"Which is your calling, remember?"* Amder's voice rumbled through his mind.

Sorry, my Lord, but… Will didn't want to repeat himself again. Not that he was mad at Amder, he didn't want to get into an argument with a God.

"I understand Will, I really do. But remember, this isn't your calling. This is a detour. One that I still don't like. I'm not comfortable with it. There is something I can't see. And I don't like it." Amder's voice seemed to intertwine with the sound of a hammer again.

What does that mean? Will did not understand where Amder was going with this.

"I'm not sure. And that I'm not sure is a terrible sign." Amder's rumble faded out, but the sound of hammering continued, and got louder. *"I will let you continue, but Forgemaster, be careful."* Amder's tone shifted from one of almost concern to a more measured one. *"I have organized passage through the Gorom held lands. The Speaker to the Sky will meet you. I will mark the location on the map you're using."*

Speaker to the sky? Will had never heard of that name, or was it a title?

"That I cannot help you with. Grimnor always has kept a very close watch on his people. I had to cajole and give up a long-held favor to get this Forgemaster. Be careful, Grimnor and the Gorom, by extension, don't mix well with those who live above ground." Amder paused for a moment, and the hammering sound ended. *"Forget I said anything. I worry needlessly about this quest of yours. I am only agreeing to this because if I didn't, I'd be out a Forgemaster. Make sure this doesn't take too long, William Reis. I have need of you in many places."*

William could feel Amder's presence vanish for now. But not completely. He had never spoken about it, but since the night of the return, in the far back of his mind, he could sense a tiny sliver of what he thought was Amder. Which would mean I carry a small part of a God within me? Not something he needed to share with those around him.

"Can we stop now? I've had a conversation with Amder again." Will spoke up, breaking what had been silence.

"Now? I guess so." Regin pulled over onto the side of the road. "What did Amder say?"

Vin roused himself. "I have to admit Forgemaster William, I find all this talking to a God strange. It makes me uneasy."

Will almost smiled at that. "If you had told me even six months ago, I'd be having conversations with Amder, the God of Craft and Creation. I'd have called you a hammer bound fool, or wondered if I was crazy."

"Where's the map?" Will asked, turning around to the back of the cart. Myriam fished it out from a small chest that was bolted to the wagon frame.

Will unfolded it, his breath catching as he saw the newly made mark of a silver mountain off a small valley.

"What is that?" Myriam asked, pointing to the mark. "That wasn't there yesterday when I looked at it."

"I didn't see it either." Regin paused. "Amder's work?"

"Yes. It's where we are supposed to meet a Gorom called 'The Speaker to the Sky'. That's all I know, except that we have passage through the Gorom held lands." Will wondered if he should say anything about the cryptic warning that Amder had let slip. *No, he said, to put it out of your mind, right?*

"That's a strange name." Myriam remarked. "But maybe it's normal for them. No one really knows anything about the Gorom, much."

Regin nodded. "As I said, I only ever saw them when taking them into meet with the upper administration in the Guild. Usually Master Reinhill."

Myriam smacked her hand against the wagon. "Sparks burn me!"

"What?" Will turned his attention from the map. "What's the matter?"

"Master Reinhill, in all the confusion of the return of Amder, and now this change, of course, I have something she let me use. I need to return it to her." Myriam frowned. "It's not mine to keep."

"What?" Will asked and gave Regin a questioning look, who just shrugged in return. "What did she give you?"

"I'm not supposed to talk about it." Myriam sighed. "She told me she'd deny ever doing it if she was asked."

Regin cocked an eyebrow at that. "What did she give you?"

Myriam looked down for a minute, and without a word, pulled a red cloak out of her travel bag.

"A journeyman's cloak?" Regin's face fell for a moment, then without a word, he shook his head.

"Why would she give you that?" Will asked, but as soon as he did, he realized the plan behind the action. Myriam would have been traveling alone, and that cloak was a form of protection. "Oh, I understand."

Regin apparently had gotten to the same place as William. "Dangerous for her, but understandable."

"But now we are going away from the Guild, and I told her I'd send it back." Myriam frowned. "I don't enjoy failing to follow through."

Will smiled at her. "Myriam VolFar. By my title as anointed Forgemaster of Amder, I say it's fine. The situation changed. When we do finally get to Ture, I'll explain to Master Reinhill."

Myriam snorted in response. "I guess that's true. Who will tell the Forgemaster of Amder that he's wrong?"

Regin chuckled. "I will! But I agree in this case. I think Master Reinhill will understand."

Will laughed. *It feels good to laugh.*

"Let me see the map. I can think of a few trails that aren't marked well in this area. Might save us some time." Vin reached out for the map as Will handed it over.

"Is it safe enough to leave the major roads?" Will asked, as Vin examined the map. "Not that I'm worried, but any slowdowns would be bad."

"Safe enough. Truthfully, the worst around here might be hungry wolves or some other wild animal. There are not enough traders that come this way to make it worthwhile. And the ones who do are heading to Dernstown, and coming back with quarried stone, not something bandits or robbers want to deal with." Vin traced his finger along the roads.

"Dernstown." Myriam said as she locked eyes with William. "I've never been there."

"Well, neither have I." Will answered and then looked away. *I've apologized enough for that. She knows why I did it. She says she understands, but yet she seems to take pride in digging me on it when she can.*

"Here, someone have a marking rod? I can mark a trail I remember that should go fairly close to this point that appeared on the map. It will take us to the north side of the Lake of the Winds, then towards the mountains." Vin held out his hand, keeping his eyes on the map.

Myriam pulled a marking rod out of some part of her bag, and a small vial of ink, handing them to Vin. He quickly traced a thin line on the map. "I can't be totally sure that this is the precise location, but it is there."

"How do you know of this trail? You said not a lot of traders come this way." Regin asked as he took the map back, examining the addition Vin had made.

"They don't. But I grew up on the north shore of the lake. Not that I have any family around there anymore. The entire village is gone, flooded out years ago when earth shakes made the lake go crazy." Vin handed the rod and ink back to Myriam. "But I remember the area still, not a lot of changes there."

William vaguely remembered some older residents of the Reach saying something about earth shakes years ago. He was thankful he never had to deal with those. Rock falls were bad enough in the Skyreach in terms of damage, though thankfully not common.

"Well, let's feed and water the horses, eat a fast lunch and then we can head towards Captain Vin's trail" Will jumped off the cart, stamping his feet to get the blood flowing again. Everything is working out the way it should. *I will save you, Duncan, this time.*

Chapter 9.

Zalkiniv spat onto the deck. Things had been going perfectly, until in the night the wind stopped, and left the boat here, stilled. He wasn't near enough to land to swim it. This was not part of his plan. He was fine for now; the blood taken by the beast was more than enough to keep this body moving and running for a week or more. Though after that amount of time, he would find it harder to keep the beast under control.

Duncan would be in no danger, at least. That shard of the man did nothing but whimper and sob occasionally. He still found it somewhat surprising that such a weak fool was able to stop Valnijz' return. Not that I'm complaining now.

He needed a plan. Based on what he could figure out by the poor-quality maps that he had taken out of the captain's bunk, he was near enough to the routes that the Saltmistresses took on their trips. He'd never really dealt with their kind. They had been slaughtered during the War of the Godsfall, and the survivors after that had avoided the Mistlands to the point of phobia. But they had magnificent ships, and more to the point, they had their goddesses' blessing.

He'd have to get close enough to the paths they took, but he might set a small fire on board, nothing too dangerous, and draw their attention. Once on board, he would rip through the crew, leaving enough to run the ship and take him to where he needed to be. A dangerous plan, though. If they managed even for a minute to get him out of the boat, that would be the end. Water and working the blood didn't go well together.

But how to get there? He was becalmed, stuck. The only thing besides this body nearby would be sea life. Fish. Silly creatures with very little blood to speak of. Useless. He paced the deck of the small ship, his annoyance growing as time passed. There must be a way, there had to be a way!

He would have to take the chance that maybe, in a rare set of luck, he could be seen by a ship, even though he wasn't close enough normally. But first, he would have to clean this body of blood. It was a disgusting step, but those not of the knowledge would not take in a man covered in dried blood alone on a ship.

Stripping down, he dived into the ocean; the saltwater rinsing the old blood off his body in a cloud of reddish brown. Blood. Dried blood. Zalkiniv quickly climbed back up into the boat, his mind racing. Blood might attract a swiftkill. A predator of the deep, more dangerous than a shark would ever be. Swiftkills were pale blue to white, and while they had a round mouth full of sharp teeth, their chief weapons were the long-barbed arms, four in total. Each six jointed arm was tipped with a sharp bone covered with a toxic slime. One puncture, and you went into spasms and shock. There was never only one puncture. As soon as one hit, the others would drive into the same target repeatedly, the barbs tearing skin and flesh until it was sure its prey was dead.

Swiftkills, though, were creatures of the blood. Yet another of the ancient experiments, prior to the fall. Bred and released to the seas to be killers. Their lack of intelligence had been their weakness and had greatly limited their usefulness. Creatures of instinct and hunger, Swiftkills would hunt and kill even each other.

If I can work the blood, I could summon them, use them to push the ship to where I need to be. But he couldn't work the blood. Not now. He had struck too many blows against the Blood God to be able to use his blessing now. Zalkiniv hadn't even tried, in his anger and hate, before the fall of the temple, and afterwards, why bother?

I must try, though. It may be the only way. Zalkiniv unsheathed the black iron knife, the blade warm in his hand, hungry. Steeling himself, he readied himself for either a scream of hate and rage, or total silence. He sliced across his palm; the edge cutting far deeper than he expected it to. A spurt of blood followed that flowed into the blade! By the blood of the dead, what was happening? He released the blade, only to discover to his wonder that his senses still were able to find it, the blood workings!

He could feel the power thrumming through him in heights greater than he had ever known, ever even dreamed of! He wanted to scream with the pure joy of it! He must be closer than ever to being a God now! He had taken so much power at the Temple that must be it. He didn't need Valnijz, he could grant himself the power needed. This was more than even the claret stones had given him back in Ture.

Tendrils of power reached down through the water, seeking and searching. He needed the creatures he knew he could control. There! And there! In short order, he found five swiftkills in varying distances from his boat. He called to them, the old rites of control still writ in their flesh. A scream of joy erupted from Zalkiniv then, the creatures came! Two were ancient, tremendous examples of their kind. The other three were of varying ages, but all were strong, powerful. He calmed their aggression towards each other with a quick working, almost in wonder as it took effect faster than he ever expected. *I am Zalkiniv, and I am power.*

***

Will sighed, pacing around the small side clearing for the fifth time. He'd eaten fast and wanted to get moving again. Regin had explained for the third time already that the horses needed more than a ten-minute rest, and so Will had to wait.

"Since you're so full of energy Forgemaster Reis, let's try some of the skills you learned." Captain Tolin took a drink from a water skin and stood. "Besides, it will be good to keep things moving."

Will wanted to plan how to free Duncan. He wanted to try to figure a way to have Myriam understand he was still the same man inside. He didn't want to work on combat training. His shoulders were already sore, and it was yet another barrier to what he really wanted, saving Duncan.

"Come, William." Captain Tolin pointed to an area closer to the trees. "Let's go."

Will let out a sigh, but followed. What else was there for him to do but follow. He might try to throw rank around, but he knew that Vin was right. He needed the training, and since he couldn't do anything about the horses needing to rest, might as well get things done that needed to be done. And Vin would ignore any rank that Will tried to pull on him, anyway.

As he approached the Captain, he took his hammer out of its loop, swinging it to both loosen up his sore muscles, and let out some pent of frustrations. The air whistled as he swung, the rushing sound strangely calming.

"Alright lad, you've slain the air. Now, show me the stance from the last time." Captain Tolin waved his hand at the patch of grass. "Go on."

Will spread his feet apart, turning his body sideways towards the Captain. He rested his weight as evenly as he was able and, remembering the ease in which Vin had pushed him over last time, slightly bent his knees.

"Better! You remembered. It took you too long, though. In a fight, you'd be skewered already. You need to sink into a basic stance as if it were second nature. No thinking." Tolin grabbed a small branch from the woods and broken it into the basic length of a sword. "This will do."

"Alright, try to hit me, William." Captain Tolin beckoned William.

Will let out a breath, and moved forward, swinging the hammer in an upward slant, trying to remember the instructions. Knock the shield out of the way, or if no shield, their weapon.

Vin stepped left, and faster than Will could process, slapped his hand with the branch, raising a red welt. "Too slow."

Will tightened his grip on his hammer and tried again, swinging sideways. Once again, Vin dodged the attack, again stepping left, and this time thrust the stick into his side. "Too slow!"

Will frowned. This wasn't working. An idea came to him, and without saying a word, he started another large swing. But this time instead of stepping forward he stepped left himself and with one hand he reached forward.

Vin dodged left again, but this time ran right into Will's hand, who grabbed his arm and pulled him forward, hard.

Captain Tolin stumbled himself then, falling forward, and laughed. "Excellent Lad! I made it easy, but you picked it up."

Will smiled in return. "Thanks!" his smile cut short by the branch smacking him again on his hand. "Ow!"

"But you didn't finish. You always need to finish the attack. Even if you don't feel in danger. You should have hit me with the hammer on the side. I was off balance, and my guard was down." Vin stopped and glanced over at Regin and Myriam, who sat talking by the cart.

"Look William. You are on edge. I know you want to save your cousin. I get it. In fact, I support it. Family is all. But don't take your frustrations out on us." Vin pointed with the stick at the cart. "We all understand. But the look on your face before I called you over here was like a storm about to break. You were angry, and obviously frustrated."

Will opened his mouth to defend himself, but closed it. Vin was right. "You are right." He finally said after staring at the cart for a long moment.

"But what, William?" Vin leaned on his branch. "Go on, say it."

Will struggled to come up with the right words. "You have to understand, I never wanted to be Forgemaster. In some ways, I still don't. I'm happy Amder is back, thrilled. But I did all this, did everything that happened in the Reach, all of this for one reason, to save Duncan." Will swung his hammer again, the whistle and air rushing by calming him again.

"I made this hammer with Dunc. He was my only family for years. He didn't want me to try to join the Guild. He wanted me to stay in the Reach. If I had stayed, none of this would have happened. My dream, my goal, broke everything." Will swung the hammer faster, harder.

"And then, after everything, Duncan died! My dream killed him. I killed him." Will felt the grief buried and swallowed leak out. "I caused this!" Will swung the hammer down, hitting the ground with a thump, which reverberated through his shoes. "And now... and now... he's not dead. He's been taken over by something, but he's alive. We are connected. I can sense him sometimes. I don't know why. But he's alive!" Will blinked the tears in his eyes out.

"If I can save him, I didn't fail. I wouldn't have killed him." Will dropped the hammer now and sat down in the grass.

Vin nodded, but stayed silent.

"Time to go!" Regin's voice cut through the air.

Will looked up to see both Regin and Myriam in the cart, waiting. He wiped the wetness off his face. "Well, at least we are making progress." And he headed towards the cart.

Behind him, he heard Vin nearly whisper the words. "Yes, we are."

Chapter 10.

Regin snapped the reins again, pushing the horses harder. Thankfully, this road Vin had suggested wasn't in overly terrible shape, though it was obvious it hadn't been used much. The ruts had more grass than rocks and sand. Still, the view was enjoyable, the long shore, the Lake of the Winds off to the right and down a slope. Every so often, he'd see a fishing boat in the distance. Picturesque.

Master Jaste would have liked it. The thought came unbidden, accompanied by a flash of guilt. *I'll never stop feeling bad about that.* Even if that night in the Reach, the night of the return, he had dealt with most of those feelings. His skin prickled as he remembered the first signs of the Valni horde. He'd never seen Valni before. A group of ten or twelve of the things had come up over the hill he and the Reachers had been waiting at.

Scrambling on all fours, howling, screaming. The noise alone had made him want to throw down his hammer and flee, clasping his ears. But he'd tightened his grip instead, and then the things had been upon them. It had been madness. Madness and chaos. Arms flailing around, each blow stronger than they should have been for such skinny and wiry creatures. He distinctly remembered a mouth trying to bite off his ear, the snap of teeth, and the smell. Rot, death, sour smells. If he hadn't been in fear for his life, he would have gone on all fours himself, retching.

Three times the Valni waves had gotten to the Church of the Eight that night. Not the full waves that the Reach proper had to deal with, but groups of less than twenty. He still was a bit in awe of the defense Captain Tolin had put together. If any more had made it through, Regin knew he wouldn't be sitting here now. None of them would be.

Yet here he was. With the new Forgemaster of Amder, Captain Tolin, and Myriam. Myriam.

Regin glanced back at the cart, watching her doze off again in the rocking cart. A smile crept to his face that he quashed as soon as he realized it. *She's an apprentice. She's too young for you, and the man you swore to follow is under her spell.*

But she was bright, talented, and forthright. In fact, she was the bluntest woman he'd ever spoken to. Yesterday, as Tolin worked with William on combat, he and Myriam had talked about smithing. He'd quizzed her on metals, ores, and techniques. She hadn't gotten everything right, but what she got wrong, she remembered the next time.

He'd been second guessing his agreement to tutor her. In truth, he'd not enjoyed being a teacher in the Guild. It wasn't in his nature he had thought to be a teacher. He'd only taken the position so he could stay in Ture, where the action was. The best restaurants, the finest tailors, the more refined entertainment. A snort escaped him at the thought. And yet, here he was, driving a cart towards the lands of the Gorom, and enjoying it.

In his heart, he had a hard time recognizing his old life. Why had those things been so important to him? He honestly couldn't remember. They merely had been. He glanced around the cart, each of his companions in various states of dozing off in the warm sun from above and the cool breeze off the lake. *They are my friends; this is important to me now.*

His eyes landed on Myriam last and lingered.

***

Will yawned and blinked the sun away as he woke up. He'd not expected to fall asleep in the cart.

"Nice to see you awake. About to stop for lunch, and then you are taking over the cart." Regin remarked next to him.

"Fine, fine." Will waved his hand, still not all the way aware. His eyes fell onto the glittering expanse of the lake. "By the sparks, that's beautiful."

"It is, isn't it? The biggest lake in Palnor." Regin agreed. "Few people, though. Dernstown has enough people for a name, but not most of these villages." Reign looked down from the path onto a small cluster of buildings as they drove past. "Well, not one that anyone knows but them."

Will wondered for a second about Dernstown. I really must go there someday. When all this is over. "Why don't more people live here? You'd think it would be well settled."

"You heard what Vin said? This place has a history of earthshakes, I think. At least on the north shore. If you had made it through my class at the Guild, your next would have been a study of world maps, and the lands they show." Regin gave forth a loud and exaggerated sigh. "But sadly, you weren't the best student."

"Or maybe you weren't the best teacher?" Will shot back, trying not to laugh.

Regin chuckled, but said nothing. Will looked around, enjoying the weather. "Where are we, at least by Vin's changes to the map?"

"If I'm right, we should stop tonight where the spur that takes us up into the Mountains branches off. Then tomorrow, hopefully meet this Speaker person. Gorom." Regin shrugged. "I'm still not clear on what we will do once we get there."

"Neither am I. Amder wasn't exactly forthcoming. And that's becoming a habit of his." Will rubbed his finger across his hammer, which, as always, was in his tool loop. "At least we can say when this is over, we've talked to a Gorom."

"I know Amder arranged this somehow, but the Gorom are a strange race, William. We should be careful." Regin glanced at the hammer Will was holding. "I hope you don't have to use that soon."

"You think we are in danger?" Will rubbed the side of the hammer with the engraving Amder had added with the edge of his shirt for a moment. "Good thing Vin is giving me combat lessons then."

Regin shook his head. "From what I'm seeing, you're more getting lessons on how to not die faster."

Will laughed then. "That bad?"

Regin shrugged, but smiled back.

"How is the tutoring with Myriam going?" Will asked and glanced back at her sleeping form behind him.

"Good. She's a bright student. If she makes a mistake, I only have to tell her once." Regin replied and snapped the reins again. "She, if we were all still in the Guild proper, would have given you a run for your money as first."

Will watched her for a moment, then turned his head away. *Be her friend for now Will, she will come around.* He turned to Regin but stopped before he spoke. Regin was unmoving, almost completely still, except for a clenched jaw.

"You all right there, Regin? Your face looks like you bit a hot coal." Will asked the Guildmaster and watched in some surprise as the man turned somewhat pale.

"Oh, uh, bit my tongue back there, bump in the road. Silly, stupid accident. Don't worry about it." Regin answered quickly but seemed to relax with the question.

Will smiled. They were making progress. Soon, they would take their shortcut and find Duncan. He knew it.

***

The boat lurched forward again, as the beasts pushing it sped up. The craft had already passed the point where he had wanted to go originally. There was no need for any subterfuge when the swiftkills made such excellent progress. There had only been one problem, and it had happened twice. Both times, the beast had nearly escaped. Working through this knife, he had taken his attention off the mental trap the beast laid in.

Both times, the beast nearly came to the fore and pushed Zalkiniv's control away. It shouldn't have happened, it couldn't happen. But yet, the beast had nearly wrested control. It had forced him to use more of the blood power that had been gathered from that stinking village on the coast to keep control.

He was no fool, and he wondered how the beast had managed it. Could it be the ecstasy of working the blood again? That was almost a constant source of wonder for him. He shouldn't be able to do this. The Scaled One should be blocking him. Valnijz should be hunting him. Though considering how insane his former master was, it was also equally possible that the Blood God wasn't even aware of what had happened in the Temple.

It could also be the working itself that was causing the control of the beast to slip. These creatures, the swiftkills, were difficult to influence. Mindless hunters, working on instinct and bloodlust, were difficult to sway. But yet here he was, controlling five of the things. That had to be it. Both the joy of working, and the working itself, had made his concentration on the beast fade out, weaken. That had to be it.

But how best to deal with that? Zalkiniv didn't want to use more of the blood power than he had to, in case he needed it when the boat landed. He'd have to release the beast to kill once they did so anyway, to replenish the power he could use. He could use workings to help, though, which would be something.

Release a swiftkill? Giving up control of one of the smaller creatures would save some power, and it wouldn't slow him by much. He could feel the hunger growing in the things. They hunted constantly most of the time, and this lack of feasting was making them harder to control.

Yes. Release one and let the others kill it to feed. An enjoyable spectacle. It had been many a long year since he'd seen a swiftkill work. Feeling out with his power, he quickly picked the hungriest of the things that now pushed the boat. One of the smaller three, it was also the one he had to exert the most control over. It must not have hunted recently.

With a mental snap, he removed his control from the beast and directed the others to kill it. The water behind the craft erupted into a froth of white water as the creatures turned and attacked as one. Their dagger like spines thrust forward, cutting into flesh and creating ripped holes as the barbs tore through the skin of the freed one. To its credit, the freed swiftkill wounded one of the other smaller ones, with one arm striking a blow that while it did not puncture the other swiftkill, it certainly scored the skin in a long ragged line.

It drove the recipient to even greater heights of rage. But it was over. The swiftkill that had gotten freed was already dead, and the others were making quick work of it. The water, which had only moments before been a tempest of wild motion, quieted and changed from a blue green to a reddish brown as the swiftkills blood flowed into the water.

The smell of death came then, of rich iron and hunger unfulfilled. Zalkiniv forced all four of the remaining creatures to share the kill, something they fought against. But they were creatures of instinct after all, and some food was better than no food. Soon, they were once again pushing the craft. Harder than before. Better, and I can keep a closer eye on the beast.

***

Duncan shuddered as the images played around him. He'd always felt somewhat uncomfortable about the sea. All that unknown water and depths. These creatures that Zalkiniv had summoned only backed his worries. Horrible things.

But what was more worrying was the beast. He was even more convinced that Zalkiniv didn't know, didn't understand what the thing was, or what it could do. Each time the beast had nearly broken control, it had not been a blind rage. Duncan could feel it. He could feel when Zalkiniv was paying attention, and so could the beast. For whenever Zalkiniv did so, the thing would rage, scream, and act as it had at the beginning. But when their captor's attention was elsewhere, the beast would be calm, calculating, and more worrisome, aware.

There was something there, some kind of mind was growing. When Duncan focused on it, gave it attention, the beast would feel like it was staring back. How he knew, he wasn't sure. But it wasn't the stare of a mindless thing. It was cold, hungry, but knowing. Intelligent. And it scared what was left of him to no end.

He wanted to hide from it. But in this endless red plain, there wasn't any place to go. Wherever or whatever this place was. And so, he watched the beast, as it sat still and unmoving, only rarely exploding into action. And worse yet, were the silent times, when he was sure the beast was watching him. Watching him and smiling.

Amder above, I was never a good follower, I know. But please, please find me, get me out of this. I want to die; I want to end this. I want peace. Haltim, I pray, forgive me. All those innocents, all those random victims, forgive me. Please, I want to be free of this prison, this flesh.

Chapter 11.

Myriam shifted in the cart, trying to not fall asleep again. The cart tended to lull her to close her eyes, but then she didn't sleep at night. She had lain there for a long time last night, listening to the fire die, the sound of William and Vin snoring. Her mind, however, had been a whirlwind.

She didn't let herself turn around and look at the two in the cart's front. Regin and William. She bit her lip for a moment in thought. The more time passed, the more she was sure she had made the right choice about William. She liked him, but not romantically. He was the Forgemaster. He was a good man. She just wished his feelings for her were more friendship and less romantic.

Things would be a lot simpler. She had caught his glances, and the smiles that broke out on his face when he did so. And this mad quest to save his cousin. She didn't blame him for trying, but Amder himself had said Duncan was under the control of something, or someone. If she were William's cousin, she'd want to be freed of it, whatever form that freedom took. If she suggested that to William, though, she knew he'd... well; she wasn't sure, but it wouldn't be good.

Regin was another problem. Working with him had been great, even easy. He was a skilled teacher. And then, the problem had arisen. She'd been looking at him, listening to his description of the smelting temperatures of more uncommon metals when she'd realized it. Regin was attractive. He was very attractive.

His smile, his long eyelashes, even his black hair that he continually raked his fingers through as a habit. She had been sitting close to him during their last tutoring session, and his voice had continually distracted her from what she should have been thinking about. So instead of the four types of flux that were used in reforging metal from the Godsfall era, she'd been distracted by the warm tones of him saying her name.

She looked down at her arms, breaking out into goosebumps at the memory. *Regin? Really?*

***

Will could barely keep his excitement contained. Meet this Gorom, take whatever shortcut through the mountains, and catch Duncan. Once he had his cousin, he wasn't sure what he would do next, but there had to be a way to fix this. With Amder's help, he would free Dunc from whatever control he was under. Then he would do whatever Amder required of him. Everything would work out.

The path the cart was on was sloping up now and had been for the last hour. Not a very steep slope, but a nice gradual rise. They were still low enough that trees were plentiful, but you would see more bare rock in places, and the air had cooled some.

"Nice." Regin said as he looked around. "It's pleasant country here."

"Reminds me of the way to Kilvar." Will remembered that trip. It seemed so very long ago, but in truth, it wasn't even a year ago. "Master Jaste spent the whole time grilling me over Dernstown."

Regin snorted. "Sounds like Jaste. He loved to quiz Apprentices and Journeymen alike. But he was a spark blessed master at knowing things. He was good with a hammer and technique, but he probably knew more than most of the Masters in the guild. He cared about the raw knowledge."

"Wish he was here. He'd be surprised at the state of everything." Will answered.

"He would both be overjoyed about the return of a Forgemaster and equally worried about the state of the Guild." Regin frowned for a moment. "I still blame myself for his death. I know I didn't mean for it to happen, but if I hadn't gone to Bracin, that dark day in the Guild wouldn't have happened."

"Regin, Bracin would have found out one way or another. And Master Jaste knew the chance he was taking when he got me to the Guild under an assumed name." Will shrugged. "If anyone is to blame, it's me. If I hadn't agreed to that madness, he'd still be alive."

"And there wouldn't be a Forgemaster, and the Scaled One would be back. You and your cousin would most likely be dead." Regin pointed out, ducking under a low branch.

Will didn't answer. Regin was right. *You can't save everyone, but Duncan, he you can save.*

Silence fell over the cart for a few minutes as they rolled up the slope, ducking the occasional tree branch. To Will, the cart path seemed a little overgrown, but it had been used. The ruts were bare of grass.

"Has anyone ever seen a Gorom without a robe? Do we even know what we are getting into here?" Vin spoke up from the back of the cart unexpectedly.

"I saw one in Ture." Will answered. "Robe covered, of course. Didn't see his or her face. Couldn't even tell really from what it was wearing."

Myriam spoke up as well. "We never saw them at my father's inn. Saw the same one William saw in Ture. That's it."

"That's what I thought." Vin's voice lowered. "Are you sure we will be safe there? I know what Amder said, but we are heading into a place that we, meaning humans, never go. Of all the races, the Gorom are the most private. We never see them, they almost never talk to us, and they hide away underground."

William thought about it for a moment. "I don't think Amder would point us into a trap, at least not without a warning."

"Amder might not plan to, but look, he's just returned to us. Does he really know what the Gorom are like? When the Godsfall happened, things could have been very different. I'm an old soldier, so I tend to be very particular. It's how I got old after all." Vin cleared his throat. "I think we should be careful."

Will wondered if Vin was right. No one knew much about where they were going. The Gorom always came to them. "We will be careful." Will spoke when he realized that Vin, Myriam and even Regin all were waiting for his response. He repressed a groan at the realization.

"Agreed." Regin ducked another low-hanging branch and frowned for a moment before a chuckle erupted from him.

"What's so funny?" Myriam asked from the back of the cart. "Potential danger at the hands of the Gorom?"

"No, I realized why there are so many branches blocking the road." Regin turned towards Myriam and Vin for a second. "Gorom are short. I doubt many men, many humans, ever come up this way. To a Gorom, there's plenty of headroom."

Will laughed. "I never thought about that." He rubbed his finger across his hammer in thought again. "And we will be careful, Vin. It's true we know almost nothing about the Gorom. But I don't think Amder would willingly put us in danger. He said something about Grimnor owing him a favor."

"Do you ever get used to it? Talking about the Gods as if they are someone you know?" Myriam asked. "I have a hard-enough time even thinking it. I feel unsettled if I think about it too long."

"Yes and No." Will shrugged. "I did at first a lot. But the fact that Amder likes to talk to me in my head makes him seem more real. I can feel him. I don't know how else to say it."

"Seems strange to me." Vin added. "But I'm solely a conscripted merchant guard."

"You are far more than that, Captain Vin Tolin." Will answered quickly. "I don't know what you are, but I know you are more than that."

Silence fell over the cart once more, the only sound the creak of the wheels as the horses dragged it ever upwards, and towards the meeting spot.

***

Jindo watched as his forces, moving faster than most people could see, swarmed through the forest. Only half the keep this time, but far more than would be needed. He hadn't taken the full force of the Curors out in quite some time. That had been their only failure. The lord had not been pleased. Jindo still remembered the punishment for his failure.

But this target was different. A minor city. Walled, but bound to a river. Jindo could not remember what its current name was, not that it mattered. Soon it would run red, like every other town. It had refused to send tribute to the keep, refused to send hunters and fighters to try for admittance.

All because Zalkiniv had failed. The word had traveled fast, merchant birds and ships had spread the return of Amder. Amder was far away in Palnor, still consolidating his power. Jindo was here, now. The town elders would learn that a faraway god would not save them.

The town came into view, and Jindo Halfman could barely contain his amusement. Fools hadn't even closed the city. The gates stood open, a few farmer's carts even came and left as he watched.

His Curors gathered behind him, awaiting his plan. Plan. There was no plan needed. Turning to the assembled forces, he reached into his belt pouch and pulled out a hooked and barbed spear head. He quickly replaced the one he had been using. This would not be a fight. It would be a slaughter. His assembled force did the same in silence.

Jindo smiled. A slaughter for his lord. He raised his spear high and pointed it at the town. With a single thrust he pointed, and the Curors rushed forward, the speed of their passing making the air rush, and Jindo's clothes move in the sudden breeze.

The screams, short and fast, came quickly, followed by more and longer ones. The stink of fear and panic washed over him. Jindo hummed a mindless tune as he entered the city. He was the weapon of Valnijz, and he would draw blood today.

Chapter 12.

Will saw the Gorom first. They had rounded a sharp turn, and the cart path had ended onto a large flat slab of hard whitestone. The edges had been carved with a complex pattern of swirls and small triangles. A huge stone overhang, supported by more whitestone pillars, even more ornate than the stone the cart was stopped on, covered the far side of the clearing. And there, under the overhang, in the shadow stood a figure wrapped in the dark red robes of a Gorom.

The Gorom was standing there, alone. Its face was hidden by the wrapped hood that covered its face, and the shade where it stood. Will and Regin exchanged glances. "Alright, we are here, but where are the rest of the Gorom? Where is the path?" Will whispered. "All I see is the trail we came up on. I don't see any out of this clearing."

"And we didn't pass any turn offs, did we, Vin? I didn't see any." Myriam asked Captain Tolin, who shook his head.

"Well, that's great. If we have to walk to where the trail is to cross the mountains, that will slow us up and not having a cart will make us slower still." Regin stood, glancing around. "I see nothing either."

Will nodded, his eyes turning again to the figure of the Gorom, who had not left its spot, and had said nothing to them. "Sparks burn me. I guess we need to find out from the Gorom then."

Will, Regin, Vin and Myriam got out of their cart, each giving a small shake and stretch to shake off the ride.

Will paused, and with a nod to his companions, walked towards the Gorom. "Greetings. I see you are expecting me."

The Gorom's head moved up, and Will took a step back. While the face was covered with cloth, the eyes were uncovered. The Gorom's eyes were pink and pale, as if even that color was a bit too hard for it to muster up.

"Yes, special of the half god, I am the Gorom who waits for you. You may call me Speaker-to-the-sky." The Gorom's voice was rough and throaty. Will had heard nothing like it.

"My name is William Reis; I am the Forgemaster of Amder." Half God? *What did this person mean?*

Speaker-to-the-sky made a small snorting noise in response, a noise that Will knew was one of dismissal. Annoyance grew. *The sooner I'm done dealing with this Gorom, the better.*

"Well, if you can show us the path for the cart to take over the mountains, we will mark it on our maps and head out on our way." Will waved his hand around the clearing. "We don't see it."

A laugh escaped the Gorom then, a harsh sound that made Will wince in response. "Not very smart, special of a half god." The Gorom laughed again, each laugh grating on Will's ears.

"What is so funny?" Will asked through teeth he didn't even realize he was clenching.

"A path over the mountains?" Speaker-to-the-sky said and stopped laughing. "We are not you. There are no paths over the mountains here."

"What?" Will felt his stomach drop. "But I was told by Amder himself that you would help us get across the mountains!"

Speaker-to-the-sky nodded. "And we will, though most Gorom are against this. The way is under the mountains." Speaker pointed a gloved hand towards the enormous stone door. "This way. You and those you travel with will come with me."

The bottom fell out from Will's stomach and with a lurch of what, nausea? Under the mountains?

"But..." Will started to object but trailed off with his realization. Amder had never said it would be a path or road over the mountains, only that the Gorom would help him cross them. *I should have realized it meant under.*

"Well, William Reis of the humans, get your companions. The less I have to be out here, the better." Speaker-to-the-sky shifted from side to side, clearly nervous.

Will nodded and walked back towards Myriam, Regin, and Vin.

"You feeling all right, William? You look pale." Myriam asked. "The Gorom tell you where the road was?"

"Yes. And no. And there is no road." Will glanced back at the smaller figure of the Gorom. "We will have to leave the cart and horse. The way is under, not over."

"What??" Regin blurted out, loud enough for the horse to stutter step away from them.

"I wasn't expecting it either, but it makes sense. We never see the Gorom above ground really, I assumed it was a road. Amder never said that." Will looked at each of the others. "Regin, are you ok with this plan?"

"I guess. Though days underground doesn't really appeal to me." Regin frowned. "And based on the size of a Gorom, maybe hunched over."

"The idea doesn't appeal to me either." Myriam added. "I'll do it, but how long will it take?"

Will's eyes fell on Vin, who, to his surprise, was nearly as pale as the cart horse's mane. "I don't know Forgemaster." Vin pulled a small rag and wiped his forehead clean of sweat, though it was a cool day in the mountains. "I…" Vin paused and lowered his voice. "I don't care for tunnels or caves."

Will nodded. He had worked in mines for years back in the Reach growing up, but days traveling underground? That didn't appeal to him either. He'd do it, but he wouldn't ask any of his companions to do it if they couldn't or didn't want to.

"None of you have to do this. Saving Duncan is my goal, my quest. I know this underground travel wasn't on any of our thoughts." Will thought about what Duncan would say for a moment. Probably crack a joke or try to diffuse the tension that had grown noticeable since he'd let them know the way they had to go.

"Oh, I'm coming." Regin answered. "I don't like the idea, granted. I swore to you to serve the Forgemaster of Amder. I'm not backing off."

"I'll go." Myriam nodded. "If nothing else, you are taking my tutor along. He's the only way I will prove I belong in the Guild." She shot Regin a smile, who to Will's surprise turned red, the hue chasing some paleness out of his face.

Vin was silent for a moment. "I've fought in wars, battles, skirmishes. I've fought professional soldiers, bandits, and wild animals. And hordes of Valni." He let out an unsteady breath. "I wouldn't be much use as a teacher and a bodyguard if I let the Forgemaster of Amder travel into the dark without me. I'll go."

Will nodded and smiled. He placed a hand on Vin's shoulder. "I know it can't be easy for you." Will didn't know what else to say. He couldn't fix the fear Vin had. He'd known a Reacher named Taron as a child who had been like Vin. Caves and mines had scared him in some deep way. He'd always said he thought the mountain would fall on him, crushing him. Taron had been a quite good smelter, and had run a profitable business, but refused to set foot in any mine.

"Well, let's get our gear. The Gorom wants to get moving. His name is Speaker-to-the-sky, apparently." Will took his pack. "We will need to split up provisions."

Myriam nodded, as they all organized what they could carry. "What does a Gorom even eat?" Myriam asked with a glance over at the hooded figure. "Did you get a look at his face?"

Will stopped packing for a moment. "No idea what they eat. And no, I didn't see his face. I saw his eyes. They are pink."

"Pink?" Regin shoved an oilcloth wrapped hunk of bread into his pack. "Strange."

Will shrugged. All of this was strange to him.

"What do we do with the horse?" Will asked. "We can't leave the poor animal here."

"I guess we should ask the Gorom, Speaker-to-the-sky, was it?" Myriam stood, shifting her pack. "The food will make this a long heavier walk."

Will nodded and shouldered his pack, along with Regin and still sickly looking Vin. "Hopefully they know what to do."

Will led the others to the Gorom, who had backed away into the shadows even more. "Speaker-to-the-sky, let me introduce you to Myriam, Regin and Vin. My companions."

"I need not know their names." Speaker-to-the-sky blurted and headed for the door. "Come."

"Wait, what about the horse?" Will asked. "Do we leave him there?"

Speaker-to-the-sky stopped walking. "Yes. We will sell him."

Will exchanged glances with his friends. They all shrugged in response. Not ideal, but there was little they could do. Will wanted to ask for the money but held his tongue. It was already clear this Gorom didn't seem to like them much.

"Come followers of the half-god. It is better for you if we get moving." Speaker-to-the-sky placed his gloved hand on the carved door and pressed in a pattern so fast that Will couldn't make it out. The door swung open without a sound, into darkness.

"Half god?" Regin asked quietly, turning to William.

"No idea." Will kept his voice even lower. "I already don't like this."

"Shouldn't we get a torch or something?" Vin asked, his voice unsteady. "I can't see anything in there."

"No! None of your lights. You will see." Speaker-to-the-sky walked forward, vanishing into the blackness.

Will swallowed and followed the Gorom, his companions walking without a word into the unknown.

***

Jindo watched as his men killed the last of the townsfolk. The river, true to his wish, ran red and would for the rest of the day. Blood flowed around his boots as the last of the townsfolk, pleading for their lives, died, their voices cut short by the hooked spear blades ripping their throats out.

Several of them pleaded for their lives, some offered money, or power, or both. One man even offered his child to serve the order if they let him go. Not that any of it did any good. What was money worth compared to the glory of the Blood God? What was the paltry power of some fat, self-styled lord, compared to the power his God had given him already? And servants? Unneeded and unwanted.

"For you, my Lord. May the blood fill your thirst." Jindo kneeled in the blood, lowering his head until it almost touched the swirling liquid.

He got no answer, not that he expected to. Not since that night, where something horrible had gone wrong, and Amder had returned. The Blood God had been silent since then. He did not believe his lord was gone for good, though. He would continue to work in the Blood God's name, for when his lord returned, he would be ready to show his God that Jindo Halfman was loyal. Jindo Halfman would be whatever the god needed.

Chapter 13.

Duncan shuddered. Or at least he thought he did. The fact was that most of the time; he seemed to not fully exist. Only if he thought of it and concentrated on being Duncan did he feel real. He wondered if that was a sign that he was slowly vanishing, that whatever he was, whatever piece of who he had been, what he had been was bit by bit disappearing. Maybe it was for the better. Anything would be better than this... pointless existence.

That same red haze seemed to cover everything, and a dusty dry feeling covered him. If it was even really his skin. He didn't hunger; he didn't thirst, and he didn't sleep. Duncan didn't know if it had been hours, days, weeks, or months since he'd forced Zalkiniv to not attack the Reach. They were elsewhere now, but where was unknown.

Worse yet, was the beast. He was terrified of the thing, and now even more than before. It watched him most of the time, a figure that looked like him, but wasn't him. A figure that was gaunt, thin, blooded. He only caught glimpses of it. Most of the time, the red haze was too thick. But he knew it was there, crouching in whatever place Zalkiniv thought it was trapped in.

Duncan knew better. He actually missed the way it had been at first. The thing had howled and screamed, and the name had been accurate. He could sense then, early on, what the beast had been feeling. Lost in a dream of death, the beast had been tricked into thoughts of killing, that it was free.

One day, that had changed. Zalkiniv had let loose the beast to use Duncan's form. Those days made him want to retch. He could feel the coiling presence of Zalkiniv wait and watch as the beast vanished. Duncan knew what that meant. He knew what he was being forced to do, or at least what his body was doing. He could watch as well, he knew it. The former High Priest of the Blood God had made sure of that. The only thing he could watch, other than the haze. Duncan, however, never wanted to look.

But when the beast had come back that day, it had been so different. It had been the first time that as soon as Zalkiniv had taken back over, the beast had stilled, and watched Duncan. And it watched him still. He hated it.

"What do you want from me?" Duncan yelled, his voice barely able to be carried in this strange place.

As usual, no answer came to him. How could it? He didn't exist. But yet, as Duncan sat in despair, the haze shifted. And for a long minute, the beast could be seen. Close, nearby. Its form as before, but something new, something that made Duncan shudder in fear now. For, in patches, here and there, something glittered in the ever-present red dim light. Scales.

"Soooon…" a whisper, sibilant and powerful, washed over him. And Duncan Reis wept.

***

Will tried to see something, anything. He'd been in dark caves, dark mines. But this was darker still. *One wrong step and Amder will have to look for a new Forgemaster already.* True blackness gripped him. He could hear the others, a mix of shuffling steps, the slight cling of metal, and the breathing. But who was who was lost in the absolute darkness.

"Speaker-to-the-sky?" Will asked, reaching his hands out, trying to find something to touch, something solid to hold on to. A wall, hopefully. The last thing he needed was his hands to find Myriam. Trying to get her to see him as the same man as before had not been going to plan. His hands finding parts of her in the dark wouldn't go well.

A snort came, the same sound the Gorom had made before. "Humans. Cursed folk." The sound of the Gorom seemed to echo off the walls. "Here."

A light bloomed, but not one that William had ever seen before. A light that shone dark blue to purple, throwing strange shadows around the room. And to Will's amazement, things around him glowed. The robe the Gorom wore, which outside had been a darkish red, now had lines of green and blue running through it in the same patterns as the whitestone slab had been outside. The walls were covered in giant swirls of glowing yellow and green.

"Now you see like a Gorom." Speaker-to-the-sky announced, and with a single motion tugged the cloth off his face and removed his hood.

Will could only stare. Speaker-to-the-sky, his skin glowed purple! One look back at Myriam, Regin and Vin only added to his amazement. Anything and everything that was white now glowed purple as well. A glimpse of teeth was disconcerting.

"How is this possible?" Regin asked, pointing to the walls. "This is amazing!"

Myriam and Vin said nothing. Will could see that at least for the moment, though Vin's unease had been banished, replaced with a wide-eyed look of what he hoped was surprise.

"We are Gorom. The light above, we dislike it. We like our light." Speaker-to-the-sky shrugged. "I will take you to the Stonefather-who-speaks, and then we go on our way."

"Who?" Will asked as the Gorom holding the glowing purple orb that had made this incredible light made his way through an arched opening that was covered with tiny points of glowing blue and red.

"Stonefather-who-speaks. He speaks for Grimnor. He is the only reason you are here." Speaker-to-the-sky paused. "We do not let humans in, this is very strange to have four of your cursed race here."

Myriam walked up, "Excuse me, but why do you keep calling us cursed?"

Speaker-to-the-sky didn't answer at first, but motioned for them to follow him as he descended a steep staircase carved out of the rock. Will was happy to have any light, even this strange one. Without it, he was sure all four of them would have tumbled down these stairs and broken bones, or worse.

"I call you cursed because you are." Speaker finally answered. "You are humans, humans are cursed."

"But you do business with us." Regin spoke up. "With the Guild."

"Yes, when we must." Speaker continued down the stairs, the purple light continuing to make various patterns glow in a strange, glowing rainbow of patterns and colors. The air grew cooler as they walked. They were getting deeper underground. How much deeper was an open question.

"Why meet with us if we are cursed, though?" Regin asked.

Speaker paused on a stone landing and turned to the four humans. "This is not my place to say. The Stonefather-who-speaks will answer questions."

"Why are we meeting with him?" Vin, who had been silent all this time, finally spoke up. "Why not take us straight to the tunnel?"

Will could see that Vin was still unsteady. He was, however, resting his hand on his sword hilt. *He thinks we might have trouble.* But trouble from the Gorom? They were strange folk, to be sure. He'd learned more about them in the last hour than he'd ever imagined, and could tell with certainty that they were unlike anything he'd ever imagined. But dangerous? He found the idea kind of silly. But then again, he wasn't the bodyguard. Maybe Vin had his reasons.

"The Stonefather-who-speaks will meet with you because he says he must. He is the Stonefather." Speaker shook his head, the bright purple sheen of his bald head glowing brightly. "I will only say this. The Gorom do not want you here." And with that, he walked on, down more steps.

Will and the others followed close until finally, after several more minutes, Speaker-to-the-sky stopped in front of a huge stone door. It was metal, but like the stone, lines of blue and red intertwined in a strange pattern of whirls and triangles. Will followed the lines with his eyes, unsure where one stopped and another began.

"You will not go through this door. I will. The door you will go through is over there." Speaker-to-the-sky pointed to a much smaller door hidden in a corner. "The Stonefather-who-speaks will meet you past that door." Speaker walked to the smaller door and touched another orb that Will hadn't seen in the dark, and it also glowed with the same dark purple light.

"Are you not going with us?" Will asked. He wasn't sure he wanted to be here. Maybe Vin was right, and these Gorom were leading them into a trap.

"I will meet you again. But you are not to go into the Heartsteen." Speaker pointed at the large doors. "For you cursed ones, it's a city. The largest in this section of Grimnors world."

Will looked at each of his friends, trying to read their faces. The strange light was giving him a bit of a headache. He wasn't used to this odd glowing world. Regin shrugged as he looked at him. Myriam nodded. Vin, however, had his mouth set in a line, a tight, firm line. Will could see that he was now gripped the sword handle tightly, instead of only resting on it.

Vin gave him a nod. A sharp nod. *Keep calm Vin, we might need you.*

Speaker-to-the-sky took the second orb and handed it to Will. "Go, the Stonefather-who-speaks is waiting."

Will took the orb. Its surface was smooth, glassy, but it was far lighter than something made out of glass would be for its size.

"Don't ask what it is." Amders rumble came. *"I know you have questions, William Reis. Go on, ask quickly. Grimnor gets annoyed if he thinks I'm too close to his people."*

Will held up a hand for a moment and turned to his friends. "One minute, Amder is talking to me."

Speaker-to-the-sky made a face as if he had eaten something long spoiled, and backed away from Will, but said nothing.

"Don't mind the Gorom. They don't like anyone much." Amder spoke quickly. *"And no, I didn't know you would travel underground. But I also didn't ask. You wanted to get to Duncan, and so you shall. You should know that he's on a boat crossing the Dawn Sea. Heading south. I am not sure why."*

That's not good! How are we supposed to catch him? Will gripped the orb tight but thought better of it. Breaking the thing would only annoy the already obviously unhappy Gorom.

"That is up to you. This is your chosen quest, Forgemaster. I am allowing it, but my help is limited. Getting Grimnor to let you through was challenge enough. Remember, I am newly reborn, and my return has shaken the balance of power. Things are... different from they were before I fell. I can't explain it." Amder's rumbled faded out.

"Well, that wasn't overly helpful." Will let out a long breath. "Duncan is on a boat, heading south. Amder doesn't know why."

"I like boats." Vin spoke up. "Open sea air would be better than this."

"There is nothing wrong with the stone cursed human." Speaker-to-the-sky waved at the smaller door. "Go, you have waited too long already."

Chapter 14.

Will stared at the smaller door. His initial surprise to this strange glowing world of the Gorom had lessened some, but even so, he felt himself unwilling to step through this door. He raised his arm to push it open and then lowered it again. *I am the Forgemaster of Amder. I can open a stone door.* Will raised his arm again and finally pushed the smaller door open. It moved easily, even though as it did so, he could see it was nearly as thick as a hammerhead. The Gorom might be strange, and not friendly, but they could craft.

Will looked back and nodded to his companions and, holding the glowing orb Speaker-to-the-sky had given him, he entered a round room, his friends following behind him. This room, unlike the others, had a unique pattern. The same colors glowed, but instead of flowing curls and triangles, this room was covered in very fine, totally straight lines. Hundreds, if not thousands, of them. Each one glowing in the purple light.

"This light is going to make me nauseous soon." Myriam whispered behind Will. He turned to look at her, but it was hard to see what she looked like. All of their skin had the same slight purple glow, though nothing like the Gorom appeared to have.

"I guess close your eyes. I don't know. It's taking me some getting used to as well." Will answered, his voice as quiet as he could make it.

"You don't have to whisper blessed of the half god." A voice answered as a new Gorom appeared from a corner, hidden in darkness.

Will blinked a few times at the sight of this new Gorom. He was, if it was a he, nearly naked, clad only in a loose robe that was open across his chest and back. His skin shone with a bright purple light. But even more surprisingly, the glowing lines that were everywhere here were on his skin! A complex pattern of interlocking squares and diamonds covered every inch of his skin that Will could see.

"Stonefather-who-speaks?" Will guessed as the Gorom sat on the floor, across from him and his friends.

"Yes." The Stonefather started at each of them, not saying anything, though when he looked at Vin, he gave forth a grunt. "These are your companions? The Stonefather is not impressed."

"What?" Will glanced at his friends again. They seemed normal, though Myriam had her eyes closed now, and he could see that Vin was still obviously uncomfortable, based on the fact that there was still some sweat on his brow, even in this cool underground room. That and the strong grip he kept on his weapon.

"I am the Stonefather-who-speaks. I speak for Grimnor of the Mountains. The Lord of the stone." The Stonefather pointed a glowing finger at William. "And you are the blessed of the half god." He moved his finger to Regin. "He is a Guildmaster in your Smithing Guild." The finger moved to Myriam. "She is…" The Stonefather paused, a frown first appearing and then it relaxed into what Will could only describe as an appraising look.

The Stonefather said nothing else and moved his finger to Vin. "And he is Stonescared. You should not have brought him here."

"His name is Vin Tolin. Captain Vin Tolin. And he is my friend, and he insisted." William answered back. He wanted to get done here, get to the other side of the mountains, and find a way to catch up with Duncan. Standing around listening to an old Gorom annoy him wasn't in the plan.

"Stonefather-who-speaks. While I thank you for letting us pass through your home, I have to wonder, why are we here?" Will walked over to the wall, rubbing his fingers over the glowing lines. "I mean no offense. Another time, and I'd love to explore this, whatever this is." He turned back to the Gorom. "But I don't have time. I must get to the other side of the Skyreach, and this is the fastest way."

"You are here, because I wanted to meet you, and give you a warning." Stonefather-who-speaks sat down on the floor. "You humans. It has always surprised us, all the other races of Alos, how you can even function. A cursed race, and yet, you thrive. And here you are, the blessed of the half god, and still you labor in ignorance and go blindly forth, as if walking into the high sun of the surface."

"Why do you all keep calling us cursed, and calling Amder a half god?" Regin spoke up. "It's getting a bit tiresome."

"Because you are." Stonefather-who-speaks waved his hand at them. "Your entire race is cursed. It's cursed because of the split, because your gods even exist."

Will and Regin exchanged glances. Will wanted to argue the point. They weren't cursed. Regin shook his head. Split? What was this Stonefather even talking about? Will could handle aggravation, but these Gorom were difficult.

Amder? Will tried to reach out to the God, but oddly couldn't seem to reach him. Will suddenly realized that since he walked into this room, he couldn't feel the god lurking in the back of his head anymore. *Amder? Can you hear me?*

Silence was the only answer Will got. He glanced at the other two of his friends. Myriam still had her eyes closed and was breathing rather forcefully. He imagined she was trying to not get sick. Tolin looked as tense as he had the moment they walked into this underground realm.

Will turned his attention back to the Gorom, surprised to find him looking at Myriam with an expression Will couldn't place. "Well Stonefather-who-speaks, can you show us the way? We want to get to the other side and get out of the tunnels here."

Stonefather-who-speaks grunted and stood. "Yes. But be clear. I will have Speaker-to-the-sky show you, but stay close to him. This is not a popular thing, you humans being here. You should be safe from attack, but..." the Gorom paused.

"Will they try to attack?" Vin spoke up for the first time in a while.

Stonefather-who-speaks shrugged. "I doubt they will strike you. But that means little here. The Stoneworld has far more dangers than you know."

The door slid open again, and there stood Speaker-to-the-sky, scowling even more than he had before. "Stonefather-who-speaks, must I do this?" Speaker-to-the-sky asked as he walked in.

"Yes. Grimnor requires us to help. Take them to where they need to go." Stonefather-who-speaks turned to Myriam again. "Open your eyes human woman."

Myriam opened them, blinking. Will could feel her eyes fall on each of them as she took in the glowing world again. *I wish she still smiled when she saw me.*

"What is your name?" Stonefather-who-speaks asked Myriam, and then to Will's utter surprise, the Gorom, who had been as acerbic and frankly somewhat insulting to him, bowed!

Myriam stepped back for a half step and her eyes widened, then locked with Williams for a moment. "Myriam. Myriam Vol Far."

"It is my honor to meet you Myriam Vol Far." Stonefather-who-speaks shuffled off then, his glowing lined tattoos fading to blackness as he vanished into that same dark impenetrable corner he had appeared from.

Regin leaned close to Will. "What was that? He calls us cursed, insults Amder, then bows to Myriam and says it's an honor to meet her?"

"I have no idea. I also can't seem to talk to Amder in this room. I tried, but the moment we walked into this room, I couldn't talk to him." Will kept his voice low. "I had no idea of what we would find here, but this, this is beyond anything I could have imagined."

"I agree. The faster we are out of the lands of the Gorom, the better." Regin stepped away.

"Come. I will guide you. It will take four of your surface days to cross." Speaker-to-the-sky stepped back into the room they had been in before, grabbing a pack he had there. "You will follow me. Do not leave the way that I lead you on. There are many things here that will eat you, or, worse."

"What could be worse than being eaten?" Captain Tolin asked. "And how narrow are these tunnels? I need to know in case... in case we are attacked, if I will have room to swing my sword or not."

"Many things are worse. Being eaten is fast, other things can take a long passage of time. And I hope you are good with a dagger." Speaker-to-the-sky smiled, and Will felt a shiver of fear quiver up his back for a moment.

Amder? Are you there? Silence. *Amder?* But no response came. Will grabbed Regin, Myriam, and Vin and pulled them off to the side quickly. "We might have another problem. I still can't talk to Amder."

"What?" Myriam asked as she shouldered her pack. "I thought you could always talk to him since he named you Forgemaster."

"I have been. It's hard to explain, but it's like there is a tiny piece of him in my mind at all times. If I think about it, I can suddenly talk to him. But since we entered that room and spoke to that Stonefather person, it's silent, I can't even feel him." Will rubbed the edge of his hammer again. "I'm not sure what to do."

"We only have two choices, William. Forward or back." Vin looked back up the way they had come down. "And while I'd prefer to be out of this place, that's not the real question. The real question is will you be able to forgive yourself if you end this quest now."

"It doesn't have to be the end; we might can still catch Duncan if we go another way." Regin answered.

"If he's in a boat heading for the southern lands, and we have to turn around, head south and take a longer boat trip ourselves, would we be able to find him? I have my doubts." Vin shrugged. "It's your choice, Forgemaster. This is your path."

"I say we stay and do this. It's far faster than the other way. And I want to see more of this place. Even if this light makes me want to lose my breakfast." Myriam spoke up. "I know I'm the least important piece of the puzzle here, but that's what I say."

"What do you mean? You are a vital part." William asked.

"You are the Forgemaster of Amder. Regin is a Master Smith. Captain Tolin is skilled with arms and fighting. He's also pretty good at strategy. I'm an innkeeper's daughter, a barely trained first year apprentice in the Guild." Myriam answered. "I'm not thinking I'm something bad, but compared to the rest of you, I'm nothing special."

"Yes, you are special!" Regin spoke up forcefully enough to have all three heads of his companions jerk back a bit. "Sorry. Never say that, Myriam. You're very special. To us. To the… well us." Regin averted his eyes and looked away.

"Regardless. I guess Myriam is right. We should move forward. Going back will take too long." Regin added.

Will didn't know what to do. If they moved forward without Amder in his head, would that be alright? Would the God return after they left the mountains? And what had changed from when they had gone into that room? He had been able to talk to Amder before in this place.

"Come cursed ones. We have much travel to do." Speaker-to-the-sky called as he stood by the enormous double doors.

Will frowned. This cursed one nonsense was still annoying. "Be right there." he called out.

"Alright, we move forward. And you all are right, I wouldn't be able to deal with it if I gave up now, or lost Duncan because I second guessed myself." Will nodded. "Thank you all for doing this with me."

"I swore an oath. And on top of it, I kind of want to see this world, no one really ever has." Regin answered.

"I will go where you go." Vin answered and then saluted, rather formally.

"And I am not going anywhere. I gave up the Smithing guild for this. I'm not leaving yet." Myriam shrugged. "And that light isn't making me as sick anymore."

Will thought she might be lying about that last part, but was happy to hear that all three wanted to come. He nodded to his friends as they walked over to where Speaker-to-the-sky was. Friends. Will realized that he meant it. Even back in the Reach, he had never had real friends. People he knew, sure. Most of them he liked. But knowing the person always had your back? And that you'd return the favor? No. Friends. He liked the sound of that.

"We are ready." Will said.

"Good. And welcome to the first and only time you will get to see the lands of the Stoneworld." Speaker-to-the-sky pushed the doors open.

Chapter 15.

Zalkiniv sat still, controlling the remaining swiftkills. One more day and night and he would be done with this leg of his travels. Find the nearest village and harvest the fools who live there. He would need an army later, of course, to lay waste to bigger towns and cities. The Cruor maybe. After killing their leader, they might fall in line. At least as a start.

He was glad for the swiftkills, though. Working the power this long was a strange experience. Before taking control of this body, in his other forms, he'd work the blood but be tired after, exhausted sometimes. The claret stones had helped, but still working at this level for this long, he had never been able to do.

I wonder if I should have stayed in the valley and searched for those stones. Their power would have been useful. The odds were, though, that the falling rocks would have broken them Cracked and useless. He didn't even need them now.

Oddly, the beast had not been difficult to control since the sacrifice of the one swiftkill. It had gone back to being easy to trick, howling in rage, lost in its delusions. The fragment of Duncan had been whimpering in fear most of the time, but that served Zalkiniv's purposes just fine. It amused him, at least, something to pass the time. And he could feed on that fear, if only a tiny bit.

The night air around him slowly grew thicker as the boat traveled on. Fog was coming in, which, while not unexpected, wasn't fully welcome. He could feel the dampness creep across his vessel as the fog closed in, even thicker with each passing moment.

Zalkiniv didn't like it. This fog came too fast, too thick. His skin broke out into tiny bumps as the fog rolled over the boat. Something wasn't right. He prepared to reach out, to divert some of his blood working into checking for danger when the telltale creak of wood made him whirl around.

Saltmistresses! A vessel, large and ornate, loomed out of the fog, running hard. Easily three times the size of his ship, the ship counted four large sails, and the hull was white with blue green stripes. It was moving fast, far faster than he was. And it was heading right towards him.

He reached out, pushing the swiftkills harder, but the Saltmistress ship came closer still. For a moment he wondered if it was sheer chance, running into a ship of theirs here, and then he saw them, perched on the ship, starboard side facing him, three huge harpoons. He was under attack.

The Saltmistress ship rode the waves with ease, and the ship cut through the water, barely making a sound itself. But he could hear them, the winches, and the rattle of chains. Drawing on the reserves of power he had, Zalkiniv began a working to strengthen the ship. He could feel the power moving out into the boards and wood, a few bright spots lit up with old spilled blood, mostly from animals. The power reacted still, though weakly.

Pushing the power into the ship was difficult. Anything not flesh was. Wood was always harder than most. Before, as Rache, he had done it in the Temple of Amder. That had been a single door, and in that case, he had been breaking it. Now, he was using the power to make the wood stronger, better. A task to which the blood working was not well suited. The resistance to his working grew, and he threw more reserves into his binding.

He released the two smaller swiftkills from his control; he needed the power. The animals, exhausted from his grip, half floated in the dark water, barely moving. It didn't matter. He must survive this attack!

Zalkiniv could barely register the sound before the first harpoon rushed out of its launcher. He braced himself for the impact, hoping the working was strong enough to withstand the blow. The water behind the ship exploded as the harpoon impacted. They had missed!

His joy was only momentary as the realization sunk in, and anger filled his mind. They had never targeted the boat; they were targeting the animals, the swiftkills! The water behind the boat erupted as the largest of the beasts came out of the water, the harpoon having fully impaled itself into its body. Thrashing from side to side, the swiftkill shook his boat as it struggled. Zalkiniv's binding was shattered as the beast threw off his working, the mortal pain cutting through his control. The boat shuddered again as the beast gave one last heave and died.

The other two harpoons lurched forth, both striking the other large swiftkill. It died instantly, and Zalkiniv, even with his newfound power, found himself thrown to the boat deck, grasping his head in pain as the workings he had held onto for days shattered and rebounded.

He could hear the winching start as the Saltmistresses pulled the bodies of the swiftkills up. He tried to reach out through the pain to establish control with the two smaller animals he had released at the beginning of the attack; the workings did not work! They flowed weakly, and his power flickered. Too much. He had used too much. He had guessed wrong.

***

Duncan watched with a small sense of satisfaction. He had been almost overwhelmed at first. The more Zalkiniv did whatever he did, the red dust and haze lessened. Not that Duncan's senses were real in this prison that his mind was stuck in. Even so, it was something. He pointedly ignored the beast, though the thing was watching him, silently.

He could feel Zalkiniv's anger, and even a small growing sense of fear. The ship, huge, blue, white, was all Duncan could sense. He had no idea who it was, or who they were, but if they could stop this madness, he was happy. Well, as happy as he could be.

He turned back to the beast, to find it staring at him, as it did often now. From violence, to screams, to silent staring. He hated it. This icy silence, calculating... It had not spoken since that one time. At least he assumed it was the beast that had spoken. It was hard to tell. The shimmer of scales on the thing had grown as well. The patches were larger.

"Well? Are you going to say something or only stare at me?" Duncan asked. He didn't feel brave. *Maybe if this thing escapes, it will end whatever this is, and I'll be free.*

The beast said nothing. Though much to his shock, the beast nodded. A single, clear nod.

"I hate this, I hate you! I hate Zalkiniv!" Duncan yelled out, his voice falling regardless of how much he tried to scream. He had no strength anymore. He still wasn't sure how he had managed to get enough control to turn Zalkiniv away from the Reach.

"I helllppp..." the whisper came again, and he knew it was the beast this time.

"Help? You help?" Duncan shivered and pushed himself to the barrier that kept him here. Never a physical thing, he couldn't seem to get any farther away from the beast than he was now. *I don't exist, that's why. I'm a scrap of a memory.*

"I help turn... Not for you, but for me." The whisper came again.

"I don't understand... what are you? Who are you?" Duncan asked, but the kernel of a thought filled him. A thought that brought new terror to him, a terror he couldn't imagine before. The beast it was playing a game this whole time. The violence, the mindless terror, that had been what, an act? The playing of a mummer's role just too...

"Convince him. My failure... He thinks I am gone. He thinks he will be a god. He is nothing. He is taking me to where I want to go." The whisper was stronger now, and Duncan knew. He knew what he was talking too, who he was talking to.

He screamed, a voice of terror. It couldn't be. There was no way it could be...

"Scream all you want, child of Amder. There is no one to help you here." The beast sat back. "Soon I will be in control, and he will join my chorus. For you know me human, you know my name." The beast smiled then, a smile full of hunger. A smile full of anger. A smile full of the knowledge of how to inflict pain.

Duncan could not believe it; he would not believe it. "I stopped you. I stopped you!"

"You stopped my first plan. A plan that would have been successful if not for his failures. He will be punished." The beast waved his hand and the cage, the protection from the beast, vanished as if it had never been. "You amuse me, human. Though I must thank you. Your act did one thing to me, it broke the madness that had gripped me."

Duncan watched in silence as the beast approached him. Wearing his own face, but distorted, tiny runnels of blood, both dried and fresh, ran down the beast's face and body. Duncan tried once again to back away more, but he found himself always in the same place. The smell came then, a fetid stink, the smell of death and horror. Duncan couldn't move. Why couldn't he move?

The beast leaned in, his face inches from Duncan's. "Say my name, human. Say my name and know me. I was never a beast. Say my name." the beast smiled again; teeth changed to sharp spikes. "Say it."

Duncan swallowed, and with a whisper, the name escaped. "Valnijz."

***

Will stood in awe for a moment as Speaker-to-the-sky pushed the doors open. They swung to reveal a cavern bigger than any he could have imagined. All lit with these strange purple lights, and glowing. Glowing with red, white, yellow, green, blue. It was enough to stop him from even breathing.

"All of Ture could fit in there!" Myriam spoke up behind him.

"All of Ture and more." Regin added.

"This is the closest you will get, cursed ones. Take a good look now." Speaker-to-the-sky pointed at the city. "One of the holy four cities of the Gorom."

"Holy four?" Regin asked. "You only have four cities?"

Speaker-to-the-sky snorted. "No. We have many, but four are holy. Four are special. Heartsteen is special. Come, you have seen it, now we go this way." Speaker-to-the-sky turned down a side passage past the doors that lead away from the city and into darkness.

"But wait! Why is it holy? Why can't we go closer?" Myriam asked as she rushed forward.

"You are humans. You are not welcome. We help because Grimnor asks. Not all Gorom will. We go." Speaker-to-the-sky shrugged and moved off at a brisk pace.

Vin caught up with Will and leaned forward as they walked. "I don't trust this. Keep your hammer ready. It will be better in these narrow caverns than my sword will."

Will somewhat agreed with Vin. While he didn't think the Gorom would not help if something happened to them, he also wasn't sure they would help to the full extent that he wished them to. And since he couldn't talk to Amder, he didn't know what to trust. Will nodded in response, holding his own glowing purple orb. His eyes had adjusted more, but he'd love a torch, or a glowstone. Something, anything than this ever present dark purple light. At first, he'd marveled at the thing, but the surprise had worn off quickly. At least it made following Speaker-to-the-sky easier, as the Gorom's skin shone bright whitish-purple in the light the orb gave off. A few random splotches of the colors that covered everything could be seen here.

"Metals! Minerals!' Regin nearly yelled as he stopped walking.

"What?" Will asked, confused for a moment.

"The colors. They shine in this light. That's how they do it. This light and certain metals shine differently!' Regin smiled, his teeth glowing in the light. "I wonder which metals glow which color. It makes sense now. I wonder if we could use this effect."

"Smart human. You have just learned what a child of the Gorom knows in its third year. You should be proud." Speaker-to-the-sky said as he waved them forward. "Come. We have far to go."

Chapter 16.

Zalkiniv watched as the Saltmistress ship sailed away. He gripped the railings of his boat as tight as he could, his rage near boiling. They had come, killed the swiftkills, and left, denying him the chance to work his revenge. He had wasted his reserves of power trying to strengthen the boat. The two smaller swiftkills that he had released from control were gone as well. One had simply died from its prolonged exertion, and the other had fed on it and fled into the deep, dark waters.

He grabbed the knife and cut his hand, dripping blood into the water, reaching for the beast, or any other beasts he could control. But nothing came. The power that had been so plentiful was now a trickle he had used too much. More blood, he needed more blood. And the only source of blood here was his own. *So be it.*

He cut again, deeper this time, down into his arms. Narrowly missing major veins. He needed the blood to flow, but death wasn't his goal, at least not his own death. The blood surged forth, and the dagger seemed to drink it in again. The black iron twisted in his grasp, moving. Zalkiniv nearly dropped the thing, but at the same moment power bloomed, a power that filled him though not as much as before.

He reached out again, searching, and found... nothing. All sea life was gone from this area. Blood curse her. The Goddess of the Seas, the Saltmistresses god, had a hand in this, he was sure. He sealed his wounds, watching them slowly close and heal, fresh pink and red, joining the crisscrossing pattern of cuts and scars that now covered this body.

He was becalmed. Still nearly a day away from the coast, low on blood for working. Hand raised, he drove the dagger deep into the wood on the railing of the ship, leaving it there, quivering. There had to be something he could do. He was Zalkiniv. He had outsmarted a God, wreaked his revenge on those who had betrayed him, and he would ascend to Godhood himself.

No weak-willed race of sailors would stand in his way. *I will not have it end this way. It shall not end this way.*

***

Will caught himself for the fourth time that day. The path that Speaker-to-the-sky was leading them down was remarkably steep in places. He was behind Regin and he'd nearly fallen into the man the first time he'd stumbled. The Gorom however seemed to never stumble, his steps sure. "Excuse me, but can we call you Speaker? Saying the whole title seems a bit long." Will called out, trying to watch his step with this blasted dark purple light.

"You can call me that. But I will not answer." Speaker-to-the-sky called back. "That is not my name."

"What is your name anyway?" Myriam said behind Will.

"Speaker-to-the-sky." The Gorom answered back.

"Oh… I thought it was a title or something." Myriam replied.

Will heard a half-said curse as he heard a foot slide across the rock. Lots of loose gravel and some slippery patches of worn stone here. At least the path was in a cave, and not some underground cliff. "I thought it was as well." Will called out.

The Gorom paused and turned to them all as they stopped.

"Humans. I am a Gorom. Not one, you cursed folk. Speaker-to-the-sky is my name, and what I do. It is who I am. If you merely called me Speaker, there are thousands of speakers. I am Speaker-to-the-sky. As much as I dislike it." The Gorom turned back and started walking again.

"You dislike it?" Regin asked. "Why do it?"

"You understand nothing. No wonder you are cursed. A Gorom's name is what they are. There is no changing it. I dislike the surface. I dislike the bright lights. Some of the other races are tolerable, but you humans are everywhere. I do not enjoy my trips to your cities. But Speaker-to-the-sky is what I am. Do you understand now?" The Gorom walked a bit faster.

Regin leaned back to Will, his voice low. "No, I don't."

Will cracked a smile. He kind of got it, but it seemed so strange to him. "Speaker-to-the-sky, why did both Stonefather-who-speaks and you say we might be in danger?"

"There are those who believe that your half god tricked Grimnor. And some who believe that Grimnor made a mistake making any agreement with a half god." Speaker-to-the-sky held up a hand for a moment.

"Stop. Say nothing." The Gorom whispered quickly, the tone in his voice going from one of annoyance to alert worry. Speaker-to-the-sky reached down and placed his palm on a patch of bare stone and then stopped moving.

Will could not even see him breathe; the Gorom was unnaturally still for a few moments. William wondered what was going on. They had seen nothing or heard anything since they had walked out of view of the Gorom city. Will glanced back at Vin and saw the man had pulled a long dagger out of some place and had unsheathed it, its edge reflected a thin shimmer of purple.

"What's going on?" Myriam leaned forward, whispering in Will's ear. Will shrugged.

"I said be silent!" the Gorom hissed, more forceful than Will had heard from him yet.

A long silence crept over them. Will exchanged glances with all three of his friends, and watched for trouble before suddenly Speaker-to-the-sky stood.

"We are safe, for now." The Gorom said and resumed walking as if nothing had happened.

"Wait! What was that?" Regin walked faster, getting closer to the Gorom. "If we need to know something, you should tell us."

"There are many dangers down here, human. Deepworms, Xendires, packs of Fallings, and worse. The Gorom can feel them through the stone. I could sense something. Deep, but very dangerous. I do not know what it was. When I return, I will tell Stonefather-who-speaks, and Knower-of-the-dark about what I felt." Speaker-to-the-sky halted for a moment again.

"More danger?" Will asked, but then, as he got closer, he saw it. The path diverged here. There were two connecting tunnels. One looked remarkably similar to the one they were on, but the other, the other seemed to drink in the light from the orb. Whatever it was made of didn't glow like everything else. It was black and made Will feel empty, cold.

"You wish to know more about this world you walk over? Here." Speaker-to-the-sky pointed at the dark tunnel. "Drendel made."

"Drendel? As in Drendel Steel?" Myriam asked, walking toward the tunnel. "They made that?"

"Yes. But step back, human. We do not go into the places of the first unless we are forced to." Speaker-to-the-sky made a gesture that Will couldn't see.

"The first?" Will asked. "We know little about the Drendel."

"No surfacer would as you bang around the roof of the world. Drendel were the first. They came before us. You find their tools sometimes, or even ingots, yes? What you call Drendel steel is their most common leavings. There are other things. Some more wonderful, and some far darker." The Gorom shook his head. "The Drendel vanished long ago. Even the Gorom do not know where, or when."

Will watched as Speaker-to-the-sky stared at the Drendel tunnel and then shivered. Will didn't like this. The Gorom was annoying, and a bit insulting, but seeing it this way... it bothered him. "Let's get going then, away from that."

Speaker-to-the-sky nodded. "Follow carefully. We are about to pass into the threads." Speaker-to-the-sky gave one long look at the Drendel tunnel before turning to the other path.

"The threads?" Will spoke up. "I am sorry, but we don't understand."

"Tight caves, lots of branches, and twists and turns. Very easy to get lost in. Get too lost and even a Gorom can't find you." Speaker-to-the-sky looked at Vin. "Put the weapon away human, in the threads, there isn't any place to fight."

Vin thrust the dagger into a waiting belt loop, but as soon as Speaker-to-the-sky turned away, put his hand on the hilt and gave Will a slow nod.

"How long are we in these threads? What's after that?" Will glanced at the dark tunnel as they slowly passed it, wondering for a moment where it led.

"Then we will come to another tunnel. I know the way." Speaker-to-the-sky answered, his voice flat. "Come, we have wasted enough time talking."

Will, Regin, Myriam and Vin followed the Gorom as the tunnel narrowed, forcing them even more to stay in a single file line. Will turned to Myriam as they walked. "Stay close. If I get too far ahead, say something."

"I will. Vin? You do the same." Myriam said to Vin, who was bringing up the rear.

Will could barely make out Vin's face, but it didn't look good to him. The man was obviously working hard to control his fears. Sweat still appeared on his face, regardless of how cool, to near cold it had gotten as they traveled farther into the stone. The man's jaw was almost bulging with the force he was clenching it with. But he never said a word in complaint.

I'll talk to him when we stop for the night. Or rest. This deep under who knew when night was. Will wasn't even sure how long they had been walking for at this point.

"Speaker-to-the-sky, when do we stop to rest and eat? I'm losing track of time." Will called out to the Gorom. He couldn't really see him, as Regin was blocking his view. The purple light of the orb the Gorom carried as well could be seen at least.

"There are some places to stop after the threads. While there are a few places to stop in the threads, I would not advise resting there." Speaker-to-the-sky answered. "Stay close, you are about to see why the threads are called that."

The narrow path they walked down turned a corner and Will understood. Every four or five cart lengths, there was a side passage from the tunnel they were in. Even small, nearly round openings in the roof that stretched out to darkness. And this stone, unlike earlier, didn't have any of the glowing lines or natural blotches. Everything was the same dark purple.

"What formed this? Why did you make it this way?" Myriam asked from behind William.

"We didn't. We found it this way. It is a subject of study among the Gorom. Are the threads a creation of Grimnor? Did the Drendel make them? Did something else? Some look like they were dug out, like some animal burrowed through solid rock. Others appear to be made by water, veins of Grimnor we call those. And yet others show obvious signs of being made by something or someone, but do not match our work, or even the work of the long gone Drendel." Speaker-to-the-sky yelled back.

Will didn't like it. And the Gorom's voice made strange echoes as it moved around them, the multiple paths and openings distorting it as faded away. He glanced back to see Vin had pulled his dagger back out and was actively trying to study each and every tunnel they passed. Will felt like joining him in doing so.

He'd spent large parts of his life in mines, but this, this was something else. He was far deeper than any mine in the Reach now. Will glanced at each opening, feeling his hair on the back of his neck raise occasionally. Did he see something move down that cave? Did he hear a scraping sound come from that opening above him?

"Stop!" Speaker-to-the-sky yelled quickly.

Will and the others stopped; Will could feel his hands getting clammy. "Why are we stopping?" Will didn't understand, hadn't the Gorom just said they would not stop here?

A sound crashed over him. A sound, a sound like no other he had ever heard. Hearing wasn't even the right word. He felt it. In each and every bone. In his skin. A sound that terrified him. A sound that made his stomach lurch and twist. And he wasn't alone. Regin scrambled to get as close to the wall as he could, turning to Will with a look of total mindless terror on his face. Eyes wide, his face reflecting back more of the light as it paled. The sound that wasn't a sound washed over them again.

"FEARSONG!" Speaker-to-the-sky yelled.

A small speck of Will wanted to ask what that was. But he couldn't. He had to run. He had to get away. Will launched himself into a side tunnel, moving as fast as he could. The sound came again, driving his feet faster. He still didn't like running, but he had to escape!

The mindless terror killed every other thought in his head. *Run away! Hide! Run!* Each step brought the knowledge that if he didn't run, he would regret it for the rest of his life, and that would not be long.

Run!

Chapter 17.

Regin tried to say something as he watched William, the Forgemaster of Amder, and his friend sprint off in a random direction. He wanted to yell at him to stop; he wanted to launch himself after him, even tackle the man. But he couldn't. His breath came in ragged gasps as total terror gripped him. Hands grabbed at the rock but slipped, unable to find purchase as his skin became slick with a cold sweat.

He watched as Will vanished, the purple light of the orb he carried vanishing with him. Another wave of the sound washed over him, and Regin dropped to his knees, trying to curl into a ball. He had to be safe, he had to… do something. He had to…

Regin managed to get himself curled up after thrashing around to get his pack off his back. He bit his lip in fear, the warm blood only driving more fears. What if some creature in the dark can smell the blood? He could be attacked right now, and he'd never know it was coming! He shut his eyes, desperately trying to push away whatever this was.

For several long minutes, Regin stayed that way. He counted his heartbeats, muscled clenched as he crushed himself into the smallest target possible. He was going to die. He knew it. All would be lost. He would die here, in this cave, far underground, far away from everyone he knew, except for those he traveled with.

Myriam. He had never told her about what he felt. What did it matter now, except one more failure on his part. Death and pain were coming for him. He fought to breathe, he fought to think.

As suddenly as the feeling came, it vanished. Regin stayed in his ball, trying to blink away the sweat and tears that covered his face. He slowly moved an arm, wincing as muscles that had been as tight as he could make them were forced to move in a more normal way. Raising his head up, Regin could see the Gorom, Speaker-to-the-sky taking long breaths of his own, his face illuminated by his orb, Regin could see the same look of relief and the residual effects of the overwhelming fear that had washed over them.

Pushing himself up, Regin looked for Myriam and Vin, but did not see them anywhere. He had seen Will run, but then the fear had taken over and he had seen nothing else.

"Fearsong. By the Stoneworld. I never thought they would use fearsong." Speaker-to-the-sky said, his voice shaky.

Regin licked the blood on his lips and forced himself to talk. "Who? What was that? What is fearsong?"

Speaker-to-the-sky looked up, blinking. "You managed not to run? Strong for a human." The Gorom looked around. "It does not appear the other humans are as strong as you. That is not good."

"Answer please... what WAS that?" Regin asked again, wiping his face clean with his sleeve.

"That was fearsong. The Gorom learned long ago, certain sounds can make you feel certain things. There are sounds that can make you sick and leave you heaving for hours. There are sounds that can make you unable to move. There are sounds that can force you to dance, but dance for hours until you collapse. And there is fearsong. Sounds that force you to feel fear. Terror. Uncontrollable, total, terror." Speaker-to-the-sky shuddered again, staring into the orb.

"Stonefather-who-speaks and I told you all there was Gorom, who did not want you here. But to use fearsong? Here in the threads? This was planned. They knew where we were. Now your friends are lost in the threads, and this is terrible." Speaker-to-the-sky stood. "I have sworn to get you all across the mountains. We must find your friends."

Regin stood finally, the fear a fading memory, to be replaced with worry. Where was William? Vin? Myriam? The thought of any of his companions being lost down here wasn't good. But the idea of Myriam being gone brought a secondary ache to his heart that he forced away. *This isn't the time.*

He let out a long breath, feeling the last of the terror flee his mind, and the last of the muscles in his body let go of the tension. *I'm going to hurt like the scourge of the Scaled One soon.* "Speaker-to-the-sky, what do we do? How do you know this was planned? How did they find us even?" the words rushed out of him. His friends were lost in this place. The more he thought about it, the more worried he became.

"They, whoever they are, must have been using the updrafts. Those smaller caves and openings in the top of the caves. I don't know how they found us. Maybe they were listening as well. It's not like you cursed humans are a quiet lot." Speaker-to-the-sky raised his head from the orb, his face not showing any trace of recent events. "And now, now we have to search. I hope the Stoneworld doesn't claim the lives of your friends. The Gorom haven't even followed all the threads to their end."

***

Captain Vin Tolin, former Captain in the Palnor army, also former Trader caravan guard lead, defender of the Reach, and before today, Bodyguard and Protector of the Forgemaster of Amder, was terrified. He had been on a knife's edge since coming down into this pit, and now he was lost. Lost in pitch black emptiness.

He'd had a tight grip on his fear, and he'd been sure he could handle it. He'd always hated being underground. Even as a small child, when he'd had to go into the cellar, he'd be terrified by it. He'd look up and be totally sure the roof could cave in on him, crushing him. Or worse, some creature would crawl out of the dark and drag him deeper into the earth, a snack for whatever horrible thing that lived down there.

Still, he'd followed William. He liked the man. Not only did he respect him, as the Forgemaster, he truly liked him. He was a good man. Young, unexperienced, and needed a thicker skin, but nothing time and life wouldn't fix. Vin wouldn't have followed anyone else down into the pits of the earth. The others were good people as well, though Vin had seen enough looks between Regin and Myriam to know what that meant. He had prepared for that to cause trouble at some point.

But then that sound had come. Right before he'd run, he'd heard that Gorom say it was called 'fearsong', an apt name for it. He'd never felt such total terror and panic before. Even defending the Reach, he'd not been as scared. As the sound had surrounded him, Vin had only been able to think of being crushed, the mountains falling onto him, everything he had ever been or would be gone, a flattened smear on a stone floor somewhere deep underground.

He'd had to get away, he'd had to run. Run where? It hadn't mattered. He'd not even given it a thought. Run! His body had responded, and he'd headed into the caves, taking turns at random, trying in his delirium to find an enormous cavern. A place where he couldn't see the top of the cave.

The small part of his rational mind knew that was stupid, but the rest of him obeyed the call of fear. But slowly, as he ran farther and farther away, the terror that had forced him to run had faded. Until finally, nearly out of breath, Vin had stopped. He was covered in sweat, panting, and in total darkness. He had more than a few places where he'd run into rock corners, pillars, and he'd tripped over who knew what more than five times in his mad scramble.

He felt his way to a nearby wall, feeling the rough touch of the rock on his fingertips. Dry, hard. No water nearby. His mind shifted into soldier mode, as he turned his thoughts to surviving this, whatever this was. Control the fear. Vin tried to think clearly. How far had he run? Did he know? Could he trace his way back to where they had been?

Doubtful. But he didn't have to sit in the darkness at least. He kept a spark kit in his pack, and he'd burn everything he had in his pack if it meant he could see. Thankfully, he'd made fires enough in the dark to not feel totally lost. True, it was darker where he was now than any traders' camp or picket line he'd ever served on, but he could do it.

He pulled the sparking kit out, followed by a small bunch of branches soaked with wax. Firestarters. He didn't use them much, and he'd almost not bought this set back in the Reach, but he was thankful to whatever god had blessed him with the good sense to do so.

Vin steadied himself, and with a strong and steady hand, scraped down the spark rod. White light flashed, and Vin involuntarily dropped the kit cursing. That had been bright. Dazzling. He blinked in the blackness; the light having made fading colors in his vision. *Fool.* Vin cursed himself. He'd been underground for no small amount of time, and the only light had been that somewhat sickening purple light the Gorom used. His eyes weren't used to anything else now.

He felt along the floor, his hands finding small stones, the firestarters, and a smooth something that he was unsure of, and finally, the kit. This time, Vin shaded his eyes as much as he could and struck again. While brighter than any noon day sun to him, this time he was ready. The white-fiery spark hit a pair of firestarters, and a small red, orange flame bloomed.

Vin kept his eyes hooded, waiting for his vision to adjust. He was in a dry cave, near a corner where it was wider. He could see where he had run from, though his steps vanished quickly, because of the dark, and because the floor in that direction was bare dry stone, so he didn't leave much of a trace. Onward, the cave became smaller, tighter. Vin was thankful he hadn't been running at full speed and tried to navigate that narrowing passage. He would have injured himself for sure in that fear laced panic.

Vin opened his eyes a bit more, thankful for the small flame. The firestarters would burn for a good hour, so he had time to look around. He glanced down. The smooth object he couldn't place was an insect shell. A big one. Larger than any beetle or bug he'd ever seen. It was nearly the size of a target shield. And of course, bone white. Vin wasn't scared of bugs, but it unnerved him a bit.

The fire might scare them off, or it might attract them. And the smell of smoke. He didn't care. He'd rather see them coming than try to fight off anything in this pitch blackness. But what to do now?

***

Myriam panted, shuddering as she tried to force herself to stop moving. Her legs quivered in response to her sudden explosion of movement. Think, Myriam. Think. She paused, trying to clear her head from the lingering effects of what had Speaker-to-the-sky called it? Fearsong? One sparks cursed name for it. Myriam wasn't the type to scare super easily. She'd never been interested in being a simpering maid, waiting for anyone to come along and save her. But that sound, it had overwhelmed her. Totally.

And now she was lost. Lost, alone, and in the dark. *Oh, so fun. Go underground with the man who loved you, but you didn't love back, the man who you wanted but who refused to want you back, and a man who was more like a father than anything else. Maybe I should have gone home after all.* She could be back at the Inn right now, dealing with an angry father, an annoyed mother and a highly disapproving Grandfather.

Instead, she was here. She felt around. The ground was dampish, but not enough to lose grip. She wasn't able to feel a wall nearby. A chamber of some kind. Explore? No. If she fell off a cliff or tumbled down a steep embankment, she'd be as good as dead. Any kind of injury at this point was a death sentence, right?

"Myriam..." a voice came. A voice she barely heard. It seemed familiar. Back in the cart, that voice!

She tried to move around, to try to sense where the sound was coming from, but no luck.

"Myriam. I know you can hear me." The voice came again. Was this Amder? She knew that William talked to Amder in his head, or at least he said he did. Normally, people talking to voices in their head was a bad thing, but William was the Forgemaster of Amder, so that sort of put him on a different footing. She was Myriam VolFar, a sort of vagabond.

"I am not Amder." The voice was… well, she couldn't tell if it was male or female, it just was. *"Myriam. Focus. I will help you get out of here the best I can. You have a great choice in front of you, Myriam VolFar."*

Who are you? Myriam asked in her head, instantly feeling foolish for doing so.

"Not yet. Soon, maybe. Hopefully. I am weak. My time is coming closer. Still, I am only a tiny fraction of what should have been." The voice quivered as it came to her.

She wondered for a moment if she was going crazy. Maybe she had run into a stone wall in the dark and blacked out, and all this was a dream born of injury. Or worse, she was dead?

"Not dead. Not crazy. And all this worry and doubt is wasting time. Listen carefully. I am whole, but only a fraction of the whole." The voice carried to her again, wavering at times, but clear.

"I am going to guide you to a safe spot. If everything works the way it is supposed to, you will find your friends. Follow the light." As if on cue, a small white-green light bloomed into existence. It reminded her of the storm bugs from back home. Little flying insects that glowed at night. The light, though, stayed still for a moment while she stood, before slowly flying off, moving in a straight line.

Do I follow it? Myriam hesitated. Her choices were small. Stay here, lost, unsure if she was some place safe or not, or follow the tiny light. Following meant she trusted that voice, though the voice confused her.

But would something or someone down here use a light like that? She didn't think so. If it was the same voice as back in the cart, then maybe, hopefully, it was worth trusting. *Well, I hope you don't walk me off a cliff, or into some strange underground lair of a nameless creature.* Myriam thought to the voice. She didn't get a response verbally, but for all the word a feeling of amusement flowed through her for a second, as she started after the small glowing light, and hope.

Chapter 18.

William ran. He'd been really afraid a few times in his life. When he'd seen his mother die at the hands of the Valni. When he'd realized that his father and his uncle were truly never coming back. When once, a few years after, it had been only him and Duncan, Duncan hadn't come home one night, he'd been keeping company with a jewel trader's daughter. William hadn't known that, of course, and had paced all night feeling sick to his stomach, afraid and worried. And of course, when he'd run from the Valni himself, the day he'd taken the crystal from the Mistlands.

This was something worse, though. This… terror. His feet flew over the stone as fast as he could go. Three times now he'd physically run into corners and almost had the breath knocked out of him once, but he still ran. The pain from the impacts would not stop him from escaping this total and absolute fear. His legs burned; his lungs had a hard time getting air. It wasn't the easiest to breathe down here, anyway. The air was often stale, old.

Still Will moved forward, the only light the same purple glow that moved with him as the orb in his hand shone on. Will glanced behind him, only for a moment, and then with an explosion of pain fell to the floor as his head contacted solid rock. The fear and terror were drowned out now, replaced with one thing, agony.

He let the orb roll out of his hand as both hands grasped his head in an automatic reaction. It filled him, a sharp white-hot pain, and for a few long moments he could deal with nothing else. He writhed on the tunnel floor, desperate for the feeling to fade. Finally, it dulled enough for him to take stock of what had happened.

He felt around his head but didn't feel blood. Good. But he knew where he had hit. There was already a massive lump forming on the side of his head. Even the barest of touch on the thing brought a spike of torment, as if a white-hot edge of a partially forged knife was being dragged across it, slowly. It brought a near scream to his lips. He only forced it down by biting his lip, drawing a few specks of blood.

No sound, not here. Who knew what lived here that the sound would bring? He sat up slowly, fighting a sudden wave of dizziness and nausea. He leaned back against a nearby cave wall, trying to think. Fearsong. That was what Speaker-to-the-sky called it. An understatement. Now he was alone, lost in the threads, injured both his side and worse, his head. His pack wasn't nearby, and he had a dim memory of it getting caught on something as he ran, and his ripping it off as he moved, leaving it behind.

He had the orb, so he had some sort of light. He had his hammer, and the clothes he was wearing, which were a nicer set of leathers, and the breastplate and the bracers they had made back in the Reach. He had a waterskin he kept on his belt; it was more or less full. He'd always had the habit of keeping one there. Mining and smithing could be thirsty work, and having to leave what you were doing to go get a drink slowed things down, or sometimes was impossible. Thank Amder for that, at least. No food though. That had all been in his pack.

Slowly, he shifted over enough to grab the orb again. *I have light, a hammer, and some water. I'm lost in a cave system. Who knows how far underground? I'm the Forgemaster of Amder, but I can't talk to the God right now for reasons I don't understand. I'm injured, alone. This is not how I wanted this to go.*

Will took his hammer out of its belt loop, thumbing the metal. It responded with a glow. It always glowed, but the effect was more noticeable now, with the silvery light contrasting with the purple light of the orb. It made him feel better, at least. Not physically, but it raised his spirits. He was William Reis. The first Forgemaster in generations. He would not die down here, alone and lost if he could do anything about it.

Slowly, he stood, using the wall behind him to help him up, grimacing at the sharp pain this caused in his head, followed by a swell of dizziness. His stomach flipped a few times, and an involuntary dry heave came. *Good thing we hadn't stopped to eat.* He wanted to take a drink but didn't let himself. Better save it.

What now? He tried to think back to how he had come, but quickly gave up. One, he'd been in such a panic he had no idea which passages he had gone into or passed by. And two, the pain in his head made even thinking a chore. He wanted to touch the lump, but was hesitant to see how much it had grown by. And the accompanying pain that would bring wasn't all that welcome. His head already felt very tight in that area, which wasn't a good sign.

Stay here? Hope someone finds him. Try to find his way back? Normally he'd stay put, but he remembered that Speaker-to-the-sky said that not even the Gorom knew the threads all the way. Staying here might mean a death sentence. He lifted his hammer and eyed the wall.

If he moved, he could maybe leave marks? Hit the wall hard enough to leave something, anything, so that he could find his way back? But that would make a sound. Did he want to attract things? Will had no answers.

"Standing here will not answer them either." Will whispered. Better to test and find out. Will examined the wall. The stone appeared to be softer than he expected upon closer inspection. Some sort of chalk, maybe? Harder than that, though. You didn't see a lot of chalk here. He'd uncovered pockets before in mines. He was never sure why or how it had gotten there, but they never really dug into them. Tendency to cave in, and never found any worthwhile minerals associated with the formations, anyway.

No, this wasn't chalk, but it was soft. Not like that rock he had smacked his head on. He wasn't sure which of the half dozen rock outcroppings he could see was the culprit, but that had been like steel. His head still throbbed. Will blinked a few times. His eyes seemed to lose focus for a moment, but cleared up. Must have gotten something in my eyes. A tinge of worry that it was something else, something worse came, but he pushed it aside. There literally was nothing he could do if it was something else.

Will hefted the hammer, the Wight Iron like an extension of his arm. He wished he could take a large blow, but there wasn't enough room. Instead, he thought back to his training with Vin. How to use his hips and center to power the blow. Not too much, but enough. His fingers flexed on the haft, and he let out a long breath. He could do this. Careful now.

Will twisted, popping his arm forward at the right moment. The hammer head smashed into the rock wall harder than Will had expected, and worse, kept going. Rock that had seemed solid gave way, falling into a blackness that seemed absolute. He tried to shift his momentum, but his lack of experience betrayed him as he stumbled forward. *Sparks, no!* Will fell forward into the now large opening in the crumbling rock, tumbling into total nothingness.

***

Regin followed Speaker-to-the-sky, as the Gorom walked a short distance, then paused, touching the rock walls. Occasionally he'd make a strange noise, like a low hum, but so low that Regin couldn't really hear it, he more felt it as a shiver that traveled over his skin. He had no idea what the Gorom was doing, but he wasn't sure he wanted to stop him.

They had been at this for a while, methodically moving forward. The only thing Regin was doing was making a mark with a glowing yellow rock every time they stopped for Speaker-to-the-sky to do whatever it was he was doing. The Gorom had handed him the rock, told him to do so, and that was it. Regin knew it was to find the way back. That much was obvious. He wished he could do more.

He took the time to examine the yellow rock as he walked. It vaguely resembled a mineral he had seen before, somewhat crystalline, not too hard, but not soft and easy to crumble. He wished he could examine it in the proper light. Actual light. His mind, worried about his friends, needed something to occupy itself, so he spent the time thinking of ways he could use this glowing rock in smithing work. Could he use it for inlay? Alloys? Could the color be enhanced or made to glow outside this purple glow the Gorom loved so much?

"Human." Speaker-to-the-sky spoke, breaking his thought. "I believe I have found the trail of one other of your kind."

"Oh! Great!' Regin responded, blinking for a moment and licking his lips, which brought a spike of pain with his recent bite marks there.

"Who? Do you know?" Regin looked at where the Gorom was, but he wasn't able to see anything different from any other cave they had passed through. It all looked the same to him.

"The one with the noisy armor." Speaker-to-the-sky answered. "He is not far, but distance does not mean much here when caves can double back and twist."

Vin, then. Good. Though he felt a moment of worry about Myriam. Accompanied by a bit of guilt for not thinking of William first. "Well, let's go get him." Regin hefted his pack again. His stomach grumbled at him a bit, but he ignored it. There was no time for that now, and anyway, he could stand to lose a bit of weight.

"Follow me human." Speaker-to-the-sky set off, his hand touching the stone as they walked.

"What are you doing?" Regin asked, genuinely curious. "What were those sounds before you were making?"

"Humans. Stone blind fools." Speaker-to-the-sky said in reply and shook his head. "Later. I must concentrate."

Regin didn't reply. He didn't think the Gorom would take too kindly to being pushed to answer. And it wasn't like Speaker-to-the-sky was doing anything wrong. He was trying to help, even though his opinions about humans and Amder still rankled Regin. The constant near insults had lost some of their sting now though. If you expected it every time the Gorom opened its mouth, it didn't shock as badly.

He followed behind, ducking under the occasional low ceiling. The cave twisted again, and Regin stopped suddenly. He smelled... a fire? The smell brought with it a release of tension. A fire would be welcome. Normal light, comfort. How had Vin lit a fire here?

Speaker-to-the-sky paused, sniffing the air. "By the glowing blood of Grimnor, that human would not be so foolish as to light a fire, would he?"

"Why would that be bad? He's in the dark, no way to see, and lost." Reign answered. "I find it comforting."

The Gorom turned to him, a scowl on his face. "Cursed humans. Never thinking. I told you all there were things down here you did not know. Things you did not understand. Things that were dangerous."

"But animals don't like fire." Reign answered. "We use fire all the time to drive animals away."

"On the surface!" Speaker-to-the-sky nearly spat his response. "Here, the smell is unknown. Here, that smell will attract. And the light will not bother those things that are blind. Not here."

Regin's skin tingled as the Gorom's words sunk in. He'd been thinking as if this was the world he knew. It wasn't. "Let's hurry then. I do not want Vin to have problems."

Speaker-to-the-sky didn't respond, but sped up his pace. Twists and turns went quickly, as the smell of smoke grew. Finally, Regin could see a difference. A slight orange glow came from around a corner.

"Vin!" Regin called out.

Speaker-to-the-sky whirled on him, anger clear on his face. "Silence!"

Regin ignored him and walked towards the glow. He turned the corner to see a small fire. And no sign of Captain Vin Tolin. The light of the fire threw orange yellow light everywhere, and for a moment Regin basked in the glow. He had to blink several times as his eyes adjusted to the firelight. Still, it brought a small measure of connection. It was real.

Regin examined the fire for a moment. Firestarters. Regin grinned, trust Captain Tolin to have firestarters. But where was the man? The ground being mostly rock didn't give any clues.

"Put out that fire." Speaker-to-the-sky's voice came from behind Regin. "Put it out now."

"But what if he needs it to get back here?" Regin asked. "I thought you said you were taking me to him, he's not here."

"I am not a cursed blind human. I am aware he is not here. He is close. He is heading back here. But he is not alone. He is being followed. A swarm of karkin follow him." Speaker-to-the-sky pulled a mace out from under his robe. "Put out the fire. The smell attracts them. The smell is on him."

Regin hesitated for a moment. He really didn't want to. He wanted this thread of what he knew. He wanted the comfort. But this wasn't his world. Regin nodded and stomped down on the firestarters, crushing the flames and the glowing bits. He ground them into the stone floor, thankful he was wearing good thick smithing boots.

The fire died quickly, the orange and red glow fading and leaving a faint shadow in his vision, and his eyes once again had to adjust to the purple glow of the orb that the Gorom carried. *I will never take sunlight for granted after this is over.*

"Pull out your weapon. We will need them." Speaker-to-the-sky said in a quiet tone. He placed the orb on the ground, a bit behind them. "Try not to break this human. Breaking it will only make things worse for both us and the other human. Very much worse. But I can not hold that and fight at the same time."

Regin felt another twist of annoyance. Would it kill the Gorom to call him by his name? *Let it go, Regin.* He'd always been a bit envious of the Masters who got to meet with the mysterious Gorom. Now? Not so much. He pulled his hammer out of its belt loop. While it wasn't made with Wight Iron and god touched like William's was, it was a well-made and serviceable smithing hammer. And unlike Will and Myriam, Regin had gone through the full combat training the Guild offered, whatever good that was.

"What's a karkin?" Regin asked, trying to lower his voice like the Gorom had.

"Beetles. I think you call them. Individually, the size of a plate. One or two, not a problem, and good eating. A swarm? A big problem, and they eat you instead." Speaker-to-the-sky pointed at the tunnel ahead. "He is almost here."

Regin strained to hear anything, but couldn't at first. Then the barest of an echo? Was that another one? Yes! Footsteps. Running footsteps. Were they heading this way? He wasn't sure. Sounds bounced around and changed here in ways he could not track. Beetles the size of plates? His mind tried to imagine that, but pushed it away. Must be the size of a Gorom plate. Which wasn't that big. It couldn't be as big as a human plate, right?

But yes, the sounds were closer. And then, out of the darkness, Vin Tolin appeared, running for his life.

Chapter 19.

Myriam followed the light. It danced and shifted around as she did so. *This is crazy. I've fallen, hit my head, and I'm having a hallucination. I know it.* Voices in her head? Glowing lights leading her to safety miles underground? All alone? An involuntary snort escaped her. But yet, her steps kept coming, and she followed the light.

"You are not crazy." The voice whispered to her. *"I understand the reasoning. But this is happening. You aren't imagining it. And if it helps, this is exhausting for me. I'm so far from where I am supposed to be. What I am supposed to be. I have never tried to touch this world this much. Hard. Very hard."*

Myriam shook her head. She had no idea what the voice was going on about, and she wasn't sure she wanted to know. Please, don't lead me over a cliff or into the jaws of some horrible unknown creature, ok?

"I said I would not, and I won't." The light bounced around as the voice came to her, but when the voice was silent, it was steadier.

Myriam wasn't sure, but maybe better to keep her mouth shut for now. The light was weak, but as her eyes adjusted to even seeing this faint light, she could make out more of where she was.

The ground reflected the light, and she could see why. It was still damp, even wet in places. She wasn't sure where the water was coming from. Even the air smelled damp. Damp and old. Stale. It reminded her of the yearly spring cleaning of the icehouse back at the inn. They'd open the place up, let the remnants of the ice melt, and then change out all the straw and insulation. It would all be wet by then and mildewing and full of rot. Her mother made her wear a strip of cloth over her nose and mouth, as to 'not inhale the foulness.'

This was like it, but worse.

Myriam froze in mid step, as the light which had been leading her suddenly rose up higher and froze. A wave of alarm swept through her. *"The one you call William. He is in danger. Great danger."*

William? What had that man gotten into now? Can we help him? What kind of danger?

"I... cannot tell exactly. I am not... this is frustrating. He is deeper than the others and injured. I can help get you to the others, but I cannot do anything else. William Reis MUST survive. Do you understand? He MUST." The voice rose as it spoke.

Myriam winced as the voice's words exploded in her head. Sparks burn William Reis. He better not get himself killed. Well, lead me to the others.

The voice, whatever it was, didn't respond, but the light moved quickly away, far faster than it had been moving before. Myriam jogged behind it, hopeful she didn't twist an ankle or worse. But the path the light led her on seemed to get drier and more solid the more she followed. The air felt less damp as well, a welcome change.

The light came to a halt again and quivered for the lack of a better description. *"I cannot go any further. It is not time for anyone other than you to see. I will give you a gift. It will help. Stay on this path. Pass three openings on the left, and then take the next one on the left. Stay straight. That will take you to them. Be careful. They are fighting."*

Who is fighting? What gift? Myriam thought at the light, when faster than she could move, the light sped right at her. She tried to throw up a hand to block it, but the tiny light moved faster. It filled her entire vision and then... it vanished.

She blinked in response and realized something. She could see. Not well, and not fully. But she could see enough to make out the walls, the floor. It was all very dim, but it wasn't total darkness. This is the gift? If it was, it was a good one.

She headed off, keeping watch for the openings like the voice had told her. She felt silly doing it, but at this point, what were her options? And if it was telling her the truth, and her friends minus William were fighting, she wanted to help. She wasn't sure how much use she'd be, but another hand can always be useful.

She passed the first opening on the left; her face making an involuntary reaction to the smell that came out of it. Sour, like rotten milk. She hurried on, keeping one hand on her own hammer as she moved faster. Second opening passed. No smell this time, at least. She stopped. Was that the third opening? Not far from the second was a crack. Was it an opening? If she made the wrong decision, she could get lost again. And she couldn't hope that whatever had helped her the first time would help her the second time. *I don't have time to waste.*

It has to be the opening. Myriam continued on, hoping she was making the right choice. Soon, she saw the last cave junction. She took a left and ran, her vision enough to make the right steps in this cave. The floor was usually smoothed rock, though here and there patches of loose gravel and small rocks laid on the floor. One critical step, one injured ankle.

She heard it then, the sound of something metal hitting a rock, followed by a muffled curse. Then more noises, and the sounds of what... it sounded like the rustle of dried reeds, but louder than any wind could make it. Her vision adjusted more, and a purple glow grew in the distance.

She ran on, drawing her own hammer. Entering into chaos.

***

Regin swung his hammer, backing away as he did, mostly so his swing didn't hit the Gorom, whose head was at exactly the right height to get hit. A sharp crack nearly lost in the din and echoes erupted as the shell of one of these bug things shattered, spraying shards of shell and a noxious smelling liquid around the battlefield.

Regin could see Vin making good work of his dagger. The man's movements were practiced and careful. And the dagger had the advantage of not spraying. What had Speaker-to-the-sky called them? Karkin? Karkin parts everywhere. Vin stopped and yelled something that Regin lost in the roar, as a fresh wave of these bug things erupted from around the corner, this time covering not only the floor and walls, but a few even crawling upside down on the tunnel roof.

Bone-white mandibles clicking. The thought of that dropping on him from above nearly made him shudder. Vin yelled again, putting his hood up. *Good idea.* If one fell on his head, at least it would fall on the hood first, maybe give him a moment to get it off of him. Regin raised his hammer again, smashing another bug, and another. Like beating out raw iron, let the blows fall. A spike of pain on his side made him whirl around, frantically grabbing at the point where it erupted. A karkin had somehow gotten under his cloak, and bit through his leathers! Not deep, but who knew what a bite could do to him. Speaker-to-the-sky hadn't said if these things were poisonous or not, though there had been little time to discuss things.

He could see the Gorom, clearing Karkin with that mace he had come up with, shiny with wetness from what passed for blood in these things. As much as Speaker-to-the-sky annoyed him, he fought well, and unlike the rest of them, had experience in both fighting in a cave, and fighting these things. Regin swung his hammer, knocking three of the bugs off the wall to his right, their bodies flying through the air and into the mass of kicking, clattering legs. To his amazement, he saw three other karkin tear one of the ones he had hit apart in a frenzy.

Speaker-to-the-sky pointed behind them, and Regin felt a sinking feeling. Not more of these things? He whirled around, ready to fight to see something that made a smile break out. Myriam VolFar was here! She ran past him, not even looking his way, and swung her own hammer in a long arc, narrowly missing Regin. He jumped back and swung his own hammer, knocking down a few more of the bugs into the mass.

He turned to Myriam to see her grabbing at her head. A karkin had fallen into her hair! Her hood hadn't been up. He tried to reach her as she frantically tried to pull the thing off, but couldn't. She was keeping it from biting her head, though. Regin tried to get closer but found himself having to jump back as the karkin, if sensing a prey not fighting back, moved in a wave towards Myriam.

He could see her smashing and kicking with her boots as best she could while she tried to dislodge the one on her head. The Gorom yelled something else, pointing down the cave where these blood cursed bugs had erupted from, but Regin could not hear him still. Regin did see Vin, however, and the man saw Myriam. Regin watched as Vin leaped into the milling biting bugs, his armor fending off the bites from the things as he quickly took his dagger and pulled Myriam's head back sharply.

For a split second, Regin thought the man had gone mad, broken by his fear of being underground. But no! Vin took his dagger and, with a few fast slices, cut off a huge chunk of Myriam's hair, and the karkin entangled in it, throwing it to the ground, and with a single motion stomping it with his boot.

Regin could feel his arm growing tired, but continued to swing, ignoring the pain in his side as best he could. At best, he could go on for a bit longer. How many more of these foul things were there? He could see Vin breathing heavily in the pale purple light. Myriam was the freshest of all of them. Even the Gorom seemed to be slowing.

Speaker-to-the-sky fought his way to Regin's side, his mace breaking through a few more shells. "We must pull back. The smell is drawing other things." The Gorom yelled, close enough for Regin to finally hear him.

Other things? Regin didn't know what could be worse than this, but if it was enough to worry to the Gorom, he had no interest in finding out. Regin stomped another bug, feeling the crack as the shell split under his boot. "Won't they follow us?" He yelled back to the Gorom.

"No. Look. We have killed enough of them; they are turning on themselves now." The Gorom smashed his mace down, injuring several more of the things.

Regin blinked, trying to make sense of the writing mass, but the Gorom was right. More and more of the karkin were attacking each other. There one bit off the legs of another of its ilk while the one it was biting appeared to be feeding on another. Regin gagged a little at the sight. He waved both his arms, trying to get the attention of both Myriam and Vin. Myriam saw him, and nodded, smashing her way back towards him, what was left of her once mid-length hair falling around her face. Vin saw him as well and stabbed and crushed his way towards the rest of them.

"We must fall back; the things are eating each other now." Regin yelled. Both Vin and Myriam nodded in agreement, as the four of them fell back, only smashing a bug when one broke from the pack to follow after them. As they moved back, the sound faded, but the smell did not. As the focus that the danger had brought wore off, the sickening stench assaulted them all. Regin could see Vin and Myriam both look as if they wanted to get sick, though none of them had eaten anything recently, which was probably a good thing.

"What were those things?" Myriam asked, holding herself up against a cave wall. Even in the purple dim light, Regin could see she looked worn. Tired.

"Karkin. Swarm hunters. They hunt in packs, though that was probably several packs. Which helped us." Speaker-to-the-sky pushed his hood back, his face showing the same exhaustion.

"How, by the blood-soaked terrors, did that help us?" Vin asked. The man was taking huge breaths and appeared to be shivering.

"Karkin packs dislike each other. Once we killed enough of them for the feeding drive to take over, they turned on each other. Allowing us to escape." Speaker-to-the-sky shot back. "Foolish cursed human, starting a fire here. What do you think drew the Karkin in the first place?"

"The fire did it?" Vin asked. He leaned against a wall and slowly slid down. "I wanted to see; I was lost in total blackness. I realized the light might draw the attention of something, but not that."

"It wasn't the light. Karkin are blind. Most animals here are." Speaker-to-the-sky touched the wall and fell silent for a moment before dropping his arm. "It was the smell. Most creatures here hunt by smell and hearing. Sight is useless for them. We are in luck. The karkin frenzy drew a pair of Adotix. They are feasting on the Karkin."

Regin glanced at Myriam, but she didn't catch his eye. "Are those dangerous?" he asked.

"Not unless you are a Karkin." Speaker-to-the-sky said. "The problem we have now is twofold. One, we are covered with dead Karkin remains. This WILL attract other things. Some, like Adotix, won't bother with us. There are deeper things that won't think twice. We need to get out of the Threads and ascend closer to the surface. Safer, though slower."

"But we can't!" Myriam nearly shouted as her eyes, once closed, shot open. "William!"

"Yes, that is the second problem. Your friend, the Forgemaster of your half god, is still missing." Speaker-to-the-sky touched the wall again and lowered his head. "I will try to delve his location."

"He's deep. He fell into danger, and he's injured." Myriam answered quickly, before closing her mouth with a snap.

"And how do you know this?" Vin asked.

"I..." Myriam's eyes seemed to dart around the area they were in. Regin could see that for her, she was agitated, stressed.

"I had a vision. I don't know how or why." Myriam answered.

"A vision?" Regin turned to her. "I thought only William had those?"

"I don't want to talk about it." Myriam answered quickly and turned her head away from him.

She's not saying something. Odd. Regin watched her for a long moment, but she seemed more interested in feeling her head and figuring out how long her hair was now.

"Vin, thanks." Myriam finally spoke up. "I couldn't get that... thing out of my hair. I should have put up my hood like the rest of you."

"Sorry for the hack job. And it was fine. You didn't have time to think about it. We appreciated having someone else there. How did you find us, anyway?" Vin took a long drink from a waterskin he pulled out. "I know I shouldn't drink this right now. But it's drink or scream. I'll drink."

"After that, fearsong thing. I found myself lost." Myriam sighed. "I have no idea how I found you all. Luck of the gods I guess."

Regin watched as her eyes darted around. She's very much keeping something from us. Regin had always been very good at reading people. It was one reason they had him teach the classes he had in the Guild. Nobles and rich merchants were always trying to get an advantage on deals with the Guild. Once you knew what to look for, it was easy to figure out who was holding something back or lying. And right now, Myriam was doing both.

"I found a wall and followed it. I got lucky and heard the sound of fighting. Once I got close enough, I could tell it was at least someone I knew, so I came to help." Myriam looked down, and pulled a small sharp knife from her boot, and starting evening out the ragged lengths of her hair.

"No time for that. We must go." Speaker-to-the-sky spoke, his head jerking upwards as he stopped touching the wall. "She is right. He is in great danger. He has fallen into Makese Folly."

"Makese Folly? What's that?" Vin asked as he pushed himself up. Regin could see the man was once again fighting with his fear of being underground. The rush and fear of combat had driven it away for a time, but it had returned.

"A great many years ago, a Gorom tried to connect several Drendel tunnels to go under what you call the Blood Moon Bay. To make a tunnel that would go all the way to the Southlands." Speaker-to-the-sky spat as talked. "He took over a thousand Gorom with him. None ever returned. We know of the tunnels, but anyone who enters never comes back. And now your friend has entered the folly."

Chapter 20.

Zalkiniv sat, staring out into the calm expanse of water as he had done now for days. He quelled the demands this body was making for food and water. It did not actually need them, but since it was normal to have them, the body wanted it. He drew on the reserves of power, now getting dangerously low to keep this form alive. His skin was thin and he could see the muscles twitch under its increasingly translucent look. Zalkiniv had never let a body he wore go this long without normal eating. He had no idea what to expect.

He would kill them. Kill every single one of the Saltmistress's ilk. Flay them. Harvest every drop of their blood, and take each corpse and burn it on land. No placing them in the sea as they desired. They had done this to him. They and the cursed sea goddess Hasseliniv. It was the only reason. First, they kill his called and captured beasts, and then leave him here, becalmed. Unnaturally so. In the days since the attack, he had been surrounded by the fog that their ships had brought. It never touched the boat or him, but it hovered, blocking any view of his boat, and his view of anything around him.

Worse yet, the water lay rock still. No wind, no currents. Even no animals came near. Not a single bird, fish, or even seaweed could be found within range of his senses. Stuck here. To be stopped by such a pathetic race as the Saltmistresses was infuriating. He had personally slaughtered hundreds of their kind before the Godsfall. And even after, when they had first done experiments with the blood mist. They were weak.

"They think I have lost. They seek to keep me here." Zalkiniv whispered. His throat was dry, and his lips cracked, so a whisper was all he could manage for now. But he was not lost. He would find a way to escape. He was Zalkiniv. He was on the path to ascend to godhood, and when he did, he would shatter the order the world existed in, and break the wills of anyone and everything that stood in his way.

His eyes alighted on the dagger, still stuck in the railing. The salt air did no damage to its pitted iron blade, to his somewhat surprise. He was no soot god follower, but iron should rust in this environment. The only current difference was that even on it, there was a slight patina of salt crystals that had dried on its surface.

There had to be a way. And he would find it. There must be a way.

***

Duncan shivered, peeking occasionally at the other. Valnijz. The Blood God itself. It wore his own face, one torn, ragged, injured, but it was his face. His form. He knew it watched him, and sometimes, it would turn towards his gaze and grin, a rictus of a smile, impossibly wide, and the skin would rip at the corner of his mouth and heal as he stopped smiling.

"I know you are watching me human." Valnijz's voice came, a near growl this time. Still perfectly clear, however. "You watch and fear, you watch and wonder."

Duncan did not answer. The Blood God had tried before to engage him in conversation, conversation that was one sided at best. How could he talk to it?

"Are you enjoying my game? I would think you would if anyone would." Valnijz asked. "Zalkiniv is sure he will ascend and take my place. MY PLACE!" The last words erupted from the figure with such force that a drop of bloody spittle came out and flew across this space they were in. Duncan watched it fly and vanish, as everything did here.

"I control the power; I control the blood. It is amusing to watch him dance for me. Even if he doesn't know, doesn't understand." Valnijz turned to Duncan. "Well? Are you enjoying my game? Answer. Or I will make sure that the Reach is wiped from the face of Alos."

Duncan winced. He did not know if Valnijz could do that right now or not. Could he risk that? This was the Scaled One, the ancient terror himself. The Reach was already dead if this thing managed to escape or take control. Duncan didn't understand everything that was going on here.

"I don't get it. Why do all this?" Duncan said, but kept his face away from the Blood God. No looking. I hate looking at that face. My face.

"I would think you Duncan Reis would understand. It's fun." The figure gave off a long laugh, half wheezing and half bubbling.

"Let me go." Duncan whispered. "I want out of all this. Keep William safe, but just let me go." He was not sure who he was even talking to. Amder? Even if Amder was back now, could the God of Craft even help?

The laughing wheezing sound continued for a minute before fading off. "My brother cannot help you. He does not even know I exist, not in this form, not yet. And you, Duncan, are the bait to bring his undivided attention."

Duncan did look this time to see the Blood God watching him closely. It was strange though, even here, Valnijz never got too close. Could he? Maybe he is not as much in control of this situation as he would like me to believe. Did he dare to push?

"Bait? Did not your High Priest try this? And it failed." Duncan spat the words out. He dared.

"Zalkiniv failed because, as in most things, Zalkiniv's pride came first." Valnijz's face, Duncan's own face transformed, hints of scales spread, until, like waves on a beach, the form was changed. Fully scaled, but yet the face was still Duncan's own. "I am Valnijz. I am the God of Blood and Rage. I will not fail. YOU will draw the precious of Amder to me. He is already on his way; did you know that? And once he is here, I will tear him apart with this very body. YOUR body. I will announce my return by destroying my killer's champion. And I will unleash a storm of blood and death upon first Palnor, and then every other people, and ever other land. Until there is only me, and those who follow me." As he spoke, the scaled form stood taller, and his voice grew harsher, sounding even more like a snake, or steam escaping from a quench.

Duncan stood as well. Let this end here. "You say that, but it's the same plan as before. You say you are no longer mad, but all I see is a remnant of a remnant, trying desperately to hold on. You call yourself a God? You are a shadow of a memory. That is all." Duncan fought to control the nervous tremble he was feeling throughout. *It's not real. None of this is.*

Valnijz merely laughed again. "I will say Duncan Reis. I can see why my brother likes your family. Maybe I'll keep you around after my victory. You do amuse me. I am a god. I can put your spirit into another body. One I can tear apart piece by piece, and then just when you are about to die, transfer it again." With no sound at all, suddenly the Scaled One was close. As close as he had ever been. The face transformed, bestial, bloody. "But never doubt, you are nothing. You are a shadow."

Duncan tried to lock eyes with what loomed over him, but couldn't. Fear gripped him, fear and revulsion. *He really is a god.* This wasn't a good idea.

"Things are moving Duncan Reis. I must make sure the chosen of Amder gets here at the same time we do. Only then will I act." Valnijz returned to where he normally was, before giving Duncan one more look. "And then, I will break the world."

***

Will hurt everywhere. His head ached worse than before, his side hurt, his legs hurt, it even hurt to breathe. He was covered with dust and debris, and worse yet, was in total blackness. Great. No purple light orb, and... he was somewhere else. He ran his hands over his chest and body, feeling for injuries. He hadn't been big on the idea of armor, but he was more than thankful for it now. It had protected his chest and wrists, at least from serious injury, though he may have cracked a rib by how much it hurt when he took a breath.

"Where's a dose of Cloud when you need one?" he said, spitting out some dry, bitter dust that coated his mouth. The irony of wanting a dose of Cloud now occurred to him, but the brief laugh he made brought forth a wave of pain. "Ow." Will muttered as he attempted to sit up. His fingers felt around his hammer! As he fumbled, he felt the familiar textured grip. As he grasped it, the faint silver glow came, dimmer than he remembered though. The light was barely enough to see anything, only that he was in a pile of rock and dust.

His head ached even worse sitting up. He raised his hand to run his fingers over his skull, but stopped. Did he really want to feel what must be a giant lump by now on his head? He carefully explored for wounds on what had been the non-injured side of his skull. A bit of dry blood, but nothing felt bad, at least not on that side of his head. Maybe a helmet would have been a good idea.

He could tell his fingers were shaking, even if he wasn't able to see them. As softly as he could, he explored the side of his head he had hit earlier. Somewhat to his surprise, it wasn't as bad as he feared. There was still a lump there, and not a small one, but the absolute fiery pain he had felt before when he had touched it was gone. It still hurt, and badly, but it was manageable pain. He was a bit more concerned about how dizzy he felt every time he moved his head.

He'd only been drunk once in his admittedly brief life. It had, as most things were, been Duncan's idea. He'd taken Will on a rest day evening to the Golden Chisel and got him to drink. And not only ale, but stronger stuff that some merchants and a few of the older miners liked. Will had not enjoyed it much at first, but as the drinks had kicked in, his objections ceased. He'd ended the night drinking some emerald green liquid that no one else had ever tried, even the innkeeper. He vaguely remembered stumbling across the main square in the Reach, unable to keep himself steady.

This was better in some ways, worse in others. Better in terms of the fact that he wouldn't have to deal with a hangover. He'd only had one of those, and he'd sworn to never have one again. Worse, because if the unsteady balance he had now was due to drink, he'd know how to deal with it. This current dizziness was because of injury, and that could be bad. Very bad, considering where he was.

He reached out, trying to find a wall to help him steady himself. He found one, but jerked his hand away as soon as he touched it. That is not a cave wall. It was smooth, straight, and ice cold to the touch. He reached back out, his fingers exploring the wall more. There were no edges that he could feel from where he was now. Simply one big smooth wall. *Where was he now?*

***

Jindo watched as the man screamed. A promising young recruit. A strong hunter, and talented with the use of the spear and net. He would make a good Curor, assuming he survived. He didn't want to be a Curor, but none of his men had, mostly.

Oh, he had gotten a few who desired it over the years. Sometimes they were madmen who did not understand the discipline and rigor that went into being one of them. Some were mercenaries, hoping to receive the powers of the blood and then sneak off to use the powers for paltry things like money and power.

The drop took care of both. The madmen usually died tearing their own flesh apart, unable to contain the additional rage and bloodlust the drop gave. The mercenaries often survived, but never left. Such thoughts always vanished afterwards. All Glory to the God of Rage and Bloodlust. What was money and the paltry power of man compared to that?

But most were like this man, hunters. Young men from the villages and towns nearby. They all hated Jindo, but he did not care. They existed to provide for the Curors. They provided food, labor, and, of course, bodies. This was the third and final hunter to go through the trial this day. The other two, a woman and another man, were finished. The woman had survived and was already learning how to use her new abilities.

The other man had died in remarkably quick fashion. The ritual had barely begun when he'd grasped his chest with both hands and, without a word, collapsed forward. Flipping him over had shown the truth. His heart had burst. He would have been a weak member if he had lived.

Jindo tapped his fingers in a rhythmic pattern, waiting for this man to either die or join them. His screams continued, as a few of the others watching exchanged glances. True, it was unusual for one to stay in the torment this long. They either died or gave in as the power of the blood cleansed them of their old life and desires. But the screams were not unpleasant. Jindo smiled as he remembered the last proper battle he had been in. He and his men had been sent on by the Scaled one before Zalkiniv had mangled everything. The city of the Red rocks had destroyed the Temple of the Blood God inside its walls. While it had sat empty and abandoned for untold years, it was still an affront.

They had poured over the city walls, each man given strength and agility far beyond anything any city guard could do. The Curors had arrived at dawn and left three days later. Every living person had died. Every man, every woman, every child. Hidden or not, the Curors had hunted them down and each sacrificed to the Master of all, Valnijz. The screams had been a wonderful chorus.

Lost in thought, he realized the man had stopped screaming. He lay unmoving. Dead then. At least his screams had been pleasing to the god.

Chapter 21.

"A tunnel? Under the Ocean?" Vin held his head as he asked that question.

Myriam watched the man. There wasn't a quiver in his voice but the signs of the stress he was under were there. But based on what they had all been through already in this insanity, she couldn't imagine how this was affecting him. *I should have gone home when I had the chance.*

"Yes. It is called a folly for a reason." Speaker-to-the-sky lowered his head and touched the wall again, as if he were in thought or prayer. Maybe both. She hated the feel of the bug remains on her skin. She wasn't a vain person, but the smell and the sticky feeling made her want to jump in a lake, take a bath, something, anything to get this off of her. It was even in her hair and was drying the already chopped tresses into hard clumps.

Not like I need to worry about that. Her eyes fell on Regin, and she rethought her previous statement. Could she deny the fact that when she had run into the fight, the sight of Regin had almost brought a cheer to her lips? He was a rough sight, as much as she was. At least he's alive. Hopefully William is alright as well.

"What are you thinking about all this, Myriam? You look like you wanted to say something." Regin asked. He fully turned towards her, his leathers and other equipment showing the same covering of karkin remains as the rest of them.

Think of something to say, quickly. "I guess I don't understand how all this happened. Fearsong? How did William get below us? How are we going to fix all this?" She took a second glance at Regin and felt some warmth drain out of her face. His side, he was injured!

"Regin! Sit. You are hurt." She ordered him to sit and pulled a very basic first aid kit she carried out of her pack. Nothing all that great, but some powered whiteroot, and a bandage should keep it from going bad, and help stop the bleeding.

"Oh? Oh yes, sorry, one of those Karkin thing's bit me on the side. I'm sure it's fine." Regin sat, though, even as he spoke. "I let it get under my cloak, and I didn't see it in the chaos."

Myriam did not answer, but pulled the cloak away, and pulled his leathers up enough to check the wound. Two straight cuts, each about a small finger in length, were on his skin. She wasn't sure why they hadn't bled more. Regin should have been bleeding all over the place from them, instead of a slow ebb. Still, she wasn't going to complain. She wished she had enough water to clean the wounds first, but there was only so much of that to go around.

"This might sting." Myriam quickly covered each cut with whiteroot, as Regin gave an involuntary intake of breath as the medicine hit the wounds. "You able to handle it?" Myriam asked, trying to give a comforting smile as she did so.

"Yes." Regin half said, half choked on the words. She knew whiteroot hurt like fire at first, but the pain faded. That with the bandage should seal them up. Though he would have a pair of scars to last him through his days.

Myriam wrapped the bandage around his torso, tight but not too tight. "There, now that should hold you together at least." She shot a smile at Regin, ignoring the flutter of nerves it brought. *I'm not a maiden in her first love. Stop that!* Her hands trembled at the memory of touching Regin's skin, only stopping when she made them into fists and put them under her cloak.

"Thank you, Healer Myriam." Regin answered with a grin and took a few preliminary deep breaths. "Ow! But doable."

Myriam unclenched her hands, careful to not let Regin see. *Why does this man draw me so?*

Myriam stood, brushing off her knees as she did so. "What was that Fearsong stuff? Why did they use it on us?"

Regin glanced at the Gorom. "I don't know if I should answer. I asked the same questions, and I'm still not clear."

Speaker-to-the-sky looked up at Myriam, shaking his head. "As I explained. Not all Gorom agreed on this. Letting you humans use our tunnels, our land, to get across the bones of the Stoneworld. I did not expect, nor did the Stonefather-who-speaks expect them to have access to fearsong."

"But why?" Myriam held her ground.

Speaker-to-the-sky rubbed his head, the purple orb making the skin glow white. His skin standing out all the more as their eyes all became used to the purple glow once more. "Do all humans follow your half god? Do all humans follow the law? All humans do not follow the same leader that I know. There are factions here as well. We are less divided than your cursed race, but separations exist. As I said, the fact that those who stood against the decision had access to fearsong, and used it in the threads, means planning, and forethought."

"What do we do now? I imagine we need to find William now. Can you find Forgemaster Reis?" Vin looked up from where he was slumped finally.

Myriam examined the man again and felt pity. He looked old. Not something she would have ever described Captain Tolin as until now.

"Yes. But I must warn you. We are heading into much more danger than we have been before. A karkin swarm is nothing compared to what exists below us. Far more dangerous, nameless things live here, in the wilds of the Stonelands." Speaker-to-the-sky waved a hand at all of them. "And we will attract more than our share of attention down below, smelling like we do."

"Is there anything we can do about that?" Myriam asked. "Not to sound too much like a damsel in distress, but I do like being clean."

Regin nodded. "This stuff, I feel like I've been dried in some horrible foul gelatinous mess."

Speaker-to-the-sky seemed to think for a moment. "I can get us to water. It is not too far from where we need to be. We can at least rinse."

Vin stood brushing a stuck karkin leg off his shoulder. "Anything is better than sitting here."

Speaker-to-the-sky nodded. "Follow me then. While it is not overly far, we may attract things as it is. Be careful, stay close."

***

Will held the hammer tight and pushing the aches and pains away. He held it as close to the wall as he could. Black. Cold, hard, and totally black. He jerked his hand away. He wasn't sure, of course, how could he be? But for all the world, it felt like, or looked, like a Drendel tunnel. Like the one Speaker-to-the-sky had shown them. Shown them and warned them about.

Sparks burn it. He needed Amder. He needed his friends. He needed… something. *I am not cut out for this. I should be out traveling the surface.* Forging and training. Bringing prosperity to all the places the former Priesthood ignored. That's what he should be doing. Not here, not this, not somewhere deep underground, lost. Injured. Alone.

Will leaned back against the wall, using it to brace himself as a fresh wave of dizziness washed over him. Was it getting worse? It made thinking painful, which was another bad sign. He had simply wanted to mark his path. How had the wall collapsed like that? Think William. Put one thought at a time and think.

The wall had been soft, but he'd thought it compacted enough and strong enough that it wouldn't do that much damage. His hammer had hit the wall harder than he'd planned, but even then, it shouldn't have done this. How could the wall collapse? It must have been weakened. Thinner than it appeared. *I should have checked.*

He'd worked in enough mines to have seen it before. A section of wall looks solid enough, but the stone was thin. It happened a lot in areas where there were pockets, open sections where gems could be found. Or in sandstone or chalk. Water or animals eat away behind the rock, leaving a section that looks solid, but enough pressure in one place, and the whole thing falls apart.

I didn't think it through. Will fought the urge to scratch his head. He didn't want to feel the lump again, regardless of how much his skin itched from stone dust and whatever else was in this place. But now what? He'd had a plan before. A plan to find the others and get out of this spark burned abyss. Chase down Duncan, save him, and then go on and be a Forgemaster.

There was no plan now. How could you plan for this? Will wanted to scream. He wanted to cry. He wanted to give up. His bones would rest here for hundreds, if not thousands, of years. Maybe forever. A legend of a fool. His hammer, still giving off the faintest of sliver glows, laid in his hand. *No, I will not allow that to happen. Not now, not after everything.*

Will gripped it even tighter. He would not die here. He couldn't. Stay and hope the others find him? Or head down the tunnel, see if he can find a way to some place safer? He examined the wall again; he had no idea what this stuff was, but it made him uneasy. The light from the hammer didn't even reflect off of it well. It all seemed dull, faded. Speaker-to-the-sky hadn't gone into detail about the Drendel. At the time Will had let it go, now he wished he'd pushed for more information. Should he explore?

He'd need more light if he was going to do that. Where had the orb gone? He'd been holding it when he'd fallen. He was sure of that. So maybe it was buried under some of this rubble. He'd grown to rather dislike the strange light the Gorom used, but right now, he'd be cheering if he found it.

Will shifted rocks aside, using the very feeble glow from the hammer as best he could. For several minutes he found nothing, only more rock, though some were damp. Water? Maybe that's why it had fallen apart. Finally, he shifted a large flat piece to find the orb. But his faint joy and finally finding the light left as fast as it had come. The thing was cracked. It still shone, but noticeably less than it had the last time he'd held it. Cracked and leaking. Leaking something slimy, and even now, foul smelling. There was still a glow, though. Fainter, weaker, but still there. Something, at least.

He picked the orb up carefully, trying to keep the crack in it pointed up, so whatever the fluid leaking out was, it would stay in. The liquid was what was glowing, anyway. What was this thing? He remembered Speaker-to-the-sky saying something about not breaking the orb, and we wouldn't like it, or something like that. Truthfully, while he missed his friends, he wasn't sure if he missed the Gorom all that much. Abrasive. That was the word. All the Gorom he'd met since they started this were simply abrasive.

Holding the orb higher, Will got a better look at the tunnel he was in. He could see where he had fallen from, a large hole in the roof, which struck him as odd. The walls, and from what he could tell, even the floor up ahead, were that strange black substance. But the ceiling here was stone. Why not the roof as well?

But he wasn't a Drendel, and who knew? He approached a wall and rubbed a thumb across the black wall. Ice cold to the touch, and smooth. *I think it's metal, but how did they get it this flat?* It looks nothing like Drendel steel. Though who knows what Drendel steel really is though. Will knew it was just called that. He'd seen it smelted, chunks of broken gears, chains, even weapons, or what they thought were weapons. All melted together and poured into ingots. Even in the Reach, Drendel steel wasn't an everyday smelting occurrence.

But this wall stuff, it was strange. Staring at the wall didn't get him any safer, though. Will held the orb as high as he could, but he couldn't see how far he had fallen. He knew he was not making the decision, though. Stay or go? Staying would be safer. Will looked down the black hallway, either direction. *I always make the safe choice. Well, usually.* And things rarely went well for him when he didn't. Getting the blood shard from the Mistlands wasn't safe, but it did not work out either.

Will hated to think about it, but had it been worth it? Yes, Duncan's life had been shattered. But he was the Forgemaster of Amder now, the God had returned from whatever afterlife Gods had, and the Blood God had been denied his return. But there was the cost. Everything has a cost, one way or another. He half remembered his Uncle, Duncan's father, saying something to that effect after his own father had sunk into his Cloud addiction.

He made one last look down the hallways and sat down. He had to stay. Leaving would be a mistake. At least for now. Until he was sure no one was coming for him. Besides, with the occasional dizzy spell he was still having, watch him wander down the hall and get injured worse, or even die this time. He knew he'd been lucky so far, almost blessedly so.

I will wait. Will sat back, working to ignore both the wave of nausea that came anytime he sat up or sat down, and his growing hunger. He did finally take his waterskin and took a long sip. He wasn't going to waste it, but if he waited any longer, he'd risked being too weak to do anything, or worse. He could do without food, but not drink.

The water was flat, but at least it was cool. And he hoped the slight grit in his mouth was just clean stone dust. He wished he could spit it out, but wasting the water would be more foolish. He wasn't sure how long he was going to have to sit here. That was assuming nothing came out of the darkness to attack him. Pleasant thought.

Chapter 22.

Regin picked his steps carefully, following along behind Myriam, with Vin behind him. And of course, leading the way was Speaker-to-the-sky. The air was already getting thicker with moisture, and as they had traveled, the stone floor had grown damp, and with that dampness came patches of some unknown mold, slippery and stinking.

Picking his steps also helped him keep his eyes on the ground, and not on Myriam. He couldn't deny the attraction he'd been feeling towards her anymore. At first, he'd passed it off to her being the only woman with them, but the more he was around her, the more he knew that wasn't the case and had never been.

She was, in truth, a very special woman. Smart, a quick learner, not scared to say what she thought. And she was very attractive, even with that emergency haircut Vin had given her with his dagger. If anything, that whole situation made him more interested. So many of the women he had chased around in the past would have screamed and cried over what had happened. Myriam had half laughed it off and then fixed it as best she could and moved on.

She'd be perfect if it wasn't for William. And that was why he wouldn't do more than admire her. He knew William still was in love with her. You only had to be in the same place with them both to see how his eyes followed her, and to see how his face broke out into a smile when she even came into view. And while she no longer returned his attraction, there was no way Regin could step into the middle of that.

"Speaker-to-the-sky, what is that thing you do? When you touch the wall?" Myriam asked as they walked.

"It's the blessing of Grimnor. We call it the delve. If a Gorom who has been granted the blessing touches the walls of the Stonelands, and concentrates, they can find what they are looking for, usually." Speaker-to-the-sky moved past a small puddle in the middle of the widening cavern they were in. "Don't step in that, tainted with blackspot."

"So not all Gorom can do it?" Regin asked as they skirted the puddle. He didn't know what blackspot was, but he didn't want to find out. After the karkin incident, the fewer surprises he had down here, the better.

"No. Few can. One reason I can is my place. Though, I never thought to be using it as much as I have been. You humans will make me return to the stone by the end of this." Speaker-to-the-sky turned around and gave what Regin could only think of as a smile. Speaker, smiling?

"How far to the waterfall?" Myriam asked. "I can't wait to get this stuff off of me." She picked at her cheek as she walked, pulling something off that Regin didn't see in the dim purple glow.

"Not far. The delve tells me we should be safe there, at least for a while." Speaker-to-the-sky answered and led them down a side tunnel, leading them down and around a curve that opened up into an even bigger cavern.

"Once we are done here, will it be far to get to the Forgemaster? You said he is alright? I don't know if we should be doing this, shouldn't we go after him first?" Vin asked from the back.

"Your Forgemaster is fine for now. He is alive, and smart, for a human, staying put. Going to where he is now, smelling like dead karkin, is a sure way to attract things that will haunt us all." Speaker-to-the-sky paused, touching the wall again, before letting his hand drop and continuing on, away from any walls.

Regin looked back at Vin and shrugged. He also wanted to get to William, but he also didn't want to be attacked by more things down here. And the Gorom was the only person who could lead them to the Forgemaster, so if he thought this was necessary, it was necessary. Vin just nodded back, though Regin could tell the man was still under stress.

"You feel alright Vin?" Regin lowered his voice as he spoke. "I know this isn't your idea of a place you want to spend time."

"I'll be better once we are out of this… place. Though being in an open cavern is better than a narrow cave. I can't see the ceiling now. That helps." Vin pointed up at the overarching blackness but stopped in his tracks. "What is that?"

Regin looked up and didn't have an answer. Lights. Thousands of tiny blue and green lights. More than thousands. "Speaker-to-the-sky?"

The Gorom glanced up, and Regin could see the scowl once again on his face. "The lights? Erch. Annoying pest."

Regin loved them instantly. It almost felt like he was outside for a moment. It was dark, it was damp, it was cool, almost cold, but the lights made it better. "I love them."

"Me too." Myriam stood next to Regin for a moment. "Pretty."

Regin looked at her. The words he was going to say stalled on his lips. He wanted to kiss her. He wanted to do more than kiss her. He could smell her. Even under all that karkin mess, he could smell a scent of… Regin fumbled for the thought. Home. Comfort. Love. A perfect fit.

"Regin?" Myriam asked, his attention shifting from his thoughts to the very real and warm woman standing next to him. "Are you alright?"

Regin blinked a few times. "Yes! Yes... sorry. Was in thought."

Myriam reached up and squeezed his arm for a moment. "Well, keep your attention here. We don't want to lose you as well." Then she fell back into line as Speaker-to-the-sky waved them forward.

Regin rubbed his arm and sighed. Attention indeed. He dropped his eyes downward, keeping them once more firmly on the steps he was taking. A short time later, a new sound came to him. One he could place. A very faint, but dull, roar.

"There. Even you humans should be able to hear that. The falls." Speaker-to-the-sky said as he picked up the pace.

Regin, Myriam, and Vin followed suit. The dull roar became louder and was joined by a blue-green glow that pushed back against the orb the Gorom carried. The light became brighter the closer they got until, as one, they stopped to take in the sight in front of them. A sight none of them would have even imagined before now.

***

Duncan watched Valnijz as he usually did, carefully. The truth was, he wasn't sure what to think of the being. On one hand, he scared Duncan to the core. There was truth in his claims to be the god Valnijz. Some deep instinct screamed at him every time they spoke to run, hide, get away. Though there wasn't anywhere to go, nor would there ever be.

But some things bothered him, some scrap of his former skeptic life kept pushing him to wonder why, if this thing was truly the God of Rage returned, why didn't he ever cross the line? There was a point he never went past. And for all his rage and terror, he couldn't seem to ever cross it. Which meant he wasn't as all powerful as he claimed.

Also, why play these games? Why did he need Zalkiniv or Duncan at all? Duncan still wasn't sure why he was here. Or where here even was. But absent any reason, he had mostly given up on wondering why it simply was. Zalkiniv had a goal to become the new Blood God. And he had a plan. But could he, could anyone actually become a god?

All of this disgusted him. He wished he had spoken to Haltim more often and understood the nature of the gods more. Though Haltim might not have known the truth any more than Duncan did. He missed the old Priest. The fool had annoyed him, and always seemed to not quite give enough information, but he had been a good man.

Duncan knew Haltim was dead. And he knew the truth, that he, under the control of Zalkiniv and his blood curse, had killed him. He did not remember it, something he found himself grateful for. So much of his memory was gone, and the gaps were even bigger from the time he gave that ruby to Rache, until he died, killed in the shaft's breaking.

Before he had woken here. Was this better? At least then he didn't remember what he had done, what he had been forced to do. Here, it was all like watching a performer's troupe. Everything that happened he could see, hear, smell. But he couldn't stop it.

"Deep in thought?" Duncan blinked as Valnijz appeared suddenly, right at the imaginary line that he never seemed to go past.

"Wishing I had paid attention more. I don't understand the gods." Duncan answered, watching whatever this was for reaction. At least seeing my own twisted face like that wasn't making me sick anymore.

"What of us? We are gods. You owe us your worship, your fealty. More than any noble, more than any king, we are the ones you should follow." Valnijz paused. "Thinking of falling to your knees and begging for mercy?"

Duncan didn't answer the question. This all bothered him. "But why?"

Valnijz changed in an instant, when mere seconds before he had been amused and even talkative, his face changed. Duncan's own features were replaced. An elongated scaled face grew as the body covered with scales and talons spiked out of its fingers.

"I am a GOD. You are a memory. A fragment of a soul that refuses to admit that you are nothing more than a parasite." Valnijz roared, its breath washing over Duncan, the smell of death and rot thick in it.

Duncan wanted to say something back. He wanted this thing, to get truly angry, to kill him. End this. But he held back. He wasn't scared. He watched carefully as the ranting, self-proclaimed god still didn't cross the same point every time. He can't. He can't hurt me. He repressed a smile as the realization came.

This may be a part of the Blood God, and in fact, Duncan was pretty sure that was true. But he wasn't the whole God. If he was, there would be no need for this subterfuge. Valnijz wouldn't need to play games. Duncan thought back on everything Zalkiniv had said to him, everything he'd seen and heard. Valnijz needs whatever it is that the priest is after, as much as his former follower does.

The more animalistic form that the Scaled One had taken roared and screamed at him, but Duncan carefully and deliberately turned around and ignored it. He may be powerless, but he wasn't stupid. Maybe there was a way to end this after all. *I'll have to protect you one more time, it seems like Will.*

***

William was tired and very bored. He'd been sitting here for longer than he wanted, getting up to stretch his legs, but otherwise sitting. He considered heading down the tunnel each way a bit for something to do, but discounted the idea. If for no other reason than the fact his light was diminishing quicker than he had hoped. He hadn't been sure at first, but whatever the orb was, the crack was very much causing it to fade. He'd lodged it in between two rocks, cracked side up, so more of that reeking liquid didn't seep out.

He could still see, but he knew it was dimmer. He'd taken a few more sips of water, but saved the rest. Mostly, he spent the time resting or examining the walls. The pain in his head still came, but with some trial and error, he'd figured out how to move it without the spikes of intense pain he'd had at first. But now it was the same throbbing ache it had been for a while. That and the still occasional wave of nausea and accompanying dizziness.

That was what worried him the most. None of them were trained in healing. He was sure Vin had picked up some tricks over the years, and he was pretty sure Myriam carried a first aid kit, but that was it. He didn't think those tricks and a traveler's kit would handle whatever this was on his head. He didn't know if Speaker-to-the-sky knew any first aid, and even if he did, did he know about treating humans? He considered us cursed anyway.

Cursed. Will didn't like the sound of that. All the Gorom had been oddly and irritatingly dismissive of Amder. That didn't even include the 'half-god' comments. He still didn't understand that. Why call Amder a half God? And why can't I talk to Amder? As much as his head still hurt, he tried to reach that little part inside that seemed to make the connection between himself and his God.

But each time his thoughts seemed to slide away, like water on oiled leather. *I could use some advice here, Amder.* Even talking to the last Forgemaster before him would be great. Oddly enough, he hadn't spoken to Simon Reis since the day he brought Amder back. Maybe the past Forgemaster finally had gotten his rest.

Will turned his musings back to the walls. The more he examined them, the more he was sure it was metal, but what kind and how it had been made were the questions that drew his attention more. That and why did it make him feel…. dark.

It was a mystery, though everything related to the Drendel was a mystery. All anyone knew, well, all anyone in the Reach knew was that they must have lived underground, and they had remarkable craft and skill. Drendel steel was the metal of choice for some applications, though it was always expensive and hard to get a hold of. He'd seen a sword made out of the stuff once. A small bucket of various finds had been melted down for making it. And while he knew little about swords, he remembered the sound the thing made as the customer had swung it. Not merely the swish of the wind, but a hum, eager and to all the world, hungry.

That was it. The guild might know more, but he'd not been there long enough to be trusted with that information. When this was over, and he'd saved Duncan, he'd go back to the Guild and do Amders' bidding. He'd look into it then, along with a lot of other things. Why did the Gorom come to the Guild sometimes? What was the arrangement with the former Church of Amder like?

His attention came back to the black wall. *I could hit this with my hammer, see what happens. I'm curious as to what kind of reaction there might be.* The thought was pushed away nearly as soon as it came to him. The last thing he needed was a repeat of before. He'd already fallen into deeper trouble once. What was below this place? Did he even want to know?

Will looked up again in the fading purple light at the hole he had fallen through. Nothing to do but keep waiting. He didn't even know if his friends were looking for him. He hoped they were alive. If Vin or Regin had died because of that fearsong attack, he didn't know what he'd do.

And Myriam? Will blinked the wetness off his face. *Stop crying. You can't afford to waste any tears.* But the idea of Myriam hurt, lost, or dead made his heart sink. Please let her be safe. Let them all be safe.

Chapter 23.

Myriam blinked in the light that newly assaulted her eyes. Though she knew it wasn't that bright, here after all this time, it seemed as if someone had sparked a forge right in front of her. The waterfall itself glowed with a pale blue luminescence, but that was only part of it. The walls around the cavern were covered with moving lights of green, dark blue, yellows. Just like the roof of the cavern before. But she could see them now. They were mushrooms? Moving mushrooms?

"Here. The water might glow, but it's clean." Speaker-to-the-sky glared at the colorful spectacle in front of him. "If I survive you humans, we must clean this place of pests."

"Pests? It's amazing!" Regin said, still staring at the spectacle.

Myriam had to agree. It was unlike anything she had ever seen, or even dreamed of. Why would anyone ever want to get rid of this? Even Captain Tolin seemed taken by the sight, as some of the age and worry leached from his face as he took in what lay before them.

"Pests. No order, no pattern. Better to cleanse than have this chaos." Speaker-to-the-sky shook his head. "You are cursed. No wonder you like this. But this is not the time. Clean up, and then we will go and fetch your Forgemaster."

Myriam shook herself, taking her eyes off the sight. "Yes. Well, Vin and Regin, the two of you can go first, then I'll go." She turned her attention to the waterfall. "You sure it's safe? What makes it glow?"

"It's safe. The light comes from the Erch. What you call mushrooms. The Erch blow off glowing spores and they stay in the water. These spores come from upstream, I'm sure the cave that water comes out of is thick with them." Speaker-to-the-sky pointed to where the water erupted from the cavern wall. "So, the spores are harmless."

"Will they make us glow?" Vin spoke up. "Could draw attention."

"No. The spores lose their glow quickly once they are out of the water." Speaker-to-the-sky looked into the pool the waterfall spilled into, its light blue glow lighting up his face. "The pool itself would be fine as well. Wish there was time, there are Romach in there. Fish. What you call fish."

Myriam joined the Gorom and looked down. There were fish. Nearly a foot long, and glowing brighter than the water itself. "What do they eat?"

Speaker-to-the-sky snorted. "The spores, what else? Now, clean."

Myriam turned to spy on both Regin and Vin, watching them dropping packs and disrobing. Her eyes moved on their own as they traced the lines of Regin's arms. He's even stronger looking now. "Regin! Your wound! Here, let me check it before you get into the water."

Myriam came towards the man, who was unclothed from the waist up. The sight grew a slight hunger in her that she pushed down. *Not the time. Or the place.*

"Oh, I'm sure it's fine Myriam." Regin stammered out, turning away from her.

"Nonsense. Let me check it." Myriam removed the bandage carefully, the cloth thankfully not sticking to the place where Regin had been bitten. She turned a careful eye to the two parallel cuts on his side. The whitepowder had done its job. Both wounds had scabbed over completely. Myriam gave in, and she lightly traced the skin by the wounds with her fingers. "Does that hurt?"

"No…" Regin half whispered.

She could hear his breath catch. *Does that mean what I hope it means?*

Her thoughts were interrupted by a large splash as Vin entered the pool, followed by a near howl. "COLD!!" Vin yelled as the man covered himself with the glowing water.

Regin jerked himself away from her touch. "I will be fine. I better clean myself up. Thankfully, we all have a change of clothes in our packs. We should have some travel rations as well. Eat something while we go find William." Regin paused. "I think you should turn around, Myriam. I need to get in the pool myself, you know."

Myriam nodded and slowly turned away. Her thoughts, though, were on the reaction her touch had brought. A splash followed by a huge intake of breath and a laugh followed soon after. Myriam chewed her lip in thought, briefly imagining the scene behind her. He's interested, I'm interested. But still… there was William. She didn't want to hurt him anymore than she already had. To his credit, he had kept it to himself and had given her space.

I'm going to have to talk to him again. That would be a conversation she did not want to have. He'd not taken the last one well back in the Reach. It hadn't been all that long ago, but yet, it seemed forever ago. But even if she talked to William, would Regin? He had his own sense of honor about things, and he, regardless of his attraction and interest, might not allow himself to do anything because of William. And he was older than her. Not a large amount, even so, older. She wasn't in the Guild anymore, at least, not right now, so the prohibition about Guildmasters and Apprentices wouldn't hold true. And since he was believed dead, Regin technically wasn't a Guildmaster, either.

A bellow and splash behind her made her sigh. Get two men in a pond and they act like they are ten. It was still kind of cute, in the 'they should know better' way. There was a time and place for that sort of thing, but this wasn't it. "Can you two men hurry up? I'd like to get cleaned up, and we need to get our Forgemaster?" Myriam yelled out. *It's a good thing they can't see my face, or they would see the grin on it.*

"Sorry Myriam!" Vin called out. She could hear puffing and the opening of packs, and it was a short time later that someone tapped her on the shoulder.

Standing there was Regin. Face red, but smelling so much better. "It's all yours. It's a bit brisk. But it feels amazing to get all that stuff off." Regin touched his wounds. "And these are fine. The scab didn't even open in the water. No need to check them."

Myriam fought the sinking feeling. He's choosing to run away. She'd have to talk to him, then if he agrees, William. She watched as Regin went back to his pack as he and Vin talked quietly. Both had their back to her, and the Gorom was… where had Speaker-to-the-sky gone? "Vin? Regin? Where's the Gorom?" Myriam looked around; the cavern at least better lit than anyplace else they had been recently.

"The Gorom is right here." Speaker-to-the-sky appeared from an alcove that she hadn't noticed. "I was cleaning myself."

"Why not use the pool?" Vin asked. Myriam winced. Vin was a great guy, but he had little tact sometimes.

"I will not bathe in the same water as... humans." Speaker-to-the-sky made a face.

Myriam sighed. More of the cursed humans' nonsense. Vin glanced at her and shook his head, and Regin only nodded. Better to let it go for now. No one wanted to get into an argument with the one person who could get them all out of this strange underground world, and back to the surface where they belonged.

"Turn around please, I for one will try to be fast." Myriam waited until Vin and Regin had turned around, and Speaker-to-the-sky gave a slight bow and returned to whatever alcove he had been at before. Why did he bow to me? Not that it mattered, but the Gorom she had finally decided were strange.

Disrobing fully, the cool cave air made her skin prickle, though it felt good to get out of the same clothes she had been in for, well, too long. Time didn't seem to matter much here. She approached the pool; the shine showing the fish, or whatever the Gorom had called them, Romach? Something like that. Cold, huh? She'd be the judge.

She took a deep breath and dove in. The water was not only cold, she nearly opened her mouth in shock and drowned. She broke the surface and let forth a long hiss. Cold? Just COLD? Her fingertips were already blueish-purple and the chattering in her jaw was already strong.

"Cold, isn't it?" Regin yelled over his shoulder.

Smug bastard. I should ask him to come warm me up, but we aren't alone. Not that he would... probably. "Yes, it's cool. But not that bad." She forced herself to say the words without a hint of a shiver. She quickly scrubbed at her skin, feeling the karkin slime, once hardened, wash off. She even grabbed a handful of sand from a shallow part of the pool and used it to scour a partially stuck piece of something off her arm.

A quick rinse of her hair, and she felt better. So much better. A real hot bath with soap and shampoo, and a razor to fix this hair of hers would be ideal, but this would do. Climbing out of the pool, her skin got colder still, but she could dry herself and get dressed soon enough. Clean clothes, clean self, and she was back to go. Her stomach, however, grumbled in disagreement. When was the last time they had eaten?

"Ready, but you said something about eating? That dip made me hungrier." Myriam grabbed her pack, slinging it on.

"Eat and walk and let Speaker-to-the-sky lead the way." Regin shouldered his pack. "You look good." The words must have been not what he meant to say, though, as he turned about four shades of red. "I mean you look ready to go, refreshed."

"Uh, huh. You look good too." Myriam answered, giving Regin a smile. "Speaker-to-the-sky, can we drink that water? Wondering if we should refill our waterskins and the like here."

"Yes. Though I'd fill it from the waterfall, not the pool. Unless you like the taste of karkin slime." Speaker-to-the-sky took a wide metal cylinder from under his robe, and filled it from the waterfall, sealing it with some sort of disk.

They filled their waterskins back to full, taking long drinks, and even filling an extra one for William, for when they found him. Myriam wondered if the water would glow even later when they opened the things. Something to wonder about, at least.

"Come humans. Follow. Be on guard. Makese's folly is a dangerous place to be. While your Forgemaster is safe for now, I cannot promise he will be before we get there. Eat and walk, we have to go." Speaker-to-the-sky started off, leading them down a winding downward slope, the cavern of the mushrooms behind them, and the blue glow of the waterfall slowly fading with the roar.

Chapter 24.

Jindo Halfman paced the room of the blood. The chamber was empty save for him, not a common occurrence. But these days nothing was common. Jindo still did not understand how that fool of a High Priest had failed so badly. All he had to do was capture and sacrifice two men. That was all.

The worst part was that Zalkiniv had at one point had both. And while Jindo wasn't sure exactly what had happened, he could guess. Zalkiniv had tried to be dramatic, or had been gloating, and had given an opening to the followers of the false one. Jindo hated people like that. Do what needs to be done, THEN gloat. None of it mattered now though, Jindo had to pick up the pieces of the mess.

One, Amder, the God of Craft and Creation, was back. And had named a new Forgemaster, one of the two men that Zalkiniv had failed to deal with. Two, Zalkiniv was dead, but someone or something had attacked the Temple of the Blood God in the Mistland wastes and wiped it out. It wasn't Amder's work, the spies and scouts were sure if it. It had been a brutal killing, but each attack had been made with a blade of some kind. Three, whatever had wiped the Temple out, had also wiped out a coastal village.

Jindo did not care about the people in the village, but that left open the possibility that whatever had attacked those places was heading here. The Cruor were on alert now for that possibility. Whatever it was, they would deal with it. Still, it bothered him that they didn't have more information. The temple had been sacked, and while he didn't know what had been taken, it was obvious who or what that had wiped it out had taken things from it.

If they were coming here, there was only one thing they could be after. The drop. The single drop of the blessed one's blood, frozen in time. Kept here, it was the source of the power for the Cruor. They eschewed the Valni and blood workings that Zalkiniv loved so much. No, the Cruor and Jindo used the blood to make themselves into more than human. Speed rivaling that of the fastest predators, deadly precise attacks, strength greater than ten men. Each Cruor was the match to a patrol of veterans.

Damn you Zalkiniv. You brought this on us. His only satisfaction, he'd never have to listen to the High Priest prattle on ever again. They would ready the defenses, deal with the attacker, and then find a way to fix this failure. The blessed one would return. The scrolls of the dead said so, and they were always right, in one way or another.

The scrolls. Written on the flayed skin of fallen Curors, the scrolls of the dead were words inspired by the drop. Jindo had written them himself once he had shared blood with the fallen. He never remembered writing them, but afterwards, he'd awaken to discover a stylus in his hand, and cuts on his arms. Written in blood, words given power. The scrolls said that Valnijz would return; it was written. Jindo wasn't unhappy though that it wasn't Zalkiniv who would bring back their lord. It would be he, Jindo Halfman.

The High Priest had always looked down on him and his followers. Mere soldiers, and Jindo no better than a stepped-up gang leader. Who is leading now?

He would make ready the men. They would end this threat and hunt down this Forgemaster. Amder may have returned, but the war was not over, not yet. Jindo Halfman would make sure of that.

***

Regin took another bite of the travel ration bar. Normally he hated these things, dried meat, fruit, other things he wasn't sure of. Tasteless and tough. Nothing he'd ever want to eat. If there was one thing in common between now and who he had been in the past, he did like his food.

But now? The bar tasted better than anything he could remember. The first bite, followed by a long drink of the still faintly glowing water from the falls, had been as near to rapture as he could imagine. When had been the last time they had eaten? It felt like forever ago. This underground world was timeless, and everything had been close to one calamity after another.

Before the pool, he'd been slowly sinking into the feeling that this was it. William was lost, and they would all die in this sunless pit. The water had helped a great deal. It had been cold and refreshing, and exactly what he needed. And Myriam. He stole a glance at her, dressed now in a set of stout travel trousers and a smithing jerkin, her hair pulled back as best as she could. Even in this light, she was, he had to admit, beautiful.

He'd been surprised at the reaction he'd had when her fingers had touched his side. The thrill had been nearly overwhelming. Regin puzzled over it. He was no stranger to the affections of women. Even in his days before, he'd found more than a few pleasant female companions. No stranger to the bedchamber. He'd made a bit of a game out of it. Different women in different cities, could he bed a woman in every town in Palnor? He wasn't proud of it now. Not that he'd ever forced a woman into that, but he'd pick out the ones that he could get what he wanted from.

He'd never had the reaction he had with Myriam. Not that he wasn't interested in her that way, he was. More than he ever expected to be. Truth if he had been alone with her at the pool, he would have stolen a few glances as she had been in the water.

He still couldn't. For the same reason. William. Everything was lost if William died. Speaker-to-the-sky said William was still alive, but would he be? This 'Makese's Folly' sounded bad. And Regin liked William. He should not move forward with anything with Myriam, at least not until he spoke to the Forgemaster. He couldn't do that to the man.

"This tunnel, this Makese's Folly. Why that name? You are Speaker-to-the-sky, we also met Stonefather-who-speaks, and you said something about a knower-of-the-dark or something. But that name, Makese? That doesn't match. Why?" Captain Tolin asked, taking a small bite of his ration bar.

Regin hadn't really thought about it, but Vin was right. Something to ponder, and something to keep his mind off Myriam and everything about her.

"Makese lost his name." Speaker-to-the-sky answered as he walked. Regin noticed the Gorom never seemed to eat, maybe he didn't have to eat as much, Gorom were strange.

"What does that mean?" Myriam spoke up. "We aren't trying to be nosey, but we are curious."

"You are humans. You are what you are." Speaker-to-the-sky snorted. "Every Gorom has two names. The name of birth, and the name of position. The name of birth is thrown away once you take your position. Unless you do something so horrible, something so wrong, you lose the name of position. Makese is the name of birth."

"What was his position?" Myriam asked. "If you can tell me that is."

"It was stricken. No one knows. It also does not matter. He lost his name. He is nothing but one of the fallen." Speaker-to-the-sky spat and ground the spittle into the stone.

"We didn't mean to offend." Regin spoke up. "Your world is strange Speaker-to-the-sky."

The Gorom said nothing in response but touched the wall and lowered his head again for a moment, before raising his head quickly. "We must hurry. I suspect the light orb your Forgemaster was carrying was broken. That is bad."

Regin exchanged glances with Myriam and Vin. Every time the Gorom said something was bad, it usually was horrible. "Lead on then." Regin nodded to the others, stowing their ration bars away.

Speaker-to-the-sky hurried down the tunnel, fast enough that all three of the humans broke into a jog. Regin wondered for a second how fast the Gorom's legs were moving, considering he was shorter than the rest of them by far. He stifled down a smile and felt slightly guilty.

They followed Speaker-to-the-sky through a series of twisting tunnels, dryer and dustier, double backs and sloping down over and over again. Regin was thankful for the delve sense the Gorom had, there was no way if Speaker-to-the-sky wasn't here that they would be able to find William.

"How you holding up Vin?" Regin lowered his voice as he spoke to the man who brought up the rear.

"I'm... alive." Vin answered. His right hand was gripping his dagger hard, and though Regin couldn't see his hand because of the gloves he wore, he imagined he was white knuckling it.

"Hold strong. We will get William and get out of this blasted darkness. And I, for one, will never set foot in a cave, tunnel, mine, or any other passage underground if I can help it. That holds true for cellars and basements!" Regin kept his voice low still, but gave Vin a grin as he spoke.

"I agree. I'd rather be on a boat for weeks than down here. I am not looking forward to traveling through a tunnel that goes under the ocean. Why would anyone want to do that? Ever." Vin shuddered. "But I do my duty. I am sworn to protect the Forgemaster of Amder, and I will do so to the best of my ability." Vin shot a small smile back at Regin. "But don't doubt for a second I've wished a time or two that I hadn't been in the Reach that day. In truth, if I hadn't had to fire those two guards, we wouldn't have been."

Regin smiled back, nodding his head. "Well, I'm sure the Reach is happy you were. As are William and I. And Myriam as well."

Vin lowered his voice a bit farther. "Are you going to tell William?"

"Tell him what?" Regin asked, unable to deny the cold shot to the gut those words brought.

"About you and our friend, Myriam. I don't blame you. She's a rare one, Myriam is. Smart, attractive, strong." Vin paused. "But…"

Regin knew it. It wasn't anything he hadn't said to himself repeatedly. He could not allow himself to do more than admire Myriam. It was out of the question.

Chapter 25.

William was bored. Sitting in a dark and getting darker tunnel, waiting and hoping for his friends to find him, wasn't how he had wanted to spend time. At least the rest gave him a chance to heal up some. The occasional wave of nausea still came, and his stomach growled all the fiercer, but he was alive, at least. The pains from the fall were mostly gone now, though he was sure he was more bruise in places than man.

A small sip of water and the pain in his stomach grew for a brief moment before fading away again. I'm going to be as thin as Duncan if this keeps up. Duncan. He wished he knew more about his cousin. Where was he? What was in control? He had seen the blood curse take over, and he never wanted to see anything like that again.

He wished Haltim was here. The old Priest would give good counsel, and William would always feel better after talking to him. He could remember Haltim's face at the end, blue black, struggling to breathe from the attack by whatever the blood curse had turned Duncan into. He wasn't sure if Duncan knew what he had done to Haltim. Will knew he'd have to tell him eventually, a task he wasn't looking forward to.

Hey Duncan, by the way, under the effect of that blood curse, you killed Haltim. Squeezed his head until his skull cracked. He didn't blame you, but figured you should know! Yeah, that wasn't the way to deal with it. In truth, he didn't know what to say. This assumed, of course, that this quest of his was successful. No, don't even think that. It will be, it must be. If he could save Duncan, everything would have been worth it. Well, mostly.

None of this was in his plan. Before stealing the shard from the Mistlands, Will's plan had been simple. Get the shard, get into the Guild, become a Mastersmith. Work wherever was needed, eventually return to the Reach, move back into the family home, get married, have a passel of kids, and retire the first Reacher to ever get into the Guild. And of course, keep an eye on Duncan's riskier lifestyle.

Everything hadn't worked out. He'd gotten into the Guild, but only under an assumed name. Using the shard had gotten him in but had also drawn a lot of attention because of the work itself and the anvil test. If he had stayed in the Reach like Duncan wanted, none of this would have happened. Duncan would be fine. None of the people killed by the Valni would have died, all those Reachers. Haltim wouldn't have died. Master Jaste would still be alive. All dead because of his dream, his goal.

Amder wouldn't be back, and that High Priest of his, Bracin would still be in power, but really, who cared? The man was evil, and corrupt, but he had been far away in Ture. Yes, based on what he knew, the High Priest had wanted to kill him and Duncan, but that had only been forced to happen after he'd told Haltim he was going to try for the Guild, regardless of what anyone thought.

His mood increasingly despondent, Will closed his eyes and leaned back against a smoother section of fallen rock. He'd moved it earlier to give himself something to lean on after leaning against the wall had made him feel strange. A cold, sad feeling. If despair could be made a thing, that's what that wall felt like. Despair. Will sat and waited and slowly, sleep claimed him in the dark.

***

Vin swallowed again, trying to force down the fear once more. At least back in that cavern, the one with the waterfall, he hadn't felt so overwhelmed. With the surrounding lights, it was almost like being outside. Almost. He could half pretend he was traveling in a canyon on a trader's caravan, stopping for a rest and bath at a natural oasis. It had been a welcome respite, even if he knew it wasn't a real one.

Now, heading deeper still and into winding tunnels, Vin could feel the fear again. All that rock above him, all that pressure. One earthshake, and they would all be buried, forgotten and lost, forever. No one would come looking for them. Not even the Gorom. They might celebrate the death of the cursed humans. At least if they were all like this Speaker-to-the-sky person.

Vin could feel his muscle get tighter and more on edge with every step. Going deeper still into this black, deadly world was not anything he wanted. *I should be sitting in a tavern in Ture, keeping an eye on the Forgemaster. Or just riding along with a merchant, watching for bandits. Not here, not doing this.* But he was here.

So, he'd keep a hand on his dagger, and hope beyond hope that each step got him closer to getting out of this place. He'd managed to keep things together so far, though it had been close at times. Truthfully, the karkin fight had been the only other time he'd not been fighting the stress. He knew fighting, even if fighting a swarm of plate sized bugs, wasn't something he normally did.

He tried every trick he knew to keep his mind off of the truth of the situation he was in, but there wasn't much he could do. Vin liked his companions, mostly. He respected Regin, though knew the man was playing with a forge fire hotter than he had ever worked by having an interest in Myriam. Myriam was a great young woman; he'd meant what he said about her. Smart, strong, talented, Myriam was, to his mind, everything he'd ever want in a daughter. If he'd ever had one.

He liked William as well, though the lad was far too prone to self-doubt and worry about how his actions would affect those around him. Being considerate isn't a bad thing, but it can paralyze a leader, and William Reis was a leader now, even if he didn't want to be. He would grow into it.

He wasn't even sure why they were on this mission. Vin knew that this Duncan person was all the family the Forgemaster had, but by all accounts, Duncan was dead, maybe. His body was being used by something, some scourge of the Blood God, but Duncan himself was dead. If Vin had known that this was the way things were going to go, he would have argued forcefully against this plan of action. His thoughts at the time had mostly been to let the lad blow off this grief and worry by doing this, and then get back to his real purpose.

He still wasn't sure how he had got tangled up in all this. He knew Amder was involved, and he'd been swept along. He wasn't much for religion, and this whole thing was not changing his mind. *Next time someone shows up with a glowing hammer and orders you around, maybe say no.*

He took his steps carefully, watching with amusement and concern as Regin purposefully seemed to glance at Myriam often. Vin wondered if he should say something to her about this. Love triangles always ended in pain, anger, and usually violence, something that he didn't want for any of them.

When we stop next, I'll see if I can say something to her.

***

Myriam stopped as the Gorom held up his hand. They had been walking for a good while, and they were far lower than they had been. She could feel it in the air. It was thick, heavy, and old. She wished they were back at the Falls. That was something she'd never seen before and wanted to explore it more. She could imagine the colors in her head, and she wondered if maybe she could replicate it in jewelry? A hair mesh maybe? Ornamental golden lace decorated with gem shards. Usually the shards were in a pattern, like a mosaic. Last time she'd paid attention to them, the rage had been flowers and vines.

But an iridescent pattern done only in blue, yellow, green and red? Could she find gem shards that would glow the right way? Her mind wandered as they waited.

"We are here, at the start." Speaker-to-the-sky said, his voice lowered. "From now on, we move quickly and quietly."

Myriam wondered if the Gorom thought they were being loud before. To her, everything seemed so quiet at times she wanted to say something to break it up. Speaker-to-the-sky would most likely fall over dead from annoyance if she broke into a drinking song from her father's inn.

"Is William close?" Regin asked from behind her, though she could feel him walking closer, finally stopping close by. She could smell him, and it wasn't an unpleasant smell. Like leather and polished steel. Strong. Safe.

"Yes. He is not too far down the passage." Speaker-to-the-sky lowered his head and touched a patch of bare stone for a moment before raising his head again. "But be warned, we are about to enter a Drendel tunnel. Things will be different there. Your Forgemaster is currently not awake. I do not know if he's asleep or unconscious."

"Different? How?" Regin asked before Myriam could get the words out.

"Drendel tunnels draw things. And dark feelings. Things we don't have names for, as the Namer-of-the-darkness refuses to come here." The Gorom waved his hand. "None of that matters. We will gather your Forgemaster, head back here, and continue on our way."

"We will be under the ocean, though?" Vin asked, his voice barely above a whisper.

"Yes. Not far under. We believe the folly goes all the way under, though no Gorom has ever made it the entire way. It is madness to even be this close to it. I will only be the fifth Gorom ever to travel, even part of the Folly." Speaker-to-the-Sky said, looking into the darkness and giving a perceptible shudder. "This is not something I want to be." He finally said. "Follow."

Chapter 26.

Will walked the streets of the Reach. The sun was shining, and a wind was blowing down the eastern slopes, and had cleared out any smoke and soot from the smelters. He loved it here. From the older parts of town with the cobble streets and glowstones, to the newer sections with the merchant stalls and high peaked roofs of the houses. His stomach rumbled as he moved. The Golden Chisel was close. He'd get a meat pie, maybe two. Then wash it down with a cold flagon of water. No ale for him.

He wondered if Duncan would be back soon. He'd gone scaving that morning, looking for a ring, or something he could sell or trade for a ring. William knew he was going to propose to his girl, the innkeeper's daughter, Faraw. He'd finally settled down some after that whole blood curse business had been solved. William wondered if Myriam was even up yet. She was about to pop, and so he let her sleep. Twins Haltim said it would be. Soon the Reis home would be full of screaming children and life. He wanted that, badly.

Will turned the corner and paused. There was a body lying on the ground. That wasn't normal. Will rushed to the body and jerked back. Falkirk Darrew! How could he be dead? Will had only seen him this morning. He'd been well, and smoking a pipe outside his house as Will had left his own home. And the wounds! The man had been torn into. Some kind of wild animal, maybe? How would a wild animal get into the Reach? Why hadn't the guards caught it?

Will stood and blinked. When had it gotten so dark? The light was dimming and dimming fast. The cool wind shifted, and brought a fetid smell, one that reeked of death and rot. Will ran towards his house. Something was very wrong. He had to make sure Myriam was alright. Fear gave his steps speed, and he sped towards his home. He passed more corpses, none strangers. Miners, smiths, merchants. All dead. All torn apart. Finally, he saw his home ahead. Myriam must be awake, there were lantern lights in a few windows.

A howling sound filled the air, as the wind grew stronger, and the sky grew even darker, if that was possible. Will was almost home when he stumbled over a corpse. An older man, armored and armed, he looked somewhat familiar to Will, but he couldn't place a name on him. His throat was torn out, his sword lay nearby, the man's hand still half grasping the grip.

Vin. Vin Tolin. Will hadn't seen him since the day Amder came back. What was he doing here? Will shook his head in confusion. No, he knew Vin well. He'd helped defend the Reach from the Valni... who ripped people apart. His fear grew. But that hadn't happened, the Valni had never attacked, had they?

Will shook his head as a pain grew in it. No, get home. Find Myriam. Hopefully Duncan would be back soon, right? The howling grew closer, the sound of thousands of throats making a sound that no human should be able to make.

Valni. A horde of Valni! It had to be. What had happened? The barrier should hold them back! A cold sweat broke out as Will stumbled the last steps to the house. Will tried the door, but it was locked.

"MYRIAM!" Will yelled. "MYRIAM! LET ME IN!" Will pounded the door with his fist, making the wood shake.

"MYRIAM!" He yelled once more, looking behind him. The sky was now pitch black towards the Mistlands. Darker than night, as if he was deep underground. The smell that came with the wind was even stronger now, and he fought back the urge to vomit. "PLEASE MYRIAM!" Will yelled as he pounded on the door one more time.

Will couldn't believe his relief when the door gave way this time, open as if it had never been locked. Will threw himself in and pushed the door closed, slamming the bar in place to lock it again. "Myriam, we have to bar the windows, hide. I don't know what happened, but the Valni are here, something failed at the barrier, I don't know…"

Will turned around and horror filled his soul. Myriam lay on the ground. Was his love dead? No, she still breathed, but standing over her was Duncan! Duncan… but not Duncan. Blood dripped from his hands, and a rictus grin crossed his face. There was a body behind Duncan, but he could see who it was.

"Duncan? What is going on? What happened?" Will's words spilled out as he pushed back the fear. This was wrong. This wasn't happening.

"Death comes. Blood comes. For the glory of Valnijz!" Duncan's words grew as he uttered them, and the very walls shook around them. The lanterns grew dim, as the light seemed to be drunk in by whatever Duncan had become.

"Dunc? Whose blood is that? What happened to Myriam?" Will moved as he spoke, creeping closer to his wife. *Please let her be ok. Please let her be alive.*

Duncan screamed, a sound that tore at his throat, a ragged sound. Duncan licked his lips, and then bit down, more blood dripping down, before kicking the corpse behind him. "Haltim, get up and say hello to our guest."

Haltim? Oh Amder. Not Haltim. The pain in his head grew again. Haltim had died back in the Temple of Amder, hadn't he? In the Heart's chamber. No, no... Haltim had been fine. He'd escaped the Temple with William. Right? William struggled to remember. As he tried to think, the ache in his head grew and was joined by a sharp pain on the side.

His attention snapped back as the body behind Duncan stirred. But it was dead! Dead! The corpse of Haltim stood bloody and pale. Haltim's head had been broken oddly. No skull should ever be in that shape.

"Valnijz wants you, William. He is triumphant. Amder is a failure, and all you have ever hoped for, all you have ever dreamed of, is a lie." Duncan leaned close, and Will could smell the scent of blood on him, rich red blood, the faint scent of iron. Will's mouth watered at the smell. *So hungry...*

"Will..." a weak sound came to William from Myriam's body. He fought back the sudden hunger the smell of blood was bringing to him. She was awake! Myriam's hand raised up slow and unsteady. A hand with blood flowing through it. She had so much. If he took some, would that be so bad? *Eat... tear... kill...*

"William.... Wake up." Her voice came again, weak, far away... so far away.

"Forgemaster Reis!" An unfamiliar voice came, strong. Vin's voice? But he was dead. William had seen his corpse right outside. Will grabbed his head as a new spike of pain came. What was going on?

"William. Wake up." Myriam's voice came again, but louder this time, and the room seemed to shiver, fade.

"You can hide William. But the Blood God will always be watching you. He will have you as he has me." Duncan spoke again and faded away. The room shook and faded into a red haze. A red haze of pain. A blackness crept along the edges, with a slight purple tinge.

"Wake up, you cursed human!" He knew that voice. Speaker-to-the-sky. William opened his eyes.

***

Duncan screamed in pain again, though he wasn't sure what good it was to do it. It wasn't even physical pain, but this horrible feeling of loss, sadness, and betrayal. And hovering just out of reach was Valnijz, nearly in ecstasy.

He had been with William, but in some horrible dream. He wasn't sure who everyone was in it, but he knew all of them were important to Will. He could still feel the echoes of Will's anger and hunger. The Blood God might not be able to get too close, but that didn't mean he was anywhere near powerless.

Duncan shuddered again, fighting back the despair that grew. He would not let this thing, a God or not, run him. He had faded out for a time, which was happening more often as of late, but when he forced himself to be more real, he had found Valnijz staring at him with a hungry smile. Duncan was sure if they had both been real, the creature would have eaten him, one bite at a time, keeping him alive as long as it could.

Thankfully, they both existed in this strange place now, and that wasn't possible. Duncan had considered himself somewhat safe as of late. Valnijz could bluster and scream, threaten and even scare him, but the dead God couldn't actually hurt him. Or so he thought. This had been proven very wrong.

All Duncan could remember was coming back here and now, to find the God with that look, and then Valnijz had done… something. Had he thrown something? Made a gesture? Duncan tried to remember, but it slipped away. But either way, the result was the same. He'd found himself inside a dream. William's dream.

He'd known it was his cousin instantly. Even if he hadn't seen him, the fact was he could feel it. The same comfortable strength, and the same stubborn outlook. It was William, all right. For a few minutes, Duncan had been happy. Happy for the first time in a long time. Even if Will couldn't see him, hear him, or even knew he was there, Duncan was with him. Home in the Reach.

For a tiny sliver of time, Duncan had forgotten everything. He was home. Then it all went bad. First the body of Falkirk. And it all came back. This wasn't a dream; it was a nightmare. Duncan could only watch at first in horror as Will's fear and despair grew. And only become more aware of the presence of Valnijz.

The fallen god was there too and was feasting on Will's terror. Duncan was powerless to do anything about it. He watched as the bodies piled up; he watched as Will ran home. He saw himself, or a version of himself, kill a woman that Will obviously cared for deeply. He saw the dead and mutilated corpse of Haltim, done at his own hand.

William had nearly broken in pain. And Duncan had nearly broken in sorrow. Thankfully, Will awoke, ending the experience. Duncan had screamed then. Screamed in loss, sadness, and deep pain. And through it all, Valnijz fed.

That was it. That was the reason. Duncan had been trying to figure it out. It wasn't Williams' pain; it was his as well. Valnijz was feeding off it. Growing stronger, more real.

"Clever man." Valnijz spoke, its form shifting.

It less and less often wore his face. More often than not, the Scaled one had a form that was all his. More animalistic, it tickled his memories. He'd seen something like it the day he'd been fully captured by Zalkiniv in the dungeons of the Temple. An… Axessed? Something like that.

"Yes, an Axessed. I should have kept them. Unswervingly loyal, deadly, and no desire to do anything but hunt and kill in my name." Valnijz stretched. "Your fears, and that Forgemaster, delicious."

"Why?" Duncan whispered. "Why do this? I am nothing. A shadow. Will doesn't…" Duncan trailed off. Of course, Will would come for him. Duncan wished he could stop him, but there was no way.

"Why? To feed. To grow. The time is close. I will free the boat, and we will travel to the south. I will be reborn. Fully reborn. You will die, of course, finally and forever." Valnijz smiled. "See, I'm giving you what you want! Am I not a merciful god?"

***

"You are a stone bound fool human." Speaker-to-the-sky said, glancing both ways down the tunnel for the fifth or sixth time since his friends had awoken him.

"What?" Will croaked the words out. Such dreams. Dark and wrong. Must be the head injury.

"You are a stone bound fool. This is not a good place for sleeping. Not that close to the walls." Speaker-to-the-sky pointed at the broken purple orb. "And doubly a fool for sleeping with that nearby."

"It's a broken light." Myriam said. Her fingers were trying to make some kind of sense of the injury on his head.

"It's not only a broken light. It's the broken light that also happens to be the egg of a Vinik." Speaker-to-the-sky again looked back and forth. "And Viniks are known to lair down near Drendel ruins and tunnels."

"Excuse me, what?" Regin said, rubbing his face.

Will was happy to see Regin. He was happy to see all of them. Even the annoying Gorom. He wasn't alone, and he would not die here. Not now.

"Viniks. Remember the karkin? Make it five times bigger, give it arms and the ability to use tools and weapons out of hard stone." The Gorom pointed at the orb. "And that's an egg."

Will had no idea what a karkin was, but wasn't about to ask, at least based on the looks passed around.

"You use eggs of these things as a light source?" Myriam asked, pushing too hard on a part of his skull that hurt, drawing a deep intake of breath from Will.

"Eggs that do not hatch. We raise the Viniks. Back above, in the holy cities. Viniks that are tamed and used for meat and milk. The Vinik down here still have their arms. And they are feral. And they hate Gorom. And that broken egg is like a beacon, or will be if any sense it." Speaker-to-the-sky reached out a hand and tried to help pull William upright.

"Let me get this right. You take giant bug things, that obviously sound kind of smart, take their eggs, milk them, remove their arms, and use them like what, cattle?" Regin spoke slowly.

Will could see the wheels turning. Regin was both disgusted and angry. Will had a hard time even grasping what was being said, but if he had heard this right, he joined in Regin's displeasure. But it was so hard to think with this pain.

"Yes. They are Vinik. We are Gorom. It is the way. Come, we must leave here. And leave that broken one." Speaker-to-the-sky pointed down the passage to the left. "Back the way we came."

Will took the offering of hands from Myriam and Regin. Standing did not make him feel any better, however, and he nearly threw up what little water he had ingested. A powerful wave of nausea came quickly, and he had to bend over, taking deep breaths.

"William, you alright?" Regin leaned down. "Can you walk?"

"Sounds like I better." Will answered. "Remind me to never come here again, will you?"

"I don't think that will be a problem for any of us." Regin held out an arm for William to steady himself on. "We should get out of whatever danger we are in."

Chapter 27.

Will still felt weak, but he was upright. As bad as he felt, he was glad to not be alone. He rarely minded being by himself, but an unknown amount of time sitting in the dark by himself wasn't something he cared to repeat. Adding injury and the ever-present fear that he was going to die there, he was glad to see others. *And I never ever will sleep in a Drendel tunnel again.* The memories of the dream had already started to fade, but even thinking about it made his guts twist.

"How are all of you? You all seem in good health." His eyes darted over his companions. "And wearing different clothes."

"We all took a bath." Regin answered with a smile. "We wanted to be presentable to the Forgemaster, after all. You able to stand on your own?" Regin removed his arm as Will nodded. Carefully nodded.

"A bath?" Will could not believe his ears. A bath? Really?

"What your good friend Regin here is leaving out is that we were attacked by an enormous swarm of bug things, Karkin, according to Speaker-to-the-sky. During the fight, we had to crush and break hundreds of the things, each the size of a large plate. We got... bug innards all over us." Myriam gave William a supporting arm to help him as they moved up the tunnel.

"That sounds... disgusting." Will said as he fought another bit of dizziness. "I hate to be a beggar, but do any of you have anything I can eat? I think part of the problem is that I'm hungry, starving."

"Here." Regin handed William a travel ration bar. "Sorry we ate as we walked."

Will took a bite and felt his mouth water nearly instantly. "So good." Will mumbled as he chewed. "Bug parts all over does sound gross, but you couldn't have come to get me first?"

"Speaker-to-the-sky explained. The smell would attract things. He just said dark and dangerous things." Regin kept his voice low. "He also said we should be silent."

As the five of them moved back up the tunnel, Speaker-to-the-sky would often pause as if trying to sense something. "We must hurry. I cannot delve here. I do not know what if anything is coming." The Gorom took out a mace, sized for him and stamped his foot.

"Delve?" Will asked, taking another bite. He felt better already. Maybe most of his weakness wasn't because of his head, it was because he was hungry.

"Gorom thing, a sensing they have." Regin said in low tones.

"Why can't you delve here? And why did you say I was foolish?" Will asked. He carefully let go of Myriam, waving her off. *And I don't have to smell her on me.* Being around her only reminded him of what he had lost, and the dream. A faint image sprung into his mind of Myriam lying on the floor, bloody and injured.

"I cannot delve against Drendel made walls! It must be stone, real natural stone. As for being foolish, you slept in a Drendel tunnel. That is bad." Speaker-to-the-sky pointed his mace at Will. "You are lucky that you did not go mad. This place plays with your feelings, your mind."

Will wondered if that was why he'd had such an evil dream. This place had done it. But it had been so real, so much more than a simple dream. He took his last bite of ration bar and chased it down with warmish old water. "I'll need more water soon."

"Oh here. We filled one up for you at the falls." Vin answered as he handed over a bulging full waterskin.

Will took it but almost dropped it as his fingers touched the sides. Cold! He unstopped the skin to take a drink and paused. Was the water glowing?

"Yes, it glows." Regin remarked, noticing Will's surprise.

"Seems the four of you had some fun times, while I sat in the dark alone." Will snorted. He could see Regin about to explain and held up a hand. "No need to explain. I wish I had been there myself. But thank you. Thank you all for finding me."

"No need to thank us, William. You're the Forgemaster of Amder. We are duty bound to help and protect you. And you are our friend." Regin gave William a slight bow.

"Well, thank goodness for that… I think." Will tried to smile, but some of the pain returned. Still, he felt much better after eating something. He took a sip of the waterskin and enjoyed the cold refreshing water a great deal, even though to him it had an odd aftertaste. Not bad, different.

"You know, in times like this, there is one thing I crave." Will smiled and looked at Regin. "I think I could use some klah."

"Oh, Amder above, not klah." Regin laughed as he walked. "Though who could guess what klah would draw in a place like this."

"I'd love some klah." Myriam added. "As long as we have my mustard chicken with it, add some flavor."

"Flavor? More like kill my taste buds." Will gave a small chuckle at the memories. The brief laugh brought pain, though. Both physical from his side, and in his heart. *Not the time for that.* Will pushed those feeling away.

"You ever had her mustard chicken, Regin? I mean, you're a food person. Trust me, if you eat that, you'll not want to eat anything for days afterwards." Will was feeling better. Food, water, and company were improving his mood and his body.

"I'd be happy with sunshine and fresh air." Vin joined in. "Though I do like klah."

Will was about to answer when Speaker-to-the-sky held up a hand, stopping them all. "Cursed humans. Be silent!" the Gorom whispered, his voice low. "We are in Makese Folly and yet you all prattle and joke as if you were going to a market fair."

Will felt his irritation with this Gorom rise. He already was more than uncomfortable with the Gorom, his acerbic attitude, his constant belittling of him and his friends, and even his race. Now, add in the new information about these Vinik, his opinion of Speaker-to-the-sky fell even more.

"Speaker, can you for once stop being a headache?" Will spat the words out with more venom than intended, his frustrations boiling out with them. "While I appreciate the guide, your attitude is horrible. You are rude, abrasive, and frankly insulting to the god I follow and my fellow travelers." Will felt better after he said the words but wondered if he had pushed things too far.

Regin and Myriam gave him surprised looks, and even Vin seemed a bit surprised. But the Gorom himself gave Will the greatest pause. Speaker-to-the-sky stood there, mace gripped tight and trembling. Was he about to attack?

"Vinik." Speaker-to-the-sky whispered, before the world roared.

***

Zalkiniv opened his eyes for the first time in nearly a day. He'd been forced to retreat into old techniques to slow down this body. It had been days now, nearly a week without water. Food as well. The power of the blood was low, and he was still becalmed here. Curse the goddess.

He had hoped a way out of this would present itself. Or that the sea goddess would take her eye off of him and he could finish his journey. She had already wisely gotten her people, the so-called Saltmisstresses to leave him. He had hoped they'd come back to check, and he'd find a way to get aboard their ship. He'd spent half a day planning how to draw the best screams from them.

The only thing that had been strange was the dreams. Zalkiniv never dreamed, at least he hadn't in several centuries. He'd used blood workings for years to provide himself with rest, and to free himself from the needs of dreaming. With the power so low now, however, he'd given up those workings, and the dreams had come back.

Most had been inconsequential. But one, one had awoken him, shaken. He'd been standing on a stone, red sandstone, with the sky full of the blood mist. He knew the spot; it was where he had almost died. Where he had been betrayed. Where the Scaled One had turned his back on his greatest servant.

But he was not alone. Across the narrow valley, there stood an altar. On that altar was the body of Duncan Reis, the very body he wore now. But worse, standing on the unmoving form, stood Valnijz. Scaled, blood covered, hungry.

The Blood God watched him, and to his surprise, gave a long blink, and then smiled. Just smiled. That was bad enough, but what scared Zalkiniv the most was the eyes. There was no madness in them. No hint of the insanity that tore through his former master. Zalkiniv had always known that the blood god was crazy. Unstable. It had made it him easier to predict. But a sane Blood God?

As he had watched, the blood god faded away and seemed to melt into the corpse of Duncan, grinning the entire time. Zalkiniv had awoken, trembling. *The Blood God is dead. Dead and gone. I have the power now. I have the control!*

Now, in the gray filtered light of dawn through the ever-present fog, Zalkiniv worried. In truth, he was not totally sure what had happened to Valnijz that night. It had been chaos. The night sky lighting up, the sound of hammers, the song of the Valni in his head, trying to keep concentration to push them deeper into the Amderite lands.

And then, the dagger, that same black iron dagger, had torn through his back, into his neck, and ended his life. Or at least had ended that life. That dagger. His eyes fell on the dagger again. A faint sheen of salt clung to it still as it sat embedded in the railing's wood. Deeply embedded. Almost part of the ship now.

The thought rolled around in his head as an idea came. Hesitancy made him think. If he tried and failed, he'd lose even more of the power. There wasn't much left that he could feel, so this would be a move of desperation. But what choice did he have? Waste away here, trapped by fog and water? He could swim, but with the fog, he knew the ocean goddess would turn him around, keep him swimming until this body gave up and drowned.

He did not have a choice. He licked his salt covered lips and bit down, hard. Blood, thick, and red came forth, but not in the quantity he had hoped for. He was going to be very weak when this was over, very weak indeed. He raised one wrist, and again, bit down, tearing into a major blood flow. Blood came then, though his lack of water was apparent. Still, it was enough. He hoped.

He fought back the weakness, and using the blood, pushed the boat forward, using the dagger as a focus. Normally, working on something like the boat was near impossible. But the dagger being nearly joined to the craft acted as a conduit. A path for the power to flow. He could feel the resistance at first, like pushing on a thin membrane inside a slave's body. He built the pressure, pushing harder and harder. And with a rush, the resistance melted away, and the boat lurched forward.

Slowly at first, and then faster and faster as Zalkiniv pushed every ounce of power he could summon into the dagger, and then into the boat. He could feel the wind as his craft moved, pushing through the fog, cutting through the trap he had been stuck in for days.

He was free. He would hunt and heal and continue with his plan. He was Zalkiniv, and he would triumph.

Chapter 28.

The tunnel exploded into echoing chaos as a huge section of the roof collapsed in front of Will and his companions. What crawled out both horrified and fascinated William. Creatures like the Gorom had described climbed over the fallen rocks, rushing towards him and his friends.

Each the size of a sheep with multi jointed legs, they looked like a garden pest write huge. Every head was covered by a single massive shell that covered most of the body. Most glowed a light purple in the orb the Gorom carried. But a few shone with bright red or blue markings. Those that had the markings seemed to hold back some, almost as if they were directing the others.

The Vinik did have arms he could see as well. *So, Speaker-to-the-sky was right.* And that turned his stomach. Longer than their legs, and coming from under the same shell, was a set of arms. And every single one of the creatures was carrying something in those arms.

The unmarked ones carried either what looked like a stone club, or stranger, still a short, curved spear. The ones with the markings carried something they were spinning. Will had no idea what they were, but didn't want to find out. His companions seemed to feel the same way, as all of them, even the Gorom moved back as the creatures swarmed in and blocked the tunnel.

"What do we do?!?" Will yelled. The creatures were making a horrible noise, a near deafening sound of buzzes and whistles, and the thunks as stone mallets hit walls and floors in a show of what, force?

"We fight or we die." Speaker-to-the-sky turned towards them, his face strangely calm. "They are Vinik. They are animals."

"They don't look like animals to me." Regin leaned close to William as he spoke, his voice only barely able to be heard over the tumult.

Will nodded. These weren't dumb animals, they were something… else. He tried to say something more, when with a rush, the Vinik moved forward as one. The fight was upon them. Will found himself trying to move away from one of the things as it swung a large stone mallet, barely missing him. Every movement brought either pain or nausea to Will, and he struggled to keep his feet. *I should not be doing this.*

His companions were faring better, though. Regin was swinging his hammer in tight blows, more knocking the Vinik back than killing them. Will didn't know what fighting the other bug things had been like, but he could tell the shells on these were thick. Heavy. *Hard to break then.*

He spared a glance at his other friends. Myriam was doing the same as Regin, though a few blows from her had crushed the legs of two of the creatures. It didn't seem to stop the Vinik, as they pushed forward, driving Myriam backward and down the tunnel.

Vin didn't seem to have any qualms about killing the things however, and had two of the creatures dead, the Vinik died curled up, reminding Will of nothing more than a dead spider. Vin was moving with practiced and careful steps, dodging and weaving back and forth, his long dagger stabbing forth, trying to find cracks in the sections of shell that covered the things. He was good at it, and a blow of his slid home into the arm joint of another creature, bringing forth a hissing whine that pierced Will's ears.

Speaker-to-the-sky also seemed to have no reservations to killing the bugs, as his mace swung forth repeatedly, cracking hard against shells, bringing forth loud reverberations in the tunnel. Speaker-to-the-sky took a blow to the side that seemed to make the Gorom stumble and fall for a moment, and Will, even though he had grown to dislike the fellow, immediately rushed to take control.

"Fall back!" Will called out, trying to keep his bearings. The battlefield was utter insanity. Glowing purple and shiny surfaces reflecting what little light there was, a crash of sound and the smash of weapons on stone, shell, and who knew what else. Will opened his mouth to yell his order again, when something struck his chest and he went flying backwards.

He had the mind to cradle his already injured head in his arms, but even still he landed hard, and it took him a long second to force his eyes to focus as an avalanche of nausea hit him. *What hit me?* The answer to that came flying past him again, as he realized the Vinik with the markings were using slings. *It must have hit my breastplate. Thank you, Amder!*

Will struggled to his feet, and turned to yell once more, when he saw it. Vin was striking again, stabbing forward, when one boot got caught up in a dead Vinik. He lurched forward, and in that second, the attacking creature swung down with a massive stone hammer.

Vin struggled to free his boot, and he threw himself down, trying to avoid the blow. The first blow he managed to avoid, mostly, though it grazed his hand holding the dagger, which clattered to the floor. Will rushed towards him, only for Vin to shake his head and stop him. Will watched the weapon fall once more and tried to warn Vin. He wanted to say something, anything, but it was too late. The hammer fell, and Vin fell with it, a wet spray splashing the wall, glistening in the dim light. Vin Tolin, Captain Vin Tolin, was dead.

Will threw his hammer down. "Drop your weapons! We surrender!" Regin and Myriam, both desperately trying not to get hit, looked at him in shock, but did as he said. Only then did they realize that Vin was down.

"Oh Amder!" Myriam tried to move to the fallen man, only to be blocked by a Vinik, its arms raised high, ready to stab her with two spears.

Regin lowered his head, shaking it slowly, with his face set in a hard line. Will wanted to say something, anything. Vin was dead. *One more death on my head.*

A yell brought his attention away from that thought as Speaker-to-the-sky was struck again and stumbled. "CURSED HUMANS! YOU FIGHT OR WE DIE!" the Gorom screamed and charged at a nearby Vinik. Much to Will's surprise, a Vinik with a single blue marking took a small bottle from under its shell and took a drink. Or at least put it in its mouth, and then without warning spit a fine spray of liquid over the crazed Gorom. The effect was dramatic, and to Will at least, unnerving. As the spray settled over Speaker-to-the-sky, a swarm of some sort of spiders erupted from the mass of Vinik, covering the Gorom.

Speaker-to-the-sky attempted to roll around to dislodge the creatures, but soon was wrapped up in some sort of web, covered from head to toe with pale green glowing strands from the tiny creatures. They only stopped once he was fully entombed, minus a bare patch where he could breathe through his nose. *They aren't killing him. They aren't killing us now. Why?*

Will locked eyes with a pale and bloody Myriam, giving her a nod. She still stood by the fallen form of Vin, breathing heavily and very pale, as evidenced by the way her skin glowed in the faint light. Regin appeared for all the world as nervous as Will was. His face was locked onto the entombed Gorom, almost slack jawed.

Will stood there, unarmed, as the Vinik surrounded him and his friends. He didn't have a choice but to surrender. They weren't animals, and regardless of what Speaker-to-the-sky said, there was no way to fight out of this, especially not now, after Vin had fallen.

The Vinik said nothing, but one took up the wrapped-up form of the Gorom and the rest herded Will, Regin and Myriam into a line and began pushing them down the tunnel. Regin attempted to take the body of Vin, but the Vinik would not let him approach it. Will pointed to the fallen body and then to himself and his friends, but the silent Vinik either didn't understand or did not care. Will glanced back at Vin's fading outline and said a silent prayer to Amder, and walked away. Wishing that the man was going to be buried under the sky, and not in this stone prison, he hated so much. He saw one of the Vinik thing gather up their weapons as well, placing them in a bag. *At least they are bringing those, but why?*

The Vinik made a quick pace, and more than once Will found himself gasping for air. His many bumps and bruises ached and more than once, he had waves of dizziness and weakness come over him. He forced himself to stay upright, though. He had no idea what would happen to him if he fell with these things here. Would they kill him? Would they wrap him up like they had with Speaker-to-the-sky? Neither was anything he wanted to be involved in at all.

They marched and kept eyes on each other. Will could tell both Myriam and Regin were exhausted as well now, but their captors didn't slow. At least they had more light. Four of the Vinik had after they had begun walking had erupted suddenly into a blue-white glow. Far brighter than the purple orbs they had been with for so long. Will, in particular, had nearly fallen three times, as his eyes had a hard time adjusting to the new radiance.

Once his eyes could see, Will could make out details that before had gone unnoticed. The features on the Vinik showed some sort of hierarchy, he was sure of it. The things with stripes or patterns in other colors were larger, and the smaller and uncolored Vinik always stayed out of their way. He could also tell that the walls, which he had assumed were black, were in fact a swirled mottled pattern of black, dark blue and red. The craftsman in him found the substance fascinating, though it still gave him a feeling of despair and sadness to look upon it.

As for the Gorom, he could see the sometimes-struggling form of their former guide being carried by one of the larger Viniks. The creature didn't seem to be very careful with his package, as more than once the Gorom was poked by a weapon of a smaller Vinik or bumped against a bit of low hanging stone. Each of these events brought forth a struggle from the bound form and a muffled sound, but it soon ended.

Topping a small pile of fallen rock, Will could see a side passage. This new tunnel was made of all rock, unlike this one. Straight and wide, Will felt a little less closed in, but he had no idea where they were being taken. He hoped there was a way out of this, but his doubts grew with each step.

***

Regin tried very hard to ignore the small rock that had in the fight got into his boot. Every step the blood cursed thing jabbed the underside of his right foot. He wished they would stop so he could get it out, but the Vinik didn't seem to be even pausing. *Not like they wear boots anyway, so they wouldn't understand.*

He already missed Vin. Captain Tolin had been a source of experience, and a steady hand. Regin knew how hard this underground passage had been on the man, and to die here? He'd wanted to take the body, and not leave it to its fate, but these bug things, these Vinik had made it very clear that would not happen.

He had been stunned when Will had thrown down his hammer and surrendered. Then he had seen the body and understood the Forgemaster's reasons. Their best fighter was gone, and they were surrounded. Amder would be no help. Will still could not talk to the God since they entered this black pit. *I hope the Forgemaster made the right choice; I would rather go down fighting than some other fate.*

The rock made keeping his mind off Myriam easier. She walked in front of him, and he could not help but wonder if this was the last time he would see her alive. He prayed and hoped that would not be the case, but who knew what they were walking into.

At least he didn't have to listen to the Gorom anymore. He hated spiders, always had, and when he'd seen them swarm over Speaker-to-the-sky, he had felt himself nearly bolt and run. All those little legs crawling over him, the feeling of being bound like a fly. What do spiders do with flies? He twitched again, trying to think of something else. He still had a small knife, it had been sheathed in the fight, and the Vinik hadn't made him remove it. *If it comes down to spiders or the knife, I will take the knife.*

***

"Be calm. You are not fated to die here." The voice came back to Myriam as they walked away from the site of the battle. She shook her head. Not what she needed, imaginary voices.

"I am not imaginary. I just cannot do much, yet." The voice had the same higher pitched sound, as if it were tiny. *"That will change. It must change. But that's not why I am speaking to you now. I know you are scared; you will not die here."*

Could have fooled me. Myriam thought back to the voice. Vin's dead. Speaker-to-the-sky is trussed up like a feast day main course. We have no weapons, William is injured, and Regin... Myriam ignored the flush of worry she felt when thinking his name. Regin isn't much better.

"I am sorry Captain Tolin has passed. I will try when I can to help... but that doesn't matter now. Be calm. Not all is at it seems." The voice faded out, leaving her feeling confused and alone. It's probably from being in the dark so much. *I hate this place. I hate it, I hate it, I hate it.*

At least they were out of those Drendel tunnels. She had noticed how much they seemed to fascinate Will, but to her, they made her sad. Sorrow and a weariness. Like the slow fading of a campfire on a wintry day outside. Here the walls were stone, but not a cave. Obviously made by someone or something, and the Vinik seemed the most obvious answer. They were even patterned after the Drendel passages. The large interlocking squares that covered the walls, like the ones before. Though made of simple stone.

Her thoughts were interrupted by a change in the Vinik. The fast walk they had been in accelerated into a run. She could hear William taking deep breaths. She could imagine all his bumps and bruises were causing him a great deal of pain. She was more concerned about his head. That lump was a serious one, and with that dizziness he'd had more than once, it worried her.

A stable hand in her father's inn and gotten kicked in the head by a warhorse once when she was little. The man had never been the same, and the first symptom had been the same bouts of dizziness and nausea. Unable to sleep, he'd become more and more delirious and finally vanished. He'd wandered off one day and been found three days later, drowned in a small pond.

Her remembrance ended as the Vinik stopped suddenly. The tunnel they were in had ended. Ended in a massive, perfectly square room. Larger than any room in the Guild she'd seen in her short time, and larger by far than the inn she'd grown up at. And the room was full. Full of Vinik. And suspended from the roof, held up with thick cords of who knew what, was the largest Vinik she'd seen yet.

Larger than eight or nine draft horses, this Vinik had the same bone white color underneath. But unlike the ones with blue, or red, or even yellow slashes of color on them, this Vinik was covered with a swirling ornate pattern of gold and silver. Or goldlace and silverlace. Her smith's eye knew the stuff when she saw it.

Her surprise only grew when, in a hollow sort of windy voice, the Vinik spoke.

"Surfacers. It has been many years since I have spoken to your kind. I believe you say, a pleasure to meet you?" The Vinik waved one of its enormous arms. "I am sorry for your loss. It is hard to control them when they are that far away."

Chapter 29.

Will didn't know what to say. *A talking Vinik?* Speaker-to-the-sky had been more wrong than ever. The Vinik were not animals. They were a people, a race. He thought about the egg he'd broken, and a sour feeling settled in his stomach. What had the Gorom done to them? What had HE done to them?

"I must ask you, why are you here? And why with one of the Vzzzderrrrttsskilk?" the huge Viniks voice changed as it motioned to the still bound Gorom.

Will could see both Myriam and Regin turn to him, letting him take the lead. *One thing I hate about being the Forgemaster.* "We did not mean to. I accidentally made a hole and fell into the tunnel; they came to find me. You killed my friend, Captain Vin Tolin."

"The word is apologize, correct? It has been many years, a long many years, since I last spoke your tongue. The younger ones are harder to control when distant, and since you were with one of the Vzzzderrrrttsskilk the bloodlust took them. If it had only been you surface people, you humans, they would have just brought you to me." The talking Vinik paused and shook its long limbs. "But why are you underground at all? Your kind doesn't live here. You scratch the surface, looking for metals and leavings. You crawl around the skin of the world."

A lump formed in Will's throat for a moment that he swallowed away. "We were here because the Gorom were guiding us across the mountains. We are traveling for reasons of our own, and this was the fastest way. There to a boat to cross the sea, then to the southern lands."

"The Vzzzderrrrttsskilk were letting you cross? And even guiding you? Who are you? They do not let anyone do this." The leader Vinik, reared up in its strange harness, before settling back down.

Regin shrugged at Will, and Myriam had a strange look of both fear and wonder on her face. Will looked back at the talking one. "I am William Reis, Forgemaster of Amder."

"Amder. I have heard this name. Amder. One of the gods-that-came." The Vinik reached down and poked the form of Speaker-to-the-sky who writhed again in response.

"You others. Your gods. We want nothing to do with them ever again." The talking Vinik pulled its clawed appendage away from the Gorom. "We made that mistake once."

"I am sorry I do not know what you mean?" Will didn't know why the Vinik was talking to them, but talking was better than spiders, or worse. And he could imagine a lot worse than this.

"I am not surprised. The Vzzzderrrrttsskilk hid their shame from everyone, including themselves." The huge Vinik let its arms hang loose. "What do you know of us?"

"Nothing. Only what Speaker-to-the-sky told us. That you were animals they raised for the light orbs and milk." Will grimaced, thinking about milk from these things, then felt a flush of shame. But would they even understand the grimace?

"Speaker-to-the-sky? Ah, so the Vzzzderrrrttsskilk still use the ways we taught them. Sad. We are the Grvvestitidel. Once we were alone. We were the first. The surface held plants and animals, but we did not live there. We lived here, and the world was our home. There were untold numbers of us then. But your gods came. We argued among ourselves. Should we welcome the new beings? Or try to stop the new ones. We tried to stop it, as we knew then more than we know now. We knew it would end our world. We failed." The Vinik stopped for a moment, before continuing.

"We hid from all at first. Hid and watched. Most of you lived on the skin, the shell. We thought this was fine. You were welcome to it. But one group, the Vzzzderrrrttsskilk, were led underground by their god. We did not know what to do. There were some who wanted to kill them all, wipe them out. But they had failed with the gods, and lost power. There were others who wanted to help, establish ties. In the end the helpers won the argument, and they reached out to the newcomers." The Vinik around the talking one who had been totally still at this point slammed weapons on the ground if they had one, and if they didn't, they slammed legs or what passed for arms.

"We took them in. They were new. We gave them an order, a structure. We gave them the names of duty, we showed them how to live here. In time, we grew to think of them as... protected ones. Friends. But they were not us. They were not Grvvestitidel. One of them convinced the others to turn on us. We had trusted them, and they came and destroyed our homes, broke our order. Stole our young and debased them, turning them into no more than lights for their homes and tunnels. Later, even more horrible things. They captured us, broke the bonds and turned entire generations of us into nothing more than things to feed off of. We were the first, but we were betrayed." The Viniks' voice grew stronger as it spoke, until by the end the sound reverberated around the stone.

"But even then, the Vzzzderrrrttsskilk were ashamed. They forgot. They erased all knowledge of what they had done. They kept the order we gave them but forgot the reasons. They convinced themselves that we were nothing more than beasts and treated us as such. They drove us down, deeper and deeper still. They made up stories about what we had to leave behind. Forgetting the truth." The large Vinik fell into silence, a silence that spread around the room as all the Vinik stopped moving.

It was an uneasy feeling that permeated the room then. Sorrow, despair, worry. "YOU'RE THE DRENDEL!" Will shouted. The idea was insane, but it fit. They were the first, the feeling... was the same feeling he got from the walls. The Vinik were the Drendel. Regin made a hissing noise and Will realized he had yelled out his realization.

"Yes." The large Vinik answered.

Did Will detect a trace of humor in that answer? It was so hard to tell with these things.

"But we thought the Drendel were gone. Vanished." Regin spoke up.

"And who told you that? The Vzzzderrrrttsskilk did. They hid the truth from themselves, and then from everyone else. In some trace of shame, they made us into something more, and spoke of us with reverence, at the same time torturing the remnants of those who had come first. We learned to hate them. It is why it was so hard to stop them when they saw you. We only wanted the Vzzzderrrrttsskilk not you all." The gigantic creature raised up again, the gold and Silverlace patterns glowing brighter.

"I am one of the last who remember. You have done us no harm. You fought to defend yourselves. You are no enemy of the Grvvestitidel." The talking Vinik poked the form of Speaker-to-the-sky "But this, this deserves to be fed to the grubs."

Will had a hard time taking all this in. These bug things were the mighty Drendel? The lost people? Myriam shrugged at him but had that faraway look on her face that she often did these days. Regin, on the other had seemed as shocked as Will felt. It was hard to face the fact that a great mystery had been solved, but you didn't much like the answer.

"What happens now?" Myriam asked. Will watched as she stepped forward, crossing her arms. "What will become of us?"

The large Vinik made a long buzzing sound, and rubbed two legs together, reminding Will of a giant cricket. But the sound this one made nearly made him grab his ears. Loud and sour note that made his bones ache.

As the sound faded, the large Vinik spoke again. "We will take you to the end of the tunnel, the far end. We will get you there faster than you could go with the Vzzzderrrrttsskilk."

"What is to stop you from attacking us?" Myriam asked, as Will winced. She could use a bit of diplomacy.

"We could end your soft skinned lives right now. But we have no hate for you. I will also only send one, one, Jusszeritick. It will not rebel at my commands." As the Vinik spoke, a large example of its kind appeared, this one having a red, a blue, and a silver slash of color on its shell. "You will cling to it like the dust of the world, and it will take you to the way out."

"And we return your weapons." The gold swirled Vinik, or Drendel, or whatever that G word was they called themselves, gave a complicated whistle and a lone creature appeared, upending a bag, their weapons clattering to the floor, except for his which made its normal low moaning tone as it struck the rock. Even the Gorom's weapons were there. Will picked up his hammer again, thankful for its smooth and solid weight in his hand. Regin and Myriam picked up their weapons as well. Will found himself almost happy that Vin's long dagger had been left behind. He wasn't sure how he would have reacted by seeing it clattering to the ground with the others.

Will and his friends exchanged glances again, and Regin shrugged. Myriam nodded, but once again changed into a faraway look. *What was she thinking about?* Will, though, wasn't satisfied. His eyes fell on the bound form of Speaker-to-the-sky. He didn't like the Gorom. And all the stories they had heard today didn't make him like the Gorom any more. But he couldn't leave Speaker-to-the-sky like this.

"What about the Gorom?" Will asked. "We are not his friends, but he saved our lives, sort of."

"A Vzzzderrrrttsskilk saved you? I find that hard to accept." The Vinik blew a long low sound, its echoes bouncing around the walls. "He will be dealt with as all Vzzzderrrrttsskilk should be."

Will swallowed. It was now or never. He stepped forward. "You took the life of our friend. Please, take him near his kind and let him go."

The Vinik erupted then. Bangs and whistles, weapons drawn, and waved around the room. Will stepped back and got shoulder to shoulder with Regin. "I may have killed us, sorry about that." He said in Regin's ear, trying to make sure he was heard over the commotion.

"Well, wouldn't be the last time." Regin muttered, but shot Will a smile.

The large Vinik let loose a blast of sound, and the room calmed. "You would ask this? For the life of this Vzzzderrrrttsskilk? If we do this, he will come here and bring his kind. They will hunt us. Drive us from this home, deeper still. I will not run again from these betrayers."

Will sighed. He didn't want the Vinik to die, but he didn't want the Gorom to die either.

Regin whispered in his ear. "Glad you're the Forgemaster, have fun with that decision."

Will grimaced at Regin and looked over at Myriam for help. Now she had her eyes closed. No help there.

Chapter 30.

The stream of sound that filled her head was almost unintelligible. Myriam had been trying to take in everything they were learning when the large Vinik, or Drendel, had said something about trying to stop the gods and new creatures. At that moment, the voice that kept appearing in her head exploded. She wasn't sure, but it sounded angry, furious.

What is the matter? Who or what are you? I think I really need to know. Am I talking to myself? Her words echoed in her mind but didn't seem to even make the stream of grumbling, angry sounds pause at all. Answer me! Myriam put some effort into the thought this time.

The stream died down, then vanished. *"It's their fault. All of this. Is their fault."* The voice was the same timber as before, but the anger and annoyance were plain in it. *"If they hadn't interfered, everything would be fine, more or less."* Myriam could feel whatever patience she had wearing even more thin. What are you talking about?

"Not yet. Not now. Soon though. Soon. I promise." The voice paused for a moment. *"You should tell William Reis to force them to let the Gorom go. The sooner these things are wiped from existence, the better."* Myriam was shocked. The voice was nearly venomous. For her own mind, Myriam wasn't sure what the right choice was. These things, these giant insect things, were the Drendel! So many times, she had wondered what the Drendel were like. Every child of Palnor, and likely all over Alos, did at one time or another. And here they were. Still alive. Hiding, damaged, changed, but still around. Still surviving.

She wondered why she didn't see any of the handiwork though of the Drendel. Drendel steel was a marvel, and yet she saw none of it here. Myriam closed her eyes in thought. *"I wouldn't bother trying to figure it out. They should stay a lost dead race for what they have done."* The voice came again, bitter still.

She pushed it away. She half wondered if she should say something to William about the voice, but thought better of it. She didn't know if it was worth mentioning or not, and she wasn't special like him anyway. He was the Forgemaster of Amder. She was an innkeeper's daughter and barely trained Apprentice. No, it's probably stress. Once she was out of this underground world, and back under the sun and stars where she belonged, things would go back to normal. No mysterious voices, no glowing lights leading to her places, none of it.

She opened her eyes to find William pacing and Regin looking down at the stone floor in thought. She glanced at the Vinik as well, most of them motionless, except the large talking one, and even that one only moving a tiny amount, slight twitches of an arm or a leg.

"If you are the Drendel, why no Drendel steel? Why no wonders of craftsmanship? The stonework is nice, but Drendel were masters of the art of the forge and metal." Myriam yelled. She needed to know. It was important. If these things were lying about being the Drendel, it might make a difference, maybe. Though knowing William, he would still agonize over the decision.

Regin looked up and tried to hush her with a finger to his lips, which, frankly, she found annoying. She had the right to ask questions; they were all in this together. Will stopped pacing, giving her a long look and nodded... Good, at least he can see the need to know.

"When the Vzzzderrrrttsskilk rebelled, they killed a great many of us. In particular, because of the kind of work they did, or we showed them, most Vzzzderrrrttsskilk worked or lived with the constructors. Our miners and makers. They killed so many that day. They targeted them. Most of the knowledge was lost then. New ones could be born, but without the training, without the knowledge and secrets passed down, the wonders stopped. The knowledge ended." The talking Vinik pointed at the bound form of Speaker-to-the-sky. "One more reason to let us deal with the Vzzzderrrrttsskilk,"

"Didn't you have written records? Scrolls or books or..." Myriam threw her hands up.

"No. We do not use such things. We know about them, but they do not work here. A Grvvestitidel is born to a position. While it is possible for one of us to do a different job, it is very rare. Or it was. Now, many Grvvestitidel must do the jobs of several." The speaking Vinik made a long whistle sound and many of the others of its kind joined in, a long mournful whistle.

Myriam approached Regin and William and lowered her voice and head. "Well, that was an answer. It's plausible at least."

William nodded. "I wish Vin were here. Or Haltim. Or Master Jaste. Or..."

"They were not the Forgemaster, William. You are. I know you don't want to make this choice, but it is your choice to make." Regin whispered, breaking into William's litany of names.

"I know. Doesn't mean I have to like it." William said as he sighed. "The two of you ARE here, though. And I value your input. Thoughts?"

"Let the Gorom go. Remember, Speaker-to-the-sky said the Gorom don't come down here. Makese's Folly and all that. Have them release him. I don't particularly like the little pain in the neck, but I don't think he deserves whatever these things would do to him." Regin answered quickly.

"Myriam?" William turned to her.

She looked up at the large talking Vinik again. "Have them release him to us. We can take him to the surface, then release him. If he makes it home, then they can figure it out between them."

William nodded slowly. "And that way we don't anger the Vinik anymore than we already have."

"Exactly." Myriam answered.

"That's a good plan, actually." Regin tapped his lip for a moment. "We save Speaker-to-the-sky from death, and yet giving these Vinik things a chance to live."

"The more I think about it, the better I like it." William reached out and gave her shoulder a squeeze. "Thanks Myriam."

She winced for a moment in her head. William never understood how strong he was, and that squeeze hurt some. *"I don't like it, but it's better than letting them kill the Gorom."* The voice in her head came one last time and faded out as the words came to her. She knew it was gone, but how she knew, she had no idea.

***

Will turned to the huge Vinik. "Release him to us, we will take him with us then."

A sweeping rattle of movement passed over the crowd of Viniks, before the large one made a long vibrating sound again, quieting the group. "You would take this Vzzzderrrrttsskilk with you to the surface?"

"Yes." Will answered quickly. "He saved us; we owe him. As you owe us for the life of our companion."

The large Vinik was still for a moment, then made a long series of reverberations with its legs again. For a moment the crowd of Vinik erupted into sound again, cracks and whistles, bangs and clatters. Then silence fell again.

"We agree. But he must not be set fully free until you are in the world's shell. Only then may you release the Vzzzderrrrttsskilk from his bonds." The Vinik leader settled back into the strange harness that suspended it in the air.

Will watched as the creature waved an arm that, for all the world, looked like a dismissal. *I guess we are going now then.*

The one Vinik identified as a 'Jusszeritick' earlier came forward. The splashes of color nearly glowing in the blue white light that was still coming off of the shells of several of the Vinik. It grabbed the bound form of the Gorom, and without a lot of care, hooked a claw around the struggling form. Will watched with some fear as the creature approached him and his companions, but as it approached, it lowered itself down.

"It will carry you. Go." The talking Vinik said and without another word, most of the Vinik filed out of the room, the clicks and scrapes of carapace legs the only sound.

Will carefully climbed aboard the creature, both fascinated and uneasy about riding on the back of what amounted to a giant insect. Regin looked a bit pale as well. Myriam looked, well... excited? He couldn't help but smile. It was one reason he loved her. She had a thirst for life that drew him. *I hope she understands me more now. I hope she sees.*

The three of them found places on the shell to hold on to, and as soon as all three were sitting on the Vinik, the Jusszeritick sped up. Will swallowed hard, as the Vinik scrambled through tunnels and corners at a rate that a racehorse wouldn't be able to keep up with. The sound of a stalactite whizzing past his head threw some fear into his mind. *The last thing I need is another head injury.*

Yet the Jusszeritick seemed to miss them all, even at its speed the Vinik made last second movements as obstacles were bypassed. He could see Regin pressed as flat as he could against the creature, his face hidden. Myriam seemed to be grinning like a madwoman, her hair flying behind her. Her hair seems shorter, strange.

Time passed and as it did, so the thrill of the strange ride dwindled somewhat. Regin never raised his head, and Will still flinched a bit when he felt like they were passing too close to something. He half expected the Jusszeritick to accidentally run the Gorom into the wall, as the Vinik had done after their capture, but the creature didn't do so. I guess the Vinik leader, or whatever it was, is true to its word.

The air grew damp, and a hint of salt could be tasted, which lasted for a long while. The Vinik they were on glowed slightly, enough to make out the walls sometimes. Usually the same Drendel made metallic tiles, though often they were covered with a strange-looking growth. They passed by so fast, though, Will could never get a decent look at them.

Finally, the slope seemed to change, and go upwards. He had no idea how long they had been traveling. The fact was that the Vinik were going to get him and his companions there far faster than he would have been able to go otherwise, which meant getting closer to Duncan and his ultimate goal.

The air grew drier, and finally, long after the thrill was finally gone, and even Myriam had stopped being excited by it, the Vinik came to a halt. It lowered its body, and all three of them slid off. Regin trembling as he did so. It placed the still body of the Gorom on the ground with a thud. Not exactly gentle, but not enough to do more than bruise Speaker-to-the-sky.

They were in a dry, wide passage, and the air, for once, smelled. Fresh, if a bit dry, or maybe dusty. The Vinik pointed with one arm, and with no other motions, turned and at a faster rate than when they had been on its back, vanished into the dark, scuttling away.

As it vanished, Will noticed that the cave they were in still had a dim light. A light that came from the direction the now vanished Vinik had pointed. Sunlight?

He and Regin grabbed the flopping form of the Gorom and, with a nod at Myriam, they headed to the light. It grew as they walked, and very quickly, there it was. A cave mouth. The light was bright, and all three blinked for several minutes. The air smelled sweet. And even the slight scent of grass could be tasted.

Will, Regin, Myriam and the still bound Gorom exited the cave. Will stood for along moment, basking in the light. He'd never been so happy to be outside in his life. Regin stood still as well, and Will could see the slight dampness on his cheeks. Will didn't begrudge him. They had been through a blood-soaked nightmare of a time, and they were free.

Myriam as well stood still, smiling in the sunlight. Will felt happy. Truly happy.

"WILLIAM REIS!" The voice of Amder thundered in his head. One anxious voice.

Chapter 31.

"What happened? Why didn't you reach out to me? Why didn't you answer?" Amder's voice echoed in a rush of words, words that William had a hard time even making out the torrent was so strong. *"Where is Captain Vin Tolin? What happened to that Gorom? You look horrible. Are you feeling alright? I can tell you are injured."*

I am hurt, but alive. Head injury. And the first question I wanted to. I tried, more than once, but you were simply not there. The connection was gone. Gone or blocked, I don't know. William tapped his head, nodding to Regin and Myriam. Amder was back.

"That's not good. I am going to have a very long talk with Grimnor. There is no reason I shouldn't have been able to talk to you. You are the Forgemaster, my chosen." Amders' voice fell as he spoke. *"I see it now. Captain Tolin died, didn't he? Ach, I'm sorry William. I am. I know you were fond of the man."*

It's fine. Well, not fine, but it happened. Lots happened. How long were we gone? Time sort of... doesn't have a lot of meaning in the dark. Will tried not to think too much on Vin. His mental list of those who had died for him was getting too long, far too long.

"And the Gorom?" Amder asked. *"I can't imagine he is happy."*

Probably not. We are going to free him and then decide on what to do next. But how long? Will nodded to Regin and pointed at the still bound and occasionally twitching form of Speaker-to-the-sky.

"*A week. The trip should have taken a few days. What happened?*" Amder asked again. This time, the sound of hammers came with his voice. William found that oddly comforting even if the god only did that when he was worried.

We went underground, met the Gorom. They don't like us much. Or you, for that matter. We started our trip, got... separated, and got found again thanks to that Gorom. Will watched as Regin used a small boot knife with Myriam's help to cut the bindings on Speaker-to-the-sky. He half wondered how strong that stuff was, as Regin really had to saw at it to get it to cut, and Regin wasn't one to have dull equipment.

Will went on, telling Amder of the Vinik, and the truth that they were the Drendel. Or at least claimed to be the Drendel. Amder never said anything, and in fact, the hammering got louder the more he spoke about the creatures. William swore he heard a muffled oath at one point, when he repeated the Viniks' words about trying to stop the coming of the Gods, but if he did, he wasn't going to ask. Amder's anger was palpable.

Where is Duncan? How much time have we lost? Will asked, as Regin sawed the last thread of spider thread off of the Gorom. Speaker-to-the-sky pulled his hood up and retreated to the shadow of the cave entrance, not saying a word.

"*When you went missing, I called in one last... favor. He's moving again, but he was becalmed. He hasn't moved as far. I even think I know where he is going. And why. But remember, it isn't Duncan. Not really. And I think I know who or what it is.*" Amders' voice, which had been getting calmer as he spoke, rose again. "*How and why I do not know, but Zalkiniv wears the skin of what had been Duncan Reis.*"

Zalkiniv? That is impossible! Zalkiniv was dead. Dead in the events that Duncan put in place that ended the return of the Blood God! Will whirled to Regin and Myriam, both who took a step back at the look on his face.

"I am aware, lad. I do not know how this happened. And I do not like it. If Zalkiniv survived…" Amder trailed off, and the hammering which had stopped returned. *"You must find him. Find him and then speak with me before you take any steps."*

What will you be doing? William rubbed the hammer at his side, the metal warm now in the sunlight.

"I will be getting some answers. I will point you where to start. Head south, away from the sea. Walk for a day and half of the next. You will find someone who can help you. Who will help you." The hammering faded out first, and then Amder's rumbling voice.

Will felt Amder's presence fade, but there was still at the very back of his mind, the seed of what he knew was the connection to his god. At least that was back.

***

Regin wiped his hands for the third time since cutting the Gorom free. Whatever that stuff was that he'd been bound in, it was tough, sticky, and unpleasant to touch. He'd have hated to be wrapped in it for whatever amount of time it had been. And as to be expected, being in that stuff for as long as he had been had done nothing to improve the disposition of one Gorom.

"You… you let them do that to me. You didn't tell them to take me back to my people." Speaker-to-the-sky scowled at Regin as he rubbed some of the residue off his cheek. "They are Vinik. Only good for eating and making lights. They are nothing."

Regin eyed the Gorom, unsure if he was saying all that for his own benefit or Regin's. The truth was not something Speaker-to-the-sky would want to face. He wouldn't if he were a Gorom. But he wasn't, thankfully. "You know the truth, Speaker-to-the-sky. You heard it. And you know it is true. You may not like it, but that changes nothing."

"It is not true. I heard a voice tell lies, but who knows what the voice came from. You could have done the voice. Cursed humans." Speaker-to-the-sky spat on the ground. "You are above the ground now. And through the mountains. My part in this farce is done. I will go back to my people, and we will seek out that nest. When we find it, we will burn it out, but take any newly hatched Vinik. More eggs, more milk, more meat."

Regin swallowed back the nausea. Hate was plain on the face of the Gorom. Hate and fear. *He is terrified that it might be true. He runs from it.* Regin looked from the Gorom to Myriam, who stood in the sunlight, almost basking in it. *It's easy to run, and hard to face things.*

Regin turned back to Speaker-to-the-sky. "You saved us. We saved you. The Gorom will have to face the past, the truth of what they did, and what they continue to do. The Vinik are not blameless either. You are Speaker-to-the-sky. You have some amount of power. Decide what you will do with that power on your trip home."

Speaker-to-the-sky locked eyes with Regin, and for a moment, Regin thought his words were getting through. But only for a moment.

"Vinik are animals to be used and discarded." Speaker-to-the-sky checked his robe and without another word re-entered the cave, walking away from Regin.

Good riddance. Regin felt a twinge of guilt at thinking it, though. At least we don't have to listen to him calling us cursed, and followers of a half god, and the like. Regin's eyes fell on William, who was still talking to Amder, and Myriam, who had been silent since they came out of the cave.

Hard choices indeed.

***

Myriam stood in the warm sun and reveled in it. They were close enough to the sea to get a slight salt smell in the breeze. Grass lay around them, and a few small bushes. Green and brown. A bright yellow sun. And she loved every single piece of it.

No more purple glow, no more damp cave air, stale and old. They were outside, and that was enough. For right now, it was more than enough. She'd helped Regin cut the Gorom free, but one look at Speaker-to-the-sky's face had made her walk away from them as the Gorom and Regin spoke. She didn't know what exactly was said, but the expressions on both faces said it all.

The Vinik. Or the Drendel, if you believe their story. And I do. The truth was hard, but hard didn't make it untrue. Her Grandfather often repeated that, attempting to make her understand that running from truth fixed nothing.

And I am running. Running from this voice thing, running from Regin, and running from William. Her attention was turned from her thoughts to William, who came to stand beside her. She examined him critically; she was no healer, but that lump on his head seemed smaller. He needed a bath; in the sunlight, she could see the state he was in. Dust and dirt clung to him, dried blood matted part of his hair, and frankly, he stunk.

"You need a bath, a real healer, and probably a good meal." Myriam pointed at William. "And in that order."

William nodded and laughed in response, bringing a smile to her lips It was the first thing he had done recently that made her feel like he was still William Reis. He'd been so wrapped up in things and trying to be strong with the deaths in the Reach, and then the chase after Duncan, Vin's death, all of it.

"I fully agree. I notice you all seemed a lot cleaner. Sometime you and Regin can tell me what happened before you all found me. But for now, let's get the Guildmaster. I see our Gorom friend has left." William kicked the ground, watching the few grass ends flutter away in the breeze. "I imagine he's going home. I hope we made the right choice."

"You made the best choice you could. Who knows what the Vinik would do. I'm not sure I blame them either. It was a tough decision either way." Myriam watched William nod slowly.

"I know. And all I can imagine is Haltim or Vin telling me that the choice is made and not to dwell on it." William took in a deep breath. "At least this is better than caves. I hate caves now."

"I'd be inclined to agree, but you didn't see some of the things we saw. Even so, this is better for us." Myriam turned to the sound of boots to see Regin walking towards them now. His face frowning. "Looks like Speaker-to-the-sky made sure to make Regin mad before he left."

Regin shrugged as he got closer. "I tried to make Speaker-to-the-sky listen, but some hate goes too deep, I guess. I assume Amder reached out to you, William?"

Myriam noticed that he wouldn't make eye contact with her. What now? A twinge of something grew in her chest. Hope? Fear? *Maybe I should stop running. I'll talk to him tonight. I can't let this unsaid thing stay there, not anymore.*

William slow nodded. "Yes. Once he calmed down, he said we needed to head south from here, and we would find a guide. And…" William sighed. "You deserve to know, but I will understand if you don't want to continue, I mean it."

"What?" Regin spoke first, though Myriam's question was right on the tip of her tongue. "We aren't going anywhere, William. You are the Forgemaster of Amder, and, more importantly, our friend. We aren't walking away. We covered this already, didn't we?"

"Zalkiniv. The body of Duncan is being used by the spirit of Zalkiniv. The High Priest of the Blood God. I don't know how or why. I thought that creature was gone and dead. But…. Zalkiniv lives." William paused. "Amder seems to think that he knows where Zalkiniv is going, but he did not share that yet. I imagine once we find this person who can help, we will find out more then."

Myriam hadn't ever laid eyes on this Zalkiniv person, but she'd heard bits and pieces. Hidden as a woman named Rache, Zalkiniv had tricked Williams's cousin, had the priest Haltim killed, tried to kill William, and had overseen the death of Duncan. Or been there. None of them were super clear on what had happened that night where the Blood God had failed.

"It makes no difference. We are with you." Myriam spoke and placed a hand on William's shoulder. Her touch brought a wince from the man with a smile.

"Watch the hand, but thank you." William smiled.

"I agree with Myriam." Regin nodded. "I swore myself to your service, and I will stand by you till the end of that service."

Strangely, William frowned at that. "I should release you from that, you know. The idea of someone being sworn to my service isn't one I like."

"Nonsense." Myriam said quickly. "In fact. I Myriam VolFar, hereby swear myself to your service." She smiled at the look of shock on both Regin's and William's face. "Now you have a barely trained apprentice in your service as well, aren't you feeling happy?"

Regin's face went from shock to worry, then broke out into laughter. "Well, now you've got two William."

William shook his head one last time. "I'm the one who hit his head, and the two of you are the ones acting strangely." He smiled, though, and Myriam noticed some tension leave him. *He was worried we would go.*

Chapter 32.

Zalkiniv almost laughed with the joy of it. Days of being stuck, and the answer had been there in front of him all that time. He had never been one to get angry about such things. Only a fool would get mad about overlooking something like that. He had made a mistake true, but he had found the solution. He would land soon; he could already see the shore.

He looked forward to the blood that would flow. First a village or a few fishermen. Renew his reserves and heal this body from its time on this cursed boat, and then find the Curors and take the blood drop. After that, he had some idea of where to go. One reason the Curors were here in the first place, why they had the drop at all, was that here in this land was the birthplace of the gods.

The actual spot where they had first stepped on this world. Before humans, before Gorom, before the Trinil, before the Saltmisstresses, before all of it, the Gods themselves had been born there. That was where he would ascend, that was where he would take the drop, and if he were right, steal whatever power Valnijz still possessed and become a god himself.

The Blood God had always been such a fool. Many times over the centuries, Valnijz had bowed before the wishes of his former lord. True, the Scaled one had almost succeeded, but his betrayal had sealed the truth. Without Zalkiniv, the Blood god was weak and impotent.

The boat slid to a stop, sliding into the sand with a soft crunch. Zalkiniv stood slowly, joints popping and creaking as he did so. He grabbed the iron dagger and wrenched it out of the wood, raising an eyebrow at the blood red residue left behind. Blood? *This is not the time, but soon I must fully examine this dagger. It is a far too important a tool.*

He nearly stumbled as he left the boat, this body having adjusted to the swells and movements of the water. He considered a small blood working to fix it, but decided not to. The blood was at a premium at this time, and he would get his land legs back soon.

He would, however, use the blood to cast a quick blood detection. He gripped the dagger and cut a small line above each eye, the blood flowing, but far slower than it should have. He worked the power, searching for life, human life preferably. Other races blood could be used, of course, he'd always preferred working human blood.

The closest, however, was a group of four Trinil. Better than some, worse than others. The main issue with Trinil blood was the blessing of their goddess. It had to be stripped of its power to detect lies and falsehoods. If he were using it without having it prepared, it would not let him change form, or lie. At least for a while. Zalkiniv was loathe to give up any advantage he might have.

He checked once more for anything closer, but the only thing in range was a village, but it was at the far end of what he could detect. They were human, at least. No, the Trinil are better. After they are taken, then the village.

He closed the wounds over his eyes, and for a moment swayed as the power left him. *Weaker than I want to be by far.* If these had been human fishermen, he would have used some subterfuge to get closer before killing them. It was only four, and he relished the idea of ending them himself. No beast, only Zalkiniv.

But since they were Trinil, that wouldn't work. He'd have to let the beast out. He had grown somewhat unsure about the thing as of late. *It seemed contained, but there were times it was too controlled.* The beast was supposed to be rage and anger made flesh, normally something he kept distracted to be unleashed as needed.

The last few times he'd checked on the thing, though, it had felt false. It had only been for a flicker of a thought, since the beast didn't exist outside his head. He must have been imagining it, loss of blood power, and the wear and tear on this form, this body.

That shred of Duncan was still there as well, whimpering and being useless. He still wondered why it was there. He had taken multiple bodies over the centuries, and never had he had a scrap of a soul stay like this one had. His only guess was that whatever forces had been released that night had allowed this shard of the man to stay. Why it chose to was something he could not understand.

***

"Soon." Valnijz paced its side of this space. Duncan watched it as he always did.

He was more and more sure of a few things. One, while this thing was the blood god, it wasn't at the same time. It wasn't mad, and it wasn't all powerful. It's a shard, like me. It was a shard of a god, so it was more powerful than he was, but it was a shard. But what was soon? He assumed it meant that it was going to take over, and then his body, HIS body, would be the vessel for the blood god.

"You are right. And wrong." Valnijz appeared right in front of Duncan, its face leering, scaled and taunt. "I will take over, and Zalkiniv will come here. Until I am done with him, then he will be devoured."

Duncan scrambled back, forcing himself back into the corner. He hated it when Valnijz did that. *Still can't touch me, though, still can't cross that line.*

"Fool. Do you want to know why you exist? Do you want to know why you are here?" Valnijz raised a single clawed finger. "Zalkiniv often wonders why you cling to existence. He doesn't know. But I know." Valnijz took his upraised finger, and to Duncan's surprise and horror, reached out, and touched him with it.

Duncan felt a lancing spike of pain as the blood gods' finger and hand crossed the imagined line. He had thought it was incapable of moving past. He convulsed, unable to control his body as waves of agony crossed over him. The touch brought pain and horror, so much that in that moment Duncan wished for anything to end it..

It was cold at first, a cold that for a tiny fraction of time felt good, then the cold became freezing, a deep dark numbing cold, then, colder still, a killing cold. The kind of cold that brings the blackness, where flesh freezes and dies.

He could feel all of it, and yet, no sound crossed his lips, and thought fled, until a long moment later, the scaled one removed his finger and his hand.

"You exist because your body demands it. For now. In each and every body he used over the years, that I, I gave him the power to control, a scrap, a shred of the person stayed. He never knew it; they were mine to play with. Some relished it, some fought it, and some begged for release." Valnijz smiled, teeth sharp and glittering in the dim red dusty light.

"He is aware of you though, the events of that night made him aware. Your noble and foolish attempt to end my return. His last gasp effort to survive." The blood god paused again; head cocked. "He is about to free me again. To kill. Good. I hunger."

"Never doubt Duncan Reis, I am a god. I can touch you. And when I take over this body, your time will come to a close. I will complete my return, and then you will be removed." Valnijz slumped off to its corner and broke into the howls and screams of the beast.

A poor actor playing a bad part. Duncan took a deep breath as the shiver still passed through him. *But I will be free then. When Valnijz takes over, I will be free.*

.

Chapter 33.

Zalkiniv shuddered, grasping control back from the howling beast. The four Trinil lay dead, though the ferocity and rage in which the beast struck had surprised even him. But the blood flowed, and now he would be ready to destroy that village, then strike at that fool Jindo.

The beast raged in its confinement as Zalkiniv fought to keep it there. It's stronger. How can it be stronger? It seemed each time he called it, something in the creature changed. *But it's a construct, a point of rage and anger. It's not real. It was never real.*

No, he was Zalkiniv, he was in control. He paid little attention to the now silent shadow that was Duncan Reis. It had great fun once feeling the man's despair and hate, but even those had faded into a simple acceptance. *He's no fun anymore.*

Using some of the fresh blood, he worked quickly, binding the form with energy and strength. His face drew into a grimace as he did so. He hated working Trinil blood; it always gave him the feeling of green. Green trees, and clean air, forests and all that nonsense. But there was power there, power he could and would use.

Strength returned to his limbs. Zalkiniv grasped the dagger and started walking towards the village, and his last stop before the showdown with Jindo Halfman and his foolish followers. His destiny was close, he would take the drop, and once at the birthplace of the gods, take the power.

***

Will half walked, half ran towards the ocean and the small stream that was emptying into it. He still hated running, but he might have found the one thing he hated more, the feeling of constant dirt, sweat, and blood on his skin. His head hurt still, but thankfully he hadn't had any dizzy and nauseated attacks in a while.

He wanted to get clean. And the ocean and the stream would do that, or mostly that. He glanced back at Myriam and Regin, who followed behind, though for once he was outpacing them. Each seemed lost in their own thoughts, but he was glad to have them both here. They each were needed. Without Vin, he would lean on Regin more. Though Regin was only a bit older than he was, he was more experienced than him.

Myriam was still a special case. He couldn't help the way he felt when he saw her. She didn't return his feelings, but maybe she would again one day. He smiled for a second, imaging Duncan's response to all this. He would crack a few jokes, tease him a bit, but Will thought Duncan would approve. Both of Myriam, and how he was handling it. So, if you can hear me Dunc, help me out a bit here!

His feet sunk into the sand, and he followed the edge of the stream to where, finally, it flowed into the waves. He had little knowledge of the ocean. He'd seen it once or twice, but that was it. Strange to think he'd traveled under it. All that water over his head, all that weight... No wonder Vin had always been on edge. He wished he'd been able to get Vin's body. He deserved to have his remains here, buried under the blue sky, not some abyssal cave.

Will waited as Regin and Myriam got closer, taking off his armor as he did so. Saved his life this stuff. He hefted the metal, his practiced eye glancing over the edges and checking for wear. Still looks fresh forged, though it is god blessed, so that sort of makes sense.

"I'm going to get clean, so the two of you, well at least you Myriam, go over that Dune?" Will asked them as he worked the ties on his shirt. He suppressed more than a few winces as muscles bruised and battered complained.

"Fine." Myriam gave an exaggerated sigh and walked over to the dune and out of sight.

"Maybe go with her, Regin? Just in case." Will asked as he fumbled with another tie. *I don't need him seeing how injured I am.* He'll say something to Myriam and then I'll never hear the end of it.

Regin paused for a minute and nodded, walking the same way as Myriam, and apparently deep in thought. Wonder what he's got on his mind so much? Will finally removed the last tie, and found his face twisted in effort as the act of removing his shirt made his shoulders ache.

Finally, getting it off made him scowl even more. He couldn't see most of his skin, but what he could see didn't look good. Spreading down his chest from his left shoulder was one nasty bruise. The edges had already faded to that yellow green color, but the higher up it was still blue black. *Great.* Thankfully, it wasn't his hammering arm.

He picked up one bracer again, hefting it. When was the last time he had done good metal work? No quests, no fighting, no running for his life. Only hammer and anvil, metal and coal, bellows and quenching. No insanity, only creation.

"Being a Forgemaster?" Amders' voice echoed again in his head. *"Welcome to the Forgemaster's lament. It seems the more you become my representative, the less forging and smithing you get to actually do. It is one reason I founded the Guild. My Forgemaster never got to actually work."*

You could have told me that, you know? I might not have taken you up on all this excitement. Will thought back as he put the bracer down and removed the rest of his clothing.

"No, you are the right choice. You know that." Amder laughed as he spoke.

Yes, yes. Fine. Will sighed and stepped into the waves, reveling for a moment in the feeling of grime washing away. Then the burning feeling of salt water in cuts and abrasions hit him, forcing him to snap his jaw shut. He could feel Amder retreat into that point in his mind, which was good. It felt right, though the fact that it felt right was strange enough.

With a gulp of air, will submerged himself into the sea, and screamed under the water. Every cut and abrasion was on fire, but at least he was getting clean. He exploded out of the water, gasping for air and taking huge gulps of it.

He quickly turned to the stream and lowered himself into the fresh water, feeling the sting get washed away. The water was warmer than he'd expected, but it did still feel good. A few minutes in the stream and Will stood. The dust and dirt were gone, and for the first time in quite a while, he felt almost normal.

He quickly dressed and found himself grinning like an idiot at the feeling of clean clothes on his skin. He still hurt, and he was tired, and hungry, but one problem at a time, right?

Packing up his dirty garments, Will took a sip of the water in his bottle, noting that it, at least, was still cool. Now some food, some rest, and we will find Duncan. Will threw on his pack, wincing again as his bruises ached, but he felt good. Happy almost. They had gone through a horrible trial, and they were still standing, mostly.

***

Regin crested the dune, leaving William behind him. Myriam stood there, and for once, she was staring at him. Right at him. *You know this is the time. William won't interrupt, and there's no one else here.* Regin wasn't sure if he should laugh or walk away.

He wanted her. And she wanted him. It was obvious. But there was William. Always William. Regin stood still for a moment. The sea breeze was ruffling Myriam's hair, and even roughly cut short, and it framed her face well. Her clothes hugged her form, strong lines, and muscles. So unlike all the soft maidens and perfumed court hanger-on's he had expected in his life.

This was better. This was what he needed. He glanced back to where William was. *Would he forgive me?*

He stood there for a long minute, his thoughts as wavering as the sea grass he stood among. He turned back to Myriam to find her standing now, right in front of him. She was biting her lip in thought.

"Myriam..." Regin said when suddenly she rushed forward and kissed him. Regin didn't hesitate and kissed her back. Feeling the rush of attraction flow through him, his skin broke into goose bumps, and a thrill fluttered up his back.

It was perfect.

***

Jindo could barely suppress his laugh when he first realized what was happening. Zalkiniv was coming. Here. The fool. Jindo knew why, of course, anyone with any mind for strategy would know. Zalkiniv wanted their power. Had he been the one to plunder the Temple in the Mistlands? He had destroyed the village on the far side of the Blood bay. Interesting.

Valnijz would not forgive Zalkiniv's failure. It wasn't in some attempt to fix his mistake. No, Zalkiniv knew things, and he knew the blood could be used. But the man had never showed any interest in the true power of the blood god, preferring his blood workings and sacrificing slaves. So no, the former High Priest would not be coming to be a Curor, not that Jindo would ever let him.

There was one place, one incredibly special place that the Blood could be used to do other things. If anyone would know, it was Zalkiniv. But the way to that place was barred shut to them, and any mortal. Doubly so to any who followed their lord. What could Zalkiniv be planning?

Jindo debated if he should send one of his men to kill his old rival. Be done with the man, here and now. Any of his men should be able to end him. But yet, Jindo held himself back. He did not like making decisions without enough information. Something else was going on. He could not see all the connections, but the pattern was there.

He would wait but wait and watch. He turned to one of his guards.

"Go, find the fool Zalkiniv. Watch him, but do not be seen, or detain him in any way." Jindo started to dismiss the guard, but paused. "If by chance, he is attacked or hurt or even killed by someone or something else on the way, do nothing, come and tell me."

The guard vanished without a word, heading north.

"And if you make it all the way here Zalkiniv, I will bury a spear in your guts myself before I see you touch the holy blood." Jindo whispered as he gripped his spear tight.

Chapter 34.

Regin pulled back first, not wanting to break contact, but he needed to think.

"Well, that's done, finally." Myriam shot him a smile. Sparks, that smile. "Well, say something. You kissed me back, so I know you didn't object. And it's not like I throw myself at men."

"Ah well..." Regin fumbled for what to say. He had sweet-talked women into more than one night of fun and passion, so why was he totally unable to think of what to say now? "I did like it."

"Liked it? You liked it?" Myriam's smile fell a bit into a small frown. "That's all?" She raised a finger and poked him, hard.

"No, it was nice!" Regin blurted out.

"It was nice??" Myriam walked away, turning her back to him.

This was wrong, all wrong. Regin went after her. "Look Myriam. I thought it was great. And yes, of course I liked it, more than liked it. You're amazing."

Myriam was very much trying to stifle a laugh, and with one look at his face, she broke into laughing. "Oh Regin. You are a fool sometimes. A good-looking fool, but still a fool."

He couldn't help but smile back, and this time, he leaned in and kissed her. He could feel her move closer, and his hand found the small of her back, pulling her in. "Nice. I like it." He whispered for a second as their lips broke.

"Shut up and kiss me again." Myriam whispered.

I feel beyond incredible. The smell of Myriam and the feeling of her in his arms, so long desired. The warm sun and the sea breeze only added to it. Being out of that hell that was the world of the Gorom. He almost wasn't able to keep a lid on how good he felt. Soon Myriam, he and William would…

"William." Regin whispered and pulled away. "Myriam, what about William?" Regin took a small step back, still touching her but needing to see her face. "I mean, William still cares for you. Deeply."

Myriam lowered her head for a moment. "I know. But… if I spend my life avoiding doing things to hurt Williams' feelings, regardless of how I feel, is that a good thing? William and I are in the past. Honestly to me, we never were. He was someone else, he wasn't the Forgemaster. That changed everything."

Regin knew she was right. She couldn't spend her life avoiding making William sad. But Regin still felt conflicted. He had come to consider William a close friend. But they weren't whatever they had been, and they were all adults. By the sparks, he was older than them both.

His thoughts were pushed back by Myriam, stepping close again. "I was so tempted to take a peek at the waterfall, even though I've heard men… say things about how cold water affects them?" Her lips came up towards his again. "Are you cold now?"

Regin barely registered his surprise at her words and had begun to try to come up with something to say back when her lips touched his again.

***

William was enjoying the breeze and relishing in the feeling of not being covered in dried blood and dirt. He had hummed an old mining tune as he walked, one of those working songs to help blows fall in place in time. Duncan was close, he was sure. Find this person Amder said could help, get Duncan, find a way to free him, and then, then life would be good.

He crested the dune, expecting to see Myriam and Regin waiting for him. He knew they both didn't have to be here, and he was profoundly grateful to both of them. His thoughts were interrupted mid step, as they came into view. The small kernel of joy he had been feeling, even with all that had gone wrong, vanished. For Regin and Myriam were there, embracing. *Lovers? How long had this been going on? Had he simply ignored it?* William dragged himself over to the other side of the crest, hiding himself from view as he tried to make sense of what he had seen.

There had been that moment, back in the Reach where Regin had said something about Myriam, but at the time he had thought it nothing more than admiration for her talents. Her smithing talents. Dark thoughts raised up as his good mood vanished, and the despair and anger for everything that had gone wrong came again.

He never should have accepted the change in Regin. He was still the same horrible person he had been when he had traveled with him and Master Jaste to the Guild. Myriam had ended things before they had really started and tossed him aside for Regin. His mood grew worse as he grappled with this new situation.

They had probably been doing this for weeks all that time alone when Regin had been tutoring her. *Sure, tutoring.* He stood for a moment, weighing his options. He could walk around them and continue on his own. Leave them to whatever they wanted to call it and go find Duncan on his own. They'd probably like that.

Amder's rumbling voice broke into his anger. *"You know that's not fair, lad. I'm no expert on the human heart, but you know that isn't true."*

William clenched his fists. He wanted to rage, to yell, he wanted to be angry. Slowly, though, he released his anger. Amder was right. He wanted it to be true, but it wasn't. He had no say here. *It didn't matter how he felt, Myriam wasn't some prize for him to own, and Regin HAD changed.* He hated it, but the truth was, they were interested in each other. It was that simple.

William sat in the sand, among the grasses and reeds, and tried to let go of the sadness that had taken over now that the anger was gone. He didn't understand how this had come to pass. Had he really been that blind? All that time together… Well, he hadn't been with this much in the caves. Had something happened then? Just when he'd thought things were going well this happens? Did they even think of him when they started this? Were they truly his friends?

"Regin is a loyal friend. Myriam as well. Don't worry lad, things will work out the way they will." Amder's voice came again.

Easy for you to say. You're a god. William thought back to Amder. He closed his eyes, feeling the sea breeze again, the skin by and under his eyes cooler than the rest of him as the tears he didn't even know had been there dried in the air. Not for the first time he wish Duncan or Haltim were here. He needed them. Now that the shock of the discovery was wearing off, his feelings calmed some. He had no place in whatever was going on with them.

Amder retreated back into the corner of his mind. William was grateful for that. He wasn't in the mood for lectures right now. He could see why Myriam liked Regin. He was an exceptionally good-looking man, and with his recent conversion, his personality matched. And it was obvious to him why Regin was attracted to Myriam. Who wouldn't be? It was simple... He had no say in it. He knew it. But he couldn't help the sadness that still gripped his heart. He stood, slowly, brushing sand off his pants. He'd better get to them. Even with whatever they had been doing, eventually they would notice he wasn't back and come looking for him.

***

Regin's hands could feel the firm muscles under her clothes as he and Myriam stood there, their passion growing with each moment. He fumbled for a moment with his shirt. "You might have to help me with this, my side and all..." he whispered into her ear.

He felt the laugh she held back more than heard it, but her fingers helped him. The touch of her hands brought a lingering tingle wherever they touched. He could feel his need for her, his desire. *What a woman.*

A clearing of a throat brought all that to an end. *William.*

Regin forcibly pushed himself away from Myriam, who caught her hand under his shirt and precariously close to his waistband. The look on her face was one of shock for a moment, but as she moved backward, she must have glimpsed William, as she turned pale for a moment, then blushed everywhere. Regin almost smiled at that, almost.

This will not be pleasant. He turned to William to see a man who he didn't know. The whole time he'd known the Forgemaster, even before the Guild, William had held an openness about him. Maybe not the most outspoken person, but he always was friendly.

This person was angry, hurt, and not the same man he had been before. Regin had never considered himself in tune to the emotions of others, but the sadness off William was physical. Arms crossed, mouth set in a hard line, and the eyes, the eyes screamed his sorrow.

"William... I... well..." Regin tried to think of something to say. He should have controlled himself. He had wanted to talk to him one on one, but have him find out this way was the very last thing he'd wanted.

"Please, don't. I have no say here." Williams's voice was low, and barely able to be heard over the breeze. "Please, just not in front of me. Not now, not yet. I'll find reasons to leave you two alone. But, please, not in front of me."

Myriam took a step toward William, but he backed away.

"No Myriam. I don't want to talk about it. Let me deal with it my way. I'm happy for you. And you, Regin. I'll come around, I'm sure. Not now though, give me some time." William shouldered his pack, staring southward. "Shall we go and find this person who Amder says can help?"

Regin felt horrible. He'd betrayed a friend. He'd sworn himself to the Forgemaster's service, and yet goes off and seduces the woman the Forgemaster loved. He wanted to say something, anything, but there wasn't much to say. He quickly tucked his shirt back in and grabbed his pack, not looking Myriam in the eye. *It had been a mistake. He should not have done it.*

Chapter 35.

Zalkiniv crested a sandy hill, the bright sun beating down on him. The Trinil's blood had dried to a delightful brownish gray, and in a pattern that was almost decorative. The sand dunes had given way to these soft rolling hills covered with brush and here and there small hardy trees. Twisted by the near constant wind, they were like claws erupting from the ground. A small stream was near as well. *Perfect, while the blood can sustain me, water and food would do this form some good, and save the power for later.*

But he was where he was supposed to be, for he could see the smoke rising from the village. He wasn't quite able to see it yet, but he was close. He could feel the blood even from here. Hot, flowing, eager. He wasn't sure exactly how many lived there, but it was not important. Nothing here could stand in the beast's way. Well, the beast and the dagger. He would watch as the beast took over and tore through the innocents. The screams and terror would spike the blood, and each drop would refill him to the point of overflowing.

There was a working that would allow him to take more power from the blood than normal, but it would also make it easier for the power to be taken from him. He still half considered it, but ultimately discarded the idea. Regardless of how he felt about Jindo, the man wasn't stupid. Stubborn, yes. A traitor to the true faith? Yes. Stupid? No.

Any opening he gave Jindo would be a bad thing. The man was a warrior. He knew strategy. It was nothing compared to the power of the beast and bloodlust, though. He sniffed the air; the smoke bringing the smell of roasting fish and sweat. Yes, some actual food would be good.

He continued on, not bothering to try to hide himself. Why bother? They couldn't harm him, and there wasn't much to hide with here. He spent a tiny bit of the power keeping the sweat off of him though. He'd never liked the heat much. While his former home was parched, dry and blasted, it had not been overly hot. Sweat would wash off the blood, and the extra fear the sight of him would bring to his new prey was worth the tiny use of the power.

He could feel them better now. Nearly fifty heartbeats came from the village. A mix of old and young, male and female. He was sure some were out and about, hunting, gathering, and maybe even some small farming. He could have waited till nightfall, and he did half consider it. Extinguish all the lights and release the hunter. The only reason he didn't, though, was the beast. He wasn't sure if the thing could see in the dark.

Daytime it was then. Zalkiniv drew the dagger, testing its edge as he did so. The salt had not damaged this blade the way it should have. The same dark dull gray color, tinged with red blood here and there. The wrappings on the hilt stained brown and shiny, hard to the touch. He could feel it beating in time with the village. His hunger grew with each beat, a hunger that nearly overwhelmed him.

He steadied himself, and with a single thought released his control of the beast. *Hunt. Kill. Feast.*

***

Duncan felt the release more than saw it. He'd taken to sitting totally still and keeping his eyes closed. It seemed to be the only way the piece of the blood god would leave him alone. There had been a few times early on when the presence had approached him, and he'd felt its hot horrible breath near him. But it had left, gone away.

He didn't know why, nor did he really care. The memory of the pain he had gone through when the creature had touched him was enough to never want that to happen again. At first, he'd found it hard, not that he could do much of anything here in this whatever place. He'd gotten used to the ever-present dried blood dust and the color red. At least with his eyes closed, he didn't have to see red.

Over time, his mind wandered. He thought about old scaving targets, places he'd only partially explored because of either time or the Valni. He thought about things he should have done differently, like women, or how he had brushed off helping neighbors and others in the Reach because he didn't like the work.

But mostly, his thoughts turned to William. He missed him. All his life, he'd told himself that he'd been the one protecting Will. He'd be the provider. That William didn't have what it took to keep them fed or safe. He'd even looked down on Will's skill and love to forging, mining, smelting, all the skills a Reacher came to naturally.

But as he'd sat there, he realized something. He'd been wrong. *Terribly wrong.* Will had been the foundation that had let them continue on. He'd held his ground on things that mattered to him, but also let Duncan's quick temper and sadness wash over him without a fight. Early on, after the elder two Reis men had vanished, Duncan had often broken into a rage. Blaming everyone and everything for them being alone.

Will had never seemed to erupt like he did. Oh, he'd been sad. He'd heard Will crying himself to sleep more than once in that first year. But the only time he'd ever pushed back hard was when Duncan blamed Will's mother for all of it. He barely remembered his Aunt. She'd been a sweet woman, that much he knew. His own mother had passed when he was a baby. A fever had taken her soon after childbirth. So Will's mother had taken a far larger role in his early life.

He remembered the feeling of her giving him a hug. A somewhat stern lecture about him wasting food when he'd tried to incite bugs into the house, so he'd not have to eat some meal. He'd forgotten what the food even was that he didn't want, but he'd laid a thin trail of honey up a wall and out a window he'd left open a crack. His Aunt had, of course, quickly found it, and she knew who had done it. She'd made him clean it and given him a talking to. She'd never raised her voice, but he'd felt bad for upsetting her. He didn't really blame her for everything, either. He'd been angry, and when the words came out of his mouth, he'd wanted to take them back.

William had stood from where he had been sitting, and poked him in the chest, hard. He'd demanded that Duncan never say that again. Duncan remembered his surprise at the reaction and had nodded and stumbled back. Of course, he had brought it up again over the years, but William had never physically responded after that first time. Duncan only did it to make him mad, if only for one reason. It kept Duncan from thinking about the truth. It had all been his fault.

All of it. He was in a prison of his own making and had been all his life. His thoughts stopped, and he just sank into his depression. This was a world he had made.

He wanted to cry and scream. He hated it. He hated all of this. He wondered if he could somehow bait this thing that called itself the blood god to end it, not for the first time.

It was then; he felt it. The presence was gone. Which meant Zalkiniv had released him again. Which meant death. He shut his eyes tighter, hoping to feel the blood rush in his ears so he didn't have to hear the screams and death of those who in the world would be destroyed.

I am sorry. I am so sorry.

***

Zalkiniv watched as the beast killed with a sense of wonder. How the thing had changed. Oh, the same delicious level of brutality was still there, but now the strikes were placed carefully. The dagger cut through at exactly the right point for the most blood flow. Victims were gravely injured, mortally so, but not killed outright unless they had a weapon. Those were dispatched in an avalanche of blows and cuts, looking more than something on display at a butcher's yard than a person.

The screams and moans of exquisite pain were transfixing. Zalkiniv had a hard time hiding his response. With each drop spilled, he felt a quiver of pleasure. Not sexual, but like a thirsty man drinking from an ice-cold spring. He wanted to bathe in it, let the lifeblood of these pitiful, weak people sustain him forever.

Soon. This was the last piece of his plan. Within an hour, the beast was done. Every person in the village was dead. Dead wasn't the right word. No, every person in the village had been sacrificed. Given unwilling to feed his desire and hunger. *The way it should be.*

Blood cultists and slaves aside, the blood of the unwilling was deeply more satisfying to him. So much fear and anger. So much sorrow and despair. He could not wait to smell it. He quickly gathered the power to push the beast back into its prison. He'd kept it in reserve for this purpose. The power flowed and…

Ended. Zalkiniv tried again, and again the power failed him. He scrambled, desperately trying to gather threads together, but the power flowed away from him. Every time he tried to grasp it tighter, it twisted away from him, snake like. *Alive.* The power should never respond that way, not to him. And there, in his dark corner, he heard it. A scream. A scream that brought the first edge of fear to Zalkiniv, a fear he had never thought to happen. A fear he'd thought he'd be forever safe from.

Another scream joined the first, and more. A thousand screams, each torn from the throat of a thousand different victims. The dark corner erupted into a red glow, and a swirling gray mist surrounded him. A voice came, a voice made of those screams, and Zalkiniv could feel his own fear, once a thin edge, cutting through his thoughts, become a torrent. *It was impossible. He was banished. He couldn't be here!*

"Zalkiniv..." the voice spoke, strong, each scream forming his name and the gray mist, now seen as faces and claws, pushed by a fetid and decaying wind. *"I am extremely disappointed in you. You fail me and pay the price and yet, try to overthrow me. You are nothing Zalkiniv. You amused me for a time... but that time is over. I will gather the drop, and with it, complete my return to this world."*

Zalkiniv screamed then, his voice joining the chorus. He felt himself being wiped away, his spirit, his mind, his very existence being torn apart. But he was Zalkiniv! He had lived for a thousand years, and he would live for more! This could not be the end for him. He tried to beg for forgiveness, to throw himself at the mercy of the Blood God. He wasn't insane now, the things they could do together!

"You will join my voice. You will live forever Zalkiniv, isn't that what you wanted?" The voice paused and gave a short laugh.

"Valnijz..." Zalkiniv whispered before the wind ripped anything but the pain away. He screamed then, a never-ending drone of terror and sadness. One more voice in the chorus, lost to the mortal world, forever.

Chapter 36.

Myriam walked slowly behind William, picking her steps carefully as the ground changed from sea grasses and sand dunes to more scrub and thorny bushes. The sun beat down on them, and she found herself often wiping her forehead and hoping she didn't get a redglow. The last thing she needed with her fairer northern skin. She would occasionally glance behind her to Regin, but every time she did, he avoided her gaze. *Men.*

She knew that wasn't the best response, but it frustrated her. She knew what she felt for Regin was far stronger than what she had felt for William, or Markin Darto, or the Forgemaster, or whatever name he was going by. *You know that's not fair.* She knew why he had done it, but the facts were she wasn't beholden to him. She had the right to choose who she gave her affection to, and while she liked William, and even considered him a very close friend, he wasn't what she wanted. What she wanted was Regin. But Regin was being Regin, meaning he was, she was sure, wracked with guilt and doubt. She wanted to stop the hike, sit them both down and hash this out right then. Get it all out in the open.

But she didn't. One, the last time she'd seen William's face, he had been on the edge of rage or tears; she wasn't sure which. And two, Regin would not go along with it, at least not yet. For now, she would put her desires away, for the sake of peace, and try to ignore it. She doubted it would work, though. Her father had once told her that between men and women, sealing things up usually ended up like a sealed-up cask of ale. Without a way for the pressure to escape, eventually it would explode, and nothing good came of that.

Maybe she'd try to talk to Regin one on one later. *Only talk Myriam, things got a little out of hand there at the dunes.* She hadn't meant to do that, but they'd been kissing and the smell of him, the feeling of him, sort of drove the caution out of her mind. *And it didn't help that my hand was nearly down his pants when William appeared.* She blushed a bit at that memory. She couldn't help it. Something about Regin made her act like a wanton dancer at a seedy watering hole. Or at least want to act that way.

She stopped short when William did, as he took a long drink out of his water bottle and turned to her. Sweat covered his forehead, but he didn't seem like he was going to scream at her, or cry.

"Remind me to never come south again. I thought I'd be happy to get out of that dark and damp world of the Gorom. But this sun is HOT." William wiped the sweat off with an exposed bit of shirt. "At this rate, the clothes I wore in the cave are going to be cleaner than these."

Myriam smiled. At least he's trying to make things normal. *That's a good sign.* "I agree. I'm more worried about getting a redglow. None of us are used to this heat."

Regin approached them, taking his own drink of water. Sweat clung to him as well, and Myriam couldn't help tracing the outline of hard muscle that his shirt clung to with the dampness.

"It would be tolerable if there were some shade, but we have seen nothing taller than mid-chest. How far is this person Amder said could help?" Regin blinked as some sweat attempted to roll into his eyes.

"He said a day and a half. So, we've got a while to go. Hopefully, we find better shelter soon. Or at least the night is cooler than the day." William shrugged in his breastplate. "This thing makes it hotter, but after the caves, I'm not sure I want to take it off. You all were right, back in the Reach, I wanted to say that. This stuff saved my life more than once in that strange dark world."

Regin laughed a short laugh, but it still brought a grin to Myriam's face. "Good. When we get back to Palnor, I'll pester you to expand it."

William shook his head. "Maybe for ceremonial reasons, but this stuff is beastly hot to wear." He paused and stroked his hammer with his thumb, starting off towards their goal, silent.

Myriam had noticed he did that when it thought. "What's on your mind William?"

William shuddered for a second and suddenly lurched over, grabbing at his head. A long hiss escaped him before he stood once more. "Something very horrible just happened. I don't know what, but...." He turned south again. "We better move." And with that, William started again, faster than before.

Regin finally looked her in the eye. "We'd better hurry then. When he gets like that..."

Myriam nodded, then pursed her lips. "When we camp, we need to talk, and you know what about, so don't act like you don't."

Regin started to object, but she turned away and followed after William, leaving Regin to take up the rear again.

***

William fought back the sickness that threatened to overwhelm him. He'd been trying to keep things normal with Regin and Myriam when the feeling of terrifying evil washed over him. He'd nearly thrown up the water he'd been drinking. *Duncan.* He had no doubt. He was doubly glad for his hammer then. Touching it seemed to clear his head, if only a little.

Maybe it was because of the spark of Amder that lived in it. Maybe it was because Duncan was there when he made it. It didn't matter. It helped. He'd been happy to also not think about Regin and Myriam. He could accept it, even if he didn't like it. What was more important, his friendships or his pride?

When they stopped for the night, he'd talk to Regin. He wasn't sure what he would say exactly, but he'd talk to him. Myriam… he wasn't sure what he could say. There was still too much raw feeling there. *No, I'll talk to Regin. Once some time has passed, I'll talk to Myriam. Maybe.*

He wondered who this person was that Amder had sent them after was. In typical fashion, Amder had been less than forthright about everything. He wondered if all the gods were that way. Speaking plainly but saying much. Frankly, it was a bit annoying when important things were afoot. Whatever that feeling had been, it was bad. Terrible.

"Yes, it was bad. And it still is." Amder's rumble echoed in his head. *"And I say as much as I can, William Reis. I think I am fairly blunt with you."*

"Then tell me where Duncan is and what is going on now. Why all this go here and do this stuff." William answered, picking his steps around some animal burrow that was hidden under a spiky plant he'd never seen before.

"One, whatever is going on with Duncan, I can't see clearly. Which is worrying. It means something is blocking me. I'm hoping that not all the gods are blocked. The person you are going to is an agent of another of my siblings." Amder's voice trailed off.

William stopped short, holding up his hand to let Myriam and Regin know. *"The last time you sent me for help from a follower of another god that didn't go exactly well, or as planned."* Days of blackness, injuries, and wondering if any of them were going to be alive soon wasn't something William had any interest in repeating. And Vin dying.

It was strange to him in a way that he was much more accepting of Vin's death than others. Master Jaste's and Haltim's deaths still hurt badly. All those innocent people in the Reach hurt as well. But Vin Tolin? He missed him, but it didn't have the same raw edge. Maybe it was because the man had been a soldier, a fighter.

"Yes well..." Amder stopped talking for a moment, and William got this feeling of panic. Near total panic. What could make a god feel that way?

"Be careful. Something is very wrong. I can't quite..." Amder stopped talking suddenly and all William could feel was his presence, though muted somehow. He tried to reach out, but like it had been with the Gorom the attempts slid off, not getting anywhere.

"William?" Regin asked from behind him.

William turned to his friends, totally not sure what to say to them. *Hey, Amder's sending us to another follower of a different god for help again, even though last time we all died. Oh, and he's vanished again, and is worried about something. I'm sure everything will be fine, and we won't all die like Vin did.*

"Amder." William paused, wiping the sweat off one more time. "He's worried about something. He doesn't know what. So, let's just be careful."

"What could worry a god? I mean, he's Amder. The god of craft and creation, right?" Myriam frowned. "I don't like this."

"I don't like it either. But at this point I don't see any other way forward." William shrugged. "But I'm willing to listen to any other ideas you all have."

Myriam shrugged in response. Regin opened his mouth to say something, but closed it again. William knew there wasn't anything they could really say. They had committed to this path when they came with him.

William nodded and started forward again, trying to remember everything Amder had said to him about where to go and what to do. In typical fashion, he'd been not overly clear, though William was pretty sure he'd be able to find the person.

They walked onward and dealt with the ever present sun. Myriam was right, they were all going to get redglow. He could feel the back of his neck and his face already being hot. Three pale red-faced northerners, sweating and dirty. Wonder how this person will react?

The only other danger was watching where they stepped. Between the ever present small twisted bushes and brush, and the strange thick leaved and spiked plants, was the evidence of animals. More and more holes, obviously dug out. They passed over one strange bleached skeleton, some long animal, with unfriendly looking fang-like teeth.

Midafternoon, or close enough, they finally saw a change in the monotonous scenery. They spotted their first actual tree, though it wasn't any tree any of them had seen before. But it was large, and gave off shade, even if its leaves were a pale-yellow green and it had a plethora of dark red tiny flowers on it.

"Can we rest there for a minute? I need to get out of this sun." Regin called to the rest of them.

"I agree!" Myriam asked. "I feel like I've been standing too close to a forge for the last hour. Let's cool off, if only for a brief rest."

William nodded. Shade would be nice. They walked toward the tree, on the lookout for whatever those tunnel making animals were but not seeing any. The only real sound was the slight buzzing noise of some insect that was exploring the small flowers. Other than that, the air was quiet, still. And hot.

The shade felt amazing as they finally entered it. Getting that burning heat off felt good, though he was sure they all had redglow now. Still, a short rest would help. They placed packs down and each sat, leaning against their bags, not saying anything.

William looked up at the tree, wondering how it got here, out in the middle of this strange flat land. The buzzing noise seemed to lull him, and he blinked in response as the weariness became more pronounced. *We could rest here, maybe sleep and get up early and get moving.* Wouldn't be as hot then. The sun would still be down. Yes, that was a good idea. A good long rest. Eat some ration bars again later, and just rest. They were all still so tired from the caves, anyway.

Myriam's eyes were closed already, and she appeared to be asleep. Regin was also nodding off, his head drooping and gave a jerk as he somewhat fought off the wave of exhaustion. William could feel himself getting more and more tired. The sun had taken more out of them than he'd thought, if they all fell asleep this fast. The buzzing sound droned on, seemingly louder, more insistent.

Sleep. Rest. Relax.

Chapter 37.

Duncan waited. Something was going on; he was sure of it. Zalkiniv had let Valnijz out, and then… chaos. He'd been dimly aware of the death of more innocents. He tried very hard not to think about it, though. If he kept his eyes closed and sat still, he could almost block everything out, almost. But after the deaths had ended, something had changed.

A howling noise, a series of screams and yells, had filled his ears. He'd opened his eyes then, at least a little to find the ever-present red dust, gone! He'd scrambled to his feet then, wondering if he was free finally. But no, he was still in the same strange nowhere place, but it was different now. The red was gone and replaced by this strange gray swirling mist. Faces appeared and vanished in it as soon as he could concentrate on them.

And the usual silence was gone as well. While the overwhelming screams and yells that came whenever the beast was released were gone, it was as if a distant echo of them remained. Each barely able to be heard. Each face he spied for the tiny amount of time he saw them seemed to be in pain, tearing at their own features. It was deeply unsettling and, more than that, scary. But it was different, which meant there was a reason.

"The reason is simple Duncan Reis. I am in control now. You should rejoice, Zalkiniv can no longer harm anyone, as he has paid the price of his hubris." A form came out of the mist, barely able to be seen, but the voice, he knew that voice. Valnijz.

"Why am I here then?" Duncan closed his eyes again and let out a long breath. "Free me. Kill me. You said once you took control, I would be free."

"Your time will come. But I need you still, Duncan Reis. Until I fully return, you are my anchor, my connection to this pitiful mortal body. But soon. I need but one thing, and then I must return to the place where I was born. There, I can fully reclaim my power and my place. This time I will not be stopped by my fool of a brother." Valnijz's voice seemed close, right in front of his face. The fetid breath filled his nose. A promise of decay and blood.

"This time I will wipe him and his people off the world, and then I will turn my sights on the others. One by one they will fall, until all this world, and whatever people that remain are mine to play with. Mine to kill. Mine to hunt." Valnijz stopped talking then but clicked his teeth.

Duncan opened his eyes carefully. He was right. Scant space was between him and the Blood God. Valnijz seemed stronger now as well. His once slim body had bulked up some, and the scales and more animalistic aspects of his body had grown. "Then you will kill me? And free me of this pain?"

A howl greeted his question, raw and tearing. The form of Valnijz stalked away, sniffing the air and gave a laugh, low and guttural. Just as sudden as the howl came, the form of the Blood God whirled back to him. "I might. I might keep you as a toy. I've grown used to having you around Duncan Reis. Maybe I'll use you the way my fool of a brother uses your cousin. He has his Forgemaster, maybe I should have my Bloodmaster?"

Duncan swallowed. This wasn't what he wanted. He opened his mouth to answer, but with a twist of a long black clawed finger, the blood god sent a streaking tendril of mist down his throat. A searing pain and a tearing agony came moments later. Duncan fell, choking on blood, coughing, each movement bringing a new fresh wave of raw red pain.

"One, I am in control here. Zalkiniv was an imperfect master of blood working. I AM the blood. Two, I doubt I would ever make a Bloodmaster. After Zalkiniv, I'm done using mortals as my pawns. Pity Zalkiniv killed that Axessed, he would have made an excellent tool." Valnijz smiled at Duncan. "Do you remember much from that time? When Zalkiniv took control?"

Duncan remembered. Sort of. So much of that was more like a barely remembered nightmare. Caught in a blood working, he had been nothing more than a puppet. Killing and maiming. *And I killed Haltim. Never forget that the old man's death was on your head.* He could still feel the man's skull in his hand sometimes, the feeling of old bones and skin giving way as he squeezed. The cracks and pops as the bones gave way.

"That was a fun death, wasn't it?" the Blood God growled. "That old priest had been giving me trouble. He'd freed you a few times thanks to Amder."

Duncan wanted to scream, he wanted to argue. His throat a ruin, all he could do was gasp and struggle to stay aware, stay conscious. *He will not kill me, he can't, but he can make me into something else. I can't let him. I won't let him.*

A searing pain covered his face as his vision returned. He knew why; the god had removed his eyelids. He tried to scream one last time before he collapsed in total despair.

"Remember this Duncan Reis. Until you die, you are subject to any whim I have." Valnijz smiled once more, and then without a sound, he freed Duncan.

The searing torment in his throat vanished so fast that he gasped from the sudden intake of air, and his eyes were back to normal. Duncan wondered for a moment if he could take this. He could not even remember what it felt like to not be in pain. What did laying on his back on a spring day in the Skyreach feel like? The feel of a hurried kiss from an admiring girl. Come to see the somewhat infamous Duncan Reis?

"I will decide your fate once I have fully returned. But for now, you will stay here." Valnijz, the God of Blood and Destruction, vanished into the sickly gray mist, the faces and movements of the stuff flowing over his form as he was removed from Duncan's sight.

Duncan sat, unwilling and unable to accept what he had just been witness to. All his sacrifice, in vain. All of this was pointless.

"Not pointless, watch… you amuse me." Valnijz's voice hissed around his head, making him shudder.

He could see then, as he could before, with Zalkiniv. But what he saw was different. There, not too far away, was a figure, robed, with a long spear. He had never seen the person before, yet, somehow; he knew he had been there all along.

"He's been watching." The hissing voice echoed around him.

Duncan watched as the figure suddenly moved, faster than any man, or thing he'd ever even thought of. Moving to a new tree, if only to keep this body in its sight.

"Come down Curor of Jindo." Valnijz yelled, and with a twist of power, pulled the man out of his tree.

As Duncan watched, the man twisted in the air, trying to break free of whatever control that had trapped him. But in moments, he stood unmoving in front of the Blood God. The figure said nothing, and as far as Duncan could tell, did not even appear afraid.

"You have been a magnificent warrior in my honor. I know you, Curor. I know every drop of blood you have shed in my name. Every soul you have given over to me. But you have something I need, Curor, something I want. And so..." Valnijz shrugged, before leaning forward and tore the man's neck open with his impossibly wide jaws.

Blood gushed as the Scaled One backed off, spitting out the skin and flesh. Duncan could only take in the sight in horror as a small tendril of blood red mist rose from the man's throat. A sight that brought a near purr from the Blood God.

"That is what I wanted, Duncan Reis. A small wisp of power, from what Jindo holds dear. The blood." Valnijz seemed to suck in this mist, and a scream echoed in Duncan's head. A scream that brought with it a flash of red.

***

Jindo awoke trembling. Something had changed. He had known that Zalkiniv was coming here. But now, something was different. Jindo stalked out of his bedchamber, moving with the power and within a few strides arrived at the other end of the keep. A small group of Curor scouts were standing there, heads cocked towards the north, as if they were listening to a faraway call.

"You feel it too. Go, discover the source of this." Jindo ordered them out. All three of the men bowed and with ritual precision bit their lips and spat the blood and spittle onto the ground. Swearing to not touch foot back in the keep until their mission was done.

Jindo grabbed a spear from a weapon rack and with a flash of his arm threw it, watching it embed itself halfway into the rock he had aimed it at. Whatever game Zalkiniv was trying, the Curors of the Blood God would stop. No mere man would take the drop from them. Ever.

What had happened to the scout he had sent to watch the man? How could Zalkiniv have stopped him? He could not have, which meant something he hadn't expected was happening. Jindo cursed the sky and waited.

***

William was home, the Reach spread out before him. It was dawn, and the torches and glows were going out slowly as the light of the new day started. It was going to be a wonderful day in the Reach. The mountain winds were already starting, and the forge and smelter smoke could not build up. It would make a good day to work.

He was happy. He had been bitterly disappointed after he hadn't gotten into the Smithing guild last year, but he'd slowly gotten over it. Duncan had finally stopped scaving and had signed on with a jewel trader as an apprentice. He already had an expert eye from his scaving days. He would be back next week, and then things would be even better.

William had turned his bitterness into energy and now owned five different mines and three large smelters. He still forged things and had been spending a lot of time fixing up the old Reis house. It would get so much louder soon. Duncan was engaged, and William was married. He'd met this girl out in town, and she'd captured him fully. A trader's daughter from the south, Rache, had become his world.

Yes, life was good. He reached up and scratched an itch on his face, smiling. Better than good. It was fantastic. Rache was out on a walk and would be home soon. He sometimes worried about her walks, but she stayed away from the barrier. Duncan would like Rache, he was sure; she loved to find old ruins, and had recently found some ruined tower she kept on about.

William scratched again, frowning for a second. Must be a spot where a spark hit, left a tiny burn. William didn't care about the ruins, but if she was happy, he was happy. Yes, everything was wonderful.

Sparks burn this itch. William felt another itch start. *I'll have to look into a waterglass.* William started down towards the Reach. He had been checking on one of the newer mines and had spent the night out there with the miners. Good bunch.

He was close to the western road into town when the first howl broke the air. Then another, then a thousand howls and screams. He knew that sound, every Reacher did. *Valni??* But the barrier! How?? He broke into a run, even though he hated it. He could see smoke rising now, but not the smoke of the forge, the smoke of things burning. *White and gray, the sign of destruction.* New screams and panic echoed around him. Men and women of the Reach flooded past him, running in terror.

William kept running. He didn't know if Rache was home yet, but he had to find her. She either was home, or she would be there soon. He had to find her! Turning a corner, he stumbled to a stop, his mind incapable of understanding what he was seeing.

Rache stood holding aloft some spear, black and bloody. Blood covered her face and body, and she screamed something in a language he didn't understand. He tried to back away, but she spotted him and did something with the spear. He couldn't move at all. Not an inch. Valni swarmed past him, each a horrible caricature of the person they had been once. They ignored him, though, swarming through the town and tearing anyone they caught apart, literally. Out of a corner of his eye, William saw Mr. Darrew fall, screaming as he failed with a maul, trying to free himself. He looked away as the man's screams ended and the sound of eating began.

Rache stood before him, a wild-eyed look of ecstasy on her face. He wanted to scream; he wanted to ask her why, or what. But he couldn't. She twitched the spear, and the tip cut a long line down his face. It burned horribly, eclipsing any other pain he'd felt. How could this be? What had happened?

Rache spoke something to him, but he couldn't hear it in the chaos of screams and smoke. She raised the spear, preparing to plunge it into his chest.

***

Will gasped for air, flailing as he discovered that he was covered with branches. More than that, he was covered with the tiny red flowers, and each one was sucking blood! He rolled and thrashed as the leaves and flowers broke off. Each tiny spot itched and burned, but he was awake and alive.

The dream clung to him. So much like the one he had in the Drendel tunnels. Vinik tunnels. It didn't matter, though. Despair and sadness had been the same. *Burn this tree.* Sparks cursed thing.

The noise must have awoken Regin as well, as the man was doing the same thing as William had been. Will crawled over to him and helped him by tearing the branches off. Will considered it a small joy that the flowers fell away so quickly once they were broken off from the tree.

Myriam was covered as well, but she had not awoken. The two men ripped the branches off her. And grabbing bags dragged her and themselves away from the tree. William could see a great many of the tiny red welts on each of his friends, and he was sure he looked the same.

"What in the fires of Amder was that??" Myriam gasped as she took deep breaths. "I had this horrible dream, and everything itched. I couldn't wake up."

"You're not the only one." William shook his head. "My dream was not pleasant as well."

Regin nodded. "I was trapped in the sewers of Ture. Tunnel borers were crawling over me, and I was bound, and rocks had been placed under my clothing. They were all trying to bore through me... it was horrible."

William nodded. He did not want to talk about his dream. It had seemed so real. *Thanks for waking me up, Amder.* But silence was the only response. He could still feel the god in the back of his head, so he was not gone, not like in the underground. Will concentrated but couldn't hear any hammers. That was good at least. Amder wasn't gone again.

Still, the lack of communication didn't make him feel comforted. If Amder wasn't talking, it meant he was doing something else. William could feel a twinge of nerves and panic crawl over his skin as he considered what could drag Amder away.

Will glanced at Regin and Myriam but said nothing. Too much has been going on. *I don't want to worry them.*

Chapter 38.

Myriam trudged along behind Regin and William. She hated this place. It was too hot, and even the plants wanted to kill them. *I could be in the Guild right now. I'd be a second-year apprentice. I'd be learning what I wanted, and I'd be comfortable, clean, and well fed. By the sparks, what was she doing here?*

"You are here for a reason, Myriam VolFar. A reason that will become clear, soon." The voice was back. And if anything, it was stronger, clearer than it had been.

"What are you? I don't want a reason, I want... Am I going crazy? William is the chosen Forgemaster of Amder. I'm just me." Myriam wanted to tell Regin about the voice. Then the picture of his face flashed in front of her eyes, one of confusion and disgust that shut that idea down.

"William Reis has a part to play. A large part. As does Duncan Reis. And you. And no, you are not crazy or strange. I chose you." The voice paused. *"You have questions. I will answer once your task is complete. I am limited right now, remember?"*

"This makes no sense. It's the heat." Myriam went to touch the back of her neck to rub it, but could feel the hot skin before she did. *Redglow.* Wonderful. She waited for the voice to retort, but there was nothing. *Just the heat, Myriam. only the heat.*

They trudged on. Though Myriam kept her head down for most of it, she took the occasional glance at Regin's backside. At least taking up the back end of the line has one perk. Her skin itched where those blood cursed flowers had been. She had refused to talk about her dream. Both Regin and William had asked, or at least hinted about asking. That sort of thing men do when they want to know the answer but don't want to seem like they are curious. Annoying that.

Not that she was going to tell them. Even thinking about it made her skin crawl. Back in the Reach, but this time she had stayed outside and Regin had gone with William to bring Amder back to life. The Valni had come and killed everyone but her, regardless of how much she tried to fight them off. They had dragged her step by step to the Mistlands, they were going to turn her into one of them. Even remembering it made her shudder. The feel of their skin on hers, the smells, the sight of the roiling red mist, reaching out to her…

The utter panic she'd felt when she'd awoken had ashamed her. She'd never been that scared before. That terrified. She glanced around, carefully following in the footsteps of Will and Regin. At least she was in the sunlight.

Late afternoon, the land changed more. The scrub and gasses were now finally being broken up by more trees. Normal trees. Pines and other evergreens from their looks. They passed another one of those trees with the red flowers, and the same buzzing sound came from it. They said nothing to each other, but William grabbed his hammer and took a wide path around the thing.

They didn't see many animals still, but it was hot. She wondered if more would come out at night. Finally, William stopped at a small rise and turned towards them. "This should be a good place to stop. Tomorrow we should find this person."

Regin unshouldered his pack with a sigh as he stretched. "Do we know anything else about them? What they look like? Why are they in this place?"

William looked down and kicked some dust off his boot. "She's a follower of the Wind goddess, which apparently is an aspect of the Ocean Goddess. At least that's what Amder says."

"Another god's follower?" Myriam threw her pack down as well. "That did not go well the last time you know."

Will half smiled as he nodded at her. His eyes unreadable. "I know. I said the same thing to Amder. He told me it would be fine this time. I have my doubts, but again, what choice do I have? Though..." He paused and grinned. "I swear unto you if she says anything about caves or going underground, I will say no."

Regin snorted and scratched one welt from the tree. "Hopefully, she's not put off by our appearance. We were clean, washed, and refreshed at the start of the day. Now we all stink, we are all dirty and we are all covered with these bite things. So... yeah."

"I will have you know Regin, I do not stink." Myriam replied quickly. "Though I do have a redglow on the back of my neck that I hope doesn't get worse."

Regin laughed but didn't reply. Not that she expected him to. Later, after William was asleep, they would talk, regardless if Regin wanted to or not.

"Let's get a fire going, if only to make sure we don't get noticed by whatever lives out here." William kept his hand on his hammer, thumb rubbing it.

"Why do you keep doing that?" Myriam pointed to his hammer. "You rub away at that thing like you're trying to polish it with your skin."

Will glanced down at his hand. "I didn't even think about it. I don't know. I find it calming. It reminds me of why I am doing this. Duncan was there when I made it. He didn't use a hammer or anything, but he worked the bellows. It… it was the last thing he and I did together before the blood curse took him."

"I'm sorry William. I didn't want to dig up sad memories or anything." Myriam patted his arm, but he pulled away quick.

"No, it's fine. Let's get that fire made and eat some travel rations." William turned away and started gathering what sticks and wood he could get.

Regin had said nothing but shook his head when Myriam tried to get his attention, and he joined William in gathering fuel for the fire.

***

Jindo stood on the keep walls, waiting and watching for any of his force to return. He had not slept anymore since he sent them out. More than one Cruor had looked at him as he waited, and only a fool wouldn't be able to pick up on the air of tension that suffused the keep.

Let them wonder. I would as well. Jindo paced, his blood enhanced speed and reflexes making him a blur to any without the gift. The scouts should have been back long ago. Hours ago. Yet, nothing. He considered sending more, but hesitated. Each Cruor was equal to over fifty men in fighting. There was not an inexhaustible supply of his followers, however.

And anything that can kill that many of mine is something to be wary of. But Zalkiniv was a shell of his former power, a scrap, barely holding on. Yet, he Jindo Halfman paced here, trying to discover what had happened to his forces. And the only unknown was that fool of a Priest who had failed and paid the price.

Jindo wasn't a scholar, but he had the scrolls. He hesitated for a moment, unsure. He did not use the scrolls much. Sometimes they told him things he did not understand, or he did not want to understand. No, he would stay here and wait. Zalkiniv was getting closer.

***

Duncan watched as the third man slumped dead. Each death brought a burst of red through the ever-thickening gray mist, and a sense of growing power. More so than a normal death, at least. He had no idea who those men were, or where they had come from, but whomever or whatever they had been, it hadn't helped them.

He had resigned himself to watching the terrors that Valnijz inflicted as he traveled south. If he tried not to watch, the blood god would punish him the same way, removing his eyelids and making him look. Better to spare himself that pain again. So, he watched.

They had been walking away from the village, covered in drying blood, when the three men had appeared. Duncan hadn't seen them move. One blink there was nothing there, the next three men, each clad in brown and grey leather, embossed with a blood red gem over their heart. *Ruby? Garnet?* He'd almost smiled at his initial reaction, almost.

He was somewhat grateful for the fact that he couldn't hear anything from the outside. Two of the men flashed long spears, points nearly touching the chest of the beast, HIS chest. He felt a tremor of recognition when he saw their design; they were identical in style to the spear of Valnijz. Followers?

For a moment, he wondered if he would be spared their deaths, but only for a moment. For as fast as the men moved, Valnijz was quicker. The Blood god seemed to flinch right, faster than Duncan could see, and the man on the right went down, his neck and part of his jaw ripped off. A fountain of blood erupted, and the grey mist flashed the first time as whatever essence these men had was taken.

The other two men registered shock, but they appeared to be well trained, which, of course, was their downfall. They both thrust forward, one high, one low. Dunc couldn't see their spears move either, Valnijz must have been able to. His body contorted oddly, and Duncan heard several crunches and snaps from inside. *My body. My poor sparks cursed body.*

The Scaled God seemed to flinch again, and both men lurched forward. Their spear points still hovered barely above his skin. But the other end, the shafts, were now both fully embedded in their torsos.

The grey had flashed red again, bright flashes illuminating the strange and grotesque forms that seemed to move in it. And if anything, the gray mist grew even thicker, stronger. He did not like the idea of it all growing to the point where he was in the mist. He wasn't sure what would happen, but he never wanted to find out. Not willingly. He wouldn't die, he knew that. He was needed. But no more pain was wanted. No more fear.

"Did you like my show?" Valnijz's voice seemed to echo around him. "They were fun. It's good to see that Jindo at least has kept the faith. My faith."

"Jindo?" Duncan truthfully didn't care who Jindo was. But if it kept him from being tortured by this thing, he was fine with asking questions. It wasn't the first time he'd heard that name from Valnijz.

"Jindo Halfman. Leader of the Cruor." Valnijz appeared in the mist. It trailed around him, nearly caressing the scaled figure. "An order devoted to me. Zalkiniv always wanted to be the only one, and in truth, he was the leader of my faith. But Jindo was my spear. Jindo didn't like Zalkiniv and Zalkiniv hated Jindo." Valnijz twisted a tendril of the grey mist around a finger then flicked it towards Duncan, smiling with a fanged mouth as Duncan flinched and pulled back.

"The Cruor have something I want. Something I need. The last liquid drop of my blood. Shed the day I learned the truth. The day I knew." Valnijz sent another tendril at Duncan, and then another. Like grey arrows, they shot towards him, though they lost speed and broke apart before they got too close.

"Knew what?" Duncan kept an eye out for any of the mist, trying to move towards him from behind.

Without a sound Valnijz was suddenly merely a hair's breadth from his face. Scaled and torn, the face ripped itself into a smile. The stink of rot, of mold and things dead for a week bloomed from its mouth. "MY truth. MY way. MY reason." And with a crack of air, the Blood God was gone. Vanished from Duncan's sight.

Chapter 39.

Will stared into the fire, watching the coals crack and fall apart. Soft woods. Wouldn't be much use for forging. *I want to make something. Anything. A hook, a fork even, just something.* A frown crossed his face as he wondered if he still had the skill. He wondered if he should talk to Regin about it, but the man was asleep and snoring, though thankfully not loudly.

Myriam was pretending to sleep. He could tell because every time he looked away, she moved. Waiting for me to be asleep, but why? Then he looked at Regin again. Ah, that was the reason, or most likely. Not that he blamed her. She had made her choice. It still hurt, but he had little say in the matter. And at least she was trying to wait until he was asleep.

"Don't worry lad. I'm sure everything will work out. But we need to talk, and not about that." Amders' familiar gravel sounding voice echoed in his head.

"Where have you been? I tried to talk to you before, but you didn't answer." William forced his thoughts inward, the heat and glow of the fire fading from his mind.

"That is what I wanted to talk about. Something is wrong." Amder appeared in front of him, or at least in his mind's eye.

"Isn't it always?" William answered back, smiling. But the smile faded as Amder shook his head, his face in a grimace.

"Not like this." Amder stuck a finger into the fire, watching as the flames turned yellow and then white, a ghostly white that William had seen only once before, the day he made his hammer.

"I had told you that Zalkiniv had taken over your cousin, Duncan. Remember?" Amder breathed on the fire and the shape changed from a small circular fire into a squared off forge. Small, but workable.

"Yes. Is there something wrong? Are we too late??" William stood quickly, brushing off his legs. *"I can wake Regin and poke Myriam, we can be gone now."*

"No lad. At least I do not think so. Again, this isn't my domain. But we are going to fix it, with my domain and your skill." Amder grabbed a heavy rock and between his heavy hands squeezed it. Will watched as it changed. Glowing and becoming soft, Amder sculpted it with a light touch, and within a fraction of time placed a small but serviceable anvil next to the forge.

"I had a great many doubts about this mission of yours, William. You are my Forgemaster. You should be in Ture. The city is still a mess. The guild is trying to find its way, but the Priesthood has completely collapsed, and along with it, most of the power structure. I've ordered the Guildmasters to reach out and work with the King of Palnor. I even blessed his spear again as a show of my backing. Made a big production out of it. Took a hint from you from back in the Reach. Glowing lights and all that." Amder stood and searched the ground for something.

"Never suitable materials when you need them." Amder muttered as he picked up and dropped several rocks and dry stones. He shrugged and pulled out a hammer from under his cloak. It was shaped like the one Duncan had found back in the tower!

Smaller, and less decorated, but still very similar. It shone golden in the white lights of the forge. Amder placed it on the anvil and crouched back down, seemingly satisfied. *"But now, now I know you have to be here. I'm afraid William Reis. I'm afraid that it's not Zalkiniv that's in control of Duncan. There is a chance, merely a chance, that it is my brother, Valnijz."*

William stepped back. *"What?? He's dead! Well, I mean he's a god, but he's still dead! Duncan killed himself to stop him."*

"I know. But I also said I couldn't fully read what happened that night. There's a chance, a slight chance, that some part of the Blood God passed through, into Duncan." Amder shook his head. *"If that's true, you will need a way to hold him."*

"I can't stop a god! I mean, I can't do again." William felt the icy knot of fear settle in his guts.

"You can. You must." Amder stood, towering over William in a way he hadn't moments before. *"There's only one thing that will bind him. Bind him long enough to learn the truth."*

William shuddered at the thoughts this was giving him. He'd only ever had the barest of contact with Zalkiniv, and still the memories made him want to spill his stomach. But to go up against the blood god himself?

William was about to argue when one-word, one name, crossed his mind. Duncan. Duncan had faced off against the influence of the God of Rage and Destruction for weeks. Even months. He had sacrificed everything to defeat the Scaled One. He had done it to save William. To save everyone.

William wasn't as brave as Duncan was. He'd always known that. It had taken weeks to get up the courage to take the blood shard from the Mistlands that had started this entire series of events. And yet, Duncan would cross the barrier without a thought. *Braver than I ever was. And faster.* William gave a small smile at the thought. Knowing that Dunc would have added that faster line on to make things less serious.

"What must I do?" William paced around the forge that Amder had made. *"What must I make?"*

Amder shifted and stood next to William, now the same height. *"Shackles. A very particular set of shackles."*

"There's metal that can bind the Blood God? What is it?" William racked his memory, trying to think of what it could be. Nothing from the Skyreach that he could think of. Something exotic. Something special. No ordinary metal. Something God touched for sure... then he knew.

He picked up the hammer from the anvil, swinging it carefully. It sang, but it wasn't his hammer.

"Yes. I am sorry William. But the only material that can hold a god is one made with the blood of another god." Amder nodded at William. *"Your hammer."*

Will lifted his own hammer in his other hand. So light, so strong. It sang to him. More than that, he had meant what he said to Myriam about it. He and Duncan had been together when he made this. Before the blood curse, before all the Forgemaster information. Before the finding of the Blade of Valnijz and the Hammer of Amder. This was the last thing that for William really connected him to those times, those days.

Will blinked back the wetness that crept into his eyes. He was going to miss it. He felt strangely like he was giving up on William Reis. He was William sure, but he was also the Forgemaster. But he knew he would do anything and give up everything to save Duncan. There wasn't a choice.

"I'll miss this hammer." Will wiped his eyes with the back of one sleeve. *"Let's get started."*

***

Jindo spotted the figure miles away. For a moment he blanched, wondering if Zalkiniv had actually killed his men. But no, the way it ran, the loping movements, eating up terrain. It moves like an Axessed. Jindo had only interacted with one of those creatures twice. Once testing his powers, and the second time right after the Godsfall, when one came to tell him.

Jindo had only been the sword of the Scaled one for fifty years at that point. He'd wanted to gather what few Cruors there were at that time and set sail for the North. Wait, he had been told. Wait. He had obeyed.

He'd waited through centuries. Other members of his order grew old and died. The blood killing them sometimes before, or rarely, when they killed for the God, dying in battle. Once sixty-five men had died when they had tried to take the City in Blue. That had been his only failure. The Scaled One gave him a year of tortured dreams and living nightmares. And when Jindo had been about to break and give in to the insanity, the Blood God had stopped.

Thankfully, he'd never been ordered back to the City in Blue. Though we could never find it again, even if we wanted to attack. The City had vanished sometime after the last attempt. Gone. Even stranger, only Jindo even remembered it had been there. Even the other Cruor who had survived that day had no memory of it.

None of that mattered now. The figure coming closer was something Jindo Halfman, leader of the Cruor, Sword of the Blood God, had never dreamed he would ever see again. Valnijz. The Blood God himself had returned.

Jindo did not know how, but he knew. Blood called to blood. And his blood was singing. Jindo leaped down into the courtyard and, using every ounce of speed, rang the call. A single ancient bell that summoned all the Cruor from anywhere they were. Thankfully, no one was too far away.

But he was here or would be soon. Jindo knew what the God wanted. He knew what was required. The Cruor would be no more after this day. *All Glory to the Scaled One, and to the new world, he shall rule.*

Jindo stood in the gathering courtyard, watching as men and women lined up. Silence filled the air, as each of them stood ready from the oldest veteran to the woman who only yesterday had survived the trial. Jindo did not feel pity or sorrow for them. No, he felt joy. The time of waiting was over. The scrolls had been right, Glory to the Scaled One.

The doors of the keep, bound in heavy timbers of nightwood and blood quenched steel, flew open, shattered by the force of the blow. There, the sun glistened off the scales that adorned the body of a god. Clad in ragged clothing and wearing an even more ruined pack.

"Jindo. Jindo Halfman. My sword. You have kept the faith, Jindo. You did not betray me." Valnijz moved with a series of twitching movements, each one causing him to grow. Corded muscles bunched under the fine scales that covered him, hands grew longer as black and white claws pushed out from his fingers.

"I thank you for that, Jindo. You have done well. Know that if I had not been betrayed by Zalkiniv, you and your force would have been the sword and pierced the world for me. The slaughter would have been glorious." Valnijz twitched again, and this time four Cruors died, each falling as their throats were sliced open with a razor-sharp claw.

Jindo felt a moment of pride, as not even one of his force moved, and no stink of fear came from them. "Thank you, my Lord. We would have lived and died for you on the battlefield. And now we die here for you. Our lives are yours to do with as you need."

"Ah Jindo. Loyal to a fault." Valnijz screamed then, and with a rage that broke Jindo's control for a second, Valnijz tore each Cruor apart. Each death releasing the blood power granted by the drop, and each speck of that power returning to the god whence it came.

Within moments, Jindo was the last one standing. Blood flowed around his boots, slowly sinking into the dusty ground. Jindo was ready to die. Ready to fall. Yet the Blood God did not move.

The form shuddered in a spasm of pleasure as it stood in a fine red cloud. A cloud that it slowly absorbed. Until Valnijz stood there again, panting, and grinning with a torn mouth and sharp and ragged fangs. "Bring me the drop Jindo."

Jindo moved then, flowing with all speed toward the most holy relic of the Cruor. He had been the one to find the drop that day. He had seen the birth of the blood god, the fall of the unnamed one into the Scaled form that stood in his keep now.

There, where it always hung, was the drop. Suspended in midair inside a crystal tube. The blood quivered inside its prison. *It knows. It knows the master is here.* Taking great care, Jindo walked with the crystal tube. He approached the Scaled one and bowing his head; he held the tube up to his god. "My lord, your blood."

The crystal was taken so fast Jindo did not know it had even left his hands. He prepared himself. He had known this time would come. The last speck of the blood was needed, and the last speck lived in him. But yet again, the blow did not come. Jindo forced the despair down. Was he not good enough for his God?

"Jindo Halfman. You are more than worthy. You have another task, at least for now. Coming for me. Coming for us. The Forgemaster of my betrayer, my brother, is near. They wish to stop me. They wish to end this. You will protect me as I claim the last parts of my power. I must take the drop and return to the Anvil of Souls. Only there can I fully return now." Valnijz hissed in Jindo's ear. A long claw traced a thin red line down Jindo's cheek, leaving a small trail of red drops.

"You will follow in three days. They must believe they have me. They will take me to the Anvil. I cannot enter without their help. Then, you will strike. Kill them all. Kill the Forgemaster and his friends. Then I will complete my return, and the world of Alos will know my rage." Valnijz spoke and then with a telltale whisper of movement was gone, leaving the crystal tube back in Jindo's hands.

Chapter 40.

Myriam awoke groggy. She had tried to stay awake, trying to out wait William. But she had gotten so tired. She blinked a few times, trying to clear her eyes and her head of the aftereffects of sleep. She blinked again as she looked around their camp. Things were different.

The campfire was gone, and in its place a small forge. Next to it was an anvil, again, not too large, but still serviceable. And standing there, back towards her, was William. But yet something was different. His hammer! The silver one, the one he had made, was gone. Replaced with a golden one. What did that mean?

"Morning." Myriam cleared her throat at the croaking sound of her voice. "Good Morning. Um…. Are you going to tell me what's going on?"

William turned around, his face serious and, if anything, resigned. Resigned to what?

"Myriam. I'll explain, but let's get Regin up first. The less I have to say on all this, the better." William walked over to the still slightly snoring Regin and prodded him with the toe of his boot. "Wake up Regin."

Regin sneezed and yawned. "I hate dust. Next time we go somewhere, can it have proper beds?" He sat up and, eyes wide, took in the same sight as Myriam had. He looked at her, eyebrow arched, and she shrugged. *I don't know anything either.*

William sighed and sat on the anvil. "I am going to be tired tonight. As you can see, I had an interesting evening."

"What happened? What is going on? Why is your hammer different?" Myriam spoke in a torrent of words. "Where did the forge come from? What were you doing?"

Regin smiled and shook his head. "Let the Forgemaster speak, though I admit I'm more than curious as well."

"Last night as you slept Regin, and you pretended to Myriam, Amder came to me." William shot her a wink.

"Oh?" Myriam wanted to ask how he knew she'd been pretending, but William was smart enough to guess why, and that wound was still too new for him.

"Yes. There is something again you both should know. I said Duncan might be taken over by the spirit of Zalkiniv, the former High Priest of the Blood God, right? It might be worse." William paused and rubbed the golden hammer with his thumb for a second before looking down and frowning at the smooth golden metal by his side.

"What could be worse?" Regin stood. "I wasn't looking forward to going up against the Blood God's own, and now you say it could be worse?"

Myriam had the same thought, but the answer came to her and she stifled a small shudder. *It couldn't be. It can't be.*

"Yes. You get it, Myriam." William rubbed his face. "The Blood god. A small part of the Blood God may have passed into Duncan. That maybe what is in control now."

"We can't go up against a god!" Regin's face had turned white, and all traces of his night's sleep gone. "William, I know we swore to help, but the Scaled One?"

"I know. Amder knows. Which is why two things happened last night. One, he gave me a way to hold Valnijz, if that's really who is in my cousin. And two, he has given you both an out." William reached into his pack and pulled out a set of shackles. Shackles that gave off a soft white glow. The Wight Iron they were made from still gave the telltale slight moan as they struck each other, a reminder of their source.

Wight Iron. Myriam knew then. "Oh William. I am so sorry."

"Yes." William hefted the shackles. "It takes metal touched by the blood of a god to hold another god. And that meant my hammer. The hammer I made with Duncan had to be reformed into these. Amder made this forge." William took the golden hammer at his side in his other hand.

"He gave me this. In some ways, it's even better than my old hammer. But it's not mine. It's not what I made with Duncan." William shook his head. "But that's not all. He gave you both a way out. When you swore your oaths to me, you marked yourself. If you fled normally, all would know you as an oath breaker. I have convinced Amder to let you both free of your oaths. There is no shame in running from this."

William turned and pointed to the southwest. "The person we are to see is that way. Only an hour or so away. We leave soon. You can stay there and be safe. She will help you find a way home."

"She?" Myriam asked, standing. She already had her answer. She was going to go with William. Why, she didn't know, but she really wanted to. She had to.

"That's what Amder said." William placed the shackles back in his bag and the hammer back on his belt. "I still don't know much about her. Amder still isn't the most forthcoming god."

Regin hadn't said anything but snorted at that. He raised his eyes to lock onto Myriam's, the questions obvious. Was she staying or leaving? What did she think of all this?

She would talk to him later, at this person's place. Whatever it was. At least there and then they would have an excuse to talk, without William there.

They broke camp quickly, though the small forge and anvil seemed so out of place. "What do we do with this?" Myriam pointed to the items. "Seems strange to leave them here."

William shrugged. "Well, we don't need them." And a small smile broke out. "And it's kind of amusing to think about the reactions of the next person who sees them."

Regin did laugh at that, but it didn't seem to improve William's mood any. They stepped carefully down the rise they had camped on. They hadn't even eaten yet, but figured they should just get to this place, wherever it is, and whoever it was.

William took point again, and Regin followed right after, leaving Myriam in the rear again. The ground changed more as they walked until, finally; they saw the edge of a proper forest. Not a large one, but actual trees and shade. And finally, a large tent structure, the sides shifting and moving in the breeze.

"I assume that's it?" Myriam asked as William paused.

"Yes." William turned towards Regin and her. "And please know, I will not think less of you if you leave. I fought Amder for your right to do so. But after this time, there's no going back."

Myriam nodded. She had to come. *Why do I feel that way, though?*

As they stood there, the tent flap pushed open from inside and out walked the strangest person Myriam had ever seen. Hair as yellow as gold wasn't that unusual, but her skin was the color of burned copper. There was something else different about her, and it took a second for Myriam to figure out what it was. The woman wasn't walking. She wasn't even touching the ground. She stood there, suspended one tiny measure above the ground!

***

William took in the sight in front of him, unsure of how to react. The woman in front of him was like nothing he had ever seen. Exotic and powerful, he wasn't sure what to think. *Except the fact that she is beautiful.* Will was used to women wearing leathers and wool. Maybe a dress or a cloak on warm summer days, but even then, northerners liked to cover up.

But this woman... her clothes were orange and green, and they flowed around her. Light, airy, and floating as she stood there. Even her hair seemed to move in small ways on its own. He was dumbfounded.

"We should probably go there; she appears to be waiting for us." Regin whispered in his ear, breaking the daydreaming William had started.

They walked slowly and carefully. There wasn't much of a path here, and while they hadn't seen as many of those empty burrows, stepping in one and breaking an ankle wouldn't help the quest. But why would there be if you could never touch the ground? *"It's a cheap trick."* Amder's voice grumbled in the back of his head.

"It's impressive. As she is". William said back. He heard Amder grumble again, but his god didn't say anything else.

"Welcome." The woman bowed, her hair moving to hide anything William might have been able to see as she moved. "My name is Lorelei. Lorelei Mistral. I welcome the Forgemaster of Amder, and his friends."

William was even more taken as she spoke. Her voice made him think of the wind rushing down the mountains back home. "Thank you. I am William Reis. This is Myriam VolFar and Regin."

"How come you never mention my last name?" Regin asked with a laugh. "I am Regin Hamsand."

"I don't know. Maybe because it sounds like the cook at a roadside inn?" William laughed at that, trying to imagine Reign cooking at an inn. It felt good to laugh. Some of the tightness in his body faded out, but returned as he remembered why he'd been so stressed to begin with.

"What's wrong with cooks at inns?" Myriam poked William. "It is a pleasure to meet you Lorelei."

"And you all. Though…. Did you have the foolish idea to sleep under a redkiss?" Lorelei shook her head as she took in the still visible myriad red specks that covered their bare skin.

"Grey-green leaves? Lots of red flowers? Makes a buzzing sound?" William asked. "Yes. You should get rid of those trees. Horrible things."

Lorelei smiled. "They are harmless, if you know what they are. And besides, they keep the Charnoth populations down. The legends say they were an experiment of the Scaled One. Many generations ago, but were thrown away as a failure." She moved to the side, waving them to enter the large tent.

"Charnoth?" Regin was the first to enter, followed by Myriam and then finally William.

"You must have seen their bones. Small animals, make lots of burrows. They are poisonous, and mostly come out at night. Mostly hunt small animals, but they are attracted to bees as well. The redkiss trees make the sound of buzzing to lure the Charnoth in, and then they feed until the Charnoth is almost dead. Charnoth hate other Charnoth outside of mating season, so already weakened, they fight and die." Lorelei floated by her clothing trailing behind her in a spinning flutter.

"Ah yes. We saw those things." William shook his head. "You know why we are here."

"Yes. But first some food? Rest? And I am sure you all want to get clean." Lorelei moved her hands, and a breeze blew into their faces. Not strong, but cooling. "And no offense, but I think you all do have a certain odor about you."

"But the Blood God…." William pointed towards the flap.

"Will be waiting. He can't go any further without you. I will explain." Lorelei raised herself up, floating now nearly two spans above the ground.

"The Blood God has returned, at least partially. A growing stronger portion of his being, his soul, lives in your cousin. He has taken full control. Zalkiniv is gone and no more. You must take him once captured to the Anvil of the Souls. The place the gods first set forth on this world." Lorelei paused, locking eyes with William.

William shrugged. "This doesn't seem all that dangerous then. We will just go off to this Anvil place, no problem." Turning to Regin and Myriam, Will raised his eyebrows in surprise, and mouthed a huge what to them both.

"You must take him there. If you do not, there will never be a way for Duncan to be free. All our destinies will be fulfilled at the Anvil." Lorelei smiled, and William smiled back. But why did he think she wasn't smiling at him?

"After you bathe and eat, I will discuss where he is. But rest assured, nothing will change without you there." Lorelei paused, giving them a small smile as she did, sinking back to the level she had been before. "Go. You will find the tent larger than you think."

Will had to admit, food, a bath, and a soft place to sleep sounded like a far better night than anything else. And trying to capture a god, even one only partially there, sounded like something he would need to be refreshed for. He nodded, looking back at Regin and Myriam, who nodded back. It was settled.

Chapter 41.

William sank into the tub again, relishing the feeling of soapy water and a gentle warmth. He had been clean only yesterday, but it felt like a year ago. Well, not fully clean. This was a proper bath. Lorelei had somehow gotten all their clothes clean as well. She even had some ointment to put on the redkiss flower bites. *How do flowers bite? Why would anyone, even the Blood God, think biting flowers was a good idea??* Whatever the ointment was made from, the stuff made the things fade and stop itching. That was enough.

He wanted to know more about Lorelei. She was a striking woman. Though there isn't much he could do. She apparently lived here, doing whatever she did.

"She's a Windtalker William. And I'm worried." Amder's voice came strong and grumbling as usual.

"Why are you worried now?" Will wiped his face with a cloth, wiping away the water.

"The Anvil of Souls. We don't go there. We haven't been there since the day we appeared in this world." A hammering sound came with Amder's words.

He really is worried. He does that when he's concerned. Will stood, glad that Amder hadn't decided to physically manifest this time. He dressed slowly, enjoying the feeling of being totally clean. There were even snacks, and much to his delight, korba fruit.

"Be careful." Amder's hammering grew louder. *"I want this business finished, there is much to do."*

Will took a bite of the fruit, savoring the flavor. He hadn't had these since he had fled Ture with Regin. *"Amder. I have a question. If the world existed before the Gods, and things were already living here, like the Vinik, why come?"*

Amder sighed, and the hammering stopped. *"We are gods. It's what we do. Don't trouble yourself about it. Just be careful. I don't trust my brother. Something is moving in the darkness that I cannot see. But now more than ever, the stakes are higher. We cannot allow Valnijz to fully return. But you have the key, William. Only you have the key."*

William could feel Amder leave again. *Very clear.* It wasn't like he would not be careful. *I wonder if Amder will ever talk to me and not say he is worried. Doubtful.* He sat on a nearby stool, wondering if he should go and find Lorelei. That meant he might run into Myriam and Regin together.

Will had purposefully taken the last bath, so the two of them could have time alone. Will knew there wasn't anything he could do or say to change the situation, but it didn't mean he had to watch them together. He tried very hard to think of anything else. It still hurt, though not as much as before.

A soft voice called out from the flap. "Forgemaster Reis?"

Lorelei. Will stood quickly, wiping korba fruit juice off his chin quickly and wiping his hands through his hair. "Yes? I'm dressed."

Lorelei entered the room, floating ever so slightly above the carpeted floors of this amazing tent. It seemed to go on forever. "Was the bath to your liking?" Lorelei slowly trailed her hands through the water, and before Will's eyes it blew away, drops at a time.

"Yes! Thank you. And korba fruit. I've only had it once, back in Ture. A Saltmistress gave it Regin and I." Will held up a fruit and took a bite. "You don't see it in the Reach."

Lorelei smiled. "I wouldn't think so. I've felt the winds in the Reach before. Cold and strong. I've heard them tell of an old city, full of men who dig in the hard ground. I, for one, will never understand that."

Will shrugged. "I love the Reach. It's home."

"I meant no offense. I have a hard time understanding how all that solidity is appealing." Lorelei tapped the air, and a small burst of cold air blew through the room.

Will immediately felt like home. The burst felt like and even smelled like home. "Thank you. But I have some questions... Amder wasn't clear. What is your relationship with the Saltmisstresses?"

"We follow the same goddess. But they follow her with water, and I and my kind follow her with air. There are more of them though." Lorelei rose higher into the air. "I said my name was Lorelei Mistral. That was only partially true. My name is Lorelei THE Mistral."

Will didn't understand the distinction, but he wasn't sure it mattered to him. "Alright."

"You do not understand Forgemaster. As you are for Amder, I am for my goddess." Lorelei rose even higher, and the room swirled with wind and scents from a thousand different places. "I came here at the behest of my lady. Tomorrow I leave. And you will head south. Cross the stream you find, then continue down the slope. It will lead you down, down to the birthplace of the gods."

Will swallowed a bite of korba fruit. *I wish had something that impressive. I had a glowing hammer at least, but that's gone.*

"Go, get some rest. The next few days will try your soul." Lorelei frowned, and a deep sadness touched her eyes for a moment. "Be careful William Reis, Forgemaster of Amder."

***

Regin spied Myriam, and ducked into another tented room, trying to avoid whatever conversation she wanted. He didn't want to be alone with her. While he felt better physically, he still felt sick to his stomach when he allowed himself to dwell on what had happened before.

He knew William had said he understood, but the guilt still hadn't faded from him. *I hate feeling this way.* Guilty for hurting my friend, but so wanting to be with Myriam. At least Will seemed to be taking it better. That Lorelei woman had at least turned his head a bit.

Regin turned to exit the room, but there, before he could move, stood Myriam. Freshly bathed as well. She smiled at him and he had a hard time remembering what his plan to avoid her had been about.

"Done running, Regin?" Myriam poked him in the chest. "Don't deny it."

"I don't. Look, it's obvious how I feel, but…." Regin looked around the room, trying to think of a way out of this.

"Obvious?" Myriam smiled. "Maybe I want to hear you say it."

Regin looked her in the eyes, and the last thoughts of running melted away. "I think you are incredible. You are strong, smart, and talented. You don't try to hide behind a pretty smile and blinking eyes. You always say what you think. I've never spent any time around anyone like you. I didn't even know anyone like you." Regin paused, trying to think of what to say next. How do I explain?

Regin continued, cutting her off from speaking. "I can't think of anything other than you when you smile at me. The way you look when it's night outside, and the moonlight catches the frame of your face. The way your brow looks when you're concentrating on getting a smithing project right...."

Myriam poked him hard enough for him to stop talking. "That's enough, now kiss me."

"But Myriam. I can't... we can't." Regin tried to resist her. He could smell her skin. *Clean, safe, warm.* Without thinking, he leaned in and their lips met. With that kiss, all thoughts of William, of how he felt guilty, all of it faded away.

His hands moved to her hips and pulled her closer. Her body, soft in all the right places, melded into his. He could feel himself being lost in her, and he loved it.

A small cough made him pull back. There at the flap stood their host. The woman, Lorelei, was unlike anything he had ever seen before. He'd at least never seen her race in Ture. He had sort of assumed that everyone came to Ture. *Though I guess that was part of my arrogance. The world is much larger than Palnor.*

"Forgive my interruption, but I need to speak with Myriam." Lorelei bowed to the two of them.

Regin looked at Myriam, her face flushed and her slightly biting her lips. *Better this way, I don't know if I can pull away from that again.* "Go with her." Regin took a step back, letting out a long breath.

Myriam looked to argue for a moment, then nodded. "We aren't done Regin Hamsand." She whispered. "Not a bit."

Regin nodded. He couldn't resist her. He knew that now. But at least, maybe delay it until all this was over with William and his cousin, all this stuff with the Blood God. Push it off till later. If there was a later. He hadn't really thought about it till then. They could all be dead in a weeks' time. Dead and forgotten.

A chill shot up his spine. "Go, then come back to me." Regin whispered back. If he was going to die in a week, did he really want to wait?

***

Myriam followed Lorelei away from Regin. That's twice now someone had interrupted them. Though the first time it had been her fault. She was ashamed to admit it, but she had forgotten about William. Not that he existed, but that he was coming back to them. When she was with Regin, time sort of didn't matter.

"I'm sorry I interrupted you. But I wanted to talk to you face to face, before the morning when you and your companions leave, and I leave as well." Lorelei led her into yet another room, red and gold, and nothing but numerous oversized pillows and other things that Myriam didn't recognize.

"Leave? I thought you lived here." Myriam sat down, sinking into one large pillow that had almost a snowflake patter of gold on red.

"No, I was here for you." Lorelei sat as well; the first time Myriam had seen her not float. *I wish I could do that floating thing.*

"I'm sure William appreciates that." Myriam looked around. "Why did you want to talk to me?"

"No. I came here to talk to you, Myriam VolFar. William Reis, Forgemaster of Amder, has a part to play, but you are the reason I came." Lorelei leaned forward. "The Gorom saw it as well. I think we all do."

"What are you talking about?" Myriam shuffled back a bit into the pillow. *Stupid thing, give me a normal chair any day.*

"The choice is almost upon you, Myriam. The choice that could remake the world." Lorelei reached out and took Myriam's hand.

Myriam nearly jerked back at the touch. The woman's hand was warm, very warm. "I am not special like that. I am an innkeeper's daughter. A barely trained Apprentice of the Smithing Guild." *Choice. The voice had used that word as well. What choice?*

"I am a Windtalker Myriam. I am the Mistral of the Goddess. I know the truth. It rides the surrounding wind. That voice you hear? The time is so close." Lorelei let go of her hand. "It will not be easy, but I wanted to meet you before it was done."

Myriam scrambled upright, rather ungracefully. *I hate pillows.* "How did you know about that?? I have said nothing to Regin or William."

"Do not worry. I will not say anything." Lorelei stood as well, or rather, she floated up and out of her seat. "It has been my honor to meet you."

"How do you know about that?" Myriam asked again. "Answer me!"

"I can't. And know, we all hope you make the right choice." Lorelei held up a finger. "I will say nothing else."

Myriam opened her mouth to demand an answer, but as she spoke blackness crept in around the edge of her vision, and the last thing she saw was Lorelei, holding up that finger to her mouth.

Chapter 42.

William awoke blinking in the morning light, completely unsure of where he was. He'd been sitting on a pillow in the Mistral's tent when he'd blacked out. But now, everything was gone. No tent, no Lorelei. He looked around and spied both Regin and Myriam. Both were asleep still, and like he had been lying on a small cushioned rug.

Their packs were by each of them, and a small bag was next to his. He opened it to find korba fruits. But that was all. No note. No signs of where their host had gone, or why. The shackles! Will opened his pack, fumbling with the closure in his rush, but there, right on top, were the shackles, right where they should be.

"What happened?" Regin mumbled from behind him. "I was waiting on Myriam and then…"

"We fell asleep. All of us." William answered, turning to Regin. "I have no idea what happened, or why."

Regin poked the still sleeping Myriam. "Hey wake up."

Myriam yawned and rolled over, then started up herself. "What? Where's Lorelei? What…" she trailed off, trying to make sense of things.

"No idea. Regin said he was waiting for you, and I was resting when we blacked out. What about you?" William reached down and took out a korba fruit, offering one to Regin, who nodded and took one.

"I was… talking to Lorelei. I don't remember why. Then nothing. I remember being surprised, but…" Myriam ran her fingers through her hair. "I remember nothing after that."

"Amder?" William tried to reach his god.

"She is a Windtalker. And like the wind, they come and go with very little warning." Amder's voice grumbled in his head.

William shrugged. Amder had been getting more and more short with him the closer they got to their goal. *He's still worried. More than that, he's on edge.* Not that he didn't understand why. If it really was the Blood God, the stakes were far higher than before.

"I don't get it, but we are bathed, were fed, rested, and healed of our aches and pains. Even my side and should feel normal for the first time in a while." Will thumped his chest plate.

"You don't remember anything, Myriam?" Regin asked as they all stood. "Nothing?"

"Not from my conversation with Lorelei, no." Myriam shouldered her pack and eyed the rug she'd been on. "What do we do with those?"

"No idea. I guess take them with us. They are comfortable to sleep on at least." Will got his own korba fruit. "Want one Myriam?"

"Sure, why not." Myriam rolled up the rug and shoved it under some straps on her pack. She took the offered fruit and took a tentative bite. "Good!"

William took his own and took a large bite. "Had these back in Ture, when Regin and I were fleeing the city. Never thought I'd get to have them again so soon."

"Which way?" Regin had his own pack shouldered, and the rug stored away. "She said which way to go, right?"

"Yes. Follow me." Will grabbed his own pack and moved south, deeper into the forest. They ate and walked, with little conversation. Will was grateful for the forest, though. At least there was shade, even if it was hotter than he'd ever thought possible. *I need to get back to Palnor. Even Ture would be better than this.* As the sun rose, they walked, until the sound of running water could be heard. Through the trees they saw it, a small stream. And in the distance a village.

"People. Hope they are friendly." Myriam looked at the water. "And that the stream there is cold, though I doubt it."

"Something isn't right." Regin looked at the village in the distance. "There's no smoke coming from there. Which means no fires. And no sound."

William nodded. Regin was right. They could see the roofs of a dozen buildings, and none had normal chimney smoke. "Let's be careful."

They walked and worked their way down the embankment and across the stream. It wasn't deep, and the only thing to get wet was their boots. Myriam went to splash some water on her face but stopped before she did so, wrinkling her nose at the water. "Smells bad."

William said nothing, but exchanged glances with Regin. As soon as they were up the other bank, he took the hammer off his belt. "I think we better be safe."

Regin and Myriam did the same. They didn't want to seem threatening, but something was very wrong here. They found a path leading towards the village, well used. But the air was still silent. William could hear what he thought was maybe a buzzing sound, so maybe one of those redkiss trees?

Then, a few steps later, the wind shifted, and the smell of death greeted them. William knew that smell. The Reach had that smell in the days after the Valni attack. But this was even worse. At least in the Reach it had been cold. Here, now, the air was thick, hot and warm.

"They are all dead." Regin looked pale. "Do we have to go this way?"

Myriam nodded. "No wonder the water smelled bad. I didn't place it at first."

William knew they had to go this way, but he had no desire to see what the inside of the village looked like. He realized the buzzing sound was insects, thousands of flies and other things. He forced down his korba fruit breakfast that threatened to come back up.

"We won't go in, though I wish there was something we could do for them. I'd say a fire, but I don't want the forest to burn." William shook his head. Leaving these people to rot in the sun wasn't a thought he wanted to have in his head.

"Can Amder help?" Myriam asked quietly. "I mean Lorelei was something to the Wind Goddess, right? She had powers. So maybe Amder can."

"Amder?" William reached out. *"Can you do anything to help these souls? I know they might not be followers, but to leave their bodies out like this... can you start a fire? Something?"*

"I don't know. I don't think I've ever tried." Amders voice came back, *"Hmmmmm..."*

With a crack that split the air, dozens of columns of white flames shot out of the skies, hitting the village in multiple places. Flames roared forth, and William, Regin, and Myriam all stumbled backwards. The flames lashed down again, and buildings exploded.

"AMDER!" William reached out as he and his friends scrambled away. *"It's on fire now!"*

"That it is. That was fun." Amder's voice rumbled. And William knew the god was grinning. How he knew, he had no idea.

"Thank you." William watched as the village burned. For a moment he was worried the fire would spread, but whatever Amder had done, the fire stopped at the village edge. But even from where they were, they could feel the heat coming from it.

"That was… why didn't he do that other times?" Myriam pointed at the village. "That would have been useful in the Gorom caves."

"He couldn't. Remember? I couldn't talk to him there. And if I'm right, I don't think he really expected to be able to either." William shook his head. "Impressive though."

Regin had said nothing, and as William turned to him, he saw the man standing with his back to the village.

"Regin?" William asked, walking towards him. "You alright?"

Regin turned towards them. "Yes, but look." He pointed into the woods, about ten spans in. A body lay there. Ripped from its face was its jaw, and a long-ragged cut had disemboweled the woman. And it was a woman. Young by the look of it.

"Oh Amder." Myriam whispered. "That's horrible."

"She was trying to flee, when… that happened to her." Regin looked away. "How could someone do that?"

"Not someone, Valnijz." Will spat. "Savage, and bloodthirsty. Look at the cuts. That was the blood god."

"How can you be sure? Maybe it was bandits or…" Myriam replied, but let it go.

"I am sure." William waved at the corpse. "There's nothing else it could be."

Myriam didn't answer as the three of them stood looking at the woman's body for a few more minutes as the village behind them.

"Let's go. We need to find Valnijz and get this done." William marched onwards and didn't look again at the body on the ground.

***

Valnijz scowled at the power that echoed over the land. Amder. His stupid and hammering brother had finally realized he was a god. It wouldn't change his plan, but it meant he was going to have to be more careful. Once they were in the Anvil, it wouldn't matter as much. He had considered killing the others outright, leaving only this Forgemaster, William Reis. The terror and fear it would have generated would have been a delicious taste prior to the Forgemaster's death.

But with Amder now suddenly realizing he could do more than simply hammer metal, that might be a bit too far to push things. Valnijz wanted to respond in kind to the display, but he couldn't, not yet. Once he had taken the power in from the drop and returned fully, he would wreak death on all.

No more armies, no more priests, no more using others to do what needed to be done. The Blood God would do it personally. But for now, he had to wait. He had to be patient. And he needed to set up these fools coming to capture him.

Taking a long sniff of the air, he smiled at the body bound at his feet. The fear was nearly overwhelming the man. He'd captured him this morning and had done nothing to him. Well, nothing physical. Valnijz had forced a vision of what was to come into the man's head. The poor fool had wet himself and spent the next long while gibbering and shuddering. Fool.

"Embrace the bloodlust. Join with it. Only in the purity of killing and blood will you ever be free." Valnijz whispered in the man's ear.

The man pulled away as much as he could, and a new spike of fear wafted to the God's face. Fool indeed. At least he serves a purpose. The god cocked his head, hearing Duncan howling in his mind. He would be glad, as much as he could be, when that annoying shred of the man was gone. Oh, he had plans for it, though. Let a little out, entice the so-called Forgemaster closer. Once they got to the Anvil, that was.

His plan was coming together nicely. Jindo would come as well, in case of the unforeseen. Valnijz had wanted to take the man's power right then. He could smell the blood, and every bit of Jindo Halfman was soaked through with the blood's power. But not yet. Jindo was insurance. The Anvil was a special place, a place of old power. Things could happen that he did not expect.

The other gods had sealed the Anvil to Valnijz after he had gone insane. And they had given the way in to themselves, and to Amder. They had never taken that away from his brother, even after he had destroyed the pitiful metal shell that Amder had worn on that long-ago day.

And now, Valnijz would use that power. Pretend to be captured. Get into the Anvil. Free himself. Destroy the chosen of his brother and those who travel with him. And there, in the Anvil of Souls, take the blood, force the drop back into himself, and rejoin the world fully.

He wondered what silly and useless thing his brother had made to hold him. Nothing could stop a god, though, even one who wasn't fully here yet. Nothing.

They were close, this band of Amderites. *It was time.* His return was close. He would be free.

Chapter 43.

Will couldn't believe, even in the shade, that it was this hot. Back when he had left the Reach the first time, heading to Ture, he had thought it hot. *What little did I know.* He missed Master Jaste. He missed Haltim. He missed Vin. Anyone who could give him advice. Regin and Myriam could advise him, and he'd listen. But both were so wrapped up in feeling guilty he wasn't sure either would be totally honest with him.

Not that Will felt good about losing Myriam to Regin. Though the truth was, he'd lost Myriam the moment he stopped being Markin Darto and went back to William Reis. The moment he claimed the mantle of Forgemaster. He'd had no choice, though. To bring Amder back, he'd had to sacrifice. A lot. His relationship with Myriam had been one more thing.

It would be better once this was done. They could have each other and have time alone. He'd step back and do whatever Amder wanted him to do. Maybe he'd send Regin and Myriam to help steer the Guild together. Away from him. He'd miss them, but if this worked, and they saved Dunc, he'd have his cousin back, and years of putting right what had gone wrong.

The more Will thought about it, the more it seemed like the right thing to do. Let Regin and Myriam go. Let them be happy. Whatever they had would never become all it could be if he was in the picture every day. Will smiled for a moment, his mind traveling back to daydreams of Myriam and him in the Reach. *Never to be, I guess.*

He stopped mid-stride, holding a hand up for his friends to stop as well. A single hammer blow had echoed in his mind. *"Valnijz is close, lad. Very close. Be wary. Even in this form, he is far more dangerous than you know."* Amder's gravelly voice moved through his mind.

"Our... goal is close. Be careful, be ready." Will pulled the golden hammer out of his belt. "Get the shackles out of my pack Regin."

He stood still, looking around, listening carefully as Regin dug out the bindings that would hold the Scaled One. The low moan of the Wight Iron carried through the air as they touched each other. "Both of you, be careful. Please." Will kept his voice low.

They crept along, the only sound the soft movements of leaves and soft pine needles. Will wiped the sweat off his face with the back of one sleeve. As they crested a ridge, William saw him for the first time in a long time. It had to be him. *Duncan.*

He squinted. No, not Duncan. Oh, it had the general shape and form of his cousin, but it wasn't him. The sun glinted off its body in a way that skin never did. And it was thin. So thin. Dunc had always been lanky, but this was almost skeletal. But it must have been strong, as it was holding a squirming man upright, off the ground. As Will watched in disgust, the figure flexed, and the man's throat was crushed, separating the head from the body. A gush of blood came, and the figure stood there, gore covered and, to his shock, gave forth a sound that seemed to tear at his ears. Not quite a scream, or a roar, it radiated one thing. Rage.

Will froze. Just for a second, but that was enough. The form turned towards them, and Will could make out its face and form better. Face torn, scaled, teeth sharp, jagged. Eyes... angry eyes. Hate-filled eyes. Without a word, it rushed forward, almost a blur.

Will stepped forward, and without thinking, moved right in front of the form. **Impact.** Will could feel the air as he flew backwards. The breastplate took most of the blow, and thanks to its forging, didn't break. The Scaled One also stumbled back, grasping the impact point. Regin rushed forward, swinging his hammer, but with a flick of its hand, the fallen god pushed him away faster than Regin could dodge.

Regin crumbled to the ground as Myriam pulled him away, keeping her eyes on the Scaled One. Will stumbled to his feet. *The shackles. Where were the god forged shackles??* A silver glint caught his eye. Thankfully, they had come to rest close to where Regin had fallen. Will rushed towards them, swinging a wild blow with the golden hammer, trying to fend off the beast they fought.

By some insane variant of chance, Valnijz must have sensed what the hammer was, because he moved back, allowing Will the time he needed to grab the shackles with his other hand. "Regin! Is he alive?" Will yelled out, not taking his eyes off their foe.

"Yes, but he's hurt. Unconscious." Myriam answered from somewhere behind him. "What do we do?"

Will gritted his teeth. There was one way, one possibility. He didn't like it, though. He wasn't sure if any of Dunc was still able to be reached in there. Will had always been stronger. He hoped Amder was stronger still.

"I understand what you're thinking. I can help." Amder's voice came to him. For once the God didn't equivocate.

He hoped Myriam would understand what he needed her to do. It would be close. As he watched, the Scaled One reached down and pulled out a long black iron dagger. Pitted and ugly. The craftsman in him recoiled from the sheer ugliness of the thing. But he knew it had power. He could feel it from here. This was not going to be a good time.

Will moved forward, rushing as fast as he could. At the last moment he pivoted and remembering Vin's lesson, twisted at his hips, and struck forward, his hammer a blur. He could feel the strength of Amder flowing into him. He could break the very earth he felt like. *I'm sorry Dunc, this is going to hurt.*

The hammer moved faster than Will could register. And with a shudder, it made contact. The form of the Scaled One fell to one knee, grasping the same place they had impacted before. Now or never. William dropped the hammer and the shackles and reached to grab the form of the fallen blood god in a bear hug. Hoping to hold him tight enough.

Valnijz screamed then, and with a lashing blow, the black iron knife struck the breastplate. Will never stopped moving. A horrible tearing sound echoed as the metal, god forged and strong tore as the knife cut through its layers. With a crack, the knife bent, nearly loud enough to deafen Will.

He had no time to look backwards to Myriam. *She better be ready and watching.* His head pounded in the aftereffects of the scream, but he had no choice. Will reached out and pulled the form of the Blood God close. But he couldn't get his hands all the way around!

The body was wearing a small pack, bloodstained and dirty, but it was big enough to cause problems. Will swore and hoped this would work. The form of Valnijz writhed and shifted. All the while, Will tried to pin his arms down. The struggle seemed impossible, until, by a stroke of luck, he tore the small pack out of the way. He wasn't even sure how he had done it, but part of a strap had gotten onto his wrist. Will gave a pull with that hand, hoping that the pack was in bad enough shape that it would give. And he was right! The pack flew off, falling to the ground somewhere off to the side of them.

There! Will's hands met, and with a mighty squeeze, he pinned the arms down, lower, lower, until the arms were behind its back. "DUNCAN! I DON'T KNOW IF YOU CAN HEAR ME. BUT I NEED YOU. FIGHT DUNC! FIGHT!" Will roared the words as he jerked his head back, trying to avoid spittle and flashing sharp teeth. *Sparks above, this thing was strong, and fast!* The form of Valnijz writhed and struggled, and it was nearly all Will could do to keep his arms locked in place, even with Amder's help.

He could see Myriam doing something. But not well. Did she understand? Had Duncan heard him? Amder above this better work!! For a moment, a single moment, he felt the strength of his foe weaken and waver. "NOW!" he yelled and held tight with all his strength. And then….

A click.

Myriam had done it. The shackles were in place. They had captured the Blood God. But now, Regin. Will turned from the captive, who was even now fighting and screaming as it buckled and twisted against its shackles. Will knew, though, they would hold. Amder's gift of strength fled, and Will could feel every bruise, but it didn't matter.

"How is he?" Will kneeled down next to Regin. "And thanks Myriam. I wasn't sure you got what I was trying to do."

"He's out cold, but I can't see any external injuries. Hopefully, he's only bruised badly. And you're welcome. I wasn't sure I could do it. My hands were shaking, I could barely make my fingers work." Myriam probed Regin's side. "I'm not a healer, but I don't think the blow hit anything serious."

"Good." Will sat, head resting on his knees, hearing the still hissing and screaming from behind him. "I hope that doesn't continue forever."

Will closed his eyes for a moment as Myriam placed a hand on his arm. "Are you alright William?"

"Yeah. Just tired. So tired. Tired of all this fighting and death. Tired of all of this. I want to have this quest be over. It was my choice, though. My decision." Will stood slowly and turned towards their prisoner. "I hope that hurts. I hope it burns you for what you did to Dunc. For what you did to Haltim. For every man woman and child in the Reach who died that night."

As he spoke, Valnijz stopped screaming and with effort flipped itself over to look Will in the face. It smiled, a horrible rictus, and laughed. A guttural, harsh laugh, but a laugh.

Will picked up his hammer off the ground and fought the urge to hit the beast. Duncan was in there still. Somewhere. He wouldn't have been able to catch him without Duncan's help, he was sure of it.

***

Myriam sat by Regin, her hands still shaking. She was sure for a few moments there that she and Regin were dead, and that William was dead as well. She had no idea how William had held that, that thing, for as long as he had managed to. The screams! Myriam tried to not think about it.

Regin was still out cold, and that worried her. And that bruise on his side looked even worse. The color had already turned nearly black. None of it looked good. "Regin, you have to wake up. Ok? We captured the... creature. You have to wake up now."

She didn't really except a reply, and she didn't get one. Will still stood over the Scaled One. The Scaled One. It didn't seem real. She was looking at a God. She'd helped bring Amder back to this world, and now she was looking at Valnijz. The Blood God. Evil. At least the beast had stopped screaming and stopped laughing. It sat sullen and looking at William, and the Forgemaster looked right back at it.

How that could be his cousin she didn't know. How it was even alive she didn't know. Gaunt to the point of looking starved to death, skin either scaled or near translucent in patches. Its face was even worse. Hairless. And its mouth, the corners were almost ripped apart, and a mouth full of jagged sharp teeth. The whole thing covered in blood. Both fresh and old. And of course, the smell.

Death. Rot. Foul and ancient. It reeked. It barely wore anything, and what it had on was nearly rotting away. Outside that pack, it had on at first. The pack. What could a god want to carry? She stood, monitoring Regin, and searched for the pack, finding it under a bush where it had lodged itself after it had been ripped off.

There was only one thing in the pack. A small metal box. She carefully opened the box and nearly dropped it. A light bloomed from inside, as a glowing yellow crystal came into view.

"Hello Myriam. I've been waiting for this moment for a very long time." She knew that voice. It had saved her life in the Gorom caves. It had spoken to her back in Palnor. And now she faced it. Whatever it was.

Chapter 44.

"Do not be scared. I am sure you have questions. I'll do my best to answer them." The voice stopped for a moment and returned with a laugh. *"Finally."*

"Who are you? What are you? Tell me!" Myriam thought in her head. She couldn't help glance at William and Regin, but Regin was still unconscious, and William was not moving?

"Let's say this conversation, no one else can hear. Not even the two cousins." The voice was flat, almost annoyed when it mentioned William and Duncan. *"I am what was supposed to be. Before the accident. Though now I know it was never an accident. It was those Vinik. Those thrice cursed Vinik."*

Myriam nearly winced at the venom the voice had laced through it as it spoke of the giant insects, Vinik or Drendel, or whatever. *"You didn't really answer my question."*

"Fine. Have you ever wondered Myriam VolFar why there are two Gods for Humans? Think about it. The Gorom have Grimnor. The Trinil, the Saltmistresses, even that Mistral you all met. Each race has their own god. Or aspect of their own God. God. Not Gods. One." The voice waited for an answer.

Myriam shrugged. She hadn't ever really thought about it. The only God humans had worth following was Amder. And Humans followed other gods. She knew people who followed Grimnor. And lots of fishermen gave thanks to the Ocean Goddess every day. *"So what?"*

"It wasn't supposed to be this way, that's the point. The day we came to this world. The day we arrived. Something happened. Something horrible. All the other Gods arrived safe at the Anvil of Souls. But when I was born. I split. The one became two. Amder and Valnijz." The voice spoke in low tones, and sadness crept into the sound.

"Even then, it was tried to make it work. Amder took the job of creation, of dealing with the external. He was supposed to take care of anything that didn't deal with humans directly. Making things, creating. Protection. Defense. Valnijz was supposed to deal with the inside world. Love, hate. Emotion. Health and healing. Persuasion. Together they would have brought your race inspiration and joy and turned those into acts of creation which would have remade the world." The voice's tone turned harsh again.

"But that was not to be. Amder became short sighted. He focused narrowly on one thing, Smithing. He abandoned all other crafts. Besides his fight with Valnijz, he stopped protecting. He stopped doing his job!" A long pause came, and the voice came again, harsher and angrier still.

"Valnijz did his job at first. Then one day, he became of aware of the question. Why two gods for humans? He tried to discover why. He and Amder fought over it. They argued, and then Valnijz left. He discovered the truth. He was never meant to be. Amder was never meant to be. The other gods knew the truth, but had refused to tell them. The truth drove him insane." The voice sighed in her mind, a singing sound that almost made her weep.

Myriam didn't know what to say. That was the reason? The true reason why Valnijz had gone mad? Why all the suffering, all the pain, all the hate had been born into this world? Into their race? *"I didn't know."* Myriam didn't know what else to say.

"Of course, you didn't know. How could you? Amder didn't. The other gods won't tell them. But they won't help me either." The voice muttered something low before speaking again. *"But now, now I can fix it. Now what was wrong can be set right."*

Myriam looked at the crystal. *"You are a god?"*

"Part of one. Part of the truth. I was reborn by accident. Valnijz is terrified of me. He knows what I am. Amder isn't even aware I exist." The voice was full of scorn. *"Both of them. Fools."*

"If he was terrified of you, why was he carrying you around? This makes little sense." Myriam considered closing the lid on this box and throwing it far away.

"For once in his miserable and long existence, Zalkiniv did something right. He knew his god hated me. He kept me to use, not knowing what I was. The box protected me from both Amder and Valnijz. The two halves of me. Now, we are close enough to the Anvil that I can hide without the box." The voice became filled with a laughing sound. *"I only now realized; I don't have a name."*

Myriam was unsure what to think about all this. It made some kind of sense. She had never thought about why there were two gods, but his reasoning was clear. And it was true the voice saved her life in the Gorom caves, and that took power. God like power? She didn't know the answer to that question.

"You can name me. Since I chose you." The voice echoed around her for a moment. *"Name me. Name me and become my chosen. The chosen of the true god of humans."*

Myriam shook her head. *"I don't want this. I don't need this. I want Regin to wake up, be ok, and to help William heal his cousin. I'm only an innkeeper's daughter."*

The voice groaned. *"You aren't making this easy for me, Myriam. I chose you. You are the one human in this world I picked. But I know you have a lot to think about. And I can feel your doubts. So, to show you who I am..."*

The crystal glowed. Bright light shone from the box. Dazzling. Myriam shielded her eyes and started to close the lid, but it would not move! Brighter again, to the point that she had to close her eyes. But even then, the light tore through her eyelids, and left red and silver spots on her vision.

"Know me Myriam VolFar." The voice whispered before the glow stopped and silence came. A silence only broken a moment later by a voice.

"Myriam? Did we win? Or are we in some kind of strange afterlife? This doesn't look like the blessed forge of Amder." Regin's voice broke the total quiet. In a tumult, all other sounds returned. Wind in the trees, a bird calling in the distance. The sound of flies buzzing around the dead body of the poor soul that the Blood God had killed before they had captured him.

Myriam turned back to Regin; the lid snapping shut on the small box as she held it. "Regin!"

Will turned back towards them. "By the sparks, Regin, I'm glad you're still alive. Don't go charging a god next time."

"We won?" Regin stood, wincing and rubbing the spot where the Scaled One had struck him.

"Yes, more or less." William pointed the golden hammer at the restrained form of the Blood God.

Regin said nothing as he took in the sight, but spat at the ground. After several moments, he turned away. "Good. I think. What next?"

"Next is me examining your injury. After that we can talk about what comes after." Myriam pointed at a tree. "Sit there at the base. And don't argue."

"I wouldn't argue, Regin. She did put shackles on an evil god. She's one tough Smith." Will cracked a smile then.

Myriam smiled back. "And don't either of you two forget it." Myriam added, waving a finger between her two friends.

"Oh, I'll never forget Myriam. How could I ever forget you?" Regin gave a half bow. "Ow! Maybe that wasn't the best idea."

"Sit Regin." Myriam pointed again.

Regin said nothing else, but sat and closed his eyes. Though a small quick intake of breath came with the act of sitting.

"Thank you." Myriam thought to the box, or whatever it was.

"You are welcome, Myriam. We are not done yet, but we are closer than ever." The voice answered back.

***

Valnijz flexed his muscles again, while the humans chattered away with each other. The shackles, however, did not give way. Which meant that Amder had done something. On top of it, he hadn't expected that fool of a Forgemaster to be so quick with his hammer. He'd only managed two good blows. One to the older man, who seemed to be up and talking now.

That bothered him. He was Valnijz. The Blood God. He knew how to kill. The man should have never regained his mind. He should have died already, bleeding out inside. Yet there he was, maybe still hurt, but very much not dead.

The other blow had been to the so called chosen of Amder, this Forgemaster. He had struck deep and strong, yet the dagger hadn't made it to his flesh. In fact, it had bent, as whatever armor that fool was wearing had stopped it. It didn't matter, of course. He had escaped that prison long ago.

None of it mattered. His plan was still going to work. Jindo was the key now, though. Jindo would come. Free him and kill the others. Maybe leave the Forgemaster one alive till the last. Long enough for him to see the eventual death of his friends. Of what was left of Duncan. Then he would join the other of his cursed bloodline.

He could feel Duncan still inside him, screaming, trying hard to contact his cousin. He wanted to badly. The desire was strong, almost impressive. But regardless of anything else, he was a man. And nothing compared to the power of a god.

Chapter 45.

Will. That had been Will. Duncan knew it. Valnijz had fought with Will, and somehow, someway lost. Or at least been captured. If Duncan hadn't seen it, he wouldn't have believed it possible. Will was a good man, but a fighter? Not possible. But yet, the face he saw had been Will's, but the face also was different. The Will he knew had been missing that edge, that sharp point that came with age and experience. The face he'd seen had that.

William Reis had grown up. The child who tried to make everyone happy, the teenager who fumbled along, unsure of himself, the almost adult who threw himself into helping everyone and ran from any hard choice, had finally become a man. *Good for you William. Good for you.* He'd seen a hint of it the last time he'd been this close to him, in the dungeons of the Temple of Amder.

It seemed too far away now. What had that fat priest's name been? Bracpin? Bracfin? Bracin. That was it, Bracin. So long ago. He wished he'd had the power to resist the control that Zalkiniv had put on him that day.

"You never would have that power." The hissing, sibilant voice of Valnijz echoed around him.

"I don't know if I would have or not, but I should have tried." Duncan knew arguing with Valnijz was pointless and was only going to end up with him in more pain. But pain had become an old friend now and held less and less sway over him.

"Fool. No mortal man can resist me. The only times you were freed was because of the workings of my worthless brother." The grey mists parted as Valnijz entered whatever this place had become. Before, when Zalkiniv had been around, it had been an endless plain of red dust, dried blood. Now it was a more depressing and dark prison.

"What do you want Valnijz?" Duncan averted his eyes, knowing he would be punished for it. Surprisingly, the expected pain did not come.

"You think your dim-witted cousin has captured me? You think my weak sibling has found a way to hold me? You are sadly mistaken." Valnijz hissed and circled the spot that Duncan stayed. There was the hint of what had been rocks here, and for Duncan it represented shelter.

"Oh? Are your hands not bound?" Duncan shot back.

"By my choice. Oh, I had to put on a convincing show for that oaf you call family. But I AM A GOD!" Valnijz whirled on Duncan and a black claw shot forth, stabbing Duncan in the arm, embedding in his skin.

Duncan screamed, then tried to stifle it. For a moment he was successful, but a strange blackness spread from the point where Valnijz's claw was stuck.

"Do not forget Duncan Reis. I am far above you. You have been an amusing tool to use, a toy to play with, but you are nothing to me." Valnijz pulled the claw out, leaving Duncan frantically holding his arm and quivering.

"Your cousin is taking me to where I want to go. That is all. I have my plans." Valnijz hooked Duncan's face upwards and looked him in the eye. *"Soon I will no longer have to abide your company, and I will grant you your fondest desire. Death. But not before you watch the end of the Forgemaster, and his friends."*

Duncan could only watch as the Scaled One vanished into the grey mists. The faces and bodies were still there, each contorting in pain as they were formed and ripped apart by their neighbors. One tried to reach out to him and slowly grew thin and dissipated as it did so, its face locked in a soundless scream.

The pain in his arm subsided as the damage done slowly vanished. All the injuries inflicted on him, whatever this 'him' was, now did the same. They healed, but each time it took longer and hurt more. As if each time some part of him was destroyed.

It didn't matter. He wanted to warn William, but he couldn't. He wanted to fight back, but Valnijz was right. He was simply a shred of a man. It was hopeless. Valnijz would win soon, William would die. At least then, in the end, he would be freed of this life.

No! Duncan shook his head. That's what he wants. He wants me to give up. *I may not be able to stop him. I may not be able to hurt him, but I can distract him. I can slow him. I just have to find the right time*. Dunc sat still and concentrated on the Reach, the mountains, the joys of finding a new treasure, the smell of the wind, the warm embrace of a new lover.

Each thought brought him more solidity. More strength. *I will not give in.*

***

Jindo waited in the keep, kneeling in the sand of the courtyard, still. The sand, loaded with the blood of the slain Curors, had hardened into something like rock in the scorching sun, but Jindo ignored that. With the deaths had come clouds of flies and other vermin, but Jindo ignored them. A small fire broke out where somewhere in the keep, a lamp had been left on most likely, but Jindo paid it no mind.

He waited for his Lord's appointed time. He waited until the moment came to help the Scaled One have his ultimate revenge on the dirty fool, Amder. He would complete his task, and in the world after the ascent of Valnijz, Jindo Halfman would be remembered as the loyal follower of his lord.

Night came, and with-it scavengers, drawn by the scent of death. A pack of Calnits at first. The dog like reptiles ignored him and started tearing chunks off the bodies of his men. Jindo did not care. The power had left them, and the flesh was simply meat.

A roaring sound accompanied by a series of low grunts did finally got his attention. A blood bear. Here? Though not creations of his Lord, Blood bears were nasty creatures. Three times larger than a normal bear, with fringes of sharp spikes that ringed its neck and down its back, the blood bear was bad enough. That the spikes were usually covered in disease and filth only made it worse.

The Calnits fled having already eaten enough, and not wanting to fight a blood bear. *Cowards.* Jindo watched the pack circle back around the blood bear and escape out the wrecked gates. He watched as the bear examined one of his dead army and ripped it apart with a paw the size of a large shield. It fed, taking huge rips out of the corpse.

Jindo wondered if it had even noticed his kneeling form when it turned towards him. Taking several steps, the blood bear grunted, and then let forth a roar. Jindo flinched a tiny bit at that sound. The blood bear was a power made flesh, and while Jindo had no doubts that any fight would end with the bear's death, there could be no wasting of time to healing. He had to arrive at the Anvil of Souls exactly when his master had told him to be there. Not a second less.

Those thoughts fled as with a rush; the bear charged at him. Jindo finally moved, drawing deep on the blood power to rush to the left. The bear's charge stopped three feet beyond where Jindo had been.

"Foolish beast." Jindo took a spear off a dead Cruor and threw it. The spear cut the air with a whine; the speed faster than any eye could see. The spear blade cut into the beast, embedding itself deep in the animal, and drawing forth another scream of rage.

Jindo kept his eyes on the thing and grabbed another spear. Thankfully, the spear was the preferred weapon in the keep, and there were lots of them. Spears could be used at range, or in closer combat. One more truth his Lord had given him. His own spear was close, but on the other side of the blood bear. Better to kill it with these others, his was to be kept for killing those who stood against his lord.

The blood bear shook itself and in a surprising turn of events did not charge. It instead scooped a corpse up and heaved it Jindo's way. Jindo had not been expecting that, and for a moment froze. That was all the time the bear needed. As with the corpse in midair, the bear charged again.

"By the blood." Jindo swore and dodged again, pulling on the blood power strongly. His arm flashed forward, and the spear flew true again, this time cutting through part of the blood bears cheek and cutting one spike neatly in half.

The bear roared again, but not in anger, but in pain. It took another corpse in its jaws and started to leave the keep, taking its meal elsewhere.

Jindo watched it leave. He wondered if he should kill the thing anyway, but decided not to. The blood bear was a hunter. A killer. It had simply picked a prey it could not beat. Still, the fight had not been a total loss.

Jindo walked to the broken spike and picked it up. Roughly the length of a belt knife, it had the most important part, the wickedly sharp point that was covered in some yellowish green liquid. Whatever the liquid was, it didn't want to come off, which suited Jindo fine. He wrapped a torn piece of cloth around the other end, making a crude handle.

There, a present for anyone who gets in his way. He didn't expect to use it, but an excellent warrior always is ready. He glanced up and down the lightening sky. Soon, very soon, he would start south, towards the Anvil, and towards the ultimate end of everything the world had become.

***

Regin sat by the fire, unable to sleep. How could he? The day's events were disjointed, a blur. He had rushed forward, trying to save William and Myriam. He'd not even registered the blow that had felled him. One moment he was running forward, his hammer ready to strike, and the next he had been sitting up, his right side in pain, but otherwise alright.

But scraps of something kept coming to him. Something in between those events. Not memories that made sense, though. He remembered voices, trying hard to understand them. Each one the voice of someone who had died. His little sister's voice, dead of the wasting death that had struck when they were kids. The voice of his grandmother who died in her sleep. The voice of Master Jaste, who had been killed by the Tempered of Amder. Other voices he didn't know. The voice of some old man, mumbling about the Reach. The voice of some old woman, screaming about betrayal.

None of them had made sense. That alone should not have kept him awake. What truly kept him awake was the form that sat, arms bound, legs tied. The form of the Scaled One. Valnijz, the God of Blood and Rage. The Destroyer and bringer of death.

That kept him awake. The form sat calmly watching them. Every so often, the form would lock eyes with Regin and bare its teeth. Its face would split in unnatural ways, and teeth, broken and sharp, would snap at the air. Regin was glad it was as far away as it was, though. The smell that came with the thing was horrendous.

"You know us. Yet you do not speak? Why." Regin whispered to the lightening air. Today would be the day. Everything would change. This Anvil of Souls place was the end result of all of this. Valnijz would be gone, Duncan would be freed, and William... William would be healed.

Regin turned his gaze towards the sleeping form of Myriam. After this was over, he and Myriam would see where things led them. William would be busy with Duncan, and finally fulfilling his purpose to bring the joy of the craft to all the people. That was the Forgemaster's purpose. Regin would help, of course, but if he and Myriam were together, he would understand if William didn't want them around as much.

No, today would mark a change in everything. He returned to watching the Scaled One, who locked eyes with him again, before giving a laugh. He had laughed before, once. This was worse. Why it laughed he didn't know, but he didn't trust it.

"It's creepy, evil. I wouldn't look at it too much." Myriam's sleepy voice came from her bedroll.

"I couldn't sleep. How could I? It's... wrong." Regin answered back. "If I'm awake, I may as well be watching it to make sure nothing happens."

"Well, since William is still asleep, why don't I give you something else to watch?" Myriam stood, barely clothed in a nightshirt because of the warmth. She sat in front of Regin, blocking his view. "The shackles will hold."

Regin tried to look around her for a moment, but Myriam had other ideas, leaning forward to kiss him again. "But William..." Regin whispered.

"Is asleep. You know how hard a sleeper he is. I'm awake, you are awake. And while the thing behind me is creepy, I know a way to take your mind off it." Myriam spoke low and stood, helping Regin up. "Take your bedroll..." Myriam smiled and walked a bit into the woods, hidden out of view.

"I must be crazy." Regin muttered, but took his bedroll and followed her, sparing one glance backward at the form of the Scaled One, who now was scowling at him.

Chapter 46.

William sat up, the fading nightmare of being hunted by a thousand Valni, all wearing the faces of those who had died already fading from his mind. Regin and Myriam were already up and sitting next to each other by the fire. Very close to each other. A momentary pang of loss welled up, but William pushed it aside. Maybe it was better this way. It would certainly put her in less danger.

His eyes fell to the also awake and scowling form of the Blood God. He'd still never spoken since his capture, though Will knew he very much could. No, he was waiting. Waiting and plotting. For what Will didn't know.

"Valnijz always was several steps ahead. Be careful." Amder's rumble came to Will. *"We need to talk, my Forgemaster. About what comes next, and what comes after."*

Will glanced at his friends, but they hadn't noticed he was awake yet. *"As good as time as any. I have questions of my own."*

A short, barking laugh came. *"You wouldn't be William Reis if you didn't."*

Amder seemed to appear in front of him, though he was translucent, like a piece of colored glass. *"Well, ask away."*

Will shook his head, Gods. *"What do we do with Duncan once we get into this place, this Anvil of Souls? No one says anything. How is it going to save Duncan? What's the plan?"*

Amder nodded slowly. *"That was the main reason I came to you to talk. But first, let's talk about the Anvil itself. You know what the Anvil is. But you asked me a question once, a question I didn't fully answer. Back at the Mistrals' tent. Why did the God's come to this world?"*

Will remembered. *"Yes?"*

"We came here because of one thing. Magic." Amder sighed and squinted at the ground, and picked up something long, black and pitted.

Will knew that thing. It was the dagger Valnijz had used! He looked back at his breastplate. The long gouge on it cut deeply at an angle. He was very thankful for the armor; it had saved his life more than he'd ever thought possible, though nothing about this adventure of his had gone anything according to plan. Then the god's words broke through his mental ramblings.

"Magic??" Will nearly stood. *"But magic doesn't exist. I mean, outside the gods. It's a fairytale, a made-up thing to entertain children."*

Amder looked almost sheepish. *"I'm only telling you all this because you are about to enter the Anvil, but that's not true. Magic exists."*

"My lord Amder.' Will paused and tried to think of what to say. *"Can you please explain? Clearly?"*

Amder sighed, a long rumble of a sigh, as he flipped the black iron in his hand. *"Magic is real. We came to this world because of it. We came to channel it to help you and the other races. Without us, magic runs wild. Uncontrolled."*

Will didn't like how that sounded, but it also seemed almost condescending to him. *"But Amder, if things like the Vinik were here before, and they used magic, why couldn't..."*

Amder cut him off. *"Do not. Magic is not for mortals to use directly. Only through us should the use of magic be allowed. It is the one thing all the gods agree on, including Valnijz."* Amder pointed at the bound form. *"Even in his insanity, he never broke that rule."*

Will didn't like this, but arguing about it now didn't seem to be a good way forward. *"Ok, let's say that's true. But what does this have to do with the Anvil of Souls?"*

"The Anvil is the place where we first arrived, you know that. But what you don't know is the Anvil is the... heart of magic for this world. Everything is different there. You may see and find things that make little sense. You may enter during the day and find it to be night inside, or the other way around. Strange visions, strange sounds, all of it." Amder pulled at the black iron and smiled a little as the piece glowed red, then yellow and finally white hot.

Will didn't know what to say. It sounded strange, but not dangerous. Just strange. *"Ok. So, it's different. But what do we do there?"*

Amder held up a finger for him to wait, before forming and moved the now almost clay-like metal. The shine was bright, but the God didn't seem to need to squint, as with sure movements he made something out of it. Then, with a smile, he blew on the object, and the glow faded. *"You use this."* And Amder held out his hand.

In his palm lay that to Williams' eyes looked like some kind of crown. The pitted iron was smooth now, but still black. Even blacker than it had been before. *"What does that do?"*

"It will draw Valnijz out of that body. But only if he is standing at the right point." Amder shook his head. "I still dislike this. The Anvil scares me."

Will took the crown from Amder's hand. The surface was smooth but had a strange coarseness if he moved his finger across it in a certain way. But odder still was the temperature. The thing was cold. Not simply cold, but near frigid. *"How do we know the point?"*

"That will be obvious. At least I think so. Once you are in the Anvil, I won't be able to talk to you. Or help you. I do not go into the Anvil. Ever." Amder turned to look at the bound form of Valnijz. "Oh, my brother. I miss you. I weep for whatever I did to turn you to this path."

The bound form raised its head until it was locked in gaze with Amder. *"Brother."* Its voice was low, hissing, and angry. *"You did nothing. You are a weak, cowardly thing. All the gods are. The lies. The half-truths become the only thing we know, and all we tell each other, and the meat we allow to worship us."*

"Brother please. Remove yourself from this poor man. Be freed. You are not mad now, I know this. I will find a way for you to be better. Whole. To be the brother you were once." Amder seemed to reach out. "Do not force me to take these steps."

"I was a lie. You are a lie. We are both lies Amder." Valnijz spat at the form of the god.

Will was somewhat shocked when the spittle landed, and Amder with a grimace wiped it off his face. "So be it brother."

"So..." William trailed off. He felt a bit out of place. Uncomfortable. He glanced at Regin and Myriam, but they hadn't moved. In fact, they weren't moving at all. They weren't even breathing!

"Calm William. They are fine. All of this is taking place... outside of what they can experience." Amder glanced at Valnijz one last time, shaking his head. *"That's all. Place the crown on his head. Once he's at the right spot."*

William nodded. *"What about Duncan?"*

But there was no answer, as Amder was already gone. His form vanished, leaving behind only the slight smell of forge smoke. Valnijz only sat there, stone faced.

Will tried to get Amder's attention again, but failed. The God would not answer.

***

Myriam worked very hard on being still. She had no idea what was going on, but she'd had the strangest feeling while sitting next to Regin by the fire, and then the conversation behind her had happened.

She'd wanted to watch it as well, but didn't dare move. She was eavesdropping on a god, and that never would do over well. Well, two gods, and a Forgemaster. Regin seemed to be frozen. Even the flames of the fire didn't move.

"That's because I wanted you to hear them." The voice returned to her head. *"It's a strange experience for me. Watching the two parts of myself argue."*

Myriam didn't respond. At least not to that. *"Magic is real?"*

"Yes. Very real. And for once, Amder was right. It needs to be controlled. By us. It's too dangerous a tool for mortals, any mortal to control." The voice seemed to tighten. *"You already know what the Vinik things could do with it. They used that power to split me."*

"But they didn't mean to. They meant to stop you, and the other gods, from coming here." Myriam pointed out. *"From their point of view, you and yours are the dangers here. You destroyed their world."*

"A chaotic and dangerous world. And whose side are you on, Myriam? If we hadn't come here, you wouldn't even exist." The voice answered back. *"Have you come up with a name for me yet?"*

Myriam didn't answer. None of this was what she expected. Or wanted. At least none of this gods and magic, voices in her head, or crystals. No, all she wanted was sitting next to her. Regin.

Her mother would have killed her had she seen her daughter a few hours ago. In the dim light of early morning, the forest had been cool, but not cold. But the bed roll had been warm enough to start and grew downright hot there for a while.

Poor Regin. Still injured, he'd winced more than once, but she'd taken control. Not that she had a lot of experience in that area. But she was not about to let him get away. Not now. Not ever.

"And you won't have to, as long as you do what I ask when I ask it. The time is near Myriam. Very near." The voice whispered in her ears, surrounding her. And without another sound was gone.

***

Duncan groaned as he watched William talk to Amder. He wished there was some way to talk to him. There were a thousand and one things he could say that he wanted to say. How sorry he was for how all this had turned out. How much he wished they were still back in the Reach. How grateful he was that William had put being the Forgemaster of Amder on hold, just to save his soul.

But most of all, he wanted to tell William that he was proud of him. That he loved him. That he couldn't be saved, but he could be freed.

"He will never listen. He is my brother's creature. And as foolish and stupid." The hissing voice of Valnijz traveled through the grey fog that grew thicker with each passing hour.

"William isn't stupid. He just wants to save me. He never enjoyed letting go." Duncan whispered, keeping his eyes away from the mist.

"Like my fool of a brother. He thinks he can make me like before. Before I knew the truth. Before I knew what was real." Valnijz walked out of the mist, more deformed than ever. His arms were now impossibly long, and almost dragged on whatever passed for a ground here.

"But once inside the Anvil, he will learn the truth. And that truth will break him. It will break him, and through him, break your cousin. Then I will end his pitiful life again, but in the Anvil, it will be forever. There will be no return. No way back." Valnijz spat. *"That is one reason why he is so afraid of the place. But he forgets so much. I know him. He will come if I force him to."*

"How?" Duncan asked, but already knew the answer. It was obvious. William.

"I will return fully. Then I will kill that Forgemaster of his. And his friends. Amder will be forced to come then. I will take the spark inside William Reis and MAKE Amder appear. And when my hand bursts through his chest, Amder will die. I will be the only one standing. And I will have all the power." Valnijz breathed in deeply and Duncan watched with horror as forms and faces tried to claw away from the god, but he inhaled them to, the faces torn apart, in silent screams.

"Your plan didn't work before. Why do you think it will work now?" Duncan was baiting him, but didn't care. There had to be a way to stop this.

"You are not here. You cannot stop me this time, Duncan. But don't despair. Once William is dead. Once Amder is dead. Once the others are dead. You will join them. I will give you what you have so desperately wanted, Duncan Reis, a death." Valnijz reached out faster than Duncan could react and ripped off Duncan's left ear.

Duncan fell to his knees screaming, grabbing at the wound. He pulled himself into a ball, trying to hide, trying to be safe. There was no blood, there never was anymore. Just the pain. The never-ending pain. But maybe it would be over soon. Maybe, maybe the Blood God was right.

No! Duncan shook himself as the pain faded. There had to be a way. There must be a way. He looked up, but the Blood God was already gone, and the pain had faded to join the aches that stayed forever. Duncan had no idea what he was going to do. He was powerless in the face of this god. With Zalkiniv, he had a fighting chance sometimes. But now?

Chapter 47.

Will surveyed the camp. They had cleaned up and broken down and were ready to head south. Towards the Anvil of Souls. He figured Amder would make sure he knew the way. *Today Duncan. I will save you today.* He knew Dunc would be exhausted, in pain, and hurt in ways he couldn't imagine. That didn't change the fact that once he was free of the Blood God, William was going to hug him.

"Who wants to take the lead?" Will pointed at the still shackled body. "I think I should be in the middle, with him."

"I will." Myriam nearly jumped off the ground. "Let me."

Regin opened his mouth but closed it without uttering a word. Though Will could see the look he gave Myriam, he was as surprised as William was.

"Alright, you have the lead Myriam VolFar." Will shouldered his pack. "Let me get our guest up off the ground."

Will approached the bound form. He wondered how Duncan's body could even function looking like it did. The thing was even more thin, paler, and in worse shape than it had been a day before.

"Get up." William kept a hand on the golden hammer at his side. It wasn't his hammer, but Valnijz hadn't enjoyed being struck with it.

The Scaled One scowled at him, saying nothing again.

"I know you can talk. I heard you. You don't have to say anything. You have failed again. And this time I will free Duncan forever. You will be banished." William fished out the iron circlet that Amder had made.

"See this? You will be bound to it. Forever. And I will see to it that this is lost, very lost. I will even go back into the darkness of the Gorom caves. Deep to the Vinik, or even deeper. I will find the darkest and deepest pit and throw it in. Then fill the whole sparks cursed thing with the hardest and heaviest rocks I can find. I'm sure the Vinik would help. You will be gone." William realized he was gloating but didn't care.

He hated this creature. Will had never really hated anything before. He might not like a person; he might not enjoy a situation. But true hate? No. But this... this he hated. For all the pain it had caused, for all the lives lost, for every single horror that had come into the world because of what sat in front of him.

"Get up." Will nearly spat the words this time, as he tore off the leg binding. The shackles seemed to somehow also make the rope unable to be removed by the thing. He had no idea how it worked, but it didn't matter.

The Scaled One smiled then, awkwardly standing. "I can feel your hate. It will make you tasty when I tear your heart out and eat it in front of your friends. Before they die as well."

Will didn't answer. There was no way this would end in the way the Blood God wanted. He was sure of it.

They made their way south, picking around the edge of the forest. It became clear that they were also descending. A subtle change, but more pronounced as they walked.

But that wasn't the unexpected thing. As they walked, things grew strange. The first change was the air. Before, it had been hot, somewhat dry, and dusty. The air had a near permanent scent of old pine needles and dirt. It wouldn't have been totally unpleasant if it hadn't been so warm. But as they moved on, the air grew cooler. And damper.

The change in the air brought a change in the plants. Before, tall pines and evergreens had been everywhere, with a mix of some strange thorny vine plant. But now, moss appeared. And even the rare mushroom. The last change was one that William didn't even see at first. Myriam did. She paused, holding up her hand.

"What is it?" Regin asked from the rear.

"Don't you see it? Look!" Myriam pointed into the woods.

Will tried to follow her finger, but all he saw were trees. Then, a tree moved. *No, a tree walked??* The tree, if it was a tree, was moving away from them, each step seeming to cling to the ground for a moment before it took the next one. They couldn't see the front, so Will didn't know if it had a face.

"What is that??" Regin whispered.

"I have no idea." Will shrugged. For a moment, the wonder of it all made him forget why they were there. Quickly he switched back to looking at their captive, but it remained still. Though its expression was not one of surprise or wonder. If anything, his captive looked disgusted.

"Leaks." The Scaled One said, near a whisper.

Myriam watched a moment longer as the tree thing vanished into the dark woods. Then she gave herself a shake, and continued on, south, and descending even more.

Will followed, his mind on what Amder had said. Magic was real. If this Anvil place leaked magic, like Valnijz seemed to think, what else might they find here? His question was soon answered. Before his eyes, a rock, a simple chunk of granite, with a growth of moss on top, stood up and waved at him with tiny arms, before walking a bit, then burrowing itself back into the ground. A squirrel, black with bright yellow stripes, leaped from tree to tree, chasing a bird that was copper colored. That wasn't the strange thing. The strange and wonderful thing was that the squirrel was wearing a belt and held a net in one hand as it chased the bird.

"Amder? This is..." William reached out to his god again. He couldn't find the words. He wanted to laugh, he wanted to nearly scream from the joy this place seemed to form inside him.

His god was silent though, and Will remembered his warning that they wouldn't be able to talk once they got the Anvil. Or near to it, apparently. What was it about all of this, this fantastical, magical landscape that brought such joy to him?

***

Myriam could barely contain herself. A walking tree? And that was the only thing she had been sure of. For the last while, she had caught glimpses of other things. Tiny people looking things, moving fast through the woods, following them. She'd also spied some bird. It had looked like a common sparrow. If a common sparrow was green and silver and left a tiny trail of golden sparks and mist.

"My half-self is right. The Anvil leaks." The voice came to her, stronger than it had ever been. *"What you see are the remains of the world, that was. The surface world that was, before we came to give order to the chaos."*

"But this is beautiful. Wonderful. Why end it?" Myriam still didn't enjoy talking in her head. How did William ever do this often?

"This? This is chaos. That walking tree? How could you build things or burn wood for fire if trees were moving and aware? That bird? How could you listen to its song if it could kill you with a single whistle? No, we came to fix it. Wild magic, untamed magic is not a good thing." The voice grew bitter as it spoke.

"And those little people you keep seeing? The worst of the lot. They never die. At least if they have magic. They just sort of spring up around magic. Fully grown, fully aware. They do not die. Nor do they create, they don't fight, they don't want for anything. They think it and they get it." The voice stopped suddenly as a rock seemed to open an eye for a moment, blinking at Myriam before closing and vanishing away.

"It's like some story book." Myriam loved it.

"It also doesn't matter." The voice came again. *"You are almost there. Be ready with the crystal. Inside, in the very middle of the circle, you will find a red sandstone pillar, cut neatly in half."*

"Circle?" Myriam had no idea what it was talking about.

"You will find it. It's where William thinks he needs to go, Valnijz too for that matter." The voice changed as it spoken. Going from sounding like a young man to an old woman. *"But listen. When I say so, take the crystal and place it on the cut pillar. That's all. Only that."*

"That's all you want me to do?" Myriam wasn't sure if she'd heard the voice correctly. Most of her attention was taken up by a set of flowers poking their heads out of the ground. Flowers that glowed blue.

"Yes." The voice shifted again, this time to a growling, nearly animal like sound. *"Put the crystal on the pillar. That's it. Easy, right?"*

"And what will that do?" Myriam tried to concentrate on what the voice was saying. That seemed too easy. Far too easy.

"If you do it correctly, I will be reborn." The voice seemed powerful now. Strident. *"I will be reborn to fix what went wrong all those years ago. And it will be because of you, Myriam VolFar. Not William, not Regin. You."*

"But what happens to William? Duncan? Amder, for that matter?" Myriam asked, but stopped moving. A cave. A cave already unlike any other she had ever seen. All the other rocks around her were grey or brown, and most were covered with moss now. But the rocks here? Sandstone. Red and yellow layers, bright and clean. No plant life grew near it.

But that wasn't the strangest part. The opening was dark, to be sure. But she'd never seen a cave entrance that sparkled like the night sky. Because that's what it was. In was the middle of the day, and yet she was standing, staring at a tiny piece of the night sky. In a cave opening.

There could be no doubt. They were there.

Chapter 48.

Regin had a hard time understanding everything that was going on. To him, it seemed the world had turned upside down. Animals he'd never seen before or ever thought possible traveled past him. Things that should not be alive were.

Then there was the feeling in the air. Each breath made his skin tingle and brought a small shiver down his back. He had very little to compare it to. The best he could come up with were two things. One, eating an impossibly good and rich dessert, where your body gives in and your eyes roll up in your head in a moment of total pleasure.

The other was kissing Myriam. He watched her as she walked. He couldn't see her face from the back, but he could see by her body. She was as nearly overwhelmed as he was. This place was incredible. He knew it had to do something with this Anvil of Souls William had talked about. It only made sense. Had the Forgemaster known it would be this way?

No, William was looking around with the same expression of wonder and delight as the rest of them. Well, interspersed with looks at the bound figure in their midst. That thing was not smiling. A sour look, one of disgust, lived on its face.

Regin would never tell William this, but he would be very glad to never see that face again. How this Duncan was still alive in that, he had no idea. Could he even be alive? Regin took a long breath, and the pleasure it brought rushed over him, driving the questions away.

Myriam stopped and turned towards them. "We must be here." Then she moved to the side, and Regin could see why she said that. A hole, a void, seemed to be suspended there, with little stars in it. All covering the mouth of a cave. *Now I have seen everything. The birthplace of the gods.*

"Yes." Regin spoke and then closed his mouth. He had no say in what happened here today. He didn't even know exactly what was going to happen. He wasn't sure Myriam did either.

"If we are here, William, what do we do?" Regin tore his eyes off the sight in front of them.

"It's not supposed to be hard. I don't think at least. I take this..." William reached under his cloak and pulled out a black and shiny circle. No, a circlet.

"I put this on the head of this thing. But it has to be done inside. At a place in the center. Amder was not clear, as usual. But it's the place the gods first stepped into this world. Only there can I pull the spirit of Valnijz out of Duncan and free him. The blood god will be in the circlet. Duncan will finally be freed." Will walked towards the opening. "But I don't see...."

William took a step closer to the void than the rest of them and was suddenly and violently thrown back. Regin rushed to his side, helping him up.

"Why do I think you were not expecting that?" Regin asked as he could see William wore a look of surprise.

"Sparks Amder, you really could be clearer on what I'm supposed to be doing here." William stood, brushing dirt and dead leaves off his clothes.

Regin turned in horror as the figure of Valnijz laughed. A raspy laugh, each laugh, brought a small spray of dark red blood to the figure's lips. "You cannot win. My stupid and foolish brother once again didn't think things through." The Scaled One's laugh grew bitter, and his face, its face, grew tight, as if the skin was about to split.

"Be quiet thing." William answered with a venom that Regin had never heard before from the man.

"I will figure this out." Will said, his voice low to Regin. "But I might need help to figure this out."

Regin nodded and followed Will, both getting as close as Myriam was, but no closer. "Well?"

Myriam picked up a twig and threw it like a spear at the void. It bounced back as well, flying between them with a zip, and landing in the woods. She picked up a rock and made to throw it, but dropped it after a moment. "You know, we all swore to never go into a cave again after the Gorom, and yet, here we are."

William nodded. "I know. Why couldn't this place be out in the open?"

Myriam picked up the rock a second time, giving the cave mouth a long look before dropping the rock again.

"Why not try the rock?" Regin asked, but he knew the answer as soon as the words left his mouth.

"Because I'd hate for us to get all the way here, after everything, and have a rock I threw get bounced back and crack your skull like an egg." Myriam smiled as she said it, but Regin could hear something in her voice he couldn't place.

Is she scared? Tired? Regin wanted to ask, wanted to comfort her. But this was new to him, this kind of relationship. And William had asked them not to, in front of him. Though this wasn't kissing, or more.

"True. I'd rather not die here. I have a long list of excellent restaurants in Ture to visit." Regin winked at Myriam and was pleased to see some of the tension leave her. But only some.

"Your stomach can wait, Regin. We need to get past this." William pointed at the void. "Whatever this is."

"It's locked, obviously. We need to figure out the key." Myriam shrugged as she answered. "Did Amder say nothing?'

Regin sat back as Will paced, thinking. His eyes wide, he reached down to his golden hammer. "Maybe?" Will whispered and held the hammer in front of him.

Nothing happened for a long minute, but with a shudder and a sound that made Regin's teeth vibrate in his skull, the void seemed to tear itself open.

"I guess I had the key." William laughed. Regin had no idea what was so funny, but kept his mouth shut. "Shall we enter?"

***

Will walked forward, hoping very much that he wasn't thrown like the first time. It had hurt. Both physically, and more so his pride. But this time he stepped in to find what appeared to be a somewhat normal, well-lit sandstone cave.

It was beautiful in its own way. Bands of yellow and orange, layered on top of one another. Some thick, some thin. The strange thing was the light. He couldn't tell where it was coming from. It just seemed to be. It wasn't coming from the outside, it went too deep for that.

Will walked out, and the other thing struck him. It was quiet in that cave. He knew quiet. He liked it often. But in there, the quiet was aware. Like it was waiting for something. A holding of breath almost.

"Come, lets' get this done." Will pushed the Scaled one forward, ignoring the hiss it brought in return. Though the blood god did not resist much, and that made him on edge some. He should be fighting every step, but yet he was willing to go. He's plotting something. But what?

Myriam and Regin followed, and the strange expectant silence covered them all. The floor was a hard black rock at least and easy walking. Will knew that was strange. This whole place should be sandstone, if it was natural. But it wasn't.

The enormity of where he was finally hit him. He was walking where the very gods had walked! He was in the birthplace of Amder, of Grimnor! They had turned this very corner he was turning. He reached out to steady himself, as the age and power of here, of now, nearly overcame him.

"William?" Myriam reached out, but he waved her off. Not because he didn't want her help, but because of what was stuck to her hand. A single grain of sand. If sand had been silvery blue, and glowing. Magic. That has to be magic.

"Myriam? Your hand." Will unconsciously wiped his hand on his leathers.

"What about my hand?" Myriam turned her palm over and froze.

"It's, well, I don't know for sure, but I think it might be..." Will took a breath.

"Magic." Myriam answered for him.

"And I think you are right. My skin almost tingles where that thing is." Myriam raised her hand up, nearly at eye level. "It's tiny, but I can feel it flowing into me."

William didn't know where she had gotten magic from, though the sights outside had made it clear they were in a very different place. "Don't get in your eyes!"

"Or breathe it in. Lower your hand Myriam. Slowly." Regin took a half step towards Myriam as he spoke. Will could see how worried he was. At least she's not another conquest for him.

"Oh hush, both of you. I think it's wonderful. A tiny spark of magic. I wonder if we will see more, the deeper we go in?" Myriam did lower her hand, though didn't brush it off.

Will didn't have an answer to her question, but then again, who would know?

"There is only one way to know. Onwards." William pushed the Scaled One forward and walked deeper into the cave.

Chapter 49.

Duncan sat very still, gathering whatever strength he could. Valnijz was going to try to kill William. And as much as Duncan wanted to rest, he could not allow that to happen. The grey mist was thicker still and had taken on a new and more disturbing pattern since they had entered this cave. The forms and faces had grown more real, more solid, and more alive.

As he watched in growing fear, part of the rolling mass of grey fog seemed to separate itself out. Long parts like legs seemed to form, then arms, and finally a deformed and wispy head. It tore itself from the rest of the fog with effort and took a single step towards him.

Duncan pushed himself backwards, but not too far. There was very little space left anymore. The grey mist surrounded him fully. Horrors seemed to shift and wave in the mist. Sometimes they fought, sometimes they seemed to weep. And others screamed a silent scream.

But this one this was new. It took another step and raised a shifting and rolling arm towards Duncan.

"Heeellllppp…." The misty figure spoke.

Duncan froze. He knew that voice. He'd not heard it for years, not since a morning, long ago. Not since his father had left the house in the Reach, to go look for Will's Da. The voice of his father.

"No. This is Valnijz." Duncan shut his eyes closed. Just when he thought he could stand up to the god, it did something like this.

"Hellllpp meee Son.." The voice came closer this time.

"Go away." Duncan spat the words from between clenched teeth.

No answer came, and after a moment He risked a glance. The figure still stood, but not for much longer. Already the outstretched arm was gone, the mist blowing away, sucked back into the boiling larger mass. The things legs and torso began to be sucked back into the mist.

"Sorrrryyy..." The voice came one last time, before the face was gone.

Duncan wanted to wretch. He wanted to scream. He wanted to punch the Blood God right in his scaled face. But he couldn't. He sat and watched as the mist that had taken the form of his father rejoined the ever-growing bank that surrounded him. And he wept.

***

Will didn't know what to think. At times, it seemed like a normal cave. A well-lit cave, but normal. Not a dank pit of a place like the Gorom or Vinik caves. But even in that, it was a bit off. First the light. The second was the size. Will had been sure more than once that the cave seemed to move. It grew to a size where they wouldn't have to crouch, they could all walk comfortably.

Myriam kept looking at her hand, and Regin kept looking at her. Will smiled. He finally had made peace with that. Oh, some small part still wondered 'what if', but he liked them both. It was alright. Maybe not as he wished, or wanted, but it was alright.

They continued on deeper, and the next oddity occurred to him. There were no side tunnels. It was a single twisting and curving tunnel. No side passages. No cracks and crevasses that led off to points unknown. He had almost gotten used to the place when he turned a corner and had to stop.

Blue light assaulted his eyes. Bright blue. He blinked and almost fell to his knees. Before him lay a stream. But not of water. But of the same blue specks that they had seen before. Millions and more of them. A stream of pure, raw magic.

"Why..." Myriam's voice stopped right behind Will as she took in the same sight. Regin must have stopped as well, but didn't say anything. The only sound was a faint hiss as the blue sand flowed past them. Straight into a wall, where it vanished. Gone.

Valnijz was the only one of them who had a powerful reaction. He twisted away from the stuff; his face locked into a grimace. Will found himself rather happy at his reaction. *Finally, something the Blood God really doesn't like. Raw magic.*

"How are we going to cross that?" Regin asked from the rear. 'There isn't a way around it and going back gets us nothing."

Will paid attention to what Reign was saying and realized he was right. The stream of magic was nearly three feet across. And no bridge or any way to cross it seemed to exist. "I don't know." Will looked around, wondering if they should go back to the forest outside and gather wood to walk across.

"It's not harmful. Why don't we wade across?" Myriam held up her hand, where she had refused to wipe off the single speck of blue.

"Walk through that? Through solid magic? If that's what it is." Regin spoke quickly. "That doesn't seem like a good idea to me. What if it's something else, and it only looks like the stuff on your hand?"

"He could be right, Myriam. You don't seem to be hurt by what's on your hand, but you don't know what this stuff is. Or maybe it's the same thing, but this much of it would hurt you." Will shook his head. "We should go back, get some wood from the forest and cross that way."

"Ask that thing." Myriam pointed at the decidedly close-mouthed figure of the Blood God.

"Would you trust anything it said?" Will pointed at the stream of magic that flowed by. "It could be hoping we'd go in and all die."

"I agree with Will. Let's go get wood and come back. There isn't a time we have to be there by, is there? Unless you can get an answer from Amder?" Regin stepped forward, his face light from below by the blue glow.

Will tried to reach his god, but the connection was as faded and unreal as it had ever been. "*Amder?*" Will thought hard, but got no reply, or even awareness the god had heard him. "Nothing. But remember, Amder said once we came here, he couldn't help us."

"Why is that, anyway? I mean the Blood God is here." Myriam asked, but her eyes remained locked on the blue glowing stream.

"I'm not sure. But since our... companion here isn't fully here, and bound to Duncan's body, maybe that's why. Amder isn't here in the flesh." Will hadn't given it much thought, but realized he rather wished he had. Having Amder here would have been a great help.

But he is here, in me. The thought echoed around his head. Will didn't know what to think, but none of this mattered. They had to get across, and that meant making a bridge.

"Do we all go together? Does only one of us leave? How do we do this?" Regin asked and turned around to head back the way they had come.

"This is a waste of time." Myriam said, and without another word, she stepped into the glowing stream.

"MYRIAM!" Will yelled, trying to reach her, but she kept on wading through the raw magic. It crested over her legs as she walked, and to his surprise, she laughed.

Regin turned and nearly pushed Will over, trying to get to her, but she was too far to grab now.

"Come on, you two, this feels amazing. It's incredible!" Myriam yelled and threw her arms in the air. They watched as she made her way across the flow, and stepped out, stomping her boots, now covered with the glowing dust.

"That was fun. More than fun. You have got to feel that!" Myriam was still smiling.

Regin said nothing at first, but then shrugged. "Well, I guess we have our answer." Taking a large step, he entered the flow. He made his way through, but giving a yell at one point. "You are right! This is... beyond words. William! You have GOT to feel this!"

Will watched as Regin made his way across and finally stepped out and, like Myriam, stomped his boots and brushed the specks of blue off of him. Or at least most. A few clung to both of them, glittering.

"They are fools. Magic has a price for mortals." Valnijz muttered. "And I will not set foot in that cursed chaos."

Will pushed his captive. "Well, you aren't staying here. Go."

Valnijz said nothing, but with a sudden leap, crossed the stream. "I will not touch it."

Regin grabbed their captive and pushed him to the floor, giving Will a questioning look.

No Regin, I did not know he could do that either. Will didn't like this. It was becoming more and more obvious that the Scaled One, while unable to use his arms and hands, was quite capable of getting away. Yet, he stayed with them. Which meant he wanted to be here.

He was planning something. But what? If they left, nothing would change. It was only here things could be fixed. Will had little choice, even if he didn't like it.

"Myriam, I hope you are right!" Will called out and, with a brave face that he did not feel in his heart, stepped into the blue glowing stream.

The feeling came instantly, though not strongly, at least not at first. It started as a thrum in his ears, then a tickle from his knees down. A strange feeling, but not overwhelming. But each step brought a greater change. The tickle became a tremor, and his legs felt like they were about to burst with energy. He hated running, but right now he would have sworn he could run all the way back to the Reach, and not be out of breath.

He was nearly a third of the way through when a largish wave of the flow washed over him. This one was big enough to splash onto his belt and his arms. The effect was immediate. The golden hammer at his side exploded into light, a bright yellow that nearly made Will stumble and fall into the flow.

The raw magic had also touched his bracers. God touched bracers. They too glowed, and much to his surprise, to sing. A wordless melody, with a rhythm that Will knew. The rhythm of the forge. The inlay glowed in different colors, based on what Myriam had used. And the underlying metal glowed silver.

Will didn't know what to do, but stepped quicker, and finally stepped out of the flow.

"Will!" Myriam took a step towards him but cocked her head oddly, as if she was listening to something only she could hear.

"I'm fine. Just, surprised." Will watched as the glow from the bracers and hammer faded, and the strange music stopped, trailing off into silence. "I did not expect that."

"I don't think any of us did." Regin laughed. "But look, we made it past. And now we know on the way back, it's safe."

"I wouldn't say safe exactly, but we can cross it I guess." Will had to admit the feeling the stuff had given him was addicting. He already wanted another sip of that power, that raw energy.

"Magic is not meant for mortals." Valnijz whispered, his eyes watching Will.

Will said nothing but couldn't shake the feeling. Maybe the thing was right. Maybe Amder was right. "Come on, let's keep moving."

Chapter 50.

Myriam was confused. The voice, this claimed god had been silent since they entered the cave. The only time it had spoken was when she went to talk to Will after he got out of that incredible raw magic stream and the unnamed voice warned her off.

"Why did you not want me to talk to Will?" She spoke into her head, still feeling very foolish doing so.

"With that much raw magic on him? With the trappings of Amder on him and full of the magic? No, there was a good chance he would know. Amder would know I was here." The voice spoke quickly. *"I do not have the time to explain everything. I require your faith and obedience. I must save my energy for my return. You remember what must be done?"*

"Yes. Put the crystal on a broken pillar when you say so." Myriam still didn't understand the why of it.

"Exactly. Everything will be made clear when you do so." The unnamed voice spoke quickly. *"You are close."*

"I don't know if I like that answer." Myriam thought, but no response came. This must be what it's like with Amder for William. Information, but never quite all the information you need. Annoying if she thought about it.

"Myriam, how do you feel?" Regin stepped up close, the cave seeming to shift again, so they could walk side by side.

"Good. Still very good. That stream was amazing." Myriam could still feel the tingles on her skin.

"It was! But let's not do it like that again? You about gave Will a fit." Regin reached out and gave her a shoulder hug, though gave a quick look to William, who was keeping a frowning face on their captive.

"What about you? Were you worried for me, Master Regin?" Myriam raised her voice a bit to a higher pitch and fluttered her eyes. "If I'd fallen, would you have come to rescue me? You're such a big strong Guildmaster after all."

Regin did laugh then, a booming baritone laugh that seemed to echo oddly through the cave. "I'd come help, but I doubt Myriam VolFar that you will ever need someone to save you."

"That's right, and don't you ever forget it!" Myriam poked Regin in the side as they made their way into the cave. This place wasn't as strange as the outside of the cave, at least, though it was odd enough.

They walked a bit further until in front of them stood something they hadn't expected. A solid wall. The way was blocked.

***

Jindo ran, using every speck of the power that he could muster. The land sped past, a blur of trees and rocks that melded into a grayish-brown blob. Each step brought him closer to freeing his lord, and nothing would stop him from such a holy duty.

He had been to the Anvil once, and only once. Hundreds of years ago, he had come out of curiosity. He still remembered the feeling of flying through the air as the cave rejected him. He had landed partially on a rock that had tried to bite his leg.

This land was not what he or anyone else could explain. But since all the oddness seemed to be around the actual Anvil, it was obvious that it came from the same place. Whatever power lived there, it changed everything outside, up to a point.

Pain.

Jindo shifted his thoughts as fast as possible back to the now, as pain forced him to stop. A tree branch. He had run directly into a tree branch. He could feel ribs popping as the blood worked to heal him. It still hurt, though. He hadn't felt this much physical pain in a very long time.

His next shock came as the tree branch that he'd run into moved. It raised up and came smashing down at the spot where Jindo had stood moments before. The branch was connected to a tree, a tree that moved.

Jindo stabbed forward with his spear, but it did little to his attacker. The blade deflected against the round trunk, striking only a glancing blow. The tree thing twisted, but this time Jindo expected the blow, and dodged out of the way. He stabbed again, but the spear did almost no damage to the thing.

This is not working. A spear isn't going to do enough to this thing, whatever it was. And if it got lucky and crushed a leg, Jindo would be in trouble. Not to mention, he didn't have the time for a protracted fight.

Jindo threw his spear down and gathered his power. He hadn't done anything like this since he was new to the blood, but it still should work. He dodged another attack, jumping up and out of the way as a branch came lashing down at the same time a root erupted from the ground, trying to grab his legs.

Good tactics, though it should have opened with that. This thing's mistake would be its end. Jindo ran then, running in a circle around the tree, ducking and weaving as the tree lashed out at him. Find the opening. Find the point.

In his next circle of the tree, he saw it. It never attacked from one small side. It always twisted from that spot to try to hit him. There. Jindo did one more pass, and gathering his power, punched forward, his hand driving with all the power he could muster at that spot.

The crack echoed over the forest, and Jindo nearly screamed himself. Bones' crushed ligaments tore in his hand as the force pulverized parts of his hand and forearm. The tree fared worse. Far worse. The blow exploded through the bark and shattered the wood where he hit it. Even more surprising, the blow's force traveled through the trunk and forced its way out the other side, tearing wood and bark outward in a spray of destruction.

Jindo pulled his injured arm close to his body and crouched ready to run away if need be, but the tree stood still, before falling, leaning towards the damage before with a series of cracks and pops, the top half of the thing fell, crashing into the woods, leaving only silence as the sound ended.

Good. Jindo concentrated on healing his arm. He pushed all he dared into that and did scream this time as bones stretch and reform. Ligaments fused back and even skin sealed itself shut where the force of the blow had forced it apart.

Jindo did not scream easily, but that had hurt. Still, it worked. He checked his grip a few times and, taking his spear from the ground where he had left it, Jindo ran again. Faster now, as he had lost some time in that pointless battle. The thing hadn't even bled. There was nothing to give to the Blood God.

Jindo soon skidded to a stop as the cave was in front of him. A cave that should not be open but was. *My lord is inside.* With those loyal to the dirty god. Jindo gripped his spear tight. They WOULD bleed, and his lord would be freed. Jindo ran through the opening into the cave, ready to kill.

***

Duncan felt strange. For the first time in a very long time, the grey fog around him had lessened. He could see past it now, back to the older confines of the space where he was. He could see the spot where the beast had been kept, the beast that had always been the Blood God.

He had no idea why this was happening, though. Standing, Duncan soon saw something else. Something even more surprising. Before, everything had been red and dusty. Then, after the end of Zalkiniv, it had changed to this never-ending grey. But there, past the gray sat a small patch of something Duncan thought was absolutely beautiful.

Blue.

A dazzling blue. After an unknown amount of time, blue was beautiful. He could feel the wetness on his cheeks as he saw it. Crying over a color? But it was amazing. It turned his thoughts to home. Of the clear bright blue sky over the Skyreach mountains, when the wind blew everything away and as fall turned to winter. A deep, wonderful blue.

But why was it here? What did it mean? He had no idea. He knew so little about this place, about why he even existed here still. He knew what the Blood God had said. That for some reason, his soul was needed to keep the body alive. At least for now.

Was that the truth? Did it even matter? But the blue was new. And new meant something had changed. He thought back to that foggy thing that had spoken with the voice of his father. He had dismissed it out of hand as a trick of the Scaled One. But maybe it hadn't been.

No one had ever seen his father again after he'd gone out that day. Could he have been captured by the Valni or others loyal to the Scaled One? He hated to think that he knew what happened to those who were. But yet, that could have been some remnant, some shred of the person who had once ruffled his hair, gave him a hug and vanished out the door.

It gave Duncan one more reason to hate the Blood God if it were true. One more reason to fight back. And if this blue glow had something to do with the lessening of the fog, Duncan Reis wanted to be closer to it.

Besides, if it killed him, the Blood God would fail now. He knew pain now, and if it only hurt, that was fine. Hopefully. Dunc ran towards the glow, tearing through a remnant wisp of the fog. Even that brief contact brought a searing line of pain that nearly made him fall over, but he forced his legs to keep moving. Closer and closer still until, with a near leap, he entered the glow and laughed.

Chapter 51.

"And now we go where?" Will shook his head. "Can't something work the first time? Just once?"

Regin shrugged, Myriam looked confused, and Valnijz laughed again. A deep laugh, old. One that should never come from anyone's throat, and very much not Will's cousins.

"What is so sparks burned amusing to you? You are my prisoner, you know. It's obvious you are plotting something. You haven't hidden it well." Will pulled the golden hammer from his belt. The glow it had gotten from its contact with whatever that blue sand was had gone now, but to his hand, it still felt different.

"My brothers and sisters did not want me to return here. Ever. I thought they had only warded the front, but it seems I was mistaken." Valnijz's face contorted, and before their eyes became even more reptilian, jaw elongating, and a horrible tearing sound came with it as skin already pulled tight gave way.

"Stop that! You're hurting Duncan!!" Will raised his hammer to hit the thing, but stopped. If he hit the beast, he was hurting Duncan as well.

Valnijz said nothing but as they watched new skin, scaled and thing grew over the bare bone. Scales grew at a rapid pace, covering any remaining plain skin. In moments, it was over. The beast that stood before them was something out of a childhood nightmare, except horribly real.

"What do we do, William?" Regin pointed at the wall. "Do we try to break through it? It appears to be sandstone. I do not think we should trust our senses here though."

Myriam shook her head. "I don't know. I simply don't know."

"What don't you know?" Will asked, poking at the wall with his free hand. It felt like sandstone. But as he touched it and a small layer of sand fell off, more returned, flowing into the spot his hand had touched.

"It appears bashing it won't help." Regin sighed and put down his pack. "So, we need to figure this out."

"Myriam? What don't you know?" William asked again.

"What?" Myriam answered and shook her head. "Sorry, I don't know what to do."

"Are you feeling well? You have seemed somewhat distracted." William looked at her carefully. She appeared fine, though she didn't seem to want to look him in the eye. "It could be that blue sand, maybe prolonged contact harms you."

"No. I'm well. Exhausted. And confused. And I think I do not want to be here." Myriam shook her head. "This is all far beyond what I thought I'd ever be involved in. I am only an innkeeper's daughter who wanted to be a Guild Smith. That was all. But I'm here, standing in a cave with the Forgemaster of Amder, and a bound god. And the cave is full of magic, which shouldn't exist. And it's the birthplace of the gods. William, I am not fine." Myriam gritted her teeth after her outburst.

"But I am here. I am here because I made a promise. But William, I have no idea what to do about a wall." Myriam closed her eyes for a moment and cocked her head, as if she was listening to something, or trying to.

"Well, I do not know what to do." Will shrugged. "But I know this isn't the place."

"I know how." Valnijz spoke again, its voice nearly gone. It was more air than sound. "Your hammer, and my blood. Blood freely given."

"What?" Will turned to the bound god.

"That will allow us to pass, and travel to the heart of this place." Valnijz sniffed the air. "It is past the wall."

"My hammer, this hammer?" Will raised up the golden hammer.

"Yes. My fool of a brother and I must have to work together to get past this wall." Valnijz laughed. "It's not a very good lock. Grimnor's idea. He was always stupid."

"Why help?" Regin pushed the form of Valnijz. "We are going here to banish you."

Valnijz said nothing and smiled. A fanged smile.

"I don't like this at all." Regin smacked a nearby wall with his hand. "This is all too much."

"I know. But I don't know what else to do." Will pointed at Valnijz. "If we leave, what do we do with him? We already know he could escape, even if he can't free his arms bound as he is. Amder won't be any help. I can't talk to him here, again. And if he escapes, how many will die by his hand? How many more are given to his thirst? And what happens to Duncan?"

"I don't have the answers. I wish I did. I wish Haltim or Vin, or even Master Jaste, were here to give advice. But they aren't. They can't be. It's up to us. Up to me. And while every spark blessed part of me screams that this is all an idiotic thing to do, I can't see any other way forward, then to do what that thing says." Will shook his head, wiping his forehead. "It's not even hot in this place and I'm sweating like a miner who dug too deep."

"But the two of you don't have to do this. You two can leave." Will pointed back the way they came. "And be together. Out there. Away from this. Away from the insanity."

"Not this again. I swore to serve you Forgemaster, and I stand by that promise." Regin answered before Myriam could. "Right Myriam?"

Myriam's eyes fell, and she nodded. "Forget what I said. I want to be here." Myriam let out a long breath and put a hand on Will's arm. "And thank you."

Will wondered what exactly she was thanking him for. "Of course. Now, let's get started."

***

"Are you there? Is this right? What should we do?" Myriam asked again in the silence of her mind. She'd been trying to talk to the strange voice since they hit this wall, and still. Nothing.

'Sparks burn you. Answer!" She asked once more, but still no answer came. Not that she expected it to.

The only thing good to come out of all this was William. He had accepted her and Regin. She could see it. At last. She gave the Forgemaster a long look. He really had grown. He was still the same heavyset, strong, clumsy man he had always been. But you could see it in his eyes. He had grown wiser. Stronger. Surer of himself, even now, when he didn't know what to do.

Back when she had first met him, back when he'd been Markin Darto, he'd always been skittish. Part of that she knew was the fact that he'd been living a lie then. But it was also obvious that part of it was he wasn't sure of himself. He was now.

He's a good man. He will make some woman thrilled. William wasn't a man to stray. He would be devoted to whomever he ended up with. Not that Regin was the type to stray, though. Her eyes caught him, and he saw her doing so, shooting her a smile that brought tingles to her skin. That man. Drove her crazy.

She wasn't even sure why. He fit. I *guess I should thank William for that as well. If he had left Regin in that cell, I might never have seen him again.* Strange how the world worked. She probed again for the voice, that feeling, but while it seemed to be there, it totally ignored her. *Should I even do this?* Her fingers found the small metal box, no bigger than a ring holder in her pocket. *I could drop this thing, and no one would be the wiser.*

But the voice saved me. *And I made a promise. I hope I don't regret it.* Myriam cocked her head one more time, trying to hear any words from the unnamed voice, or god she guessed she should say. Unnamed. It wanted her to name it. Why me? Why does a name matter? She didn't have the answers to any of it.

Still, she turned her attention from her introspection and worry to William and Valnijz. Valnijz. Thinking too much about what the bound figure represented made her both want to be sick and also made her want to kick the thing. Hard.

Will had pulled his golden hammer out and was speaking to Valnijz in a low voice. Why did he even trust that creature? But as William said, they had no choice.

She watched as Valnijz bit its own lip, blood flowing down its scaled chin, and onto the hard-black stone floor. Oddly enough, the blood that landed there seemed to flow into cracks in the floor in like an alive creature, as if it was seeking a way out on its own.

Will held his hammer under those drips. As each drop struck the hammer, a point of golden light erupted. It reminded her of the crystal in her pocket. Only not as strong. A few more drops and Will pulled the hammer back and, without a word, struck the wall.

Sandstone collapsed, falling away from his blow like a wet sheet of parchment. It was impossibly thin. A good sneeze should have broken it. But here, nothing was normal.

"Let's go." Will kept a firm grip on the hammer and pushed their companion through. Myriam followed, and she heard Regin come in behind her. It was time.

***

Duncan felt better than he had in, well, longer than he could remember. Whatever this strange blue light was, he wanted more. Months of pain, months of fear, unending days of sadness seemed to melt away. For right now, at this moment, he was Duncan Reis again.

He could still watch, though, and he didn't like what he was seeing. He knew Valnijz would make his move soon. That Jindo person would be here. They were almost at this center place. This Anvil of Souls. He was sure William loved the name; it would have spoken to his blacksmith heart.

To Duncan, it seemed a bit formal. Why not call it the first place? Or something like that? Not that what it was named really mattered. What mattered was what was going to happen there. He had to be ready. He wasn't fully aware of what he could do to stop things, but if he could even through a momentary stall in the Blood God's plan, that was good enough for him.

He watched as they came around a bend to an opening that seemed to grow as they looked at it. Concentric rings covered the floor, leading to the center of the room, where a half-sized pillar stood. Carved out of the same sandstone that this place seemed to be made of, but cut neatly in half, it was a bit out of step with the surroundings.

For unlike the rest of the place, this half pillar was covered with engravings, carvings, and writing the likes of which Duncan had never seen. The words and pictures seemed to move as well, the longer he looked at them, but blinking helped them snap back to whatever they had looked like before.

A creeping sensation of cold and death assaulted him, and the grey mist, what was still left of it, flashed with red here and there. Duncan wasn't sure, of course, how could he be? *But if I had to guess, Jindo was here.*

Chapter 52.

Jindo ran, not bothering to look at the strange wonders around him. The blue sand, the shifting tunnel, and to his highly tuned senses, the faint song that seemed to echo through everything. None of that mattered. He must free his lord.

Jindo burst into an open chamber, and finally saw his opponents. One tall man, wearing only traveling clothes, and holding a hammer. Holding it in a typical defensive stance, the man had the look of someone who at least had some training.

The next was a younger woman. She didn't even hold her weapon and had her back to the tunnel he had come from. Fool. She was looking at the pillar in the middle of the room. Jindo's blood enhanced senses could see her eyes dart over it, the skin at the edges of her mouth and eyes getting pulled tight for a moment. *She's surprised.*

And there, by his lord, his master, his god, stood a young man holding a golden hammer. And this must be the Forgemaster. He held the hammer like a club. No good training then. Jindo let his eyes examine the man. Strong, but maybe not too quick. The hammer itself also stood out, golden and with a fading glow. A hammer from a god. Jindo knew blows from that hammer would hurt and might not heal. Not that he thought the man had a chance to even touch him. But the real prize was the figure who was in front of this Forgemaster. Scaled muscles clenched, hands bound, Valnijz.

Kill the helpers, free Valnijz, and then kill the Forgemaster. Simple. Jindo moved like oil over water, his feet gliding more than stepping. He pulled his spear back and threw it, aiming at the larger man who held his hammer well. The spear flashed forth, the point nearly splitting the air with a whine that would have made many a person grit their teeth and hold their ears. The target whirled, inadvertently giving the spear a bigger target as he moved towards the source of the noise.

The crack that echoed through the cavern surprised Jindo and he took a moment to register what had happened. The Forgemaster had stepped in front of the spear. How he had managed to be there was unclear, as he seemed unsteady. Jindo's eyes flew to the only other thing close enough to do so. Valnijz.

But no. The eyes. It was Valnijz in form, but the eyes. Something or someone else was looking at him through those eyes, but whatever it was fading already. In the barest sliver of time, he looked back at the Forgemaster. The spear had hit his armor, and more in point, it had hit a long rent in his armor; the point had caught there, but the spear had broken, the force of the impact too much for the shaft of the spear, and it had broken off.

Jindo smiled then. His blow might not have done exactly what he hoped, but it did not matter. The shaft of his spear had broken and flown. Right into the side of the large man with the hammer.

***

"REGIN!" Myriam screamed as Will tried to get his bearings. He'd been standing behind Valnijz, with Regin nearby, when he'd been pushed by the Scaled One into his friend. He'd stumbled, starting to stand up, when something had struck him. Something hard. He'd partially spun with the blow, whatever it was breaking as it hit the chest plate.

Then the scream. He turned to Regin, only to see the man down on his knees. A shaft of black wood was embedded in his side, and blood was already on his lips. "Regin no!" Will forgot about everything else for a moment and rushed over, joined by Myriam.

"Regin! Say something. Hold still. I..." Myriam grabbed Will's shoulder. "Do something! Amder must save him!"

Will was stunned. He reached out, trying to talk to his god, but got nothing. There was nothing he could do. "I can't." Will whispered.

Regin tried to talk, talking a gasping breath, but blood bubbled forth instead. Regin's hand grabbed Will's shoulder, and he nodded at Will before turning to Myriam. He took a long breath, gasping for air.

"Please William. Help him!" Myriam was on the verge of tears. Will wished he could do something. Anything. But he knew it was too late. The shaft had broken into his lungs. He was a dead man already. All Will could do was put a hand on Myriam's shoulder and watch as Reign took one last breath and died there on the floor. Regin fought to take a breath, gasping for air, but it was no use. Eyes wide, he looked at both of them, a look of fear and sadness flitted across his features. One last half gasp and Regin lay still.

Myriam threw his hand off, turning on him with a ferocity that he'd never seen her display before. "You could have saved him! Why didn't you save him!"

"I couldn't Myriam. I wanted to." Will answered before she collapsed onto him, her voice breaking as she spoke. "Why William? Why..."

"Because he needed to die. You will join him, and then this Forgemaster, though I will relish his death. I may even let him speak to the shard of Duncan that I've had so much fun with. Would you like that, William Reis?" Valnijz's voice broke through their sadness.

Will didn't know what to do, but Myriam did. Before he could react, a growl broke from her throat, and she rushed towards the Blood God, her hammer held with both hands to smash him, only to halt at the appearance of another man from nowhere. If it was a man. He looked nothing like any man Will had ever seen.

A thin man, a man who must have thrown the spear. A man that looked like he was dead already. Grey skin, pale eyes. The only thing that stood out was the man's lips. Blood red, they stood out like a red gash on an otherwise lifeless face. But that wasn't the worst part. The man held something. Something silver. Shackles. Valnijz's shackles.

The Blood God was free. Will knew. This was the plan the Blood God had in mind the whole time. He knew this person was coming. He wanted us to get him into here. He couldn't have done this alone. He used us. He used me. *And I let him. What have I done?*

"Jindo. Instead of killing the other one right now, disarm them both. Show them your power. I want an audience for my ascension. Then, I will kill them myself. I'll make him watch as she dies, and then I will kill him, so he joins my eternal chorus." Valnijz snapped his teeth for a second at William. "I will enjoy adding your screams to my voice."

Jindo stepped forward and then everything was once again a blur of motion. William was thrown backwards, as his belt was cut, and the hammer thrown to the far side of the chamber. Myriam's hammer was thrown by itself, but the result was the same, both were weaponless now.

Jindo pulled a long clear cylinder out from under his clothes. It wasn't too large, but what William couldn't keep his eyes off of was the single red drop of blood floating in it. What had Amder called it? The drop? Jindo held it forth with a reverence that William didn't share.

Valnijz stepped to a point, a clear spot in the circles. For a long moment, nothing happened. Then, he took the cylinder from Jindo and crushed it. The drop seemed to hover in midair for a fraction of time, and Will held his breath. A vibration struck the room, and the blood seemed to shatter in the air, flowing into the form of the Scaled One.

Valnijz screamed then, and Will found some pleasure in knowing that this at least hurt the vile thing. The scream did not last long though, as the form went down, silent, kneeling on the ground. In the quiet, Jindo turned towards William and Myriam, pulling some long sharp bone from behind his back.

"Do you know what this is? This is a barb of a fully grown blood bear. One poke, and your blood will burn. Your skin with start to die. Even a scratch has been known to kill in total agony. I tied a man up once to test it. He screamed for five long days as the foulness did its work. Not a weapon of war, not usually, but in service to my lord, all weapons are acceptable." Jindo approached them, each step measured.

"My lord? May I?" Jindo asked, while keeping his eyes on them.

"Yes. A suitable end for them." Valnijz answered. The Blood god was still recovering from whatever he had done, but it was clear he couldn't be for long. Even as the words left him, each one was stronger, with more malice and hate joined to each word. Barely above a whisper, but it held power.

Jindo seemed to hesitate, and then pain. Two furrowed cuts on each of them. Long red and just deep enough. How had the man moved that fast? Will tried to think, but the pain crawled up his arms and became worse as it moved. Fire like molten metal traced up his arms with the pain. Normal pain he could handle, but this? Will could barely move, it overwhelmed his senses. Could he even use his hands to put the crown on that head?

"Jindo." Valnijz spoke quietly, but Will could hear his voice clearly now. "You have been an excellent weapon. But your blood is needed. You are the final speck of the blood."

The figure who was Jindo froze for a moment, but bowed. "My blood is your blood. In life or death, I serve."

Valnijz stood then, and Will could see the change already. The body, which had been nearly broken and wasted, was strong now. There was a hard strength about its form, and while it was still thin, it radiated power. Without another word, an arm surged forward and ripped out Jindo's throat. The form of this Jindo person, already hated, collapsed with a faint sound, as if he was an empty husk, not a man.

The blood flowed out of the fallen form, and up the body of the Blood God. Rivulets of power seemed to join with it, transforming the body beneath as they passed. All was lost. Will swallowed in fear. He had failed. How could he stop this?

"Good." Was all Valnijz said as the man's blood flowed around him. "I have returned!" Red mist flowed from the very rocks into the body of the God of rage and destruction, as Will watched in horror.

***

Myriam couldn't accept this. Regin was dead? The Blood God had been freed? They knew the evil thing had been planning something, and yet they had still failed to counter it. Regin dead. She wanted to scream, she wanted to hurt something. She wanted to blame William. Blame Amder. Blame anything.

It wasn't their fault. But Regin was dead! And the pain! The cuts on her arms started on her hands and had not been large. But thin black and green lines were already moving up her arms, tracing her skin in torment.

She barely paid attention as Valnijz spoke to the man who had killed Regin. What did it matter? When the vibration struck, even she gave it her attention. She reached into her pocket, feeling the small box there. Maybe this unnamed god could fix this. Maybe. Regin could live again.

Horror grew as she realized what the red mist that had entered the room was. The blood mist from the Mistlands! How could it be here? Now? That was thousands of leagues away. But yet, here it was. It flowed around her and William, all but trapping them. The fear grew in her mind, only being challenged by the pain that came in ever stronger waves up her arms. Her hands still seemed to work, but each movement brought a new spike of fiery agony.

Valnijz had won. The mist lessened, and as it did, the sense of dread grew. The full force of the evil of the Scaled One hit her. A wisp of a waking nightmare, one of despair and fear crossed her senses.

"NOW!" the voice in her head screamed, shocking her into movement. Her fingers forced the box open, and she grabbed the crystal. She could see Will standing surprised behind her, and Valnijz reach out, his hand coming closer. Her hand held the crystal forth, and to her surprised Valnijz recoiled, and for the once she saw the terror on its face. Abject fear. *FACE THIS YOU SCALED BASTARD!* The crystal left her hand and rested on the pillar.

And the storm began.

Wind howled around the chamber as sand flew, stinging her skin and eyes. Will rushed towards her, his face full of questions, but this was not the time to ask. He had somehow grabbed his hammer and held it tight.

Then, with a sudden jerk, William was held in place, and a silver glow suffused him. Likewise, Valnijz was held, and a red glow covered his form.

"Thank you, Myriam. And now, in this place, what was wrong can be set right. The two will be one." The voice came, but not in her head, but all around. Valnijz tried to scream then. She could see the muscles in his neck grow tight. Will's eyes darted around but closed and a horrible shuddering began as the power of Amder, all the power of his god, flowed through him and into the crystal.

Likewise, the red mist, which moments before had covered the area, flowed back out of Valnijz and into the crystal, which glowed. Brighter and brighter still. It was oddly like watching drains swirl away, except it was the Gods themselves, being drained away into that crystal. Into that voice, into.. a new God?

Myriam shielded her eyes, and a growing awareness filled her. She knew the other gods had come. Come to see their long-lost kin be reborn. Myriam closed her eyes. Her job was done. The pain that came with the fire on her arms now controlled everything, and it was all she could do not to scream and shiver as it grew ever stronger. *I am going to die, but at least I have my revenge.*

Chapter 53.

Will hurt. He could barely hold on to himself. A roaring, screaming overwhelmed all his thoughts. The screams of a god. Amder was dying. And with the gods' end came his own. He had come so close, but to no avail. Duncan was lost. He'd seen Myriam do something, and everything had changed.

"Will?" it was Duncan. Will could not see him, but he could hear him.

"Dunc? Is that you?" Will searched, near frantic to find his cousin. But to no avail. He couldn't see anything.

"I'm sorry Will. I tried to stop him. I could dislodge him for a moment, only a moment, and throw you out of the way. But you weren't the target. I failed. Your friend died anyway." Duncan's voice was still Duncan, but each word came slower, weaker.

"It's ok Dunc. Really. I don't know what is happening. We live through this; we will go home to the Reach and stay there." Will meant it. Without Amder, his promise would be over. And he could go back to being William Reis, from the Reach. If I don't die here. What had happened? What had Myriam done?

He hurt so much now. The cuts had gotten wider, deeper still. A wound that festered in minutes instead of days. He wanted to weep from it. He wanted to weep for the pain he knew Duncan must have gone through, not just for a day, but for months at a time. The roaring of the surrounding wind grew, as he could feel the essence of Amder being pulled through him. It burned like his very bones were engulfed in flame.

"No Will. That is not to be. "Duncan's voice dropped. "I'm tired. Tired of pain, tired of fighting. Tired of it all."

Will tried again to see anything, but he had a hard time thinking. "Duncan, listen to me…"

"I'm using whatever this power I found to talk to you now, Will. But I can't do this anymore. Let me go, please? I need to rest." Duncan's voice was even quieter now, the voice of someone on the edge of sleep.

Will wanted him back, but… Duncan had suffered enough. "I'm fine Duncan. Rest. I love you." He yelled the words, hoping that Duncan could hear him. Will held on, trying to find any way to survive. The wind blew sand and small rocks that cut into his skin just as much as the wounds did.

"And I love you. I'm proud to be…" Duncan's voice ended, and the pain overwhelmed any thoughts Will had of surviving this.

***

Myriam watched in silent terror as Will and Valnijz's forms became nothing more than glowing blobs of power. Power that the crystal sucked in with ever-increasing speed. *What have I done? Have I killed William, as well as myself?* The chamber was shattered, and a large pit had opened up near to where she stood, a pit filled with that glowing blue sand. *Magic.*

A scream came, but not a voice she knew well. It was deep, strong, and sudden. With a thousand thunderclaps going off at once, the crystal shattered. And from the base of the pillar, a figure grew. The blobs of power that had been feeding into it faded, leaving the body of Valnijz and the body of William Reis lying on the dusty floor.

The air crackled as the figure grew. "I am reborn. The shattering has been undone." The figure spoke then, and not in her head. It was the same voice, but stronger, more powerful. "All that remains is to be named. Once that is done, I shall take my revenge on those disgusting creatures who caused my downfall. And then all the lands will know, the true god of humans has returned. You shall be my prophet Myriam VolFar. All will know your name."

'Name me!" the unnamed god pointed at Will's form. "He lives. I shall show you my power." Myriam watched as the figure grew more solid, and wore a grey cloak, and a hood over its head. It raised a single gloved hand, and waved it over the form of William Reis, which as the shadow of the hand touched it, took a series of short coughing breaths. The lines of fire on her arms stopped growing but did not disappear. Will's must have done the same as his face relaxed, the struggle with the agony abated for now.

"Name me! Name me so that I might fully live." The unnamed god stood in front of her, head bowed, ready for her benediction. The new form waved his hand over her, and the pain that nearly kept her from speaking faded. At least enough for her to move and think. But he didn't remove the damage. Why wouldn't he heal her?

The air was still now. And the only sound was the coughs and gasps as William took breath again.

"What about Regin? Can you bring him back as well?" Myriam looked at the body, the spear shaft still protruding from the side of his chest.

"No. He died before I fully returned." The unnamed god shrugged. "But I will find a suitable replacement."

Replacement? Myriam felt her anger grow. *Replacement?*

"Maybe even myself. You could be the living bride of a god. But you must name me!" The figure pointed at her. "Now!"

Myriam felt like she was at the edge of a chasm. She could either run back or fall forward into the unknown. This was it. Her eyes went back to the fallen form of Regin. *I am sorry. I am so sorry.* She moved her gaze back to William, who had sat up now. He looked horrible, but he was alive. His expression was unreadable though. He held his hammer still, but the golden shine was gone.

Amder dead. Myriam could barely wrap her head around it. All that work, all that danger, all that effort. All those deaths, all made worthless, by her hands.

"Name me!" The figure yelled again, and pain spread across her body. Lines of fire seemed to travel across her body, and down her harms to her hands. Raw black lines grew again, weeping blood.

"Name me! I can be kind, or I can be cruel." The unnamed god shrugged. "I saved you in the caves. I gave you advice. You are mine."

Resolve hardened her heart as she turned to the unnamed god. "You want a name?"

Myriam ran forward, grabbing William and rushing towards the pit. Rushing towards the pool of raw magic. The figure behind her yelled something that she didn't listen to. With a deep mid-air breath, she and William plunged into the pit with one thought on her mind.

Get us out of here, and to some place safe from the gods. Myriam felt her body spasm and raw magic flowed into the wounds on her body.

And with a flash in her mind, she and William were gone.

***

The unnamed god stood still, growing increasingly angry. Not at its prophet, but at itself. *Trusting a human who had been through that much trauma. Why had I done that?* It was unnamed. *Only Myriam could name it, as it had decreed. I was a fool.*

Maybe not a fool exactly, but I should have thought it through better. She would have named him if he had brought back this Regin person. She didn't even have to know that it would have been a fake until after she had done her job.

But he'd told her the truth, and now she had fled. Fled with that, William Reis. Fled into the stream of magic. She might die there, but she might not. Myriam was a remarkably strong-willed person, and magic would respond to that.

Which made it dangerous. And maybe, it made her dangerous.

The unnamed god watched as the projections of its brothers and sisters agreed with the plan formed in his mind. They each faded out, leaving the unnamed god alone. First, he would take vengeance on the Vinik, and then, magic itself. Which meant the Anvil and one other place. It had appeared in his mind the moment he had been reborn. The only place outside the Anvil where magic was still strong and still used.

The City in Blue.

The story continues in 'A City in Blue.'

If you have enjoyed this story, please leave a review at Amazon. Reviews are the lifeblood of any self-published author. Thank you, and Happy Reading!

Link for Reviews of this book:
The Anvil of Souls

--Joshua C. Cook
Nov 11, 2021
https://www.joshccook.com

Glossary

Amder – the god of the Forge, Craft and Creation. One of the two gods of humanity. Recently returned to the world of Alos by the actions of William Reis and his friends. Had previously been dead, killed in battle with his brother, Valnijz many centuries ago.

Anvil of Souls – The location where the gods first appeared in our world, it is also one of the last two locations of 'wild' magic found in Alos.

Blood bear – A bear only found in the southlands near the Anvil of Souls, it appears as a bear with long bone spikes, some have speculated that the bears were normal bears changed by the power of the Anvil.

Blackspot – a mold only found deep underground that turns any water it grows in caustic and capable of destroying skin and flesh.

Calnit – a scaled pack hunter/scavenger. Around the size of a fox. Will always go for the easy meal.

Captain Vin Tolin – a veteran of Palnor, Vin Tolin is an old soldier. He directed the defense of the Reach during the Valni attack the night of the Return. Working as the defacto bodyguard to William, and training him, Regin and Myriam in combat.

Charnoth – a burrowing hunter, Charnoth are poisonous and have large fangs. Outside of meat, they only eat honey and bees.

City in Blue – a nearly forgotten place, the City in Blue is the only place outside of the Anvil where Magic seems to exist in its 'natural' state, and not filtered and controlled by the gods.

Cloud – a drug that dulls all emotions and pain for several hours. Often abused by those wishing to escape loss, take too much and you lose the ability to feel anything for the rest of your life. Called "going to the sky" those who have gone too far, wander off and die, unable to feel hunger or thirst.

Curors – an order of warriors devoted to Valnijz, the God of Blood and Rage. Unlike the Priests near the Mistlands, the Curors use the power of the blood to make themselves into living weapons. Not many survive the process, and as a result their numbers are lot large. Faster and stronger than any normal human by a large factor, the Curors fight for their god.

Delving – a race talent given to the Gorom by their god, Grimnor. Delving will allow a Gorom to sense through the stone what is around them, and the general location of whatever they are seeking is. Not all Gorom are blessed with the Delve.

Drendel – a lost race, known almost fully by the metal artifacts they left behind, it was recently discovered that they are not lost, they are the Vinik.

Drendel Steel – a blueish grey metal only found underground, and only in cast and made forms. Must be melted down to be used for anything else. Very hard, strong, and does not rust. How to make Drendel steel is unknown.

Duncan Reis – William's cousin, who stopped Valnijz from returning at the cost of his own life. Once afflicted by the blood curse that left him a wrecked and tortured man.

Earthshake – earthquakes.

Erch – A mushroom that glows and is capable of movement. Found deep underground near water. The Gorom consider them pests and an annoyance because their glow has no order.

Fearsong – a weapon of the Gorom. A sound that regardless of race seems to cause total and abject terror and an overwhelming desire to escape and run away. Very deadly when used underground as the hearers will run in a blind panic through caves and tunnels, uncaring of where they go.

Gorom – a short race who live underground, the Gorom are somewhat xenophobic. They try to keep all contact with other races to a bare minimum. They breed Vinik for eggs, and milk. They do not accept that the Vinik are an intelligent race. Gorom have a strong attachment to order and structure.

Jindo Halfman – Leader of the Curors, and the first of their order. Disliked Zalkiniv and considered him a fool. The first to use the 'blood' to give himself powers, he is almost as old as Zalkiniv.

Karkin – an insect the size of a plate, karkin travel in swarms. Blind, they are attracted to smells. IF enough die, they will frenzy and turn on each other.

Klah – a thick very garlic heavy spread that is very popular in the Reach and close to the Reach. Most other parts of Palnor and Alos think it's rather unappealing.

Korba fruit – a fruit that the Saltmistresses trade in, it is sweet, juicy, but not sticky. The Saltmistresses refuse to say where it comes from.

Lake of the Winds – The largest lake in Palnor. The city of Dernstown lies on its southern end. The northside of the lake is under populated due to the sometimes catastrophic earthshakes and floods that have hit in the area.

Master Jaste Noam – Former Guildmaster who got William into the Guild under an assumed name and was at one point the Master that Regin was assigned to on his final Journeyman training. Killed in Ture during William's escape.

Myriam Volfar – a guild apprentice who once had a relationship with William Reis, Myriam considers herself nothing special. She fled the Guild when she realized it was utterly compromised by the Priesthood of Amder. Currently traveling with both Regin and William.

Nightwood – a jet black wood that is nearly as hard as Drendel steel. Grows only near the Anvil of Souls.

Rache – the name Zalkiniv used when working to capture both Duncan and William Reis.

Redglow – sunburn

Redkiss – a strange tree that is covered with tiny red flowers. Always generates a buzzing sound to attract Charnoth. Known to give any humans who are foolish enough to sleep under the tree horrible nightmares. Sleepers will awaken to find the flowers of the tree attached to them and sucking blood through their skin.

Regin Hamsand – Former Guildmaster of the Smithing Guild. Young and smart, Regin was also highly arrogant and not well liked. Somewhat recent events have changed his outlook on life, and he is a new man.

Romach – the Gorom word for fish.

Saltmistresses – a race that follows the Sea Goddess. They are also exclusively female. Have an unknown relationship with the Windtalker, as they worship different aspects of the same goddess.

Speaker-to-the-sky – a Gorom who is tasked with interacting with other races. Does not enjoy such activity. Also acted as the guide for William and his friends during their trip through the Gorom lands.

Swiftkill – creatures of the blood, the swiftkills are an ancient creation. Not easy to control, swiftkills live to hunt. They are called swiftkills because they use a set of natural bone harpoons to stab and tear their prey apart in a matter of minutes before feeding.

The Blood/The Drop – a single drop of blood from Valnijz. Unlike all the other blood spilled it did not turn to mist and seems to have other powers and abilities. Owned and controlled by the Cruor and Jindo Halfman.

The Scrolls of the Dead – semi prophetic scrolls written on the skins of dead Curors by Jindo Halfman.

Trinil – a race of tall thin beings that follow the forest goddess. It is impossible to lie to a Trinil, they always know if people are telling the truth or not.

Valni – men and women transformed by the blood mist into monsters. Their numbers are much diminished after the night of return when many perished in the fighting in the Reach, and more died after the barrier went back up upon Amder's rebirth.

Valnijz – The Blood God, the Scaled One, God of Rage and Destruction. His return thwarted by the actions of Duncan Reis who paid for it with his life, Valnijz is thought to now be unable to ever return.

Vinik – a race of intelligent underground insects, they claim to be the first race on Alos, predating the arrival of the gods. The Gorom and the Vinik have a deep hate for each other.

Waterglass – a mirror

Whiteroot – a basic antiseptic and astringent used to clean and bind wounds. Hurts like fire when applied for first few moments.

Whitestone – A bright white stone that often has thin lines of Silverlace flowing through it. Not common, but highly prized for both its attractiveness and its strength.

William Reis – Forgemaster of Amder. Young but talented beyond measure, William is the Forgemaster of Amder, and carries part of his divine spark.

Windtalker – an order or a race (no one is totally sure which) that follows the wind goddess. Very rare, and almost never touch the ground. They all have skin the color of burnt copper, and hair tends to be blood to auburn. No one has ever seen a male Windtalker. Have an unknown relationship with the Saltmisstresses as they worship two aspects of the same goddess.

Zalkiniv – The former High Priest of Valnijz, Zalkiniv was killed and sacrificed to the Blood God for his failure in capturing both of the Reis bloodline. Old and very canny, it is not known what happened to his spirit.

Printed in Great Britain
by Amazon

18746605R00243